HELEN YENDALL has had dozens of short stories and a serial published in women's magazines over the past twenty years and now writes female-focused WW2 novels. She's a member of the Romantic Novelists' Association.

She studied English and German at Leeds University and has worked in a variety of roles: for a literary festival, a university, a camping club, a children's charity and in marketing and export sales. But her favourite job is the one she still has: teaching creative writing to adults.

Although a proud Brummie by birth, Helen now lives in the North Cotswolds with her husband and cocker spaniel, Bonnie. When she's not teaching or writing, she likes reading, swimming, tennis and walking in the beautiful countryside where she lives.

Also by Helen Yendall

A Wartime Secret

The Highland Girls series

The Highland Girls at War
The Highland Girls on Guard

The Highland Girls Report for Duty

HELEN YENDALL

ONE PLACE. MANY STORIES

HQ
An imprint of HarperCollins*Publishers* Ltd
1 London Bridge Street
London SE1 9GF

www.harpercollins.co.uk

HarperCollins*Publishers*
Macken House, 39/40 Mayor Street Upper,
Dublin 1 D01 C9W8

This paperback edition 2025

1

First published in Great Britain by
HQ, an imprint of HarperCollins*Publishers* Ltd 2025

Copyright © Helen Yendall 2025

Helen Yendall asserts the moral right to be
identified as the author of this work.
A catalogue record for this book is
available from the British Library.

ISBN: 9780008603311

To the memory of the 641 brave women of the Canadian Red Cross Corps Overseas Detachment, who crossed the Atlantic and served in Britain and continental Europe during WW2.

Chapter One

Blantyre Forest, Highlands of Scotland
25th December 1943

'I cannae believe they made us work on Christmas morning!' Flora said, as she and the other Macdonald girls queued up outside the dining hut. They were surrounded by dozens of other lumberjills, jostling for room and keen to get in out of the cold.

Seffy slapped her playfully on the shoulder. As leader girl for Macdonald hut, Seffy was responsible for morale and Flora – the youngest, at just sixteen – often needed a nudge in the right direction.

'Buck up, Flo! It was only a half-day and it's done now!'

Enid was jogging on the spot to keep warm. 'It was mean, though,' she said. 'Even the POWs had the day off today.'

'I've been praying for snow,' Belinda said. 'So's we'd be snowed off for Christmas.'

Morag snorted. 'You'd nae chance of that! It's too cold to snow!'

Tattie strained her neck to see over the girls in front. 'I dunnae care about any of that. I just want ma Christmas dinner. I'm starvin'! I hope the portions are big. We've earned it!'

There was no arguing with that. The girls had been up since first

1

light, felling, snedding, dragging trees and burning brushwood.

'Oh, look, there's Jean!' Seffy said, catching sight of her copper-red hair. 'Where's she going?'

Jean was a measurer and had been working deep within another part of the forest that morning. She'd got back later than the others and had told them to go on without her while she had a wash and brush up. Now, she'd meekly joined the tail end of the queue, twenty yards away.

'I say, JEAN!' Seffy beckoned her nearer. 'Come on, you! We're over here!'

'I dunnae like to push in,' Jean murmured, blushing furiously and apologising as she edged her way through the gaggle of girls until she reached the Macdonald gang.

'Oh, you silly sausage,' Seffy said. 'We saved you a place. I'm sure no one minds a bit!'

Seffy glared at the girls standing behind them, daring them to object but no one did.

Jean adjusted her beret. 'Aye, well, thanks.' She nodded at Flora. 'What's up wi' her?'

'Still sulking about having to fell trees on Christmas Day. I've told her, a long face never won a war!'

'Aye, you might try to smile, Flora,' Jean said. 'If we're merry at Christmas, we're showing the enemy we're winning the war of nerves.'

'And today's going to be such fun, Flora,' Seffy said. 'We've got the pantomime this afternoon, starring yours truly!'

'And there's to be a surprise over lunch!' Tattie said. 'Cook told me!'

Flora brightened. 'Mebbe Miss McEwen's gonna dress up as Santa!'

Everyone laughed at the thought of their dour supervisor doing anything so frivolous.

'Aye and she'll hand out presents to all the good girls,' Tattie said.

'That counts us out, then,' Seffy said.

'No, I reckon Jean qualifies as a good girl,' Morag said. 'And if Grace was still here, she would too.'

'But as for the rest of you ...' Seffy said, shaking her head. 'No chance!'

'I dunnae care!' Enid said. 'Who wants to be a good girl, anyhow?'

They'd reached the dining hut entrance now and Flora was the first inside. At the sight of the Christmas tree on the far side, she gasped and stopped, causing an immediate traffic jam.

'Cor, look at that!'

It did look rather marvellous: adorned with real candles and standing like a sentinel in the corner of the room.

'You chose well, Jean!' Seffy said, as Morag huffed and thumped Flora on the back to make her move.

Jean looked pleased. 'Aye,' she said. 'I went miles into the forest to find the right one, but it doesnae look bad, does it?'

It was a perfectly symmetrical Douglas fir, not too sparse or too bushy and exactly the right height, so that its top branches grazed the ceiling. There were other decorations in the dining hall – paper chains swinging from the rafters and wreaths of holly and ivy on the walls – but the tree was the star of the show.

'Let's bagsy that table next to it!' Enid said, and the girls scampered across the room and threw themselves down on the seats.

'Aw, it's awful bonny!' Flora said, gazing at the tree.

'Don't get too attached to it,' Jean said. 'It's going to the saw mill next week.'

Seffy laughed. 'Oh, Jean, don't spoil it!'

'I'm only saying! You can't afford to be sentimental about trees.'

'I think Scottish trees make the best Christmas trees in the whole world!' Enid said.

Jean wrinkled her nose. 'Actually, the Douglas fir is native to North America. It was brought over in the nineteenth century by ...' Her voice trailed off. She must've realised no one was listening. They were too busy laughing at Belinda, who'd placed a bunch of mistletoe on the table.

'In case anyone wants to kiss us,' she said.

'As Jock's the only man around – a happily married grandfather, I might add,' Seffy said, 'I think it's rather unlikely!'

'Aw, never mind. We can dream!' Flora said.

For the next couple of minutes, she and Enid screamed with laughter as they held sprigs of mistletoe over their heads and practised puckering up.

Seffy smiled. This was her first proper Christmas as a lumberjill. She'd rather not think about last year and Hazel's terrible accident; that festive season had passed by in a miserable blur.

This year, she was going to make up for it; this was going to be a super Christmas.

'You know—' she said, waiting until she had everyone's attention '—I really do think we should make the most of this time. The newspapers are awfully optimistic, aren't they, Jean? They say it'll be the last Christmas of the war.'

'About time too!' Enid said, thumping the table. 'We've had three in wartime already. Or is it four?'

'This is the fifth,' Jean said.

'So we have to enjoy ourselves,' Seffy said. 'We mightn't all be together like this again.'

Especially if her request for a transfer to England was accepted. A little thrill coursed through her at the thought of it. She should be getting news any day about a move to the New Forest, in Hampshire.

Callum was down there, somewhere on the south coast and she wanted to be nearer to him.

She'd only seen him once since his company had moved out of Blantyre Forest, almost eight months ago. They'd met up briefly in August, in Gretna Green. The fact that he'd travelled so far to spend just two hours with her, was proof – surely – that he liked her too.

She had no claim on him – he was engaged to a girl back home in Canada – but Seffy couldn't shake off the feeling that they were meant to be together.

Since Gretna, they'd exchanged a few letters.

She'd started the correspondence by congratulating him on his recent promotion. He'd replied, asking about her part in recapturing a group of errant Italians. He'd heard about it from his pal Gordy, who was married to lumberjill Grace.

Seffy had written back and pointed out that she'd now seen more enemy action than him and he was supposed to be the soldier!

Neither of them had mentioned the passionate kiss they'd shared as Seffy's train had pulled out of Gretna Green. She was starting to wonder whether she'd imagined it.

It was tricky, holding a torch for someone when you weren't sure if your feelings were reciprocated. It was simply a matter of hoping for the best and holding fast to the inkling you had, that the chap concerned actually liked you more than he dared say.

Now, as Seffy gazed around the table, she got a lump in her throat. She'd hated Blantyre at first but now she had proper chums here and she loved the work. It wasn't quite the same since Grace and Joey had left, but it would still be a wrench to leave everyone. She supposed, at some point soon, she ought to tell them her plans.

'Is that right, Jean?' Morag was asking. 'Is the war nearly over?'

Jean listened to the wireless every day and often stood in the village shop, poring over every newspaper until she got thrown out for not buying one. She knew everything about the progress of the war.

Seffy would rather read the society pages. It cheered her up to read the engagement and marriage notices and to feel reassured that, despite the terrible times they were living through, life still went on.

Jean nodded. 'Aye, the end is definitely in sight.'

The girls grinned and Flora gave a little cheer.

'The Red Army's making inroads, Mussolini's gone, of course—' Jean said.

'—and the Italians have thrown the towel in,' Belinda said.

'Though they still haven't released the POWs,' Enid said, tutting.

'I read the other day,' Jean went on, 'that there's no power on earth that could now prevent the Allies defeating Germany.'

Flora punched the air and cheered again.

'But—!' Jean raised her hand. 'It also said that our forces – and those of our allies – "may have to endure the greatest sacrifice of life which they have yet suffered."'

The girls fell silent.

Seffy felt an icy-cold chill cover her body. 'Don't say that, Jean. For goodness' sake, it's Christmas!'

Everyone looked sombre now. They all had fathers, brothers, friends or sweethearts who were serving.

Honestly, she could swing for Jean. All that 'sacrifice of life' might well be true but there was no need to say it.

'Watch out, here comes trouble!' Flora said.

Seffy had never been so pleased to see Miss McEwen marching towards them: a most welcome diversion from talk of the depressing war.

The supervisor scowled at the flickering candles on the tree. Perhaps she was worried about the risk of fire.

'Dunnae fret about those candles, Miss McEwen!' a girl on the next table said. 'We've buckets o' water on standby!'

'I should think so too!' Miss McEwen said. She looked as though she were going to say something else but someone called her from the kitchen and she swept past without further comment.

Seffy inhaled. 'It smells wonderful!'

'Aye,' Flora said. 'I'll never tire of that pine scent.'

'Not the tree, silly, the food!' Seffy said. 'I wonder what's on the menu? Oh, here comes Joey! Budge up, Jean!'

Joey shrugged off her coat and sat down, thanking Jean for making space on the bench.

'Good of you to join us, Mrs Stirling!' Seffy said, grinning. It truly felt like Christmas, now that her chum was here.

'Aye, we thought you'd had a better offer,' Belinda said. She had to shout over the babble of excited lumberjills. 'Seeing as you're a married woman and pals wi' all the toffs these days!'

Joey shook her head. 'I was invited to Lady Lockhart's and to Seffy's auntie's but if I cannae be with Ralph today, then I only want to be here with you lot!'

'Quite right too!' Seffy said.

Strictly speaking, as she was no longer in the Women's Timber Corps, Joey shouldn't be here. She'd reluctantly had to resign when she'd married dashing Major Ralph Stirling. Seffy had stuck up for her, pointing out that Grace hadn't left when she'd married Gordy, her Canadian soldier. But it wasn't quite the same: as Ralph came back between missions and Joey had a hearth, home and a part-time husband to care for, she was no longer considered mobile. Rules were rules: she'd had to give up her job.

But as Ralph was currently overseas with his regiment and Joey was a particular favourite of Miss McEwen's, she'd been allowed back for Christmas dinner.

Joey poured herself a glass of water and looked around. 'Merry Christmas, one and all! Aw, but it's a shame Grace isn't here. Have you heard from her?'

'Yes,' Seffy said. 'We had a Christmas card. She says she's well but if she gets any bigger, she won't be able to fit through the door, so we're praying it's not twins!'

Joey winced. 'Och, no, you wouldnae wish that on the poor girl. Double trouble!'

Everyone laughed.

'I suppose you were hard at it this morning?' Joey asked. 'I bet it was freezin' out there!'

'It was rather bracing,' Seffy said, 'but it was also great fun. I could hear the felling team singing carols and apart from 'Silent Night' which they absolutely slaughtered, they weren't half bad!'

'And *someone* had a visitor!' Belinda said, nodding at Tattie.

Joey laughed. 'Private Nowak, by any chance? Tomasz to his friends?'

'Got it in one!' Seffy said.

Tattie's sweetheart, Tomasz – one of the guards from the nearby POW camp – had turned up in the forest that morning with a present for Tattie, carefully wrapped in brown paper.

'Aw, it's all right for some!' Enid had complained, her bottom lip jutting out.

But then Tomasz had crossed the clearing and handed Enid a similar-looking parcel, from Giovanni, her Italian beau.

Seffy had thought wistfully of Callum. Oh, what she'd give to see him stroll into the forest, just as Tomasz had done, to wish her a Merry Christmas. She'd pictured him, lithe and tanned, his blue eyes fixed firmly on her and that knowing smile, twitching at the corner of his lips.

She didn't give two figs about a present: simply to have him here would be enough. She missed him so much, there was an actual pain in her chest. Was that what they meant by heartache?

Tattie and Enid were lucky that their chaps were nearby. Even if Enid's was a POW, she saw him more often than Seffy could see Callum, who was hundreds of miles away. And although he had a habit of turning up when least expected, it was too much to hope he'd make it here, to the Highlands of Scotland, at Christmas time.

She wondered what he'd thought of the little parcel she'd sent him for Christmas. Inside, there'd been a handmade card, a letter and a pocket-sized Penguin book of short stories. She'd spotted it on a station bookstall when she'd made the trip to Greta Green with Grace.

It had seemed ideal because he'd told her once, when she'd mentioned a favourite book of hers, that he didn't have the concentration for anything too long. She didn't expect him to read it, but she hoped he might keep it and enjoy the little message inside.

She hadn't even had a card from him, which was disappointing but not entirely unexpected. The mail was often unreliable. He might be on manoeuvres or have been redeployed elsewhere. Or perhaps, as he'd done before, he'd considered it time to draw back and think of his fiancée in Canada.

Seffy's close friendship with Callum had always been of a yo-yo nature. Friendship? No, it was definitely more than that, but she was never quite sure what to call it, even to herself.

Joey was nudging her. 'Hullo! Is anyone home? I said, how are the horses?'

Seffy snapped out of her reverie. 'Oh, sorry! Yes, they're all absolutely chipper. I gave them an extra scoop of bran mash as a Christmas treat. And a pat from you!'

The girls had worked together on the dragging team, with the horses, before Joey had left the Corps. She seemed happy enough now, living in a cottage on the Blantyre estate and keeping herself busy whenever Ralph was away, but Seffy knew she missed her old life as a lumberjill.

'Here comes the grub!' Enid yelled, standing up for a better view. 'And – oh, ma God! You'll never believe who's gonna be serving us!'

Chapter Two

'More gravy over here please, Miss McEwen!' Seffy said, making the others snigger at her nerve.

Jean thought Seffy would do well to keep her head down and her nose clean where Miss McEwen was concerned. Last summer, the supervisor had been obliged to reinstate Seffy as leader girl, when the girl she'd chosen over her had turned out to be a rotten apple. Miss McEwen almost certainly resented Seffy for it. But of course, keeping her head down wasnae Seffy's style at all.

They were halfway through Christmas lunch: goose, roast potatoes, stuffing, neeps and piles of other veg. The cooks had really worked wonders with the rations. According to Enid, there was still figgy pudding to come.

But the icing on the cake – and the surprise they'd been promised – was seeing Miss McEwen and their foreman, Jock, waiting on the tables.

Miss McEwen had entered into the spirit: she was wearing a frilly white cap and a pinny over her breeches. But she still glared at Seffy as she thumped the jug of gravy down and received an exuberant, 'Thank you so much!' from Seffy in return.

'They do it in all the armed services,' Jean told the others, as they ate their meal. 'Officers always serve the lower ranks on

Christmas Day.'

'So they should!' Morag said.

'Hey!' Enid said, leaning across the table. 'You're never leavin' that potato, are you, Jean? Remember, "A clear plate means a clear conscience"! Here, pass it over. I'll finish it off.'

'Now, we must have a toast,' Seffy said, once the food had been devoured and Jean had started stacking the empty plates.

'Fill up your glasses and all rise!'

When they were ready, Seffy raised her tumbler. 'Merry Christmas to us all! Let's count our blessings and look forward to the New Year with hope in our hearts!'

'With hope in our hearts!' the girls chorused.

You had to hand it to her, Jean thought, Seffy was good at public speaking. She had a clear, confident voice. She'd never need a loudhailer.

'What's everyone looking forward to in 1944?' Belinda asked, when they'd settled back into their seats.

'Release of the POWs!' Enid said.

'My wee sister's getting married in the spring,' Jean said. 'Wi' a bit of luck, I'll make it to the wedding.'

'And I'm to be a godmother!' Seffy said. 'Someone actually trusts me to be a good influence! The christening's in London, next month. I'm hoping to get there.'

'London?' Morag said, blowing out her cheeks. 'It'd take days just to get there and back. Do you have that much leave?'

Seffy opened her mouth and closed it again, looking suddenly uncertain.

'There's summat else, isn't there, Seffy?' Joey said.

Seffy toyed with her glass. 'Ah, yes. I – well, I've been meaning to tell you for yonks and now's as good a time as any.'

She flashed a smile at Joey, who nodded encouragingly.

'I've applied for a transfer—'

'A transfer?' Tattie asked.

11

'Yes, and as Miss McEwen will only be too glad to see the back of me, I expect I'll be off soon. And that's why I thought I could make it to the christening: I might be down there by then. You see, I've applied to go to England.'

'England?' Enid said, aghast. 'Whyever would you want to go down there?'

Jean knew why, or at least, she could hazard a guess. Seffy had a beau in the Canadian Forestry Corps company that had worked nearby but which was now based on the south coast. She must want to be closer to him.

Unlike most of the others, who missed the glamorous Canadians and the dances they used to hold in their camp, Jean was glad they'd gone.

There'd been an incident one night, with one of the Canucks, in the woods. It'd been a misunderstanding, and probably her own fault, but if Grace hadn't come to her rescue, heaven only knew how it would've ended.

She closed her eyes for a second to block out the memory. The other girls were still talking about Seffy's move south.

'Do they even have trees in England?' Flora asked. 'Is it no' full of cities?'

'Of course there are trees!' Seffy said. 'There are lumberjills working all over the place, from Yorkshire and the Lake District right down to the New Forest. I read about it in the *Land Girl*.'

'Aw, well, if it's in the *Land Girl*, it must be true,' Morag said.

'I suppose we should be grateful the Timber Corps even got a mention,' Jean said. It was a particular bugbear of hers that the Land Army always seemed to take precedence over them.

As she stood up to carry the stack of plates back to the kitchen, her mind was whirring. Seffy was leaving!

Whoops! As she'd started to cross the hall, she'd stumbled, only just saving the plates as they'd started to slip from her hands. She cringed at the thought of the delighted cheers that would've gone up if they'd smashed over the floor. She could never understand why folk did that.

'Do you need a hand, Jean?' Joey called.

'No, I can manage, ta!'

She might only be a measurer, not used to hard labour like the others, but she didn't want them thinking she was a weakling.

An idea had struck her like a thunderbolt. Seffy's leaving was an opportunity for someone. Macdonald hut would need a new leader girl! And there was no reason why it shouldn't be her.

'A word, if you please, Miss Ferguson.'

Jean's heart sank. Not now. She was standing in a group next to the wireless, waiting to listen to the King's Christmas message. She'd been looking forward to it. But as the national anthem played, and before the King had uttered a word, Miss McEwen had tapped her arm and led her away to a quiet corner.

She fixed Jean with a hard stare. 'Miss Ferguson, how would you like a transfer away from here?'

Jean was taken aback. Seffy was supposed to be moving, not her.

'There's a gang of lumberjills moving to a new felling area, in need of a leader girl—' Miss McEwen went on.

Jean perked up. That sounded promising.

'—and I've been asked to release Miss Mills. In fact, she's been particularly selected for the task.'

Not her, then, but Seffy. Seffy was leaving, after all. But what did this have to do with her?

'I shan't mention her being "the chosen one", and please keep that to yourself too, Miss Ferguson. The girl already has a high enough opinion of herself. But word's got around, amongst the powers that be, that Miss Mills has a gung-ho attitude and is up for a challenge. They're convinced she's the right person for the job.'

Jean frowned. Whatever Miss McEwen might think of Seffy, there was no denying she'd made a name for herself in the summer when she'd braved a forest fire and helped bring those errant Italians to book. But goodness, this job must be summat out of the ordinary if Seffy had been selected by the top brass.

'So … where exactly do I come in?' Jean asked.

'The gang needs an experienced measurer – a good one – so I'm asking you. You're ma first choice.'

First choice. She felt a warm glow, not only at the unexpected praise but at the thought of moving. She was ready for something new. The trees would be different; there might be hardwoods. And she'd get away from that part of Blantyre Forest that she still couldn't walk through without trembling.

'But – it's not England, is it?' she asked.

Miss McEwen gave a throaty laugh. 'England? No! What d'you take me for? You'll have your work cut out, mind, dealing with Miss Mills. She could try the patience of a saint, that one, with her airs and graces.'

That was unfair. Seffy was one of them these days. Often, Jean forgot she wasnae even Scottish. Aw, but she might need some gentle handling, when she heard the news. She wasnae going to be happy. Not when she had her heart set on going to England.

Jean glanced at the huddle of girls standing around the radio set. Seffy was easy to spot: taller than most, with her unmistakeable mop of curly blonde hair. She and Joey were sniggering, like a couple of schoolgirls.

Jean felt a sudden stab of guilt, as though she were in collusion with Miss McEwen.

'If you dunnae think you're up to it, Miss Ferguson, there are other measurers I can ask. Lassies who'll jump at the chance.'

That was true enough. If she turned this down, someone else would simply replace her. This was a golden opportunity: she should grab it with both hands.

'Would I be the only measurer?' she asked.

'No, there's a lass who's had some training but needs supervision. You'd be the senior measurer; a position of immense responsibility. Reporting directly to the acquisition officer from the ministry. If he spots your potential, who knows where it might lead?'

Jean liked the sound of that. 'Aye, all right. I'll do it.'

'Good! Now, I want you to be my eyes and ears in the new place and keep Miss Mills in your sights. I'm no' happy about the girl being let loose like this. She's bound to slip up and the moment she does, I shall be hauling her back here. Then there might be a chance for you to take over as leader girl.'

Jean felt queasy. She might've known there'd be a catch.

'So, a fortnightly report is what I'll be needing from you, Miss Ferguson. Can you manage that?'

Was she being asked to spy on Seffy? That wasnae fair! The transfer didn't seem half as exciting now.

'There'll be more money in it. Perhaps I haven't made myself clear, Miss Ferguson: you're being offered a promotion.'

When Miss McEwen told her how much more, Jean was torn. How could she say no to that? She'd be able to send money home. It wasn't long 'til Mary's wedding and her folks were feeling the pinch.

'But you'll need to gi' me your word. A fortnightly report?'

Aw, it'd be all right. She could write reports well enough and what could Seffy possibly do that'd be bad enough to be brought back to Blantyre in disgrace?

She gave the slightest of nods.

'Best not tell Seff – Miss Mills – today though,' Jean said. That was one thing she would insist upon.

The strains of 'God Save the King' were crackling out of the wireless. The speech was over; she'd missed the whole thing.

The girls were singing along to the national anthem with gusto. Seffy looked as though she didn't have a care in the world. They couldn't tell her now; it'd ruin her Christmas.

'Could it wait 'til Monday morning?' Jean asked. 'Only, we're puttin' on the panto in a wee while and Seffy's the principal boy. I wouldnae want anything to … erm, put her off.'

They'd been rehearsing *Cinderella* for weeks and Seffy in a sulk would ruin everything.

The supervisor pursed her lips. 'Principal boy, is it? She'd have to be principal summat or other. Aye, I suppose it can wait until then.'

She turned to leave.

'Oh, Miss McEwen,' Jean called softly after her, 'I forgot to ask. Where exactly is it we're going?'

Chapter Three

'Oh, no, you don't, fella! SCOOT!' Juliet said, sliding the compartment door shut in the soldier's face. 'SCRAM!' she added, for good measure, shooing him away.

Missy winced. Did her sister have to be so darned loud? The other passengers were watching them, although of course, being British, they were pretending not to and no one said a word.

Through the glass, the Tommy grinned, raised his hands in defeat and backed away. He'd followed them down the corridor from the moment they'd boarded the train. He'd even tried coming in here, where there were just two free seats, between a soldier and an old dear. Where did he imagine he was gonna sit, on their laps?

But now, at last, he'd gone.

Juliet tossed her canvas bag onto the luggage rack and threw herself into a seat so hard that she bounced.

Missy looked down at her own bag. If she waited, one of the fellas would surely offer to help. The airman next to the window was already half out of his seat.

17

But Juliet was glaring at her, eyebrows raised in a 'Don't you dare!' expression. Missy quickly picked up the bag – cursing herself for bringing so much for what was, after all, only a two-day trip – and heaved it onto the rack.

She sat down beside Juliet and hugged her overcoat tight. It wasn't exactly warm in here. She stole a glance at the other passengers, who – now the show was over – were getting out their knitting, newspapers and books. The airman sat back, took a cigarette from his top pocket and lit up.

The train started to pull out and Missy exhaled. What a relief to be getting away from London and those infernal raids for a while. With any luck, it wouldn't be so bad on the coast.

This was the second British train she'd been on and it was no different from the first: dirty, noisy and packed to the hilt with troops in every shade of khaki and blue. She and Juliet were in uniform too and she'd thought – wrongly, as it turned out – it might've afforded them some respect.

To be fair, most of the fellas they'd encountered had been polite. But there were also fresh, unsavoury types, like the guy who'd followed them and others, who, even if they didn't catcall or tail you, stared as though they'd never seen a woman before.

Missy pulled off her hat and held it in her lap. She'd wanted to wear her own clothes today. The green wool dress or maybe the blue one with the lace collar. Callum had always liked her in that.

But Juliet said everyone wore uniforms, even off duty and they should be proud. So, she'd put on the khaki tunic with the Red Cross emblem on the sleeves and the matching skirt with a black belt, grateful she could cover it up with the overcoat. She felt a fraud because they hadn't started work yet.

They'd arrived in England on 20th December and had spent a week settling into their temporary home at the Maple Leaf Club. They'd sorted out ration books, registration cards and banking, and celebrated a strange, makeshift kinda Christmas.

The Club was staffed by girls from Canada, who were proudly

providing a 'home from home' for off-duty troops in London, where fellas could even get a bed for the night.

They were a great group of gals but it was still tough, spending the holidays with a bunch of folk you barely knew.

And now they'd been granted a week's leave before transferring to the hospital. As one of the married girls, Juliet had been able to request a spot near her husband and by luck, she and Missy had been assigned to the same place. It was something else for which she had to be grateful. She'd probably be paying her sister back for the rest of her life.

They'd only travelled a few miles when the train slowed and jolted to a stop. Travel here sure was frustrating. The trains stopped constantly and the station signs were all blacked out, so you had no idea where you were.

But it was still better than being on that darned boat.

That thirteen-day voyage to England had felt like thirteen weeks. Thank goodness for the other girls. They'd been a good bunch and the shared experience of stormy seas, awful food and the constant fear of German U-boats had sealed their friendships from the off.

Missy had introduced herself as 'Miranda' which had made Juliet smirk.

Someone said it was a real pretty name and Missy explained how Mom had liked Shakespeare growing up, so she'd called her first daughter Juliet and her second Miranda, after the girl in *The Tempest*.

'Miranda, is it, now?' Juliet said later, when they were alone in their cabin.

Of course, she didn't expect Juliet to call her anything but 'Missy'; she'd called her that for twenty-three years, after all. But to everyone else, she would be Miranda. No more baby names. She was a grown woman; she needed a grown woman's name. This trip was a chance to kinda reinvent herself, if that didn't sound awful modern.

But goodness, she should stop thinking of this whole experience as a mere trip; it made it sound like a day's outing, when it was actually the journey of a lifetime.

She'd never have come, if it hadn't been for Juliet's spirit of adventure. Although they weren't poor, they didn't have the kind of money you usually needed to go overseas. Juliet had seized on the idea of going to Great Britain with the Red Cross Corps because not only would she be nearer to her husband, Verne, it was also a wonderful opportunity to travel.

Missy wasn't convinced. Sure, she'd love to be with Callum again and it would be nice to see something of the world before they settled down but the thought of going all that way, in the middle of a war, was terrifying. She'd never been out of Canada. Heck, she'd hardly ever been out of British Columbia.

But she couldn't bear to be left behind. When Juliet had started pestering Mom and Dad to let her go – because you needed parental permission before the Red Cross would allow it – Missy had insisted she was coming too.

It'd been the same when they were kids. Wherever Juliet went, Missy had followed. It was a family joke: Missy was Juliet's little shadow.

Apparently, she'd gotten to the age of two and had never spoken a word, so Mom had taken her to the doctor and said, 'She's mute, she doesn't speak.' Then the doctor had pointed at Juliet and said, 'There's the reason, right there.'

Juliet had spoken for both of them and in a lot of ways, she still did.

Missy was still wondering whether 'tagging along' (in Juliet's words) had been the right thing to do. There'd sure been a lot of disappointments so far; she hoped there weren't more to come.

When they'd finally sailed up the estuary towards land, that had been the first let-down. Missy had stood on deck with the others, holding tight on to the railing, to get their first view of England.

'It looks just like Canada!' someone had said, and it was true.

The train was moving off again.

Juliet nudged her. 'Excited? You sure don't look it!'

Missy pulled a face. Her stomach was whirling like a carousel and she was feeling both happy and scared. The moment she'd been yearning for was – all being well – just an hour or so away. Two whole days with Callum after two years apart. It was kinda daunting.

'Hey, but don't blame Verne if Callum's not there,' Juliet said. 'I know he'll do his best, but …' She shrugged.

Juliet had told Verne he had to bring Callum along because she had a surprise for him. But there were no guarantees he'd be able to convince him to come.

Missy wasn't sure whether she was doing the right thing. What if Callum showed up but it wasn't the romantic reunion she'd dreamed of? He might be cross with her for not telling him her plans. They were engaged, after all. He'd probably think big decisions should be made together.

And he might've changed. War and travel and two years apart could do that to a person. He mightn't be the same boy she'd known and loved almost her whole life. It was impossible to tell from his infrequent letters. Sure, he couldn't say much about how he spent his days or where he was stationed, because he had to keep the censors happy. He always said he was 'fit and well' but was that because he didn't want to worry her?

She'd tried to follow the advice in women's magazines, to keep letters 'jolly and full of fun family news'. Maybe his instructions were to always say he was 'fit and well'?

Were they telling each other the whole truth? It felt as though any real troubles or emotions had been kept firmly under lock and key. And, despite their letters, they'd lost touch.

Missy glanced at Juliet. Surely she must be a little apprehensive too? But she was gazing out at the passing scenery, lost in thought. At least they had something better than bomb damage to look at now. The countryside, although bare and wintery, was pretty.

The only sign that perhaps Juliet wasn't as relaxed as she seemed, was the jiggling of her crossed leg.

She suddenly turned in her seat towards Missy. 'Hey, I've been meaning to say something to you for a while,' she said. 'I know you'll be tempted, but don't marry Callum out here, will you?'

Missy was taken aback. 'What d'you mean?'

'It'd break Mom and Dad's hearts to miss your wedding. Wait until we're all back home, huh?'

Missy's chest tightened. Why was her sister always so darned bossy? It was nothing to do with Juliet what she did or didn't do over here.

She made a vague murmur and then changed the subject. 'Can we go to the restroom when we arrive? I wanna fix my hair and face a little.'

'Sure, if we get the chance. But I'm guessing the guys'll be waiting on the platform. And they'll swoop us straight up into their arms!'

Juliet laughed a little wildly and caught the eye of the airman in the corner who smiled at her.

Missy's stomach did a loop-the-loop at the thought of the fellas waiting on the platform. Maybe she should've told Callum she was coming. She'd wanted to, many times, but she'd always stopped herself. She'd begged her sister not to tell Verne. He was in Callum's unit and he'd have only let the cat out of the bag.

'OK,' Juliet had said. 'But why the big secret?'

'I just don't wanna jinx anything. I'd rather wait 'til I'm on British soil and then surprise him.'

But there was more to it than that. If she didn't announce she was coming to Europe, she could always back out. Because, even though she'd insisted on leaving with Juliet – and she'd done the training and drills, had the physical exams and the shots for various diseases – she'd had cold feet, right up to the day they'd left.

Darn it, she was spoiling everything with these dark thoughts. This should be one of the best days of her life. Callum loved her: he'd be over the moon to see her!

Hadn't she crossed an ocean and risked torpedoes to be with him? He'd be so proud. There was no need to tell him she'd been terrified and full of doubts the whole voyage.

She'd made it, she was here, and very soon she'd be with Callum again.

Chapter Four

At breakfast on Monday, someone passed a message to Jean and Seffy, asking them to report immediately to Miss McEwen's office.

Jean shot up, leaving her porridge half-eaten, but Seffy took a moment to spread another piece of toast with margarine, fold it in half and tuck it into her pocket. The wintry weather made her constantly hungry; Miss McEwen would have to wait.

'I wonder what the old dragon wants?' Seffy said, as the girls hurried across camp. 'It can't be anything too terrible because you're involved, Miss Goody Two-Shoes! You've probably never had a dressing-down in your life!'

She nudged Jean and laughed. It had been a top-hole Christmas and she was in a buoyant mood. Her performance in *Cinderella* had been a triumph and the fun hadn't ended there. On Boxing Day – which had fortunately fallen on a Sunday – she and Joey had been invited for another hearty lunch, this time with her Aunt Dilys and Marigold. They'd had goose again.

She patted her stomach. 'You know, I've eaten so much goose over Christmas, I think I might be about to sprout wings!'

Jean didn't laugh. In fact, she was looking decidedly uncomfortable. Perhaps she knew more about this mysterious summons than she was letting on?

She tapped her watch. 'We'll be for the high jump if we keep her waiting.'

'Come on, then, let's run!' Seffy said, and they raced towards the hut.

Once inside, Seffy took a moment to catch her breath and gaze around. 'Office' was rather a grand title for what was effectively a shed with a couple of desks and chairs. It had a single paraffin heater and a primer stove to boil the kettle for tea.

The supervisor was sitting behind her desk, puffed up with self-importance. She beckoned them over.

'I've news for you both,' she said, without any preamble. 'You're away to Ballamar!'

Seffy's stomach dropped into her boots.

'What do you mean, "away"?'

'You're being transferred. The two of yous.'

But to somewhere called *Ballamar*? Not Lyndhurst or Ringwood, the places she'd been hoping for in the New Forest?

'Where's Ballamar?' she asked.

'It's in Aberdeenshire,' Jean said. She didn't sound surprised by the news. 'I've always wanted to go there. It's near to Balmoral, Seffy. You know, the royal estate?'

Seffy glared at her. So what? She didn't give two hoots about the royal estate. Wherever this stupid place was, it was still in Scotland.

'I don't understand,' she said. It was an effort to keep her voice level. 'If you remember, Miss McEwen, I specifically asked for a transfer to the south coast. To the New Forest.'

Miss McEwen was running her finger down a list of figures. She looked up. 'Aye, ye did. And I – *specifically* – havenae forgotten, Miss Mills. And if you make a good job o' this, we'll see if that can be arranged. But this comes first. You're to stay there until the job is done! And there are no horses, so you'll no' be part of a dragging team. I hope ye can remember how to fell a tree!'

Seffy's chest tightened until she thought she might explode. When had this been arranged and why hadn't she been consulted? It was outrageous!

It hit her then, in a flash: this was the wicked witch's revenge for her heroics during the summer! Miss McEwen must still be fuming about having to eat humble pie in front of the whole camp. She was getting her own back.

Miss McEwen was looking at her with narrowed eyes. 'Five trees! Do ye know the significance of that, Miss Mills?'

Seffy shook her head.

'I do!' Jean said. 'The ministry has worked out that five trees are required to keep each soldier fighting in this war.'

'Correct! THAT'S how important your work is! Do soldiers on the battlefield question their superiors? I think not! And as a soldier of the forest, Miss Mills, you should not be querying why you're being sent to Ballamar!'

Seffy took a step backwards. Gosh, she'd never seen Miss McEwen so furious.

'It's not exactly Ballamar, is it?' Jean said. 'Where we're being sent, I mean. It's a hamlet a mile or two away.' She nodded encouragingly at Seffy. 'But it IS to the south of here!'

Seffy frowned. Jean seemed to know an awful lot about all this.

'How far south?' she asked.

'About fifty miles.'

Fifty measly miles? A mere hop, skip and a jump! She'd still be hundreds of miles from Callum. And to add insult to injury, there was now no chance of her getting to the christening in London. This was a disaster of the highest order.

'Can't we all move?' she asked. 'Why are Jean and I the only ones being sent?'

The supervisor sighed. 'No, you can't all move! The others are needed here and there's already a gang in the new place, including

27

a measurer. They're newly trained and ready to go. They simply need a leader – that's you – and another, more experienced measurer.' She nodded at Jean, and then, infuriatingly, turned back to her paperwork, as though she considered the matter closed.

Seffy tilted her chin. She would not give Miss McEwen the satisfaction of seeing how upset she was.

'May I ask how big the camp is?'

Miss McEwen looked up. 'Who said anything about a camp? You'll be in billets. Your first has been secured for you by the divisional officer. If you need to change, or when the time comes to move on, it's up to you to find a new place.'

'We'll be in private houses?' Jean asked.

Miss McEwen pulled a face. 'Aye, that's the usual meaning of billets, Miss Ferguson! Aren't you supposed to be the brainy one?'

Billets? That would certainly be very different from the camp.

'You'll soon realise how easy you've had it up to now, being in a camp,' Miss McEwen said.

Easy? This place was hardly The Ritz! And the girls' board and lodgings were docked from their pay; no one was doing them any favours. But it wasn't worth getting into a quarrel. She'd had run-ins with Miss McEwen in the past and she'd usually come off worst.

'Billets might be fun!' Jean said.

Seffy had a sudden vision of a sweet, grey-haired landlady fussing over them, steaming hot suppers at the end of a working day and cups of tea in bed on Sunday mornings.

Plus, there'd be no pesky supervisor breathing down their necks. They could come and go as they pleased, without having to beg for late-night passes. There'd probably be a key under the door mat. Total freedom!

On reflection, being billeted mightn't be too bad.

And she'd be felling trees again. As much as she'd loved working with the horses, she missed parts of her old job. Nothing could beat the feeling of yelling, 'TIMBERRRRR!' as a ten-ton tree tilted, groaned and came crashing to the ground.

'All the arrangements have been made. You leave on Friday morning,' Miss McEwen said.

'That's New Year's Eve!' Seffy said.

'That's Hogmanay!' Jean said, at the same time.

They looked at one another and smiled.

Miss McEwen sniffed. 'The ministry is laying on a car to take you. I'd have put you on the train myself, but there you have it. Now, we have a day's work ahead of us! Time to crack on!'

As much as she was trying to think positively about this unexpected transfer, Seffy felt completely hollow.

Thank goodness she hadn't mentioned a possible move south in her letters to Callum. She'd decided to hold back in part until the transfer was confirmed but also because she was concerned about appearing too keen. It was a chap's role, after all, to do the running.

But in any case, her plans had been shot to pieces. Who knew if Miss McEwen would even keep her word and have her moved south once this Ballamar business was over? She was so disappointed, she could cry.

But she wouldn't. She'd only look a complete ninny if she cried, and besides, it wouldn't solve anything. She blinked hard and gave a small cough. She could act – she'd proved it in the pantomime – so she would jolly well act her socks off now.

'Very well,' she said, looking straight ahead. 'Aberdeenshire, here we come!'

She could feel the others gazing at her, no doubt surprised at how well she appeared to be taking the news.

The girls left the office in silence. Jean gave Seffy a sympathetic look before rushing to fetch her bicycle and head off to work. Seffy stuck her hands into her overcoat pockets and found the toast she'd saved from breakfast. As she set off towards the stables, she ate it in large mouthfuls, hardly tasting it. She'd give herself indigestion but she didn't care.

It was only when she was sure she was alone, deep within the woods, that she leaned her forehead against the rough bark of a fir tree, kicked the base of the trunk and let out a loud – and most unladylike – 'AAAAAGH!'

'I'm leaving on Friday!' Seffy announced, as the girls sat around the campfire at morning break. 'I'm being banished to Ballamar!'

Enid almost fell off the log she was perched on. '"Banished to Ballamar"? It sounds like a film!'

'Aye, a thriller!' Flora said.

Seffy huffed. There was nothing remotely thrilling about what lay ahead, she'd put money on it.

'What happened to England?' Morag asked. 'Weren't you supposed to be going down there?'

Seffy felt irked. Wasn't anyone going to say they were sorry she was leaving?

'Where is Ballamar, anyhow?' Tattie said.

'Jean knows,' Seffy said. 'She's coming too. Here she is now. She'll tell you exactly where Ballamar is. I expect it'll be like a gulag in the middle of Siberia.'

Tattie hugged her mug of tea. 'It cannae be any colder than here. I woke up in the night and ma hot water bottle had fallen out o' the bed and frozen solid!'

'Oi, Seffy, did you say Jean's leaving too?' Flora asked. She clapped her hands in delight. 'That's two more empty beds in Macdonald hut! They'll have to let me stay in camp now, won't they? I'm gonna ask!'

Every cloud, and all that, Seffy thought. Flora's long-held wish to move out of her mother's house and into the camp might be about to come true.

'We'll certainly miss you. Both of you,' Belinda said.

'I don't want you to go,' Tattie said, sounding genuinely upset. 'How long will you be away?'

Seffy smiled at her, gratefully. 'I mightn't come back. If

The rising swell of land had looked the exact same as the home-land they'd left two weeks earlier.

When they'd disembarked in Liverpool and she'd had solid ground under her feet, that had felt good, though. The relief had washed over her like a hot shower. But her buoyant mood hadn't lasted long.

As they'd travelled by taxi to the railroad station, the devastation had come as a shock. Sure, there were pictures in the papers, but until you saw it with your own eyes, you could pretend it wasn't happening. There were craters in the ground and so many build-ings reduced to nothing but rubble.

All credit to them, the British were still going about their busi-ness, picking their way through the ruins like it was nothing out of the ordinary. She supposed you could get used to anything, if you had to.

But could she? It had made her stomach flip wondering how many people must've been inside those buildings when they'd been hit. She'd asked herself what in God's name she and Juliet were doing here. They must be crazy. They'd been safe in Canada; so far from the fighting.

Everyone had felt it. The girls' cheery chatter had stopped and they'd gazed out of the cab windows in silence.

London had been the same – a wounded city – and it had been rainy and grey there too, although as someone pointed out, it was winter, so what could they expect?

And then, there were the raids.

When the sirens went off, as they did most nights, the girls had to leap out of their warm beds and go stand in a damp cellar, leaning against a cold stone wall, until the all-clear sounded.

In the distance they could hear the sounds of planes, ack-ack guns and explosions, as bombs were dropped in another part of the city. All you could do was pray that another night they wouldn't be dropping on you.

everything goes to plan and Miss McEwen keeps her word, I'll go straight from Aberdeenshire to England and join a gang down there.'

Finally, they seemed to have grasped what she'd been trying to tell them: that this was goodbye.

They were silent for a moment. The only sounds were the crackles and spits of the fire and Morag, slurping tea from her tin cup.

Enid suddenly piped up. 'Aye, well, remember what Vera says!'

'Vera who? Is she new?' Flora asked, hopefully.

'No, you daft sod! Vera Lynn, of course!' Enid said. She broke into, '"We'll meet again, don't know where, don't know when …"' and a few of the others joined in, swaying in unison from side to side.

Seffy wasn't sure whether they would meet again; it was a sobering thought.

Jean had propped her bicycle against a tree and made herself a cuppa. She squeezed into a space on the log between Seffy and Belinda.

'Where's this Ballamar place, then, Jean?' Tattie asked.

'It's still in the Highlands, only a couple o' hours away, in Aberdeenshire. It's on the River Dee and—'

'All right, Jean!' Morag said. 'We dunnae need a geography lesson!'

The others laughed and started to chat amongst themselves about other things.

'Did you know about this transfer, Jean?' Seffy asked. 'Before, I mean?'

Jean pushed her glasses up and took a sip from her mug before answering. 'Miss McEwen mentioned something on Christmas Day, aye. Aw, dunnae look at me like that! I didn't want to spoil your Christmas by telling you then. I knew you'd be upset.'

Seffy sighed. Jean was right: it would have ruined Christmas.

31

'Oh, blast the woman!' she said. 'Why couldn't she have chosen someone else? Miss McEwen hates me.'

'Och, she doesn't!' Jean said. 'Maybe she thinks … well, maybe you're the best girl for the job?'

'Codswallop! This is her way of putting me in my place. But we'll show her, won't we, Jean? Let's hope the gang are good workers and we can get the job done quickly. Then, in no time at all, I'll get my wish to move to England. What do you say? Can I count on you?'

Jean seemed to hesitate for a second, before nodding.

'Sure, you can!' she said. She clutched her mug and kept her gaze fixed on the flicking flames. 'Sure,' she said again.

Chapter Five

The South Coast, England
27th December 1943

'This is it!' Juliet said, as the train pulled into the station and the guard called out the name of their stop.

Missy's stomach lurched.

The airman leaped up and insisted on retrieving their kitbags and carrying them onto the platform. As he placed the luggage down, Juliet was all smiles and thank yous, but it was making Missy jittery. Imagine if that was the first thing Callum saw: a strange fella hanging around. He might get the wrong idea.

It was a relief when the airman left them. There was still no sign of the fellas amongst the porters and passengers milling about on the platform.

Juliet bit her lip. 'Oh, boy, they were supposed to get here before us. Their train must've got held up. So much for running into their arms, huh?'

'I guess it's not like the movies,' Missy said.

They decided against going into the Ladies' Waiting Room in case they missed the guys. Instead, they stayed put on the cold platform, getting buffeted by people rushing by. Missy tucked her hat inside her kitbag, and ran her hands through her hair, fluffing it up a little.

Finally, the train pulled out and they were the only ones left.

Then they heard a yell.

'Heyyyyy!'

Verne. There was no mistaking that voice. Big Verne was lolloping towards them, in his green CFC uniform. He had his cap in one hand, arms spread.

He seemed to be alone.

Juliet screamed in delight as he reached her and almost smothered her in a bear hug. Her hat went flying. Then he bent to give her a passionate kiss.

Missy's shoulders fell. Callum wasn't here. The disappointment was like a thump in the stomach.

Darn it! She'd completely messed up. And how was she gonna bear spending the next two days with those lovebirds?

Oh, but – wait! Her heart soared. Yes! He was there! He'd been a few yards behind and her view had been blocked by Verne's large frame. He looked a little different in his uniform – taller, somehow, and real grown-up – but it was Callum, unmistakeably him.

Oh, goodness, her legs had turned to jelly. She couldn't move or even speak. Instead of running into his arms, as she'd planned, she was rooted to the spot.

His face lit up as he spotted her. He dropped his kitbag, took a few long strides forward and then, he was there: all six foot one, two hundred pounds of him, enveloping her in a hug.

Boy, that felt good. She was safe; she was home. She wanted to melt into his arms and stay there forever. He tucked her head under his chin for a second, holding her tight, breathing in, as though he were inhaling her.

'Wow! How did you get here? Oh, and you smell real good,' he murmured, and Missy laughed, glad she'd spent yesterday evening washing and setting her hair.

He pulled back and grabbed her hands, then leaned in to kiss her but she turned her head at that moment and instead of her lips, he kissed the side of her ear. They laughed. It was kinda clumsy and embarrassing. But what did it matter? Like she'd said to Juliet earlier, this wasn't the movies.

Missy squeezed his hands. 'Did you guess? That I was the surprise?'

'No! When Verne said I had to book a forty-eight and come with him—'

'He didn't wanna do it, did ya, buddy?' Verne said. He and Juliet were standing nearby, arms wrapped tightly around each other.

Callum laughed. 'I didn't get why he needed me. Unless it was to carry his bag! Then I thought maybe he was too scared to go see his wife on his own!'

They all laughed at the thought of big Verne, who had biceps like Popeye, being scared of anything.

Callum smiled at Juliet and said hello, and she nodded back, cool and not overly friendly. She was probably too wrapped up with Verne to worry about social niceties.

'I had no choice but to say I thought the surprise might be you, kid,' Verne said. 'Sorry, I kinda ruined it, but it was the only way to get him here!'

Missy didn't care. She didn't even care that Verne was still calling her kid. Nothing mattered; nothing could spoil this.

'Glad you came now?' she asked Callum, looking up at his gorgeous face and those sea-blue eyes.

'Absolutely!' He held her out at arm's length and gazed at her. 'Look what I got!'

He hugged her again, real tight and when he pulled back, they simply stared at one another and laughed.

It was a kinda nervousness, she supposed. It wasn't like Callum to be nervous, especially not with her. It gave her a moment of doubt but then it passed.

Two years was a long time; they needed to get to know one

another again. They were a little shy but they'd get over it soon enough.

Callum looked her up and down and a slow smile spread across his face. 'Say, are you in uniform, Missy Gilbert?'

She laughed and lifted the hem of her overcoat, giving him a glimpse of khaki skirt. 'I might be!'

'Show me later,' he murmured in her ear, and her stomach lurched. When did he get so fresh?

He pulled back, shaking his head in apology. 'Oh, jeez, I don't mean—'

'I know,' she said, stroking his arm. He only meant when they got indoors and she took off her overcoat, nothing more.

Juliet had made it very clear that she'd booked one double room at the boarding house for her and Verne, and two singles for Missy and Callum. They might be engaged, and Missy knew some girls wouldn't hesitate to go all the way in a situation like this, but she was saving herself for her wedding night.

'Hey, did you get thinner?' she asked, touching Callum's face. 'Aren't they feeding you?'

'Sure, we get plenty. A lot more than the British on their rations. But, we're always on the move, I guess.' He stroked her hair. 'Your hair got long.'

'Yours got short!'

She liked it, it suited him. She reached up and ran her hand over it. 'It's kinda spiky.'

'Come on, let's get outta here,' Callum said.

He hoisted his bag over one shoulder, tucked hers under his arm and reached for her hand.

Verne and Juliet were full-on necking. They sure weren't feeling shy with one another. Verne was practically eating her alive. Yuck.

'Hey, put her down, buddy,' Callum said, laughing.

'I wish they weren't here,' Missy muttered.

'They won't hang around long.'

Sure enough, when they'd disentangled themselves, Verne

muttered something to Callum, then he and Juliet walked off arm in arm to find the guesthouse.

'You've got the address, right?' Verne called back. 'See you down for dinner at seven!'

Missy exhaled. Alone at last.

'Shall we take a stroll?' Callum asked. 'The sea's that way. I spotted it from the train. Or is it too cold?'

In truth, she'd rather find a cosy tea shop – the one thing she truly liked about England, so far, were the tea rooms – and sit in the warmth, holding hands over the table. But Callum always had to be outdoors.

'No, it's fine, come on,' she said.

There was a chilly breeze, but it was refreshing to walk hand in hand along the promenade and look out at the pretty pebbled beach, even if it was behind rows of barbed wire.

Callum pointed towards the sea. 'See that line of wooden poles? That's the kinda thing we were timbering for, up in Scotland. They stop the enemy landing, by sea and air.'

He gazed out at them, lost in thought. He almost looked as pleased to see those darned wooden poles as he'd been to see her.

'That's great, honey,' Missy said, tugging him gently back towards her. 'But, anyhow, the voyage over was a nightmare. I'd imagined we'd be sailing on a huge ship, like a cruise liner?'

'And weren't you?'

'No! It was a tiny ship, the HMS Cavina, a requisitioned banana boat! Even the crew were nervous. We felt every wave. I was still moving and swaying a couple of days after we landed.'

'Same here! It's the weirdest feeling, right? Our crossing was real rough too. And it was spring, not winter, so it was probably worse for you. Oh, boy, I was sick as a dog.'

'Me too! Well, not like a dog,' Missy added quickly, in case he thought she'd become coarse. 'But at least my luggage arrived safely. One girl's bag went over the side when the stevedores were tossing the gear ashore. And you know, a group of Red Cross girls got held up in New York City, waiting for an escort ship? They spent a couple of days there and had a marvellous time. That wouldn't have been so bad, huh?'

She was gabbling now but it was the novelty of finally being able to talk to him. She couldn't stop.

'You'd have liked to see New York?' he asked.

Missy nodded. It had rankled when she'd heard about those girls. Why couldn't that have happened to them? To see New York City, now that would've been something.

But in case Callum thought she was more interested in seeing the world, than in seeing him, she said, 'Oh, but I wanted to get over here as fast as I could, so … no, I didn't really wanna get held up in New York.'

They walked on a little further.

'Sorry I didn't write much.' He winced, as though bracing himself for a ticking off.

'Yeah, see what you made me do?' She let go of his hand and prodded his shoulder. 'I got so fed up waiting on mail from you, I had to come speak to you in person!'

She'd forgiven him for his sporadic letter writing. Callum wasn't keen on reading and writing. Not that he was stupid: he was cleverer than almost anyone she knew. Still, it was a pity he didn't like books. She'd often thought it would be nice to read the same book and then write to each other about it. Some of her girlfriends did that with their fellas overseas. She'd imagined it would bring you closer.

She'd suggested it in one of her letters. Did he want to read *For Whom the Bell Tolls* or, if that was a little heavy, maybe a mystery by Agatha Christie? If he told her which one he preferred, she'd send him a copy and get one for herself at the same time. And when they'd both finished it, they could write and tell each other which parts and which characters they'd liked best.

But he'd never answered that particular question, so she'd guessed the answer was no.

'It's good to see you, Missy,' Callum said. 'I've missed you. It kinda feels like I'm dreaming!'

That was what she'd wanted to hear: that he'd dreamed about this moment and now she'd made it real. She felt suddenly lighter, as though the worries of the past few weeks had dropped away.

'I'm gonna be so near, we can see each other all the time!' she said.

Was it her imagination or had his smile faltered a little?

'Not all the time, of course,' she said quickly, 'because we'll both be on duty but when we can get leave at the same time. We're moving to the military hospital next week. It's not far from here. It's in a place called Basingstoke.'

Callum smiled and told her he'd heard of it and sure, it wasn't far from his camp. A short train ride away, that was all.

An elderly man and woman coming the other way walked slowly past. The two couples wished each other a good afternoon.

They were probably like us once, Missy thought: young and in love. Her whole life with Callum stretched before her. This would be something to tell the kids one day: 'Guess what Daddy did in the war? And Mommy too!'

'Are you surprised?' she asked. 'That I'd do something like this? You see, when I thought 'bout you coming home, I got worried. You'd have seen the world and had adventures, and what would I have done? Stayed home, knitting woollies for the troops? And that might've made a gap between us. So, that's partly why I've come: so we can share a little of the same experience.'

Callum stopped and turned to her, shaking his head.

'Wow, that's real thoughtful, Missy.'

He was looking at her with a new kind of respect. She didn't deserve it because, in truth, those were Juliet's words and Juliet's reason.

'I don't want a husband who's a stranger when he comes back from the war!' she'd said, when their parents had expressed doubts about her going to Europe. It had done the trick: Mom and Dad had practically fallen over themselves to sign the papers.

'Hey, you and Verne seem real friendly these days,' she said, as they continued along the promenade.

Back home, the fellas had never got along, which was a pity because there'd been no chance of double-dating and one day, Callum and Verne would be brothers-in-law, after all.

Callum gave a short 'Ha!' and laughed. 'We're not, believe me. I had a punch-up with the fella a few months back and almost got put on a charge.'

Missy laughed along but inside something twisted: a worry. Callum never fought. Correction: Callum never used to fight.

'You were in a fight? What was all that about?'

He was looking down at his boots now and shaking his head. When he looked up, his face had closed down.

'Aw, nothing much. We're good now. But Gordy's still my best buddy. You remember Gordy Johnson?'

'Sure, I do! Little Gordy! I always liked him. And he got married to a Scottish girl, right? You sent me the cutting. I thought his bride looked nice. Kinda homely looking. Oh and tall! Taller than Gordy! But … yeah …'

She tailed off, not wanting to admit how she'd pored over the photo, picking out the CFC men she knew from home but mostly staring at Callum, already looking so different in his uniform.

He'd been gazing straight into the camera, mouth set, and she'd wondered what he was thinking. Was he thinking of her and their future wedding day? Or was there a local girl who'd caught his eye? Maybe he was thinking about her.

'And now they're havin' a baby!' Callum said.

'A baby! Wow! But—' she blushed a little '—how did that happen? Didn't your company leave Scotland a while back?'

Callum laughed and looked a little embarrassed too.

'Let's just say, Mr and Mrs Johnson managed to have themselves a second honeymoon. A few days at the border and… whaddaya know – there's a baby on the way!'

Missy laughed. 'Tell Gordy congratulations from me, will you?'

She wondered what Callum thought about Gordy getting married over here and becoming a father. Because Callum wanted that too, she was sure of it. Hadn't he always told her that family was everything?

His ma had died when he was just a kid and his dad – a wastrel and a drunkard – had died a few years back. That was partly why he was so close to her folks: they were the family he'd never had. It was one of the things she loved about him: the respect he showed her mom and dad.

An awful thought crossed her mind.

'Gordy's planning on coming back to B.C. though, right? He's not staying here, once the war's over?'

Callum frowned 'No, they'll come back to Canada. Wife and baby and Gordy. We're all coming home one of these days, sweetheart.'

'That's good,' Missy said. 'You know, I'm glad you've got pals like Gordy here, in the same company. And that you're not too lonesome.'

'When you're this far from home, the army becomes your family,' Callum said.

Missy stopped and pulled him towards her for a kiss. She didn't even care if anyone saw.

'But I'm here now, darling,' she said softly, as they drew apart. 'And I'm all the family you need.'

Chapter Six

30th December 1943

Callum cleared his throat. 'The reason I wanted to see you, sir…
I've come to ask, if there's any chance—'

Hell, he was beating around the bush, the exact thing he told
himself not to do.

'"Any chance", Staff Sergeant?' Coomber said, from behind his
desk. 'Any chance we'll be across the Channel by next Christmas?
Any chance Hedy Lamarr will come visit the troops or someone'll
do us all a favour and shoot that son of a bitch Hitler?'

He gave a short laugh and banged his pen on the edge of the
desk. Callum liked Coomber but since he'd been promoted to
captain, he'd gotten a little too big for his boots. He thought he
was funny.

'Hey, you're not after a pass out for tomorrow night, are you,
Staff? Because all the New Year passes are long gone!'

Callum pushed his chest out and clenched his hands behind
his back. 'No, it's nothing like that. I'm officially requesting a
transfer, sir. Back to Scotland.'

He'd battled with this for the past three days, but there, he'd
finally said it.

'Scotland?' Coomber sounded incredulous. 'Don't tell me, you're missing the rain?'

'No, sir.'

'The cold, is that it? You know, couple o' years before we pitched up, they raised hundreds of timbermen from British Honduras to work in those forests. Can you imagine coming from the tropics to the freezing north of Scotland? Course, those guys couldn't cope. Got sick. Had to send 'em all home. It's a tough place. That rain's the real killer. And you wanna go back?'

Coomber was one of the better senior officers. He was fair and he listened, for the most part. But Callum was getting kinda irritated with the guy now. Why didn't he give him a straight answer?

The captain stood up, placed his hands on the desk and leaned forward, so that his face was only a foot away from Callum's.

'What's all this about, Staff?'

'There's a girl, sir. In truth, she's my fiancée.'

'Ah.' Coomber wrinkled his nose, straightened and looked down at his desk. 'Another lassie left in Scotland! You should be talking to the padre about this.'

'She's not Scottish, sir. She's Canadian, from my hometown, Invermore. She's … well, she's come over.'

He had Coomber's attention now. 'She's in Europe? How in tarnation did she manage that?'

Callum bit the inside of his cheek. She wasn't merely in Europe; she was in England. He was half expecting her to turn up in the Nissen hut next to his and tell him she'd moved into camp.

He'd thought she was thousands of miles away, he'd thought he had time to figure this all out, maybe not even think about it properly until the war was over. But his old life had suddenly collided with this one; something had to give.

He moved his tongue inside his mouth. He could taste blood.

'She's in London, sir,' he said. 'At the moment. But soon she'll be moving to her posting in Basingstoke. That's a few miles along—'

'I know that! I'm just trying to establish how in hell's name she got there!'

For the past three nights, as he'd lain in his cot, unable to sleep, Callum had asked himself the same question.

'She's a volunteer, sir. She's come over with the Red Cross.'

Coomber's frown faded. He looked impressed.

'OK, that makes sense,' he said. 'That's a mighty brave and honourable thing to do, don't you think?'

'Oh, yes, sir, it surely is.' Hope was draining out of him. He gave a bitter smile. 'But I didn't know she was coming.'

That had sounded pathetic. He'd had one chance and he was messing this up.

'You didn't know? She just turned up?' Coomber shook his head and gave a low whistle. 'I dunno 'bout you, Staff, but I don't allow myself to think too much about the folks back home, else I'd go "barmy", as the British say. I'm betting you were focused on keeping everything in check and suddenly, your girl was there, right in front of your eyes!'

'That's kinda how it was, sir, yes.'

The captain picked up the photograph of his family. As he gazed at it, his eyes softened.

'If I thought there was any chance of getting Mrs Coomber here and I could guarantee her safety, why, I'd ask her to do it in a heartbeat. Mind you, I'm not sure she'd be brave enough to try. You remember being on a ship in that ocean, praying the escorts are up to the job, right? It's pretty unnerving, when you think about it.'

Callum nodded. 'Sir.'

Coomber put the photograph back on the desk and sighed. 'Let me get this straight: your fiancée has come over to serve her country and to be with you, and it's a bad thing because …?'

Callum shuffled his feet and resisted the urge to look down.

'I feel rotten, sir, but I can't do it. I can't see her every couple o' weeks, on weekends or whatever, and pretend everything's all right when—'

He stopped, hoping Captain Coomber would fill in the gap, but no, he was gonna make him say it.

'—when there's someone else, sir.'

He'd mumbled that last sentence; it had come out in a rush.

He fixed his gaze on the desk in front of him: the photographs, the fountain pen lying on the blotter, the packet of Winchesters. Coomber didn't smoke but he always had a pack, a lighter and an ashtray on his desk for those who did. Callum didn't smoke either but he reckoned he could manage a cigarette now.

Coomber got up and started pacing the office, hands behind his back.

You didn't talk about this kind of stuff in the army, leastways, not with your superior officer. But he was grateful to the captain for listening to him, anyhow. No one could help him, he knew that. He had to do this himself. He had to pluck up the guts to do the right thing.

'This other girl – not your fiancée – I'm assuming it's a Scots girl? A lassie?'

'Not Scots, sir. But British, yeah. She's a forester, a lumberjill.' He felt an unexpected surge of pride, thinking about Seffy. He was bracing himself for a reprimand, though. They'd been warned often enough about getting involved with British girls.

'You haven't made her any promises, this British girl? She's not … in trouble?'

'NO! No.' No promises, nothing spoken. But unfinished business, for sure, he thought.

'And she's still up there in Scotland?'

He nodded. 'Yeah, she's in Blantyre Forest, where we used to be.'

There was silence for a few seconds, then Coomber inhaled and said, 'Here's what you need to do, Staff. Forget her. She is gone, ancient history!'

That was easier said than done.

'How long have you known your fiancée?'

'Forever. Her folks have been real good to me. They kinda

45

brought me up. I owe them everything. I guess I'd be letting them down, too.'

'Yep! You'd be letting everyone down. Your fiancée, her family, your country and hell, you'd be letting down the CFC! We're honourable men in the Canadian Forestry Corps, don't you forget it. This woman – this fine Canadian woman – what's her name?'

'It's Miss – it's Miranda Gilbert.'

'Right, so Miss Miranda Gilbert has risked her life to be with you, as well as doing her duty, serving in that excellent institution, the Red Cross. I'd say you've got yourself a mighty fine lady there. A mighty fine wife-to-be. Only a numbskull would say otherwise. And if she were my daughter, I'd sure as hell be expecting you – her intended – to do the right thing.'

Callum nodded. His shoulders dropped. He wished he'd never asked for this interview. It was one thing to be told when to get up, what to wear and eat, when to march, when to shoot a rifle. But the army sure didn't have the right to control your whole life.

Maybe he would've been better off talking to the padre, after all. But the padre couldn't give him what he wanted; only Coomber could do that.

He'd guessed, when Verne had said he needed to book a forty-eight and come to the coast, that Missy must've come over with Juliet. But he still hadn't really believed it until he'd seen her with his own eyes.

Jeez, he'd have bet a year's wages on Missy never doing such a thing. Which only went to show, you never really know a person. Not deep down.

Five minutes later, he'd been dismissed and he was standing outside Coomber's office with the captain's final words ringing in his ears. 'Do the right thing, Staff Sergeant!'

But what was the right thing? His head was saying one thing, his heart, another. Hell, he couldn't do anything until he'd spoken to Seffy.

Chapter Seven

London, England
30th December 1943

'Oh, gee, that is *so* adorable!' Missy said, holding up a tiny white cardigan. 'It's got the darlingest mother-of-pearl buttons!' She turned to the other women standing around the trestle table. 'Isn't it cute?'

'Sure is, honey,' Sylvia murmured.

This was Missy's favourite chore at the Maple Leaf Club: assembling layettes for British women married to Canadian servicemen.

She was probably driving the others crazy. They were all 'veterans' – they'd been in London a while and this was simply another routine chore for them.

She and Juliet had only used up two days of their week's leave visiting the fellas on the coast and in theory, they could've set off to see different parts of the country. Some of the other Red Cross girls were doing just that: they'd requested hospitality and were staying with British families who'd offered to host them.

But Juliet was determined to see as much of London as possible, so they were staying here a few more days, before they transferred to the hospital. There was a limit to how much sightseeing Missy could manage, so today she'd left Juliet to it and instead, she was helping out with chores at the Club.

Making beds was the worst: there were dozens to be made every day, with heavy army blankets that were hard on fingers and nails. But this – sorting and packing up the layettes – was fun.

'Imagine,' Missy said, stroking a pink satin dress, 'you've fallen in love with a handsome Canadian, you've gotten married and now you're having his baby!' She felt a twist of envy for those unknown British women, who seemed to have all a girl could ask for.

'How long have you been going with your fella, Miranda?' Sylvia asked.

'Oh, forever! He's the only boyfriend I've ever had. He's practically the only boy I've ever known!'

Dorothy curled her lip. 'Jeez, honey, he sounds more like your brother than your lover!'

'Boring,' Sylvia agreed. 'Say, I could introduce you to some real men, if you like.'

Missy was taken aback. These girls should think about a person's feelings before they spoke.

'Oh, no, Sylvia, that's kind,' she said, 'but I'm OK.'

'What age are you, Miranda?' another girl asked.

'I'm twenty-three.'

'Hey, you're a baby! You really should sow some wild oats before you settle down. That's what we wish we'd done, don't we, Sylvia?'

'We sure do! After all, there are plenty of fish in the sea.'

'And it's a mighty big sea!' the first girl said. 'Hell, it's an ocean!'

When the raucous laughter had died down, Dorothy said, 'You know, some of these layettes are for pregnant British women who *aren't* married to the father of their child.'

Missy felt a jolt of surprise and then shame on behalf of her compatriots. Why weren't they making honest women of the girls they'd gotten in the family way?

'Aren't the fellas allowed to marry their British girl?'

'Sure, they're *allowed*,' Sylvia said, 'but not if they're already married and have a wife and family back home.'

Already married? That was shocking.

'Poor things,' Missy said.

'Yeah, they probably have no idea. The Canadian wife is in the dark about the British girl her husband's courting, and the British girl probably has no idea that the fella she's fallen for is married. And the next thing—' Sylvia shrugged '—she finds out she's in the family way.'

Missy swallowed. Gee, what a mess.

She had a horrible thought. Was Callum capable of something like that? Would he ever pretend she didn't exist, like some of those married fellas must've done? No, he wouldn't, would he?

'You're looking kinda strung out,' Dorothy said. 'Not doubting your own fella, are you?'

'Oh, no! We're actually engaged and—'

Dorothy laughed. 'That don't mean jack, honey. Oh, boy, you're straight outta the backwoods, ain't you? A ring don't mean a thing! Not when fellas are so far from home!'

Missy hid her left hand behind her back. She didn't actually have a ring. Not yet.

'Did he ask you to marry him just before he set off for Europe?' Dorothy asked.

Missy nodded, uncertainly.

'Thought so. Dozens of 'em did the same. A kind of insurance policy, I guess, so neither of them would consider themselves at liberty to find comfort in someone else's arms.' She held up a blue bonnet and tutted. 'Didn't always work, though, did it?'

Hot tears were pricking Missy's eyes. Who did this girl think she was? She didn't know anything about her or Callum.

'He's not like that,' she said, tilting her chin.

Dorothy put her face right up close to hers. 'How do you know what your fiancé's been doing over here? You don't think he's been dancing, flirting with a stranger? This is wartime, honey.

49

Rules have gone out the window!'

'You know,' another girl said, 'I hear British girls are snapping up all our available men!'

Missy's stomach dropped. 'Are … are they?'

'Yeah. They don't have men of their own no more. They're fighting in France and places like that. There are no fellas left in the British Isles, except old guys and young boys. No men, except OURS!'

Missy put her hand to her chest. Not her man, no way.

'And it's not just ours, it's the Yanks too,' Sylvia said. 'British girls wanna get themselves a better life once the war ends.'

The tight knot in her stomach pinched.

'If I were you, Miranda,' Sylvia continued, 'I'd get that fiancé of yours down the aisle as soon as you can!'

'Oh, yes!' Missy said, glad her sister wasn't around to hear this conversation. 'That's exactly what I intend to do!'

Chapter Eight

Aberdeenshire, Scotland
31st December 1943

On Friday, as the girls were being driven to Ballamar, Seffy was subdued. She was slumped in her seat, gazing out at the passing hills and low-lying cloud.

Jean sat quietly beside her, occasionally turning to glance out of the window to check that her bicycle hadn't fallen off the boot rack.

'You're not anxious? About the transfer?' Aunt Dilys had asked, when Seffy had told her the news. 'When I was your age and in the Women's Forestry Service, we were always being moved around. We were like a merry band of nomads. It'll do you the power of good, Persephone. One doesn't want to stand still in life! Always move forward, that's the ticket!'

Perhaps that was true. A change was as good as a rest. And of course, Seffy wasn't anxious *per se* about the transfer, but she was anxious to get the work done as soon as possible, so she could move south.

She sat up properly in her seat. Slouching would give her round shoulders, as she remembered from deportment.

At least she had Jean for company. She wouldn't have put it past Miss McEwen to have sent her away quite alone.

Jean was clever and well-meaning. It would've been more fun with Joey but there were worse gals to be stuck with. She really ought to speak to the poor girl and not sit here moping for the whole journey.

'How long do you think we'll have to stay in this new place?' she said, knowing how Jean liked to be asked for her opinion.

'Impossible to say. I'll know more once I start calculating the amount of standing timber to be felled. But I expect it'll be a few weeks, at least.'

A few weeks. She'd definitely miss the christening. She'd have to write to Emerald and suggest she might want to choose a different godmother.

It would be spring, then, at the earliest, before she was granted a transfer down to England. She didn't relish seeing out the rest of this perishing winter in Scotland but the thought of spring was comforting. Lighter evenings, sunshine, blossom and birdsong. And spending time with Callum, of course. It would be worth the wait; it was definitely something to look forward to.

'Did you bring the whisky?' Jean asked.

The previous evening, Aunt Dilys had held a farewell party for the girls, during which she'd presented Seffy with a bottle of Lagavulin.

'Amber nectar, for you, madam!' she'd said, thumping it down on the table. 'Consider it a leaving present.'

Seffy had gazed at it, astonished. 'No, aunt, honestly, I can't take that!'

'I insist! I've got gallons of the stuff and I don't touch it, save for a wee snifter on Burns Night and even then I hold my nose.'

'Oh, well, in that case, thank you very much,' Seffy had said.

She wasn't overly enamoured with whisky either, but it would've been rude to refuse a second time.

'It's always handy for a hot toddy,' Dilys had said. 'If you catch a chill or a cold, put a little honey and a dash of lemon in a glass. Add hot water and some of this and Bob's your uncle! It's a cure-all.'

Seffy had smiled. It was kind of her aunt but how in heaven's name would she come by honey or lemons in the middle of rural Aberdeenshire?

She looked at Jean. 'Yes, I did bring the whisky. My aunt was so insistent, I wouldn't have dared leave it behind! Why?'

Jean shrugged. 'Only that it's Hogmanay and we could have a wee dram tonight, if you fancy one?'

Seffy supposed a toast to the New Year wouldn't go amiss. It would be a time to reflect on the past year too and remember absent friends.

The car had stopped at the top of a steep lane. There was a row of neat grey stone cottages to one side and open countryside on the other, as far as the eye could see.

'I cannae go any further doon there,' the driver said. 'I'll never get up again. Not wi' all that ice.' He sighed. 'And there's more weather comin' in. It won't be long before it snows.'

'Very well!' Seffy said, opening the car door. 'We'll get out here, then. Would you mind giving us a hand? We seem to have brought everything but the kitchen sink.'

As well as their luggage, the girls had brought a big box of tools: a crosscut saw, a couple of axes – one small, one large – a paring knife and a bill hook. They'd even filched a billycan for making tea and some tin mugs.

Their destination – Laburnum Cottage – was the last house in the row, nestled in a dip at the bottom of the hill. The driver had been right about the ice. The girls skidded down the lane, loaded up with their belongings, while he stood at the top, watching them. So much for giving them a hand.

Once they'd deposited their bags and cases next to the rickety gate and the faded 'Laburnum Cottage' sign, they struggled back up the slope to collect Jean's bicycle and the tools, which the driver had removed from the car.

With a farewell grunt, he got back inside and reversed fast up the lane, as though he couldn't wait to get away. Seffy was glad she hadn't tipped him.

'It's a good thing we're strong and capable, Jean. The days of chivalry are over. Now do be careful on the way back down. It'd be a fine to-do if we broke an ankle before we'd even got inside!'

There was no sign of life in the cottage. The curtains and blinds were still drawn, even though it was almost midday.

'I hope no one's died,' Jean said.

There was a patch of garden at the front, enclosed by a wooden fence and a gate which came off its hinges when Seffy tried to open it. She propped it up against the post.

'This way!' a woman barked from somewhere to the side of the building. 'Round the back!'

The woman was leaning on the doorframe. She was younger than Seffy had expected: mid-forties, at a guess, an attractive, buxom woman, even in her housecoat and slippers. She had rollers in – at this time of day! – covered by a red headscarf and she was holding a feather duster aloft, like a conductor's baton.

'Hullo,' Jean said. 'Mrs Harris?'

'Aye,' the woman said. 'Bring yerselves inside. Are those tools?' She pointed the duster at the box. 'Put them in the shed first. Mind the fishing rods! The bicycle can go in there too, next to mine. Don't be bringing dirty tools into ma house, now, especially not today!'

Once they'd deposited everything in the shed, the girls returned to the house and introduced themselves.

Mrs Harris looked them up and down. 'Land girls, is it? I hope you're better than the last two. I dunnae want any more rough girls, mind.'

'We're not rough!' Jean said. 'My colleague here is the daughter of an Earl.'

Seffy nodded. 'It's true, I am.' This was hardly the time for false modesty. 'My name's actually "Lady Persephone Baxter-Mills" but ever since I joined the Women's Timber Corps, I've been known as "Miss Mills."'

Mrs Harris looked unimpressed. She wiped her hands on her housecoat. 'Blondie, you're clearly English but where are you from, Red?'

'Glasgow,' Jean said.

'A toonser,' Mrs Harris said. 'I thought as much. Now, it's two weeks' rent in advance and I'll need your ration books.'

Goodness, they hadn't even unpacked and she was demanding money. It was awfully businesslike and rather dispiriting. So much for a sweet old landlady fussing around them. Seffy couldn't imagine this woman bringing them tea in bed. Or if she did, she'd want paying.

Once the finances were sorted out to her satisfaction and she'd tucked the money inside her blouse, Mrs Harris said, 'You'll be wanting to see the room.' She jerked her head at the ceiling. 'First door on the left.'

Seffy left Jean making polite chit-chat about the weather and lugged her case up the stairs. Gosh, they were practically vertical; it was like scaling Mont Blanc. The whitewashed walls were cold to the touch and she wondered, with a sinking heart, whether this place ever got warm.

At the top of the stairs, she turned left, pressed the latch and opened the bedroom door. The room had beams and a low ceiling. She'd have to remember to duck. But the latticed windows had a nice view over the rolling hills and although small, the room was neat and clean.

There was a rag rug on the floor, a mahogany wardrobe in one corner and a double bed, covered in a crocheted blanket, which lent a bright touch. Against the back wall stood a dresser with a mirror, a china jug and basin.

Seffy sat on the bed and bounced, making the springs squeak. Rather on the hard side, but not bad. Yes, this would do nicely.

There was a creaking on the landing and Jean put her head around the door.

'I'm having this one,' Seffy said.

Jean staggered inside and hauled her bag onto the bed. 'Ha, very droll. We're sharing. Did you no' realise?'

'What? I've never shared a bed with anyone in my life! Are you quite sure?'

'Aye, she's just told me. There are only two bedrooms. The other's hers. It's against the rules, of course. It's one o' the conditions of billets that we're supposed to have our own bed.'

Jean didn't seem unduly concerned. She had lots of siblings: she'd probably doubled-up like this before. And it was too late to do anything about it now. Mrs Harris was brusque and rather scary, and if they refused to share the bed, they'd have to get their money back and try to find a new billet before nightfall.

'It won't be forever,' Jean said.

'Yes, we shouldn't carp. There are people suffering worse conditions than having to share a bed or put up with a—' Seffy lowered her voice '—strange landlady.'

'Aye, she's rude.'

'Fancy calling us "Blondie" and "Red" when she hardly knows us. And I can't understand half of what she says. What's a – what was that she called you?'

'A toonser? It's someone from a town. I suppose, to her, living in such a remote place, anyone's a toonser. By the way, the privy's at the bottom of the yard. And—' Jean looked under the bed and brought out a ceramic chamber pot. 'We've got one of these!'

Seffy laughed. 'That, is strictly for emergencies only. Agreed?'

'Agreed.'

Seffy looked at the bed. 'We can top and tail, if you like. Let's just try not to kick one another in the head in the middle of the night!'

Once they'd unpacked, they went downstairs, in search of a cup of tea. The kettle was whistling merrily on the hob and there was ham and bread on the small kitchen table for lunch. They devoured it. The bread was rather stale and the ham had a greenish tinge, but Seffy was so hungry she didn't care.

Mrs Harris bustled around them. She scrubbed the sink, dusted the plates on the dresser and swept the floor, nudging their feet with the broom until they lifted them up.

'What a day for yous to arrive, eh? While I'm redding the whole house for Hogmanay!'

Seffy gave Jean a questioning look.

'Cleaning the house from top to bottom,' Jean explained. 'It's bad luck to start a new year with a dirty home.'

'Aye, that's it,' Mrs Harris said. 'It's like a spring clean. Start the New Year as ye mean to go on! When I've finished here, I've got to go up to Mr McIntyre's place and do the redding there!'

It was a relief that this frantic activity was only for today. If their landlady was always this house-proud, muddy footprints and sopping overcoats might've been an issue.

Mrs Harris stomped through the kitchen and out of the back door, carrying a panful of ashes.

'Now,' she said, as she returned and slammed the door. 'I expect you'll be going out tonight. It is Hogmanay, after all!'

She took a tin of polish and a duster from the cupboard under the sink and darted out of the room again.

Seffy pulled a face at Jean across the table. She'd rather hoped to spend the evening listening to the wireless or some records. There was a coal fire in the living room, she'd glimpsed it through the open door as they'd arrived. But Mrs Harris clearly wanted them out of her hair.

'This reminds me of a B&B my family stayed in once, in Saltcoats,' Jean said.

'Saltcoats? What a funny name!'

'They used to harvest salt there, from the Firth of Clyde. It was

57

the first time my whole family had been away together. Once we'd had breakfast, we had to leave the B&B and we weren't allowed back until five o'clock. We roamed around all day, freezing cold, trying to eke out our holiday spends in tea shops. Ma wee brothers and sisters cried the whole time.'

'That sounds horrendous! And that was supposed to be a holiday?'

That decided it. They were not going to have a Saltcoats experience, being ordered out of the house at all times of day and night.

'Now, Mrs Harris, about going out,' Seffy said, when the woman reappeared. 'To be perfectly honest, we're fagged out and—'

'The Drover's Inn is two minutes that way!' Mrs Harris pointed down the hall. 'Left out the front door. It opens at five.'

A pub? Whatever poor opinion Mrs Harris had of them, surely she didn't expect two unaccompanied young women to venture into a strange pub?

'I hardly think—' Seffy said.

'It's perfectly respectable! I go in there myself!'

Seffy raised her eyebrows at Jean and gave the tiniest shake of her head.

'Aw, and I forgot to say,' Mrs Harris said, with a distracted air, 'a fella called in and left a message for yous earlier. Now, what did he call himself? Burke! Aye, that's the fella. Face like a weasel.'

'That's the acquisition officer,' Jean said. 'His name's Mr Burke.' She sat up straight and tucked a strand of hair behind her ear.

'He said he'd meet you in The Drover's Inn tonight at eight sharp.'

The girls looked at one another.

'We shall have to go,' Jean said.

Seffy sighed. 'Yes, I suppose we shall.'

Chapter Nine

Jean lit the way with her torch as the girls made their way to The Drover's Inn. She was glad she wasn't alone. She'd had a fear of the dark ever since that awful night at the Canadian camp and she couldnae shake it off.

'It's ridiculous!' Seffy said. 'Who arranges a meeting on New Year's Eve, in a pub!'

'Maybe Mr Burke's leaving the area,' Jean said, 'and it's his only chance to see us. I expect he travels a good deal, supervising different gangs and negotiating with landowners.'

She was hoping to impress the fella. Who knew, as Miss McEwen had said, where it might lead?

When they arrived, the pub was in darkness but they could hear voices and music coming from inside. Seffy opened the heavy oak door, they pushed their way through the blackout curtain and – oh, what a pleasant surprise!

The place was crowded, a fire was blazing in the hearth and someone was playing an accordion. Most of the customers were old fellas, perched on stools around the bar, or standing, waiting to be served, but there was also a lively group squeezed together around a table, playing dominoes.

'This isn't too shabby, actually, is it?' Seffy said.

Much of the lively chatter had stopped as the girls had walked in. Heads had turned. It was hardly surprising: they were strangers here and female, too. Seffy, with her willowy frame and shock of blonde curls, probably always made men look twice.

Someone aimed a long, low whistle in their direction.

'Ignore that,' Seffy said.

Gradually, the curious stares subsided and the villagers returned to their conversations and their drinks.

Mr Burke was sitting up at the bar, a grey-haired fella of about fifty. He had a long, narrow face and close-set eyes. He was wearing a green tunic and breeches, which marked him out as either a gamekeeper or a woodsman, and it turned out he was the latter.

'Mr Burke?' Jean asked.

'Aye?'

'Jean Ferguson.' She extended her hand. 'Women's Timber Corps.'

Seffy put her hand out too. 'Miss Mills. Also Women's Timber Corps.'

He stared at them, his face quite blank.

'We were asked to meet you here at eight for our briefing?' Jean said.

'Oh, aye!' he said, as the penny finally dropped. 'Of course! Sit yourselves down.'

They hadn't shaken hands and there wasn't anywhere to sit. Every stool was taken and this wasnae the kind of place where men would offer their seats to women.

Mr Burke carried on knocking back his beer and didn't seem to notice. The girls had no choice but to stand, one on either side of him, and lean against the counter.

'You'll be wanting a drink,' he said, and before they could utter a word, he'd ordered two halves of shandy.

They raised their eyebrows at one another. It would've been nice to have been asked.

What a numbskull he'd turned out to be! And to think, Jean

had expected to be in awe of him. Why were fellas always such a disappointment?

Once they'd been served with their drinks, Mr Burke looked at Seffy appraisingly. 'So you're the English lassie who rounded up the Eyeties, eh?'

Seffy looked puzzled. 'If you mean the Italian POWs then yes – Miss Ferguson and I were both involved in that little fracas but how—'

'What is it we're here to do?' Jean said, cutting Seffy off.

Miss McEwen didn't want her to know she'd been specially selected by the bigwigs and it had sounded as though Mr Burke was about to spill the beans.

'Ah, right.' He shifted on his stool. 'The landowner's name is Finn McIntyre. Biggest landowner in these parts.' He sniffed. 'New money. His grandfather was an industrialist.'

'And what about the woodland?' Jean asked. She didnae give two hoots how the landowner had come by his wealth.

'It's mostly mature Scots pine,' he said. 'But there's also an old oak wood, surrounded by young pines.'

Oak? That sounded promising. Plenty to get their teeth into.

'And I understand there aren't any horses?' Seffy said.

'Aye, the trees are brought out by tractor.'

Seffy's face lit up. 'Goody! I'll have some fun with that!'

'No, the saw mill laddies drive the tractor. In fact, those are some o' them over there.' Mr Burke nodded at the table of domino players.

There were a couple of weather-beaten old men, two young lads of about sixteen – too young to be in the forces or drinking in a pub, for that matter – and a man of about thirty-five, whose thatch of hair was an even brighter shade of red than Jean's own.

'The ginger fella is Mr Galbraith, head sawyer.'

Jean wondered whether they should ask to be introduced but at that moment, the head sawyer fella let out a whoop as he won a game, and his pals erupted into shouts and laughter. They'd had a skinful. Perhaps it'd be better to make their acquaintance when they were sober.

'So, what is it you want us to do?' Seffy asked.

Mr Burke shrugged. 'The usual: felling, burning brushwood, cross-cutting. And getting the gang up to scratch.' He took a gulp of his pint and wiped his mouth with the back of his hand. 'They're a wee bit green. They've been training on the job. This is their third workplace but they've, er … still got a lot to learn. And you'll need to assign one of the lassies to the saw mill. The pay rate's higher there, so you shouldnae be short of volunteers.'

'So, one lassie's to go to the saw mill and one's a measurer, working with me. How many does that leave?' Jean asked.

'There are six of them altogether. So that'll leave four fellers.'

Jean nodded. Five felling trees in total then, including Seffy.

'You might come across the odd conchie,' he said. 'I think there's mebbe one at the saw mill. You know what they are, don't you?'

Seffy tutted. 'Of course. Conscientious objectors.'

'Aye, well, you're no' to talk to them.'

'I beg your pardon? We're forbidden to talk to the conchies?' Seffy sounded outraged.

'Aye, that's right. No one talks to them.'

'I thought the gang might've been in here tonight?' Jean said, quickly changing the subject so that Seffy didn't get into a row.

Mr Burke swallowed. 'The gang? Erm … no. They wouldnae come in here. Now, there's summat I should probably explain.'

That sounded ominous.

'Go on,' Jean said.

'Afore ye can start felling, there's some clearing to be done.'

'Clearing?' Seffy narrowed her eyes. 'How much?'

'Aw, a wee bit. Mr McIntyre resisted having his woods felled for some time, but in the end, of course, he's had to give in.'

'So they've been requisitioned?' Jean asked.

'Aye. A couple o' years back a copse on his land was felled. Some fellas volunteered to do it in their summer holiday. Schoolboys, teachers, students and the like. They did their best but …' he sighed, 'they didnae have the experience.'

'You mean they botched it?' Seffy said.

Burke nodded. 'So this time around, McIntyre took some persuading. He's not awful keen on having any more of his woodland taken. I only got him to agree on condition that this, er … copse is cleared for replanting before any more felling takes place.'

Seffy looked grim. This wouldn't affect Jean's measuring work but everyone knew clearing was a back-breaking and thankless task, not half as satisfying as felling.

'What'll happen to the saw mill while we're in this copse?' Seffy asked. 'We won't be supplying them with wood.'

'There are other Timber Corps gangs in the area,' Mr Burke said. 'The fellas have enough to do. But once your gang starts felling, they'll need more hands on deck, which is why you need to assign a lassie to the saw mill.'

He stayed for a few more minutes, gave them contact details for the divisional and welfare officers, wished them the best of luck and then, with obvious relief, knocked back his pint and left.

Jean had the feeling he hadn't been entirely truthful with them.

'What did you think of him?' she asked Seffy.

'An absolute chump! Burke by name and berk by nature! I wonder how he knew about the Italian breakout though?'

'Aw, I expect word's got around. I thought he was a chump, too. How do men like him get jobs like that?'

'What do you mean, "men like him"?'

'Incapable,' Jean said. 'And daft.'

Seffy laughed. 'Yes, quite. I suppose all the capable and sensible men have joined up, so there's no one else to do it!'

'I could do it! I could do that job better'n him!'

'But you're young, Jean and you're a girl and with the best will in the world—'

'I know they wouldnae let me. But I still could!'

'I don't doubt it for a moment,' Seffy said.

She'd sounded so sincere that a wave of guilt washed over Jean. Seffy was kind and loyal. Which was more than could be said for her. The thought of that blasted fortnightly report was hanging over her. She wished she'd refused to do it but she hadnae dared and it was too late now.

She glanced at her watch. It was only eight-thirty and she was in no rush to get back to the cottage.

'Shall we stay and have another drink?' she suggested.

Seffy was climbing onto the stool Mr Burke had vacated. 'Absolutely! And one of our choosing this time! Oh, look, there's another stool. Grab it, Jean, then we'll both have one.'

They ordered two port and lemons and sat up at the bar amongst the locals, letting their legs swing.

'Right,' Seffy said, shuffling forward on her stool. 'Let's recap on what we've learned. The girls are green, the landowner's tricky and we've got to clear a site before we can do anything else. I'd been looking forward to felling but instead, we've got to tidy up the mess that others—'

'Men!'

'Yes, quite, that men have left behind.'

'Sometimes I think that's a woman's role in life: tidying up the mess that men leave behind,' Jean said. 'And that includes war.'

Later, as they made their way back to the cottage, the girls linked arms, for warmth as well as safety: the path was uneven and already frozen solid.

'I've been wondering why none of our gang were in the pub,' Jean said. 'I've worked out there are four possible reasons.'

Seffy giggled and squeezed her arm. 'Oh, you're a hoot! You're like Miss Marple in the Agatha Christie stories!'

'Jane Marple? The old maid detective?'

'Don't be offended, it's a compliment! Because you're so good at deducing things, Jean. Come on, then, tell me.'

'Mebbe their digs are too far away or they're too young to go into a bar or they've no money. Or – and this is my favourite – they're God-fearing lassies who consider alcohol to be the work of the devil.'

'Or they knew bumbling Burke would be there and wanted to avoid him at all costs!' Seffy said. 'Anyhow, we'll meet them in the morning and I expect we'll find out then.'

Laburnum Cottage was in darkness. Mrs Harris must've already gone to bed. The back door was locked.

'I'm surprised,' Jean said, rattling the handle. 'I thought country folk would happily leave their doors on the latch.'

Seffy bent down, lifted the mat and patted the ground underneath until, with a cry of delight, she held something up.

'Hurrah! At least one part of my imaginary billet was right! The key's under the mat!'

The range in the kitchen lent the room a cosy warmth, so Seffy fetched the bottle of Lagavulin from upstairs and they sat at the table. They'd found glasses in the press and had a wee dram to warm themselves up and toast the New Year, even though it was still a couple of hours away.

'It's not so bad, if you knock it back quickly,' Seffy said, after her second dram.

Jean shook her head. 'That's a terrible waste. This is quality whisky. It deserves to be savoured, not gulped down like a dose of castor oil!'

'Can you believe it's almost New Year?' Seffy said, nodding as Jean offered her a refill. 'I wonder what 1944 has in store for the Timber Corps?'

She laughed, pleased with her little rhyme.

Jean looked at the clock on the wall. It was only ten-thirty.

'Hmm, still a little while to go,' Seffy said. 'Shall we stay up and wait for New Year, sing "Auld Lang Syne" at the tops of our voices and wake Mrs Harris?'

'We'd never do it. She told me she has a milk stout before bed and she sleeps like the dead. We could do first footin' at midnight, although by rights the first person over the threshold should be a dark-haired fella and we dunnae have one of those.'

Seffy sighed. 'I'd actually prefer a nice fair-haired chap with a deep Canadian drawl but there's no chance of that either. Oh, don't mind me, Jean. I think that whisky's making me morose. As for all this New Year malarky, I honestly don't think I can be fagged. Can you?'

That was a relief. Jean was ready for her bed. 'No, let's turn in,' she said. 'Mind, it's gonna be freezing up there. No wood burner, remember!'

'We're going to miss that, aren't we?' Seffy said. 'I'm going to ask my father to send a pair of his long johns. I'll get a pair for you, too, Jean.' She stood up. 'Right, we'd better make a dash for it.'

'And sleep with half our clothes on.'

'And forget about having a wash.'

Before they faced the arctic conditions, they rinsed and dried their glasses and put them back in the press. They didn't want to get into Mrs Harris's bad books on their very first night.

Chapter Ten

London, England
31st December 1943

It was New Year's Eve and Missy wanted nothing more than to have a hot bath and an early night. She and Juliet had been sightseeing all day. The traffic in London was horrendous – you surely had to watch your step – and it was one more thing Missy didn't care for over here. But, despite her protests, Juliet had dragged Missy all over town. She was plum worn out.

'You carry on,' she said, when some of the girls who were making plans for the evening, invited her along. 'I'm gonna turn in. I'm dead on my feet.'

Dorothy – the awful woman who'd been so rude to her yesterday, as they'd packed layettes – rounded on her. 'Not so fast, young lady. It's New Year's and these fellas are on leave. They've got money to spend and they wanna have some fun. After everything they've been through, I think they deserve that, don't you? So you go right ahead, put on your lipstick and your dancing shoes. I don't care if your feet are on fire, you're comin'!'

Juliet was standing nearby and Missy gave her a pleading look but she turned away.

Missy sighed. She didn't want to fall out with anyone, or have them think she was a bad sport. What choice did she have? She got ready and went out with the others, trying to smile, even though it was the last thing she wanted to do.

They started the evening at the Trocadero, with cocktails in the lounge. She was persuaded to try a White Lady for the first time and she had to admit, it was real good. Then they went downstairs to the Grill Room and had a tasty dinner, with white wine.

'Let's have a ball tonight, Missy,' Juliet said. 'It's our last chance to be out in London for a while.'

Juliet was gonna miss the place. But apparently their new posting wasn't far away and they could come back on weekends. They'd been told there would always be a bed for them at the Maple Leaf Club.

Juliet knocked back her drink. 'Come on, we're going someplace else to dance!'

Outside, in the dark, the streets were teeming with people, although it was kinda weird, the way the dance halls and restaurants were blacked out, as though there was no one in them.

Somehow, one of the fellas in their group spotted someone from his unit across the street and hollered to him and asked if he wanted to come with them.

They were shortly joined by a couple of other girls – Canadians too, one from Ottawa, the other from Alberta – and by then they had quite a crowd.

Everyone was greeted with hugs and smiles, like they'd known one another forever, and boy, it was like a party on the street before they'd even got to the dance hall. Although there was no light seeping out, they could hear the music way before they arrived at the venue.

It felt unreal. Here she was, little Missy Gilbert from Invermore B.C., celebrating New Year's in a strange country, on the other side of the world. Even stranger to think that when it turned 1944 here, for a few hours after that, it would still be 1943 back home.

Missy's heart sank as she suddenly spotted Dorothy, skirting around the edge of the dance floor and making her way over. She stopped in front of Missy and blew a smoke ring into the air. 'Still dead on your feet, honey?'

'No, I'm having a good time, thanks, Dorothy.'

Because it was true, she'd forgotten about being tired. But she felt guilty, having fun without Callum on such a magical night of the year. She wished he were here too.

It had been hard leaving him all over again, when she and Juliet had headed back to London after their trip to the coast. But at least they'd made arrangements to speak on the telephone. That'd bridge the gap until the next time they could be together.

Later in the evening, she and Juliet got talking to a lieutenant from Montreal. He peered at the insignias on their sleeves.

'Red Cross? Say, are you gals nurses?' He held up a finger. 'Can anyone kiss this better?'

Missy sighed. If only she'd had a dollar for every time a fella had asked them that. She was sure Callum would never say anything so cheesy.

'Sorry, we're not nurses,' she said, gently pushing his finger away.

'The Red Cross Corps needs volunteers to do all manner of things,' Juliet said. 'We're helping rehabilitate injured Canadian troops in a military hospital.'

'Although we haven't started yet,' Missy said. 'We go to our posting next week.'

She hoped he wouldn't ask what they'd be doing because Missy wasn't entirely sure. Juliet had probably told her and she'd only get snarky if Missy asked again.

'What made you ladies wanna come over and do your bit?' the fella asked.

Missy let Juliet answer. Everyone asked them that and she always gave the same reply.

'Well, we're sisters,' Juliet said, 'and as we don't have brothers, we felt an obligation to play our part in the war effort.'

He looked impressed. 'Sisters, huh? Say, you don't look much alike!'

No, Missy thought. Juliet is the curvy, pretty one and I'm the little scrawny one.

'Bet your folks weren't too happy 'bout the two of you going overseas in the middle of a war, right?'

Juliet laughed. 'You betcha! But you know, our folks are great. They'd never try to stop us doing what we want.'

Missy felt a twinge of that now familiar guilt. She didn't deserve this soldier's admiration. Truth was, she hadn't come over out of any sense of obligation or patriotic fervour. No, sirree. She'd come for one reason only and it was a lot more selfish than that: she'd come to be with Callum.

A little while later, Juliet took great delight in teasing a G.I. from Ohio.

'Boy, Canada was in the war two years before you fellas showed up!' she said, emboldened by drink. 'We were standing side by side with Great Britain from the off!'

It was true, of course, but the American didn't like hearing it. He turned away from Juliet and offered to buy Missy a drink.

Girls were in short supply, the fellas were real friendly and you had to take care, else you'd have so many drinks bought for you, you'd end up under the table. A girl could get swept along by so many compliments and constant attention.

Missy always made sure to tell the guys straight up she was engaged, so it was crystal clear that any chat, drinks or dancing, were purely on a friendship basis.

'What's that? You're engaged?' the G.I. asked, leaning in, so he could hear her over the music.

'Yes, my fiancé's here with the Canadian Forestry Corps. He's—'

He'd grabbed her left hand. 'What, did you lose your ring, honey?'

Missy flushed scarlet.

'Oh, there wasn't time to get a ring before he left.'

She'd told Callum she didn't mind but that hadn't been strictly true. Were they even properly engaged without a ring? Now she wished for one more than ever, if only to prove to fellas like this that she truly was off the market.

The G.I. scratched his head. 'Did you say your fella's in forestry? There ain't much call for that in London, is there?'

Some of the other Red Cross girls standing nearby laughed.

'No!' Missy said, raising her voice over the band. 'He's not in London. He was lumbering up in Scotland.'

How dare this guy look down his nose at Callum. Perhaps he thought he wasn't in uniform?

'My fiancé is actually a staff sergeant,' she said. 'As well as being lumberjacks, the guys in the CFC are infantrymen and—'

But the American had turned away, either bored or unimpressed by Callum's credentials. He'd already started chatting to a British woman in a Navy uniform.

How rude! Missy had never felt so stupid, sitting at a bar talking to herself.

Her eyes filled with tears. Why was she even bothering to converse with these dumb-ass fellas? She didn't wanna be with anyone but Callum.

Oh, but it was so frustrating. She'd assumed England was so small, they'd see each other all the time but she didn't even know when they'd next be able to meet up.

It was nearly midnight. A couple of the girls came over and dragged Missy onto the packed dance floor for the countdown.

'Ten, Nine, Eight …!'

In a few seconds, everyone would be cheering, hugging and kissing. It would be 1944.

Missy sent up a silent prayer. *Please let this New Year be a good one; please let the war be over soon.*

As midnight struck, she would make a wish. And if it came true, what a marvellous journey home that would be at the end

71

of the war. She'd be a married woman, with a wedding band on her finger. And maybe even a baby in her arms.

Chapter Eleven

When Seffy came down for breakfast on New Year's morning, the first thing she saw was the bottle of Lagavulin on the table. She covered it with a tea towel – it was making her stomach heave – and tried to eat the brose that Mrs Harris was dishing up. It was porridge by another name, and the best you could say about it was that it was hot and filling. It also had the consistency of wallpaper paste.

'Sleep all right, girls?' Mrs Harris asked.

They said they had and agreed politely that it was a comfortable bed. Although *two* comfortable beds would've been preferable, Seffy was tempted to say.

'Actually, Jean,' she said, 'sharing with you has one definite advantage: you radiate heat like a human hot water bottle!'

Jean pushed her glasses up. 'Do I really? I suppose I must have a high metabolic rate.'

'Quite,' Seffy said, lifting a spoonful of brose to her mouth. She caught Jean's eye across the table and they laughed.

'You know what that means, don't you?' Jean asked.

'Of course!' Seffy said, indignantly. 'Well, no, to be honest, but there's no need to explain. I get the gist.'

Later, they set off to meet the gang. The sky was grey, it was starting to rain and Seffy felt rather queasy.

'Do you have a headache, Jean?' she asked.

Jean looked perky and was striding out purposefully. 'No! I've never felt better! Why, do you?'

Seffy nodded. She'd totted up what she'd drunk last night: a shandy, a couple of port and lemons (downed at high speed) and at least two drams of whisky. No wonder she felt poorly. Sensible Jean had stopped after one dram and was quite clearly none the worse for wear.

As they rounded the bend in the lane and spotted the gang huddled together in the gloom, Seffy gasped.

'Good grief, what a rag-tag crew!'

At least dopey Mr Burke had got something right: the girls were at the appointed meeting point – the bus stop at the edge of the village; and at the specified time – eight-thirty, just as it was getting light. And as far as Seffy could see through the drizzle, they each had an axe, saw or bill hook, so they'd come prepared to work.

But they were certainly a motley bunch. They were wearing civvies for a start.

'Where are their uniforms?' Seffy muttered.

'Mebbe they don't have any?'

'We were issued with ours on our first day!'

'But we were in a camp,' Jean said. 'These lassies have been all over, living in billets and learning on the job, remember.'

Not one of them was properly dressed. They were wearing a mixture of overalls, sweaters, slacks that were too short in the leg, headscarves and battered lace-up shoes. Not a beret in sight and their overcoats were thin and threadbare.

A girl at the front – so petite she looked like a child – didn't even have gloves. She was cupping her hands and blowing on them for warmth.

They looked awfully young. Late teens, Seffy estimated. A stout girl, whose mop of curls was escaping from her headscarf, was older: probably in her early twenties, closer to her and Jean's age. From her stance – legs wide, arms crossed – and the peeved look on her face, Seffy thought she might be trouble.

Jean had spotted her too. 'I'm prayin' that one's not the trainee measurer,' she said.

Seffy shifted the heavy haversack on her shoulder. She'd brought tools, a billycan and mugs for making tea. 'They look like tinkers,' she said. 'They don't even look particularly clean!'

'Shhhh!' Jean said. 'Mebbe they could only bear a cat's wash this morning too.'

That was a good point. It'd been so cold when she and Jean had got up, they'd only given their hands, faces and necks a cursory wash.

As they reached the girls, Seffy did her best to smile and sound jolly. 'Good morning, Lumberjills! A happy New Year to you all!!'

There were a few murmurs in reply but one girl was too busy yawning, without covering her mouth, to speak.

'I'm Miss Mills, your new forewoman and this is Miss Ferguson, senior measurer.'

'Jean,' Jean said, smiling. No one smiled back.

'Are there any more of you? Is anyone missing?' Seffy asked.

The girls shook their heads sullenly. There was a chill in the air that had nothing to do with the temperature. Resentment, Seffy sensed. And suspicion.

'Are we no' good enough as we are?' the stout girl asked.

'Of course! I simply wasn't sure how many of you to expect,' Seffy said, taking the list of names that Jean was holding out. 'And you are …?'

The girl folded her arms and glowered. 'Ma name is Peggy Gorman.'

'Right. Quick roll call. Peggy, you're obviously here. The rest of you, when I call your name, please shout, "Here!"'

'Eileen! Isobel! Rona! Myrtle! Brenda!'

She tried not to mind that they all said a barely discernible 'Aye' instead of a loud 'Here!' And one of them – Brenda – said nothing at all.

'Brenda?' Seffy repeated.

The small girl – gosh, she couldn't be more than about four feet eleven – put up her hand. 'Aye, that's me. B-b-but everyone calls me Tich,' she stammered, so cold she could barely speak.

Seffy nodded. 'Very well. Tich it is.' She pulled off her gloves and handed them to the girl. 'Here, put those on.'

'I cannae take these.'

'It's just a loan,' Seffy said. 'I've got another pair back at my billet. Now, it's too cold to stand around, so let's make a move, shall we? Chop, chop, if you'll pardon the pun!'

They stared at her blankly.

'You're English!' Peggy said.

'Correct! Can't do anything about the accent, I'm afraid. Do shout if you can't understand. But I've been here a while now, I'm almost an honorary Scot, wouldn't you agree, Jean?'

Jean nodded uncertainly. She looked as stunned as Seffy felt. They'd expected the girls to be inexperienced but they hadn't expected them to be hostile. Blast that Burke fellow. He might've given them fair warning.

'Right! Quick march to the … erm, site!' Seffy said, shooing them as though they were a herd of geese.

No one moved.

There was no time to check with Jean, so Seffy turned and started to lead the way, taking long strides down the lane and hoping she was heading in the right direction.

Last night, when boring Mr Burke had explained how to find the site, Seffy hadn't been listening. She'd started watching a game of pontoon that some chaps were playing on a nearby table.

Jean caught her up.

'Is this the right way?' Seffy muttered. She'd look a proper Charlie now, if they had to do an about turn.

'Aye. And the lassies are coming. Albeit at a snail's pace. I suppose we should make allowances. Perhaps they were out somewhere last night for Hogmanay?'

'You mean, it's a case of the morning after the night before?'

Jean shrugged. 'Mebbe.'

She hoped Jean was right and the girls were simply tired and hungover. Otherwise, they truly were going to have their work cut out.

The clearance site was even worse than Seffy had expected.

'That?' she asked Jean, gazing at the wilderness that stretched in front of them. It was a dense, ten-foot-high tangle of brambles and branches, stretching parallel to the lane for a hundred yards. There was no telling how far back it went.

Whoever had felled the trees here, had removed the branches and tops but had left them piled up in heaps, to rot. And the rest of the wasteland was a confusion of bracken, weeds, ivy and lichen.

Jean grimaced. 'Aye, this must be it. So much for a "copse", eh? You could keep POWs behind that and they'd never escape. It's like an enchanted forest! *Beauty and the Beast.*'

Seffy rolled her eyes. 'It's certainly beastly.'

She braced herself. The girls had almost caught them up. They were scowling at the jungle to their left and then at her and Jean, obviously wondering why they'd stopped and what this unholy mess had to do with them.

'Where are the trees?' Peggy demanded.

'Aw, noo! Don't tell me we're doin' a clearance jobbie!' the frizzy-haired girl, Myrtle, said.

Tich let her bill hook fall to the ground. 'That's no' right! We've been well and truly stitched up!'

Stitched up? Oh, how Seffy would like to tell them that she and Jean felt exactly the same way.

'We *will* be felling,' she said, firmly, 'in due course. But first, it's been agreed with the landowner that we'll clear up this patch.'

'I KNEW it!' Myrtle said, nostrils flaring.

'"Patch"?' Tich said. 'That's no patch! It's at least the size of a football pitch! It's a jungle! There'll be beasties in there. Rats and God only knows what!'

'It's hardly a jungle,' Jean said, reasonably. 'It's about two acres. It'll only take a couple of weeks, depending on how well you work.'

Peggy put her hands on her hips. 'How well *we* work? What'll you be doin', then, Gingernut? Havin' a party?'

The others giggled.

Gingernut? Who did the impertinent girl think she was talking to? The absolute nerve of her!

Jean put a restraining hand on Seffy's arm. Probably just as well; she might've said something she'd regret.

'I'm a measurer,' Jean said, flinching slightly under Peggy's glare. 'I'll be assessing the felling site to the south of here, with whichever one of yous is the trainee.'

She looked relieved when Rona, a pale, dark-haired girl at the back, put up her hand. She was one of the quieter ones and she looked sensible.

'How much training have you had?' Jean asked.

The girl wrinkled her nose. 'A week's worth. Looking at maps and a wee bit of working out the cubic contents of a tree.' She shrugged. 'Not much.'

'That's nae problem. I'm here to show you the ropes,' Jean said, smiling. She turned to the others. 'While you're clearing this area, Rona and I will be in another part o' the forest, assessing the felling site for volume, extraction routes and a stacking ground. Each tree will have to be measured for its cubic—'

'Aye,' Peggy interrupted. It was probably going over her head. 'Well, don't be getting all toffee-nosed on us now, will ye, Rona, just 'cause you're a fancy measurer?'

Rona shook her head so vigorously that her headscarf started to slide off.

Seffy coughed loudly and stepped forward. 'Perhaps, Jean, as we've got our work well and truly cut out here, the two of you

78

could help us out for a while before you start measuring?'

Jean nodded. 'Aye, we could do that, nae problem.'

'Good!' Seffy said. 'And I'll be here the whole time, working alongside the rest of you. If we put our backs into this, we'll soon get this site cleared and ready for replanting.'

There was silence. The tension in the air was almost tangible.

Peggy curled her lip, turned her gaze on the wasteland and with a stamp of her foot said, 'Aye, well, good luck to you, Miss Sappy Mills, because I, for one, am NO' DOIN' IT!'

Seffy jerked her head back, shocked, as if she'd just been slapped. Had she heard correctly? Or was this some kind of prank? But no one was laughing. Peggy had spun around and was glaring expectantly at the others.

Tich was the first to speak up. 'Me neither. I won't do it. It looks dangerous!'

'Aye, count me out too,' Eileen said. 'I've done summat like this before. The brushwood had been left for ages, same as here and when we set fire to it, hundreds o' ticks rained down! Like a plague out o' the Bible! We had to have tick-picking sessions to get them off each other.'

The three girls who had still to declare their intention to work – or otherwise – grimaced at the story of the ticks, but said nothing.

Seffy was too taken aback to speak. Were they actually refusing to do this?

As the gang of girls huddled together, whispering frantically, Seffy exchanged helpless glances with Jean. Even if the remaining girls were prepared to defy Peggy, it wouldn't be enough. They needed the whole gang, working together, to have any chance of clearing this site within a reasonable time.

Seffy sidled up to Jean. 'You know,' she murmured, 'my aunt told me once to "Always expect the unexpected."'

And this was certainly both unexpected and unprecedented.

The gang of girls was on strike.

Chapter Twelve

'I think we should go to church in the morning,' Jean said, as she and Seffy lay in bed on Saturday night.

'To pray for deliverance from this place?' Seffy asked, pulling up the crocheted blanket. 'Or to give thanks for the delightful girls with which we've been blessed?'

Jean tugged the blanket back. 'I think it's important to lead by example and start the New Year as we mean to go on.'

She could tell from the silence at the top of the bed that Seffy was thinking about it. 'Very well,' she said. 'We'll go. Those little minxes might give us the surprise of our lives and turn up too!'

It'd been an awful blow this morning when the lassies had refused to work. Of all the things Jean had imagined happening in this new posting, that hadnae even crossed her mind.

Once Peggy had started the rebellion, one by one the girls had followed suit. Within minutes of arriving at the site, she and Seffy had found themselves standing quite alone. The girls had taken their tools and marched off, presumably back to their billets. They'd been so determined, there hadn't seemed any point in trying to stop them.

'They're testing us, Jean,' Seffy had said, watching them

disappear around the bend in the lane.

'Aye, reckon they are. What'll we do now?'

Seffy lifted up her bill hook and turned to face the wilderness. The drizzle had turned into proper rain and the wind had picked up. 'We're going to work, Jean! This rubbish won't clear itself!'

Jean gasped. 'But we cannae do it by ourselves! It'll take a month of Sundays!'

Especially as, unlike Seffy, she wasn't used to this kind of manual labour. She wouldn't say it, but she was afraid she mightn't be up to the task.

'Should we no' report them? And, I dunno – get their pay docked, at the very least. Or have them sacked?' Jean asked.

She'd already started to think about the first report she would write and how best to phrase it so that no blame could be apportioned to Seffy.

Seffy's shoulders slumped momentarily, then she rallied. 'Let's have no talk of sacking. If they leave the Corps, we'll have no gang at all. It could take yonks to get replacements and there's no guarantee new girls will be any better. These girls, believe it or not, are better than nothing. We just have to work out how to get them onside.'

They spent a good couple of hours hacking at the tangle of bushes and branches. Some of the brambles were as thick as Jean's wrist and covered in ferocious-looking thorns. She got scratched, even through her gloves.

It was hard work but they soon had a big pile of wood and greenery to show for their efforts. They'd hardly made a dent in the so-called 'jungle', but it had felt good to be doing something.

The rain had eased off again and once they'd made a semblance of a clearing, they built a fire to boil water for tea and to dry themselves off as best they could.

'I always say a cup of tea makes everything better,' Seffy had said. 'Even without milk or sugar!'

Jean had smiled and agreed with her. Good old Seffy. She was never downhearted for long.

On Sunday morning, the girls donned their full dress uniforms in readiness for church: breeches, shirt and tie, green jersey, knee-length woollen socks and lace-up shoes, with a Mackintosh over the top and the all-important green beret.

'I always feel so smart when I'm togged up like this,' Jean said.

Seffy was adjusting her beret in the mirror. 'Absolutely! Smart and proud.'

They asked Mrs Harris for directions and set off towards the kirk at the other end of the hamlet. It was a cold but bright morning, and although Jean was stiff from yesterday's exertions, she hoped the walk would soon loosen up her aching limbs.

'Did you ask Mrs H if she was coming too?' Seffy asked, as they picked their way along the lane, dodging puddles and patches of mud.

'Aye, and she said, "I dunnae dare. I might be struck doon"!'

Seffy laughed. 'That wasn't bad, Jean. You got the gruff voice spot on. But what a queer thing to say! I wonder what she meant?'

Jean shook her head. She had no idea.

The church turned out to be a tiny granite building, with only a handful of pews, crammed with folk in their Sunday best.

There was no sign of the gang.

'Actually, I'm glad they're not here,' Seffy said. 'Scruffy, lacklustre individuals. They're hardly a credit to the Corps. Do we really want them out in public?' She pursed her lips. 'Now, where on earth are we going to sit? The place is packed.' She stretched up on tip-toe to look over the heads of the congregation. 'Oh, there! The front pews are empty. Come on!'

An elderly fella sitting nearby, called out huskily, 'You'll no' sit there, if ye know what's good for ye!'

The girls stopped in their tracks.

'What did he say?' Seffy asked.

Jean wasn't surprised she hadn't understood. The accent in these parts was broad. Jean was having trouble understanding it herself.

'He says we shouldn't.'

'But the pews are empty!' Seffy said.

'You still cannae sit there,' a woman – presumably the man's wife – said, leaning across him. 'They're reserved for the McIntyre family.'

Jean nudged Seffy. 'That's the landowner.'

Seffy crossed her arms and pouted. 'And where is this very important McIntyre family? There must be a dozen of them, at least, if they need that much room!'

'Land girls, are ye?' the man asked.

'No. WTC,' Jean said.

He repeated the letters slowly. 'WTC? Women's Tank Corps? That's a new one on me!'

'Women's Timber Corps,' Jean said. 'We'll be felling trees around here soon enough.'

'Felling trees?' another old fella said. He lifted his trilby and scratched his head. 'That's nae job for a woman!'

Jean wished she and Seffy could slink off somewhere. They were making such a scene, standing in the aisle while everyone stared at them.

The rector had taken his place at the pulpit and was adjusting his cassock.

'Here, you'd best squeeze in wi' us,' the woman said. Everyone in the pew shuffled along. 'And there is no family,' she added in a whisper. 'There's only him.'

'Miserable old so-and-so,' Seffy said, as they walked home after the service. There was a fine mizzle in the air now and it was bitterly cold.

'The fella who thinks we're not up to the job?'

'Him too. But I meant McIntyre. He doesn't use those pews

but he won't allow anyone else to! I'd like to give him a piece of my mind!'

The next moment, a scarlet open-topped car sped past, horn blaring. It came so close, the girls had to leap out of the way and only narrowly avoided a ditch. Seffy's beret flew off and as she bent down to retrieve it, she muttered something most unlady-like under her breath.

The car had screeched to a halt further up the lane. It was a two-seater, shaped like a boat. The driver appeared to be waiting for them.

'I've got a horrid feeling that's him,' Jean said. 'Mr McIntyre. Who else would have a car like that and the petrol to drive it?'

It was as though Seffy had conjured him up.

They walked cautiously towards the car. Jean wouldn't have put it past the maniac to suddenly start reversing at them. Clearly, he fancied himself as a racing driver: he was wearing goggles and a leather driving cap. His greying hair was awful long: it was sticking out below the cap.

Villagers and church-goers were calling out, 'Good morning!' as they passed the car. Some of the fellas were tipping their caps. The driver was acknowledging them with nods and a raised hand.

'TIMBER GIRLS!' he shouted suddenly, peering at Seffy and Jean in the rear-view mirror. It wasn't a pleasant greeting. Not only had he got their name wrong but he sounded cross.

'LUMBERJILLS!' Seffy called back.

As they reached the car, Jean's knees suddenly felt weak. If this was the landowner, it wasnae the best start to a working relationship. She hoped Seffy wasn't going to carry out her threat and confront him about the empty pews. It was no concern of theirs. And from what Mr Burke had said, Mr McIntyre needed to be handled with kid gloves.

'So this is where you've been hiding yerselves,' he said. His goggles were steamed up and he didn't bother to wipe them. It was a wonder he could see anything.

'With all due respect, sir,' Seffy said, 'we've just been to church and now we're walking down the road in broad daylight. We're hardly hiding!'

The man's face was half hidden by the goggles, but from what Jean could make out, he was middle-aged and stern-looking. As she glanced down into the driver's seat, she noticed he was sporting an emerald-green kilt.

'Finn McIntyre,' he said, curtly, by way of introduction. 'I assume you two are in charge of the rabble?'

'If you mean the gang from the Women's Timber Corps,' Seffy said, 'then yes, I'm the leader girl. Miss Mills.' She nodded at Jean. 'And my colleague here, Miss Ferguson, is the senior measurer.'

Jean tried to smile at him but the man was barely looking at them.

'I dropped in at the site yesterday,' he said, 'and there wasnae a soul to be seen! And the place is still a complete shambles. Do you no' work on Saturdays?'

That explained his bad mood: he thought they'd been slacking. Thank goodness he hadn't arrived in the middle of the argy-bargy and witnessed the girls storming off.

'Actually, we did make a start yesterday, sir,' Seffy said, with exaggerated politeness. 'We cleared a huge amount of debris. I'm surprised you didn't see it, piled up and ready for burning. But it was a half-day and the weather was bad, so we called it a day an hour or so early. We'll start properly tomorrow.'

Would they though? Seffy sounded awful confident, considering they currently had no gang to do the work.

Mr McIntyre drummed his fingers on the steering wheel. 'Think you can knock them into shape?' Before Seffy could answer, he added, 'Because I have it on good authority that this is their last chance saloon. They've seen off two of your ilk already. Perhaps it'll be three in a row!'

'Or perhaps it'll be third time lucky!' Seffy replied, without missing a beat. She beamed at him. 'I can assure you we'll do our very best.'

Jean swallowed. *Last chance saloon?* She *knew* Mr Burke hadn't been straight with them! And what was that about seeing two girls off? He must mean leader girls. Ma God, the gang was rotten to the core and no one could manage them! This was the reason Seffy had been brought here. Jean remembered now: Miss McEwen had told her the powers that be thought Seffy would be 'up for a challenge'.

Mr McIntyre wasn't returning Seffy's smile. Even she couldnae charm this fella. He slammed the car into gear and revved the engine. 'I'll be keeping a close eye on yous!' he said. 'And I shan't allow you anywhere near my woodland 'til I'm happy with your clearing work. I'd have preferred to have men on the job but—

'—there are no men,' Seffy said.

Jean's chest tightened. What a cheek, considering the men who'd done the first round of felling had made a complete mess of it. But she didn't dare say it and judging from Seffy's silence, neither did she.

'One more thing,' Mr McIntyre said. 'There are twenty deer on my estate and there'd better be twenty when you leave!'

He put his foot down, the engine roared and he sped off, wheels squealing. They watched the car career up the lane and disappear from view.

'Well,' Seffy said, blowing out her cheeks, 'what a charmer!'

'Another man who thinks we're useless. Ma God and he thinks we might be poachers too!'

Seffy shook her head. 'Nutty as a fruitcake.'

'But what he said, about the gang seeing off leader girls and last chance saloon an' all, was that the ramblings of a lunatic or was he telling the truth?'

'Why would he lie?' Seffy said.

Her mouth was set, her eyes were downcast and for the first time since they'd arrived, she looked seriously troubled. 'Blast that Burke fellow for keeping us in the dark! You know, Jean, I think we've been dealt a rum hand. A very rum hand indeed!'

Chapter Thirteen

First thing on Monday morning, Jean and Seffy headed for the clearance site, on the off-chance the girls had had a change of heart.

Mrs Harris had agreed that Seffy could borrow her bicycle – 'just for today, mind!' – as she wasn't working at McIntyre's house until Tuesday.

'Did I hear her say her husband's away in the Navy?' Seffy asked, as they pedalled side by side, cracking frozen puddles under their tyres. 'Maybe she's having a torrid affair with McIntyre? And that's why she daren't set foot inside a church for fear of being "struck doon"!'

Jean frowned. 'Mrs Harris and Mr McIntyre? I cannae imagine it.'

In truth, neither could Seffy. It was hard to picture the dour Scotsman of yesterday – strangely flamboyant, with his sports car and his bright kilt but also surly and disapproving – falling in love with anyone. He was a grump of the highest order. No wonder he had no family to fill the church pews and was all alone in the world.

As they got nearer to the wasteland, Seffy sniffed the cold air. 'What're you doing?' Jean asked.

'I'm hoping to catch a whiff of woodsmoke. The girls might already be sitting around the fire, waiting for us.'

'And pigs might fly!'

Sure enough, when they pulled up in the lane next to the site, there were no signs of life. They didn't even bother dismounting but circled their bicycles, until they were facing the way they'd just come.

Jean gazed dejectedly at the brambles. 'I swear they've grown since Saturday.'

'Never mind that now,' Seffy said. 'Let's go and flush the girls out of their billets! You've still got that list of names and addresses, haven't you?'

Jean tapped the basket at the front of her bike. 'Aye, safely in there. Mrs Harris gave me a rough idea of where the houses are. One or two aren't that far from the cottage.'

'Right, let's round them up!' Seffy started pedalling towards the village. 'Who's first?'

'The nearest is … aw, I'm afraid it's Peggy Gorman!'

At the tumbledown cottage where Peggy was lodging, the door was opened by a kindly-looking old lady with grey curls and a hunched back.

'Miss Gorman?' she repeated, in a croaky voice, when they asked for Peggy. 'I'm afraid you cannae speak to her. She's still tucked up in bed.'

'In bed?' Seffy said. 'But it's almost nine o'clock!'

'Is she sick?' Jean asked.

'Och, no! And from the way she puts her food away there's nothin' wrong wi' her appetite! I think she's plain worn out, poor lass. It's the change of air, you see. I've told her to sleep as much as she likes 'til she gets used to it. Are you pals of hers? She'll be awful sorry to have missed ye!'

Seffy turned and mimed a scream at Jean, just as the old woman said, 'Wait, now. I think perhaps that's her.'

She disappeared into the hall.

'Aren't you sorely tempted,' Jean murmured, 'to charge up those stairs and drag Peggy out o' bed by her jimjams?'

The woman was back. 'No, it was only a door banging. Miss Gorman must still be in the land o' nod!'

Clearly Peggy had this poor woman wrapped around her little finger. She was eating well and having lie-ins, as though she were on holiday! Why couldn't she and Jean have been billeted here?

'Now, can I gi' her a message?' the woman asked.

Seffy turned to Jean. 'Do you have paper and a pen in that magic basket of yours? I'll leave a note.'

There was every chance the old lady might forget to mention their visit and Seffy wanted Peggy to know they were on her trail.

She scribbled a message, folded the piece of paper in half and handed it to the woman. 'If you wouldn't mind giving this to Miss Gorman when she … er, emerges … I'd be grateful. It's an invitation.'

'Aw, that's nice. I'll be sure to see she gets it.'

'An invitation?' Jean said, as they pushed their bicycles down the path. 'I'm surprised you didnae give her a warning. Or at least a ticking off!'

'I don't think that'll work with Peggy. It'll only make her dig her heels in even more. No, I think this is a case of "Softly, softly, catchee monkey", Jean.'

Seffy waited until they'd both gone through the gate and remounted their bikes, before she spoke again. 'Once we've rounded the girls up, I thought we'd invite them to a powwow. You know, peace talks.'

Jean laughed. '*Powwow*? You do know we're in the East of Scotland, don't you? This isnae the Wild West!'

The next port of call was a farmhouse where both Rona, the trainee measurer, and frizzy-haired Myrtle were billeted.

A stout woman of about thirty – presumably the farmer's

wife – was dragging sacks of coal across the yard.

She stopped at the sound of their squeaking brakes and scowled. 'If you're looking for those wee scamps, they're in the barn. They're supposed to be clearing the place o' rats but—' she sighed '—heaven only knows what they're up to. Are you their bosses?'

Seffy swallowed and gave the smallest of nods. She hardly dared admit it.

'Aye, well, someone needs to tek 'em in hand! They're a disgrace!'

Without waiting for a reply, the woman continued to drag the sacks over the cobbles.

Seffy and Jean pushed their bikes towards the barn at the far side of the yard.

'She's right,' Jean said. 'They are a disgrace. They're blotting the copybook of the whole Timber Corps.'

'And they're letting down those of us who are putting our heart and soul into the war effort. Those men who think women aren't up to the job? Well, the girls here are proving them right!' Seffy said.

She was incensed now and quite ready to give them a piece of her mind, but when they reached the barn and peered inside, there was a surprise.

Reclining amongst the stacked straw bales, looking utterly miserable, were not only Rona and Myrtle but the three other members of the gang.

'Tich, Eileen and Isobel,' Jean said.

As the farmer's wife had surmised, rat-catching appeared to be the last thing on their minds. They were stretched out amongst the bales, looking as though they'd been there for hours.

Myrtle jumped when she spotted Jean and Seffy and dropped the piece of straw she'd been chewing. She murmured something to the others and they swung their legs off the bales and sat up.

Rona leaped to her feet, blushing and brushing chaff from her slacks. At least she had the grace to look ashamed: she couldn't meet Seffy's eye. There was hope, she thought, for Rona.

'Morning, girls!' Seffy said, brightly. 'We're just checking everyone's digs are up to scratch. Rona and Myrtle, you're lodging here, aren't you? Everything all right?'

'No, it's crummy!' Myrtle said. 'We're on camp beds in the damp cellar. There's water coming down the walls! And if we get ill we'll have to leave straight away because the woman has her bairn to think of!'

Eileen waved a dismissive hand. 'Try living in a place wi' no electricity or running water. It's like summat from the Dark Ages. If I want to have a wash, I have to go out to the well, fifty yards from the house, wind up a bucket full o' water and lug it back inside!'

'You lot have got it easy,' Isobel said. 'I reckon our digs – mine and Tich's – are the worst of anyone's. Tell them, Tich!'

'We cannae even unpack our bags!' Tich said. 'Our landlady's hiring out our beds during the day to men who work nights in some place or other. She's getting double rent!'

'What?' Jean said. 'You mean, you're sharing beds with strange men?'

'They're no' in the beds at the same time as us!'

Seffy sighed. 'No, Tich, we realise you're taking it in turns with the beds. Are you saying you don't have a room or even a bed, to call your own?'

Tich nodded. 'And once we've had our measly breakfast, we have to get out o' the house and we're no' allowed back 'til dark.'

Which explained why they'd gathered here, Seffy supposed. A warm barn, out of the wind and cold, wasn't a bad place to be if you were bunking off.

'Surely someone must have approved these lodgings before placing you there?' Jean said.

Eileen make a scoffing sound. 'Aye, the district officer was supposed to check them first. But she didnae.'

'We should be used to it by now,' Myrtle said. 'The billets we had in the last two places were no better. We cannae compete with the men, you see. They earn more 'an us and they can pay higher rents.'

No wonder they were fed up. Shoddy billets, low pay and no uniforms. Goodness, Seffy thought, the girls had had a tough time of it since joining the Corps. But she mustn't start feeling sorry for them. Whatever conditions they'd found themselves in, it was still no excuse for refusing to work.

'Look,' she said, 'we got off on the wrong footing on Saturday, so how about joining Jean and me for a drink tonight?'

'Tonight?' Isobel said. 'Have ye not come to badger us back to work?'

Back to work? They could hardly go 'back' to something they hadn't even started.

'I think we need to have a proper talk first,' Seffy said. 'It's cosy in The Drover's Inn. We can sit next to the fire.'

Tich frowned. 'The Drover's Inn? Wha' is that, a pub?'

'I dunnae go into pubs, me,' Eileen said, and Isobel agreed.

'We've no money for drinking,' Myrtle said. 'Once we've paid our board and lodgings, there's not much left over.'

Seffy was tempted to remind them that if they continued their strike, they'd be even worse off because their pay would be docked. But now wasn't the time. They were terribly down in the dumps.

'It *is* a pub but it's a decent enough place,' she said. 'Jean and I were in there the other night and no one batted an eyelid.'

'We'll stand you a drink each, won't we, Seffy?' Jean said. 'Just the one, mind. We're not made o' money!'

The gang went into a huddle and muttered amongst themselves. Seffy and Jean exchanged exasperated glances. Honestly, Seffy thought, what was there to discuss?

After a minute, they separated again.

'What about Peggy?' Tich asked.

'Aye, we cannae leave her out!' Eileen said.

'Don't fret about Peggy,' Jean said. 'We've left a message at her digs.'

'Her *very* nice digs,' Seffy added. 'I'd say Peggy's landed on her feet there. So, what do you say?'

'All right,' Myrtle said. 'Tell us where it is and we'll be there.'

'Good!' Seffy said. 'Shall we say six o'clock? No, let's make it earlier. Let's meet at five-thirty!'

Chapter Fourteen

Seffy and Jean were sitting next to the fire in The Drover's Inn when the girls arrived. For all their apparent coyness about venturing into a pub, they stormed confidently inside, like regulars.

Seffy waved. 'Over here! We've got chairs for everyone.'

'We shan't be needing one for Peggy,' Jean said. 'It doesn't look like she's come wi' the others.'

The barman jerked his head at the old chaps sitting around the bar. 'Mind your language now, fellas. The lassies are here!'

The men watched as the gang made their way across the stone floor to reach Seffy and Jean.

'What're those fellas gawking at?' Tich demanded, throwing herself into a seat next to the fire.

'They're not used to women in here. Especially not women in slacks,' Jean said.

Seffy thought it was more likely that the chaps simply couldn't believe their eyes. The girls looked like scarecrows: scraggy-haired, with dirty boots, ragged overcoats, and trousers at half-mast.

Although she was glad they'd deigned to turn up, she was wondering, once again, how she'd ended up responsible for this unruly rabble.

'Is Peggy no' here?' Myrtle asked.

'Oh, I expect she'll turn up in her own good time,' Seffy said. 'Now, do sit down. Shandies all round? Jean, can you give me a hand?'

'You must be the lassies due to work on the McIntyre estate,' the barman said, as he placed their drinks on a tray. 'I remember you now, from Hogmanay.'

Seffy decided against telling him that she and Jean had already made a start on the site, without the rest of their gang. It would raise too many questions.

'Finn McIntyre's tellin' anyone who'll listen that you won't be around for long,' the barman continued. 'Says you won't get as far as fellin' any of his precious trees. He's hopin', eh?'

Blast that McIntyre chap. He really was the giddy limit. Seffy had hoped to find an ally in the landowner but there was clearly no chance of that.

'Peggy's a no-show, then,' Jean murmured. 'We couldnae even tempt her with the thought of a free drink.'

Seffy winked. 'Let's wait and see.'

It was a few minutes before Seffy could start addressing the gang. They were squabbling over seats and complaining about the fire, which wasn't burning well enough for moaning Myrtle's liking.

In the meantime, the pub was filling up with locals, and from the far end, came the steady thud of darts being thrown at a board.

'Put another couple o' logs on that excuse for a fire, will ye, Tich?' Myrtle said. 'It's goin' out.'

Tich rolled her eyes but did as she was asked and after a minute or two, the fire was finally blazing away to Myrtle's satisfaction.

'Right,' Seffy said. 'Down to business! Firstly, we're wondering why you don't have Timber Corps uniforms. Where are your sou'westers and gumboots?'

The girls looked at one another.

Isobel shrugged. 'I dunno. I've never had either.'

'We were offered uniforms but they wanted us to fork out for them ourselves,' Tich said. 'As if we could afford that!'

'Aye,' Rona said. 'Because of our age, we're on the lowest pay rung. Except Peggy. She's older than us.'

Yes, Seffy thought. Older but definitely not wiser.

'Molly and Shirley had uniforms,' Rona said. 'And a couple o' the other girls who … left.' She bowed her head.

Seffy exchanged a glance with Jean. She wouldn't ask about 'Molly and Shirley' and open up old wounds, but it sounded very much as though there'd been other girls, aside from the leader girls, who'd been driven out by this lot.

'So we wear our own clothes,' Eileen said. 'But you know, we've never even been offered extra coupons.'

'But don't you feel the cold?' Jean asked. 'Some of your coats look awful thin.'

'I fold up old newspapers and tuck them inside my jumper,' Tich said. "Dunnae laugh, it works!'

'And if you get bored, you've always got summat to read, eh?' Eileen said.

'Aye. But when you start sweatin', the ink runs,' Tich said. 'Once, when I was getting undressed for bed, I found a headline printed on ma vest!'

As the girls shrieked with laughter and suggested all manner of unsuitable headlines for Tich's vest, Seffy and Jean exchanged hopeful looks. The gang had actually worked, then, at some point. Tich had even managed to work up a sweat.

Away from Peggy's bad influence – and in a warm and convivial setting – it was possible to have a reasonable conversation with them. And even a laugh.

'There must be something we can do about their clothes,' Seffy muttered.

Jean placed a warning hand on her arm. 'Dunnae promise anything we can't deliver.'

No, Seffy thought, but there was no harm in saying she'd *try*.

'Why did you enlist in the WTC?' Seffy asked, once the girls had stopped sniggering over Tich's vest.

'In the wha'?' Myrtle asked.

'The Women's Timber Corps!' Jean said. 'This! The reason we're here!'

'Aw, I see,' Myrtle said. 'Well, ma pals were being sent to work in munitions factories down in England. I knew the call-up papers would be coming any day and I didnae want to do that.'

'Me neither,' Eileen said. 'I suppose we wanted to stay in Scotland, so we jumped afore we were pushed.'

'I was frettin' about the medical,' Tich said. 'Being so wee an' all. But the doctor only asked if I had varicose veins and when I said no, that was it, I was in! I worked in a horrible printing press before, earning two and six a week and a box of chocolates at Christmas.'

'I used to be a hairdresser,' Isobel said. 'That's why I've got soft hands—'

'Aye, and how many times has Peggy told you to rub soil into them?' Myrtle said. 'That'll harden them soon enough!'

Isobel pulled a face. Presumably, she liked her soft hands. 'I applied to be a hairdresser in the WAAF but they turned me down. Hairdressing's considered a luxury, it's no' reserved, so I had to enlist. This came up and someone told me we'd have picnics in the woods every day, so …' She shrugged.

Picnics every day! If that wasn't so ridiculous, it would be funny. Everything was starting to make sense. None of these girls had volunteered for the Timber Corps because they loved the outdoors: they'd enlisted to avoid being sent to munitions factories or because they thought it was a better option than what they were doing before.

But at least they'd cheered up. They'd become quite animated as they'd explained why they'd joined the Corps. Maybe no one had ever asked them before.

Rona glanced shyly at Jean and Seffy. 'Why did you two join up?'

97

'I was due to go to—' Jean stopped herself and Seffy guessed she'd been about to say 'university' but had thought better of it. 'It was my da's idea. He was all for me doin' ma bit.'

'And my brothers enlisted in the RAF and I felt left out,' Seffy said. 'They were getting far too much admiration from the parents for my liking. Plus, I've always been quite outdoorsy.'

Happy days. Fly fishing on the River Ayr with her brothers Tol and Percy, or riding glossy thoroughbreds around their father's 1,000-acre estate. Probably best not to mention that now.

'But I had no idea how hard it was going to be. I think the heaviest thing I'd lifted before I joined the Corps was the flap of an envelope!' The girls laughed. 'Anyhow, what've you been doing with yourselves today?' Seffy asked, casually. She picked up her glass and took a sip.

There was an uneasy silence, then Rona said, 'Nothin' much.'

'It's been a wee bit borin', to tell the truth,' Tich said.

'Our landlady expects us to trap and poison rats,' Isobel said. 'The farm's riddled with them and she says they're "doin' Hitler's work".' She shuddered. 'But I just cannae do it.'

'Me neither,' Rona said. 'I'm too squeamish!'

'She shouldn't expect that of yous, in any case,' Jean said. 'That's a job for the anti-vermin squad.'

Isobel's eyes widened. 'Is that right? Is there such a thing?'

'Definitely,' Jean said. 'Tell your landlady you're in the Timber Corps and she should get herself a land girl if she wants a rat-catcher.'

'I will!' Isobel said. 'Thank you, Jean.'

The timing of that conversation couldn't have been better, Seffy thought. She rubbed her hands together and sat forward in her seat. 'Now, Jean and I have been working on the clearance site again today—' she looked imploringly at the gang, sitting in a semi-circle around her '—but we can't do it for much longer without you. I know you're not awfully keen on the idea of clearing but once it's done, we can move onto felling which is heaps more fun! What do you say?'

The girls looked nervously at one another. They still didn't look convinced.

'If we try to get you kitted out properly,' Seffy said, 'and if we try to find better billets, will you agree to start work?'

Before anyone could answer, Peggy's outraged voice boomed across the bar, 'HOW LONG HAVE YOUS ALL BEEN HERE?'

'Ah, Peggy! Glad you could make it,' Seffy said, standing up. Everyone in the pub was staring.

Peggy looked furious. 'The note said to come at six!' she said, stomping over to join them. She delved into the pocket of her dungarees. 'I have it here somewhere.'

Seffy made a show of tutting and sighing. 'Did I put six? Oh, silly me. I told this lot five-thirty. Must've got muddled. Never mind, you're here now. Sit down and I'll fetch you a shandy.'

When she returned with the drink, Peggy had commandeered her seat and was preoccupied with a pipe, carefully sprinkling tobacco into the bowl.

Seffy watched, as Peggy struck a match on the bottom of her shoe, lit the pipe and started puffing away like an old man.

At least she'd stopped ranting.

Jean had retrieved another chair from somewhere and she placed it down next to Seffy.

'Thank you, Jean,' she said. The smell of pipe smoke was filling their corner of the pub now and Seffy breathed it in, surprised to find she liked it. The rich, comforting smell took her back in an instant to happy childhood holidays at her grandfather's house.

But enough, she was getting distracted.

'Peggy!' That was enough to get everyone's attention. 'I've been talking to the girls about the clearing work and I think we're about to come to an agreement.'

Everyone was silent. Seffy was praying the wretched girl wasn't about to scupper everything.

Peggy yanked the pipe out of her mouth. 'Wha' kind of an

agreement?'

'If Jean and I do our absolute best to resolve the uniform and the billet issues—'

'"Billet issues"?' Peggy queried. 'What's up wi' the billets?'

'Yours might be all right,' Eileen said, tartly, 'but ours are awful.'

'And if I promise to try to sort it all out,' Seffy continued, 'will you all agree to start work, from tomorrow morning?'

Peggy sucked the end of her pipe and looked at the others. They gazed back, bright-eyed, hopeful.

'Can we, Peggy?' Tich asked. 'We could gi' it a go?'

Peggy considered it for a minute, puffing slowly on the pipe and glaring at everyone. She saved her worst glower for Seffy.

'Mebbe,' she said.

She stood up and that was clearly the signal for the gang to leave. They all got up and stood near the bar. Those who had them, put on their coats and headscarves.

'What're they doin'?' Eileen asked the barman, peering at the other side of the pub.

'They're playin' darts.' He let out a short laugh. 'What, do yous want tae have a go?'

'Aye, why not?' Peggy said. 'It's only chucking pins at a board, after all!'

'Aw, fightin' talk!' he said. 'Don't let the lads hear you say that. They're awful serious about their arrows!'

Peggy shrugged. 'I'm good, me! Ma uncle ran a tavern in Motherwell. I used to play all the time.'

Seffy grimaced. Peggy had a grim, determined look on her face. Any minute, she'd probably insist on joining in, whether 'the lads' liked it or not. Luckily, though, Tich started tugging on her sleeve and Peggy was soon persuaded to leave with the others.

When they'd finally trooped out, Seffy threw her head back and blew out her cheeks. 'Heavens above, that was hard work! And I still only got a "mebbe" out of it!'

'You've sown a few seeds of dissent, though,' Jean said. 'They had no idea Peggy had bagged herself the best billet. Plus, they're getting bored. Good idea of yours, making sure Peggy arrived after the others.'

Seffy shrugged. They wouldn't know whether her scheming had worked until the morning.

'I didn't expect to have to nanny them like this!' she said. 'Do you know who they remind me of? The Lost Boys.'

Jean frowned. 'In *Peter Pan*?'

'Yes. They've fallen out of their perambulators and come to Neverland! Except they're girls, not boys, of course. Oh, my, what have we been landed with?'

Jean shook her head dolefully. She picked up her empty glass and held it up to Seffy. 'Another?'

'Yes, good idea. Something stronger than a shandy this time. You know, I'm absolutely not a giver-upper but at this precise moment, I'm quite tempted to throw the towel in!'

Chapter Fifteen

'When's Grace having the wean?' Jean asked the next day, as she and Seffy set up the fire for tea. She wasn't overly interested in bairns but she was doing her best to distract Seffy.

It was late morning and despite their best efforts, the newly christened Lost Girls hadn't turned up for work. She and Seffy had spent the last few hours tackling the wasteland on their own again. They were weary and disheartened.

'Erm … let me think,' Seffy said, from her position on the ground. She was lying on her front, setting a match to the leaves. 'We were in Gretna in August so … the baby must be due in May.'

'I was surprised when Grace announced she was expecting,' Jean said. 'She was always so adamant she didnae want to bring a bairn into this war.'

Seffy blew gently on the flame until, with a snap and crackle, the leaves curled and started to burn and a tiny flame travelled up the pyramid of twigs over them. The wood underneath would soon be alight.

She shuffled backwards on her elbows and stood up. 'Yes, but she changed her mind. She told me if anything happened to Gordy, she wanted a child to remember him by.'

Jean swallowed. That was an awful poignant reason for starting a family. And being reminded of it now, was probably not the best way to cheer up Seffy. She'd been trying to give her a boost all morning. Seffy was usually the one keeping up everyone else's spirits, but it had clearly hit her hard that, despite everything she'd done to get the girls to work, she had – in her words – 'failed miserably'.

Jean sighed. She wasnae used to making chit-chat. She'd already blathered on about her wee sister's wedding, asked about Seffy's pal – the glamorous-sounding Emerald – who'd asked her to be godmother to her baby and now they'd talked about Grace. What else was there?

She yanked off her balaclava – she was getting too warm in any case – and held up a handful of hair. 'Tell me truthfully, do you think I should have a perm?'

Seffy wheeled around. 'YES, I do! Deffo! I mean, your hair's the loveliest colour – it actually reminds me of a chestnut mare I had once – but it is awfully straight, Jean. A little bounce and curl would make all the difference! It could be your crowning glory!'

Jean frowned and let her hair fall back into place. 'They're ever so costly, though, aren't they?'

Seffy patted the curls beneath her beret. 'No idea! I've never had one. Mummy says I have her to thank for my natural curl.' She peered at Jean's hair. 'Can't you just put curlers in at night?'

'No, ma hair's so poker straight, it makes no difference.'

'It'll have to be a permanent wave then! Ah, but you said they're dear. How much are we talking?'

'A fortune!' Jean said. 'A girl in our street had one. She took her copy of *Picturegoer* to the hairdresser's and showed the girl a photograph of Rita Hayworth and said she wanted to look like that. It cost ten shillings.'

Seffy gasped. 'Golly, that's half our weekly rent! But was it worth it? Did she end up looking like the gorgeous Rita?'

Jean sighed. 'I dunno. Probably not.' She tugged at her hair disconsolately. 'I shall just have to live wi' it, I suppose.'

'HULLLOOO!' A man's strident voice rang out through the thicket, making the girls jump.

'Curses,' Jean said. 'That's the landowner fella! He'll think we've been doing nothing but making tea all morning!' She held up the balaclava. 'I'm tempted to put this on back to front, so I don't have to see him!'

'We're over HERE!' Seffy called, with obvious reluctance.

Mr McIntyre had no idea how to get into the clearing and the girls smiled as he thrashed about, fighting his way through the undergrowth, muttering oaths. It took ages until he emerged, red-faced, wielding a walking stick and pulling a bramble from his overcoat sleeve. He was wearing a deerstalker hat – like Sherlock Holmes, Jean thought – wellingtons and his dark green kilt.

'There you are!' he said, irritably, scratching the five o'clock shadow on his chin. He had an obvious limp and as he stood on the other side of the fire, he leaned heavily on the stick. 'What's all this I hear about a strike?'

Jean gasped. He knew! And he'd no doubt inform Mr Burke, so she'd have no choice but to put it in her first report. Darn it! It was exactly the kind o' ammunition that Miss McEwen had been hoping for.

Seffy was taking her time hanging the billycan on the frame of sticks over the flames.

'Good morning, Mr McIntyre,' she said eventually, without looking round.

He quickly pulled off his hat. Goodness, Jean thought, his greying hair almost reached his collar. He needed a haircut, as well as a shave.

'Aye, good morning,' he said. 'Is it true? Have you lost the foot soldiers? Are you two captains the only ones here?'

What could they say? It was obvious that they were.

'May I ask, sir, who told you?' Jean said.

He tapped the side of his nose. 'I have my sources!'

'Mrs Harris!' Jean said, and he didn't deny it.

Blast the woman! She must've overhead her and Seffy talking about the gang and passed the information straight to Mr McIntyre.

The instructions on the government posters were quite right: 'Keep Mum', 'Loose Lips Sink Ships' and all that. You never knew who was listening.

Mr McIntyre looked hopefully at the billycan. 'Any chance of a cup of tea?'

'I'm afraid not,' Seffy said. She sat down next to the fire and gave him a quick, insincere smile. 'We only have two mugs. As you've just pointed out, there are only two of us here.'

Jean knew it wasn't true, about the mugs: they had enough for the whole gang. But Mr McIntyre wasn't to know that.

He looked surprised by the way Seffy had spoken to him. As a laird, of sorts, around here, he must be used to everyone tugging their forelocks and never saying no to him.

Jean wouldn't have dared herself but good for Seffy for refusing to kowtow to him. The fella was rude: it was no more than he deserved.

As they waited for the water to boil – and for Mr McIntyre's next move – Jean sat on one of the tree stumps they used as a seat.

The fella was staring at Seffy, as though seeing her for the first time. Of course, on Sunday when he'd nearly ploughed them down, his fancy driving goggles had been so steamed up, he probably hadn't been able to see much.

Seffy didn't seem to notice how Mr McIntyre couldn't take his eyes off her. She gazed around the clearing until, finally, her eyes lighted on him and she nodded at his kilt. 'That's a nice tartan. I like the mossy green with that white overcheck. It's jolly smart.'

He opened his mouth and closed it again, the wind clearly taken out o' his sails. 'Aye, well, it's a McIntyre huntin' tartan.'

'And are you hunting? Apart from us, I mean,' Seffy said.

Mr McIntyre's brow furrowed and he cleared his throat. Seffy had done her best but he clearly wasnae going to be sidetracked for much longer.

Jean cocked her head. She'd heard something. Or had she imagined it? It'd sounded like folk coming along the lane. The other two had been too busy discussing kilts to hear.

'So, anyhow, what're you going to do about those reprobates?' Mr McIntyre asked Seffy. 'I've heard they've refused point blank to work!'

'No, sir! You've heard wrong!' Jean said, standing up. She blushed, as Seffy and Mr McIntyre stared at her in astonishment. She wavered then. She wasn't entirely sure if … but – yes, it was! It was the sound of lassies' voices. And they were getting closer.

'Here they are now!' she said.

Peggy came first, arms flailing as she fought her way through the bushes and into the clearing. She was followed, with much shrieking and wailing, by the other five girls. They were still a rag-tag bunch and their expressions were surly but none of that mattered: they were in their work clothes – such as they were – and they'd brought tools. They were here.

'Ma God, what time d'you call this?' Mr McIntyre exclaimed, pulling out his pocket watch. 'It's nearly midday!'

Seffy had leaped to her feet and was standing between him and the gang.

'Who's he?' Peggy asked.

'This is the landowner, Mr McIntyre,' Seffy said. She turned to him. 'It's all right, sir, we weren't expecting them until now.'

He huffed. 'Well, you might've said! Where've they been, all this time?'

Jean held her breath.

There was a flicker of uncertainty on Seffy's face, but then, with perfect confidence, she said, 'They had to be measured for their Timber Corps uniforms!'

Mr McIntyre looked at her doubtfully. He was probably wondering – as Jean was – exactly who was supposed to have done the measuring.

'Their *dress* uniforms,' Seffy added. 'Which are only for special occasions and for a few other bits and pieces, for day-to-day working.'

'They are going to be working, then?' he said.

Peggy harrumphed and Jean felt the tension in the air. Any minute now, Peggy would explode or turn on her heels and leave again. They had to get rid of the fella. Fast.

'Of course they are,' Jean said. She was worried about saying the wrong thing and making him even crosser but she forced herself to continue. 'And if you dunnae mind, sir, we'd like to get on. As you know, we have an awful lot to do.'

'Can we no' have a cuppa first?' Tich asked, and received a nudge in the ribs from Rona. 'I was joking!' she said, but Jean wasn't so sure.

Mr McIntyre gave a curt nod. 'I'll leave ye to it. Dunnae forget to bag up any pine cones you find. For seeds.' He gazed around, dolefully. 'This'll all be replanted in due course.'

'Not by us,' Peggy muttered.

'If you go past the stack ready for burning – there on the right – aye, that's it, sir,' Jean said, 'there's a way through onto the lane. It's easier than … erm, the way you came.'

He tipped his deerstalker at her and then turned to Seffy.

'Come for tea at my place, Miss Mills,' he said, waving his stick and making it sound more like an order than an invitation. He nodded at the billycan over the fire. 'As we didnae manage to have one here.'

Seffy blinked hard and didn't reply.

'I'll come if she won't!' Tich said, and received another nudge from Rona.

'Shall we say this Saturday, at three o'clock? Mrs Harris will tell you where to find me.'

Seffy pursed her lips. 'That's awfully kind but I'm afraid I'm otherwise engaged this Saturday.' She tilted her head and gave a tut of regret.

Mr McIntyre looked bemused. He was probably wondering what Seffy could possibly have to do, here, in the middle o' nowhere, that was so pressing.

'I see,' he said. 'Another time, then?'

'So long as it's not during the week, because, obviously, I have to work. And on Sundays, we're busy with church,' Seffy said.

McIntyre let out a long breath. He clearly hadn't expected this to be quite so difficult.

Some of the girls were nudging one another and giggling. Jean couldn't help but smile too. She looked away in case anyone saw her.

'Of course,' he said. 'What about the following Saturday?'

Seffy nodded. 'Thank you. I shall look forward to it.'

Chapter Sixteen

Seffy blew out her cheeks, as McIntyre limped off into the thicket.

Gracious, he'd asked her to tea. What a surprise.

She hoped Jean hadn't taken the hump. She might've thought that, as one of the 'captains', she should've been invited too. But it was better this way. Seffy needed to launch a charm offensive on the chap and it would be easier to do it alone. Jean could be rather too direct at times.

Peggy was scratching her head. 'What was all tha' about?'

'He's asked her to tea!' Tich said. 'And to be fair to the lass, she didnae make it easy for him!'

'Never accept the first date a man offers you,' Seffy said.

'*Date?*' Jean queried.

'Not that kind of date,' Seffy said. Gosh, Jean was such a pedant. 'Appointment, suggested time. Oh, you know what I mean!'

'I wonder what his missus'll have to say about it!' Myrtle said.

'Don't be silly, Myrtle,' Seffy said. 'For a start, there is no missus and it's a business meeting. I expect he wants to talk over our plans for felling his forest. How we'll calculate its value and when he'll be recompensed. That kind of thing. Nothing for you to worry about!'

'Should Jean not be there too?' Rona asked. 'If you're going to talk about assessing the woodland and all o' that?'

Oh, goodness, that was all she needed: one of the gang – and Rona, too, whom she liked – stirring up trouble.

'It's all right, Rona,' Jean said. 'Seffy and I work closely together. We'll discuss it all, before and after. I don't need to be there.'

Seffy gave Jean a grateful smile. They were putting on a united front. Excellent.

'What was all that about uniforms?' Eileen said. 'I wasnae measured for any uniform!'

Peggy rolled her eyes. 'No one was, dopey! It was a ruse to get the fella off our backs.' She looked at Seffy. 'But you are gettin' the uniforms, like you promised?'

Give us a chance, Seffy wanted to say. It had only been discussed last night. Did Peggy think they were miracle workers? But she painted on a bright smile and said, 'We've put the wheels in motion!'

That was true. Last night, when they'd got back from the pub, they'd agreed that Jean would write a letter to the divisional officer.

Seffy had thought a telegram might strike a more urgent note, but Jean wanted to include more detail than a telegram would allow. She'd explained that she wouldn't ask the girls for their sizes, in case it raised false hope, instead she would 'measure' them, as she did with trees, estimating their height and girth, then draw up a list of what was required.

Now, Seffy clapped twice to get everyone's attention. 'As Jean and I have worked like billyo all morning and we were about to have a brew, we might as well all have one. But then, to work!'

Tich cheered and the others – even Peggy – brightened a little.

As the girls squabbled over the mugs in Seffy's haversack, Jean pulled her to one side. 'I thought you wanted to get this clearance done in double-quick time?'

'I do!' Seffy said. She'd been filled with a restless energy ever since they'd arrived, which had made the gang's rebellion even more infuriating. But clearly, Jean thought she was being too soft.

'But they'll be expecting a cuppa every day now, before they do a stroke o' work!' Jean said.

'And would that be so terrible? I know that wasn't how we did things in Blantyre but we make the rules here!'

Seffy watched as Jean grappled with that idea. Jean wasn't used to making rules: she was used to following them.

They sat around the fire, warming their hands on their mugs of tea.

'Dunnae work us too hard, will you?' Eileen said.

'When'll we stop for lunch?' Isobel asked.

Seffy and Jean rolled their eyes at each other. Heavens above, the girls hadn't done a stroke of work and they were already hankering after a break.

'I thought, twelve-thirty for lunch,' Seffy said. 'Have you all brought a sandwich from your digs?'

'She means a piece,' Jean translated and the girls nodded.

'Peggy's got a mutton pie,' Myrtle said.

A pie! Lucky thing. All Mrs Harris had given her and Jean was a meagre 'jammy piece' wrapped in greaseproof paper.

'And she's got a flask o' tea!' Myrtle said. 'Wi' milk and sugar, if you please!'

'Aye, and if you're nice to me, Myrtle the Turtle, I'll gi' you a sup of it,' Peggy said.

Myrtle grinned. 'Truly? Will you?'

'Nah!' Peggy said, and screamed as Myrtle launched herself at her. The mugs and tea went flying, as they rolled around on the ground, getting dangerously close to the fire and pulling one another's hair.

Seffy wasn't sure whether they were play-fighting or really scrapping but from the way Eileen and Tich sprang up and expertly dragged them apart, it wasn't the first time this had happened.

She shook her head at Jean and mouthed, 'Savages!'

The girls might've turned up for work but there was still a

long way to go.

Later that day, Seffy cupped her hands around her mouth and yelled, 'Isobel, where are you? ISOBEL!'

'There!' Jean said, pointing to the raised billhook in the middle of the tangle of brambles. Once they were deep within the thicket, the girls were completely hidden. Getting them to raise a tool in the air was the only way to find them.

'All present and correct!' Seffy said. 'The good news is, they're finally working—'

'—and the bad news is,' Jean said, 'they're not exactly falling over themselves to get it done.'

Seffy tutted. 'They're no-hopers! I keep smelling tobacco. Peggy can't be doing much chopping if she's puffing away on her pipe. And there's so much giggling in that part of the copse; Tich and Myrtle can't be doing a thing! Quite honestly, I should be writing down the names of the worst offenders and reporting them.'

'You'd have to write them all down, in that case,' Jean said. 'Why don't you?'

'Because if we push them too far, petulant Peggy will simply march them all off again. Strike number two!'

Seffy's sense of satisfaction when they'd finally turned up this morning had soon been replaced by one of utter frustration. As well as smoking and giggling, they were working at a snail's pace and she was constantly having to chivvy them along.

She and Jean had collected up the meagre amounts of deadwood that the Lost Girls had managed to hack down and added them to the pile for burning, most of which had actually come from their own efforts.

'Over here, girls!' Seffy yelled. 'It's time to light this pile of deadwood!'

The gang appeared almost instantly. There was never any delay when they were told they could down tools.

They looked warily at the pile of brushwood.

'Dunnae ask me to go anywhere near that!' Peggy said.

'No, you can all stand well back,' Seffy said. 'If anyone's going to get showered in ticks, it'll be me, all right?'

'All right!' Tich said, happily.

Seffy suspected that everyone – hopefully with the exception of Jean – would be tickled pink if something awful happened and she ended up covered in creepy-crawlies.

But the pile went up in flames and started to crackle and burn without incident.

'Sorry to disappoint!' she said, holding out her arms for inspection. 'But I seem to be insect-free!'

Chapter Seventeen

Basingstoke, Hampshire, England

Missy could see her breath, like smoke, as she stood in the phone booth, inserting coins into the slots. There, one more penny. That should do it.

It was a queer system. You had to guess how long you'd be on the line and how much that might cost, and remember to press button B to retrieve any leftover coins. There usually were some coins unused at the end.

She'd called Callum a couple of times from London and their calls hadn't been long. Once they'd asked each other how they were doing, confirmed they were missing one another and enquired about news from home, conversation had gotten a little stilted.

There! It was ringing out. She'd arranged to call at six on the dot so hopefully, he'd be waiting in the call box at the other end.

'Hi, Missy?'

That was his voice, smooth as honey. She pressed button A and felt a wave of relief as the call connected. 'Callum? Can you hear me?'

'Sure.'

Swell, it had worked. And the line was so clear, it was as though he were standing right next to her. Thank God, for the times they lived in. Not the war – no one could be grateful for that – but for marvellous inventions like the telephone.

'Are you there now, in Basingstoke?' he asked. 'What's it like?'

'Seems real nice. We haven't explored yet, we only got here a couple of days ago. We've been settling in at the boarding house and finding out what we'll be doing at the hospital.'

'Will you be in an office? I can imagine you behind a desk.'

No. Another disappointment. She'd have liked to work as a secretary for one of the top brass, answering the telephone, keeping the filing neat and making coffee for her boss.

'No, but it's OK. We're working with the injured men. Oh, and you'll never guess—' she stifled a giggle '—we're General Duties Officers. We've got officer status!'

'No!' He laughed. 'Do I have to salute you?'

'Crazy, right?'

Callum was really proud of making staff sergeant but he'd had to work hard for it, while she'd been handed a rank for doing nothing more than volunteering in a military hospital.

'And as we count as civilians over here, we have to do a fire-fighting course,' she said. 'Then we'll be on fire-watching duty at the hospital one night a month.'

'Wow, Missy. You're getting involved in all sorts.'

He'd sounded impressed.

She and Juliet had been introduced to their work by a real nice girl, Laura from Toronto, who'd been working at the hospital for a couple of months already.

'Mornings are spent in the Red Cross Room,' Laura had explained, 'organising activities with the Up patients. That's the fellas who are well enough to get outta bed. We get them to do handicrafts. Yeah, really! Lots of fellas turn their noses up at first. Grown men, knitting and making soft toys and leather belts? But it gives them a focus, helps them forget their injuries. Once they get involved, they get real competitive, trying to beat one another to finish a project and start the next. And once a week, we organise ping pong and darts contests.'

'And what happens in the afternoons?' Missy had asked.

'We do our tours of the wards. There are hundreds of patients to get round, so we're each allocated a few wards on a rota basis.'

She was going onto the wards alone? Missy's mind had raced. She and Juliet had done courses in first aid and home nursing when they'd joined the Red Cross but the thought of blood and gore had given her the collywobbles. If she saw stuff in the hospital she wasn't prepared for, she'd most likely pass out.

'They haven't let you loose on the wards, then?' Callum asked.

'No, we're starting tomorrow.'

Missy clutched the receiver in both hands and turned away from the girls now standing in line outside. Apparently, if you took too long over your call, someone would bang on the glass. It was hard to believe – the British, on the whole, being so polite – but Laura swore it'd happened to her.

But no way was she gonna rush. Since the New Year, she'd been mithering about her lack of an engagement ring. She needed to raise the subject.

'Say, Callum, I was wondering,' she said, carefully, 'did you bring your ma's necklace with you, over to Europe?'

He surely had: he never went anywhere without that precious keepsake, the only reminder he had of his mother. It was an opal, strung on a beautiful gold chain and Missy had long admired it.

There was a pause and for a moment, she thought the connection had cut out. Then Callum said, 'Yeah, I brought it. Why d'you ask?'

'I was thinking it might be nice to turn it into an engagement ring. That way, even though your ma's no longer around, it would make her part of everything. What d'you say?'

Darn it, the line had suddenly started to crackle.

'Honey, I can't hear you,' he said.

She repeated it a couple of times but he still couldn't hear and eventually she yelled, 'WE COULD GET IT MADE INTO AN ENGAGEMENT RING!'

Gee, this was hardly romantic, and the girls outside were giggling now. They must've heard. Shoot, she'd sounded desperate and clingy. She should've waited until he'd raised the subject of a ring.

'Never mind!' she said into the receiver, not knowing if he could hear. 'Let's talk about it next time we meet up.'

They said their farewells. Missy put down the receiver and pushed open the heavy door. She was out and away as fast as she could, without looking at the girls waiting outside.

It was only when she was halfway back to the boarding house, that she remembered she hadn't pressed button B.

Chapter Eighteen

There wasn't much time to dwell on the telephone call because the next day Missy and Juliet started work in the hospital.

They spent the morning in the Red Cross Room with the Up patients. They were a game group of young fellas, who, despite their crutches, slings and eye patches, were full of life and ready for some fun. There was a lot of teasing and laughter in that room. Missy was surprised how much she enjoyed it.

What wasn't so enjoyable was meeting the two sour-faced British women who were already working there and clearly resented their presence.

'I call them "the Limeys",' Laura said, when the women disappeared to make refreshments. 'Take no notice of them. They probably think we're here to do them out of a job because the Red Cross pays them and we're volunteers. But there's plenty of work for all of us. Mostly they camp out in here, drinking tea and leaving the ward rounds to us. But I let them have the officers' wards. They think it makes them special but the officers are real demanding. Quite frankly, they're welcome to each other!'

Laura offered to accompany Missy on her first tour of the wards.

'Just this once, mind,' she said, with a smile. 'From tomorrow you'll be on your own! OK, here's your cart.'

It was packed with handicraft materials and what Laura called 'goodies' for the fellas, 'to give some comfort to a lonely fella and bring a smile to his face!' As well as ditty bags filled with soap, combs and shaving stuff, the cart was full of stationery, craft materials, newspapers and books, gum, cigarettes and candy.

'The Limeys call them "trollies", by the way, and pretend not to understand when you say "cart".' Laura rolled her eyes. 'But whatever they're called, the guys perk right up when they come round. It's the highlight of their day. See, we're not nurses; we're not gonna change dressings or jab needles in them. All we're offering is a friendly face and a chat.'

Laura and Missy took it in turns to push the trolley down the corridor to the Nissen huts in the grounds, where the bed patients were housed.

'I'll give you some tips for keeping the fellas in check,' Laura said.

'What d'you mean?' Missy said, and Laura laughed. She must've sounded terrified.

'They're injured patients and pretty much bed-bound, Miranda!'

'Of course,' she said. 'They can't exactly jump on me, right?'

'No! But bear in mind, they're lonely, bored and a long way from sweethearts,' Laura said. 'Most haven't seen a woman in a long time, so they flirt and sometimes overstep the mark. Be friendly but firm. Oftentimes, they'll say something to provoke you and if that happens, I always say something like, "We're all married ladies, corporal. There's not much you can do or say that'll shock us."'

'But I'm not a married lady!'

Laura laughed. 'Me neither, but it's easier, trust me, if they believe we're off limits. There's still horseplay and larking around, but if they think you're hitched, the fellas won't push it too far.'

Their first port of call was the Burns Ward.

119

Laura must've sensed Missy's apprehension. She stopped the cart outside and said, 'It's not so bad. Just don't look shocked or show any pity, OK? That's the last thing they want.'

Missy nodded.

'Oh and you'll notice they call us 'Sister', as though we're some kind of nurse,' Laura added. 'I've never bothered to correct them.'

As soon as they stepped inside, fellas sitting up in rows of identical beds started whooping and cheering.

'They make you feel like a movie star, these fellas,' Laura said, laughing. 'Afternoon, guys. Now, calm down! This here is General Duties Officer Gilbert. She's gonna be sharing these rounds with me, and I hope you'll extend your usual courtesies to her.'

There was a chorus of 'Sure, we will!' and 'Welcome, Officer Gilbert!' and Missy blushed as dozens of fellas stared at her.

Laura glanced at one of the occupied beds and frowned. 'Has Fletch gone, Chas?' she asked the fella in the next bed, and he nodded.

Laura turned away and murmured to Missy, 'That's another reason for staying detached. Get too friendly with anyone and you'll only be disappointed when he's suddenly gone without the chance to say goodbye.'

'But it's good news, right, when fellas get discharged?'

'Sure. But I worry they'll be sent straight back onto the front line.'

Missy nodded. She hadn't thought of that. She sure had a lot to learn.

Laura swung back around to face the fellas, a cheery smile on her face.

'And who do we have here?' she asked, addressing the fella who was now occupying Fletch's bed.

He was sitting up, leaning back against the pillow. His pyjama top was half undone and his whole head was swathed in bandages, with only a gap for his mouth. His hands were bandaged too.

'He don't say much,' Chas said. 'Won't even tell us his name so we've named him Rabbit.'

Missy swallowed. Boy, he must've been badly burned to be wrapped up so completely. The bandages were tied on the top of his head, with two ends sticking up, like rabbit's ears.

'This is the Sister, like we told you, man,' Chas said.

Rabbit didn't react. His breathing was laboured, as though he'd run a mile. Missy thought she'd never seen someone so young and big – he seemed too long for the bed – look so exhausted.

'She's got all sorts on her cart, there,' Chas said. He nodded at Laura. 'Tell him, Sister.'

Missy watched, as Laura pushed the cart nearer to his bed. What would she offer him? He couldn't see, of course, so books or newspapers were out, so too were any handicrafts: he couldn't use his hands.

'All righty!' Laura said. 'I've got gum. Do you smoke? I've got Winchesters or Sweet Caps—'

'Nothin' for me,' he said quietly, not moving his head from the pillow.

'No? Well, maybe next time. We come round with the cart every day, just so you know.'

'What, he don't want nothin'?' Chas asked.

Laura shook her head.

'Heck, I can't force him!' she said quietly to Missy, and they moved on to help other fellas on the ward.

Chapter Nineteen

Aberdeenshire, Scotland

Jean was trying to get back to the cottage before dark. As she pedalled harder, going as fast as she dared down the bumpy lane, she cursed herself. How could she have misjudged the timing of her errand so badly?

They'd spent a couple of days now hacking away at the copse and burning the brush, and although the gang's work still wasnae up to scratch, they were making some progress. Seffy had agreed she could leave the site early today, to cycle to the post office in Ballamar. There was an ivy-covered letter box at the end of their lane but Jean suspected it wasn't often emptied. Her request to their divisional officer for uniforms was important and she wanted to send the letter as soon as possible.

Seffy had given her some letters of her own to post. Before she'd dropped them into her bicycle basket, Jean hadn't been able to resist glancing at the addressees. There was a letter each for Grace and Joey, and one for Seffy's pal in London, no doubt sending her apologies for the christening. And that Canadian fella too, Staff Sergeant Callum Fraser. There was a letter for him.

'Noo! Not again!'

Every time her tyre hit a big hole, the dynamo jumped off the back wheel, plunging her into near darkness. She had to keep dismounting and reattaching it, which was delaying her even more.

The setting sun was turning the sky burnished gold and the trees along the ridge were black silhouettes, like sculptures. It was awful pretty but she didnae have time to stop and admire the view. She was still a long way from home.

Another hole, another BANG! But this time – thank God – the dynamo stayed on. She pressed on, standing up on the pedals, hoping to spot and avoid the ruts in the lane. But her eyesight was poor at the best of times and in this half-light she struggled to make much out at all.

Suddenly the bicycle started to slow, as though it were dragging something. Jean's heart sank. She knew that sensation. Aye, the back tyre was almost completely flat. A puncture. That was all she needed.

There was no point trying to cycle any further; she'd only ruin the tyre. She dismounted and started to push. She tried not to think about the trees, looming large in the gloom on either side of the track and where anything – or anyone – might be lurking.

The woods were silent now. The chirrups and calls of birds preparing to roost for the night had stopped. There was no sound but her footsteps on the rough ground and the faint click of the bicycle's wheels.

She tried to work out how much slower in percentage terms it was to push a bicycle rather than ride it. But even numbers couldn't distract her. Because she *was* afeared, there was no denying it. She didn't believe in ghosts or things that went bump in the night; there was a logical explanation for most things. But after that horrible night in the woods, with that fella, when she'd been pinned to the ground, too terrified to even scream, she wasnae the same person any more.

She could hear herself breathing heavily.

Just get to the end of the track, turn sharp right and you'll almost be back.

There was a sound ahead. A footstep or a boot, scraping on the ground. She felt a whooshing sensation in her chest and her heart started hammering, her breath was coming in short, sharp bursts.

A man was walking towards her.

Don't be daft; calm down. You'll gi' yourself a seizure. It's only a fella going home for his supper, same as you.

He was nearer now. Tall, young and dressed in overalls. He had a small knapsack slung over one shoulder. A workman. Almost twice her size.

Just say good day and walk past. Dunnae let him see you're afraid.

She tried to remember the unarmed combat moves she'd learned in the summer. She'd once knocked an Italian Fascist out cold with a chin jab. But that'd been months ago; she doubted whether she could do it again.

He was nearly upon her now, walking with a jaunty, purposeful air. Surely not the manner of someone who wanted to harm her? If only the bike was on the other side, forming a barrier between them. As they drew level, she hardly dared breathe. She flinched as he moved his hand. But he was only lifting his cap.

'Afternoon, Miss.'

Jean nodded. They'd almost passed one another, when he stopped.

'Is summat up with your bicycle? Shall I take a look?'

'Aw … no. Don't tr-trouble yourself …' Her voice had sounded quiet and quaking. But he'd already dropped to his haunches and was pressing on the back tyre.

'Flat as a pancake!' he said, standing up again.

Jean jerked back, almost letting go of the handlebars. Should she run? No, she couldn't leave her bicycle and all her things in the basket.

'Shall I walk you home?' he asked. 'You're new round here. You might lose your way.'

She hesitated. Her first thought had been to refuse. But it was almost pitch black now and the fella seemed all right. He was well-spoken for a labourer and although that was no guarantee he wouldn't hurt her, somehow, she doubted he would.

'Are you a conchie?' she asked, as the thought suddenly struck her.

'I am. I work at the saw mill. Alec Reid is the name.'

'We're not supposed to talk to you!'

Aw, God. She'd blurted it out without thinking. She wouldnae blame him if he took offence. But when he spoke, she could hear the smile in his voice.

'I'm used to the silent treatment. Let me do all the talking and that way, you won't get into any bother. Agreed?'

Jean nodded, her lips shut tight.

He laughed. 'I'll take that as a yes. You're one o' the timber girls lodging with Moira Harris, aren't you? Come on. I know where she lives.'

He seemed to know everything. It was a small place, she supposed word got around. It was good of him, though, to go out of his way to help her. He might be a conchie but she was still grateful to him.

When Jean opened the back door of Laburnum Cottage, a delicious smell of rabbit stew wafted out.

Seffy and Mrs Harris were sitting at the kitchen table.

Seffy shot up out of her seat. 'Jean, where've you been? We were getting worried!'

'Aye, we thought the bogeyman must've got you!' Mrs Harris said cheerfully.

Jean sighed. 'I completely lost track of time.'

'Aye, well the bright lights o' Ballamar can do that to you!' Mrs Harris said. 'Come in, then, lass, don't stand there, letting all the warmth out. Oh! Now, who's this?'

As Alec Reid stepped out from behind Jean and pulled off his cap, Mrs Harris's face fell. 'Oh, aye, I know who you are.'

Her tone had changed completely.

Jean could see him properly now, in the pool of light falling onto the doorstep. He had a shock of dark hair and an open, round face. She'd never met a conchie before. She wasn't sure what she'd expected but not this: a perfectly ordinary fella, not much older than her.

He was looking hopefully at the stew steaming on the hob. There was more than enough in that pot for four, but judging from Mrs Harris's sour tone, there was nae chance of her asking him to stay for supper.

'Mr Reid walked me back,' Jean said. 'I got a flat tyre coming through the woods.'

Mrs Harris nodded. 'Aye, well, we'll wish you goodnight then, Mr Reid. I'm sure Miss Ferguson is obliged to you.'

He twisted his cap in his hands. 'I could come back in the morning, before work, and fix that puncture, if you like?'

There wasn't time to even consider the offer: Mrs Harris was already starting to close the door.

'No need,' she said. 'We've men around here who can do it. Real men, mind!'

She slammed the door shut.

Ouch, that'd been rude. Jean hadn't even thanked him or wished him goodnight. What must he think of her? But then, he was a conchie; he was probably used to it.

Mrs Harris had returned to the range and was stirring the casserole vigorously with a wooden spoon.

'Conchie,' she said. 'Works up at the saw mill with my—' she stopped herself '—with the fellas up there. Now, this supper's ready. Miss Mills, might I trouble you to lay the table, please?'

After supper, Jean wheeled the bicycle into the kitchen and borrowed a couple of forks to mend the puncture.

'Mind you don't bend 'em!' Mrs Harris instructed. 'And no

making a mess of ma kitchen!'

Seffy sat at the table and watched, as Jean turned the bicycle upside down, onto its saddle, filled a bucket with water, and set to with the chalk, sandpaper and a sticky patch.

'You're so clever, Jean. I wouldn't know where to start!' she said.

'When you've had as many of these as me, you know what to do. Look, there's another patch.' Jean pointed to the inner tube. 'And another there.'

Seffy looked around, checking they were alone. 'Mrs H was rather off with him, wasn't she? The conchie?'

Jean shrugged. 'He's a social pariah. They all are.'

'But even so,' Seffy said. 'Poor chap. I thought he seemed pleasant. And gentlemanly.'

'Aye,' Jean said. 'I suppose. I do feel rotten that I didnae even thank him for walking me back.'

'Oh, I shouldn't worry. I expect our paths will cross again. Did you find out much about him?'

'No. I didnae speak to him.'

'Whyever not?'

'Because Mr Burke said we weren't to.'

Seffy laughed. 'And was Mr Burke there, checking up on you? Hiding behind a bush?'

'No, but it's the principle.'

'Are you telling me you walked back in total silence?'

'No. He talked and I listened. In fact, he told me—' Jean shook her head. 'Aw, nothing.'

'Do you always stick to the rules, Jean?'

She didn't answer for a moment. She was concentrating on pushing the patched-up inner tube back inside the tyre.

Finally, when it was done, she nudged her glasses up her nose and said, 'Ye know where you are with rules. If everyone stuck to the rules, the world wouldnae be in half such a mess. If it were up to the conchies, we'd all be speaking German now. We'd be overrun with Nazis.'

Seffy was like a dog wi' a bone; she wouldnae let the subject drop.

'I'd have expected better from you, Jean. Why won't you talk to him? Not simply out of politeness. I think you'd enjoy the challenge.'

'You mean, I should have a debate with him? "What's the answer to Nazism, if not brute force?"'

'Exactly that!' Seffy said. 'You're judging him without having heard his side of things.'

Jean shook her head. She didnae want to fall out with Seffy. They'd simply have to agree to disagree on this one.

She stood up, deftly attached the pump to the inner tube and started to reinflate the tyre.

'He'd have done that for you,' Seffy said. 'Alec Reid.'

Jean wrinkled her nose. 'Aye, so he said. But it's nae bother. I can do it myself.'

Seffy sighed. 'It must be awfully lonely, being one of them. You have to respect their moral courage. Sticking to one's principles isn't necessarily the easy option.'

'I cannae condone it.'

'I suppose it rather depends on their reasons for not wanting to fight. If it's for religious reasons – you know, not wanting to break the commandment "Thou shall not kill" – I suppose I can understand that.'

'But if it's out o' pure cowardice?' Jean said. 'It's not right. Not when our lads are serving king and country, risking life and limb. And if the only way I can show ma disapproval is to refuse to speak to the fella, then that is what I shall do.'

Chapter Twenty

'Aye, aye! Tools down is it, ladies?' McIntyre yelled, an unmistakeable note of glee in his voice.

Seffy threw her hands in the air, in exasperation, as the landowner appeared on the edge of the clearing. This was at least the third time he'd pounced.

'I curse the day I told him the best way through the thicket,' Jean muttered.

They'd been working hard on the site for a few days now and progress was slow but steady.

The Lost Girls lived for their breaks, so Seffy didn't dare reduce them but the moment they stopped work, McIntyre appeared, as though he'd been hiding in the bushes, waiting to catch them out.

Usually, Seffy managed to distract him and send him on his way, but today, before she could say a word, Peggy leaped to her feet. Her tea splashed over the rim of her mug and onto Myrtle sitting below, who cursed, loudly.

'For God's sake, man!' Peggy roared. 'We sat down five minutes ago. We havenae stopped all mornin'!'

Myrtle's swearing combined with Peggy's outburst, did the trick. He looked quite taken aback at being talked to like that by a mere girl. Even a little scared.

He raised a hand. 'I'll leave you to it, ladies!'

Then he backed off and disappeared the way he'd come.

Peggy sat back down, with a satisfied nod. 'Bullies!' she said. 'Ye have to stand up to them!'

Seffy put her hand over her mouth. 'It takes one to know one,' she whispered to Jean, with a giggle.

'You're in a good mood today,' Jean said. 'Considering everything. Was that a Christmas card I saw you with earlier? A wee bit late, isn't it?'

'Better late than never!' Seffy said.

Jean was right: she was on top form. She'd had a Christmas card and a letter from Callum that morning: a warm and funny letter that had filled her with optimism for the future.

Judging from the postmark, he'd sent it just before Christmas – to Blantyre camp – but it must've missed the Christmas post. It had been redirected from Morayshire to Laburnum Cottage, which had caused a further delay. Callum would have her new address by now, so that shouldn't happen again. But what a relief to know he hadn't forgotten her. She'd read the letter about twenty times over breakfast; she knew parts of it off by heart.

Thank you so much for the present, he'd written. *I won't open it until the big day! So sorry I haven't sent you a gift for Christmas. It sure was my intention and I have something real nice for you but I don't trust the post, so, if you don't mind, Seffy, I'll wait until we're together again (hopefully before next Christmas!) and give it to you in person.*

She was thrilled at the thought. Not of the present – delightful though that would be – but at the thought of being with him again. With any luck, she only had to wait a few more weeks.

Jean knocked back the dregs of her tea and stood up. 'Shall we get back to it, then?'

Seffy clapped her hands. 'Come along, girls, time to work!'

No one moved.

'Must we?' Rona said. 'I'm worn out!'

'Aye, and it's freezin'; Tich said, looking longingly at the fire.

'Mightn't we clock off a wee bit earlier today?' Isobel asked. 'That way, we'll be fresh for tomorrow.'

Jean sighed heavily. *Clock off earlier?*

She'd had her doubts about Seffy's softly, softly approach and now the lassies were taking advantage. She could see the frustration on Seffy's face. A minute ago, she'd been happy as Larry, now she looked tense and pale.

A flurry of snowflakes drifted down. It happened every half hour or so but stopped after a minute. As though, like the Lost Girls, the snow couldn't decide whether to stay or go.

Seffy folded her arms and glared at the gang. 'Have you any idea how essential our work is? We're not in these woods for the fun of it! Timber is the prime commodity in so many industries!'

The lassies were looking at her blankly. She might as well be speaking double Dutch.

Jean gave a small cough. 'Layman's terms, Seffy,' she said.

Seffy scrambled to her feet, so she was towering over the girls seated around the fire. She started to pace around them.

'Right, let's take the mines. Mines are where we get coal, you understand?'

'Course we do!' Eileen said.

'Aye, we're not eejits!' Peggy said.

'Without our work, the mines would close! The trees are used for pit props, to hold open the seams. And without mines, there'd be no heat or power. The munitions factories, that make weapons to help us win this war, couldn't operate.'

'And mining's just one industry that needs timber,' Jean said. 'There's shipping, aircraft and railways too.'

No one spoke. They still looked glum and now they looked disinterested as well. Aw, this was useless. Appealing to the girls' better natures wasn't doing the trick.

Jean fished a well-thumbed book out of her overcoat pocket. She held it up. 'Rona, can you tell everyone what this is?'

Rona looked uncomfortable. Perhaps she was fretting about being called a 'toffee-nosed measurer'. But eventually, she said, 'It's a *Hoppus Ready Reckoner*.'

'Correct! This is what Rona and I'll be using to calculate each tree's cubic capacity, as I tried to explain the other day.'

Peggy shrugged. 'Aye, well, bully for you two. But that has nothin' to do wi' the rest of us!'

Jean stood up, so she was standing beside Seffy. 'It depends how interested you are in getting paid more. When we do our calculations, we can estimate the amount of timber that a tree will yield. And those of you who are felling will be paid on that basis.'

Eileen's head shot up. 'We'll be getting paid for each tree we fell?'

'Aye, you'll be getting piece work out here, instead of a fixed amount,' Jean confirmed. 'So the sooner you get this clearing done and start felling, the better.'

The Lost Girls gazed at one another. Finally, they looked animated.

'More money?' Tich asked, eyes wide.

'More money,' Jean said.

'How much more?' Peggy asked.

Jean told them, and Eileen almost went cross-eyed trying to do the maths.

'It's about twenty per cent more than you're earning at the moment,' Jean said. 'It depends, of course, on how hard you work.'

'That's loads more!' Isobel said.

'We could get better billets!' Eileen said.

'We could go to the pub!' Myrtle said.

There was a change in the air, Jean could sense it: a feeling of hopefulness.

Seffy raised her thumb at Jean as a sign of 'well done,' and said, 'Let's have no more talk of knocking off early. Let's grit our teeth and get on with it, shall we?'

The girls immediately got up and started rinsing out their mugs in the bucket.

Only Peggy was staying resolutely glum.

'I dunnae think we've won her over yet,' Jean said.

'Oh, don't you worry about her,' Seffy said. 'I have a plan for Peggy.'

Chapter Twenty-One

Basingstoke, Hampshire, England

It was suppertime at the boarding house. Everyone else was downstairs in the dining room; Missy was curled up on her bed, sobbing.

There was a gentle knocking on the door and when she didn't answer, it slowly opened and Laura came in.

'Hey! This won't do! Sitting up here all on your own and – *crying*? What's up, Miranda?'

Laura sat on the edge of the bed and waited until Missy had dried her tears.

'You haven't had a run-in with Matron, have you?'

Missy shook her head. 'Why, is that likely?'

Laura wrinkled her nose. 'She can be a little sharp. She runs a tight ship! You know, she actually has the rank of "major"? But underneath the tartar exterior, she's probably quite nice. So, if not Matron, what's up? Aren't you hungry, is that it? Do you feel unwell?'

Missy shook her head. To tell the truth, she was ravenous.

What she was feeling was a kind of sickness inside. They'd been in Basingstoke for a week now and for the last few days she'd wanted to cry the whole time, for reasons that she couldn't quite define. It was worse when someone was nice to her. The tears bubbled up, and as much as she wanted them to stop, she couldn't. And even when she wasn't blubbering, there was a constant hard lump in her throat from holding back the tears.

'Shall I go get your sister?' Laura asked.

'NO! Please don't. I don't want Juliet seeing me like this. She didn't want me to come here in the first place. She said she didn't wanna babysit me and she didn't think I'd hack it.' Missy managed a wry smile. 'Looks like she was right, huh? I couldn't bear to hear her say "I told you so!"'

'All righty, I won't say a word. You're homesick, I reckon. I went through that too. It's kinda different here, the culture takes some adjusting to. The British and their funny ways, huh?'

Missy nodded. Oh, boy, she was so glad she wasn't the only one.

'The way they say, "Ah, another colonial!" when they find out you're from Canada! You know, someone said to me recently, "Well done, at last you're getting rid of that awful twang!"'

'Your accent?'

'Yeah! The cheek of the guy! When they say that thing about being a colonial, I always wanna reply, "We didn't have to come over, you know! We're volunteers!"'

'And besides, we haven't come to help the British,' Missy said. 'We're here to support our boys.'

'That's right! Look, it's tough, especially at first. You're away from everything that's familiar and you're missing your folks. Also, this place and the job—' Laura shrugged '—it's not always what you'd expected, right?'

Missy nodded, feeling a swell of gratitude towards Laura. That was exactly it. She'd never been away from home before and now she was thousands of miles away, with no chance of getting back any time soon.

Oh, boy, she was all mixed up. She should be ecstatic: she'd arrived safely in Europe and been reunited with Callum, but

135

instead, she was sad and she couldn't shake it off.

'Isn't your fiancé over here?' Laura said. 'That must be wonderful, being so close!'

Missy nodded. 'Yeah, his unit's not far away but I've only seen him once so far and that was two weeks ago. Sure, there's the telephone but that has its challenges!' She laughed. Gee, she was doing nothing but complain. 'But we're gonna see each other on the weekend. Only for the day, mind but—'

'Swell! That's something to look forward to, right?' Laura looked around. 'At least we've all got our own room. And yours is pretty, with that view out over the garden. Wait until the spring. Everything'll look a whole lot better.'

That was true: she wasn't seeing England at its best. She liked the place – although everything was in miniature – but it would be better when it wasn't so cold and rainy.

Oh, she should stop griping and count her blessings. She was away from London and the bombs, her room here was nice and the boarding house was walking distance to the hospital, which was real handy. Some of the girls had to cycle or catch the bus. And their landlady was kind, nothing was too much trouble.

She must've looked brighter because Laura said, 'Now, are you coming down for something to eat, before it gets cold?'

'They're not waiting for me, are they?'

'No, don't worry. I told them to go right ahead and start.'

'OK, now I'm worried there mightn't be anything left!'

They laughed.

'I'm pretty sure I know who you mean,' Laura said.

A couple of the male boarders – Mr Barker and Mr Jones – were in the habit of eating their food real quick, putting their cutlery together and then staring hopefully at the women around the table, as they finished their meal. They reminded Missy of the dogs back home.

She pinched her cheeks and bit her lips to give them a little colour and fluffed out her hair. 'Do I look OK?'

'You look perfect!'

Missy followed her out of the room and closed the door behind them. They trotted down the stairs together. She was real nice, Laura; she'd made her feel so much better. She was gonna be a real good pal over here, Missy could tell.

Chapter Twenty-Two

Aberdeenshire, Scotland

When the girls got back to the cottage after work one afternoon, there was a large cardboard box on the kitchen floor, addressed to Jean.

'Uniforms!' she said, triumphantly. 'That was quick!'

'It certainly was,' Seffy said. 'And the timing's perfect, as we'll soon be felling. Oh, but let's not put the bunting out until we've seen what's inside.'

Jean tore open the box and pulled out a gabardine Mackintosh with one hand and a gumboot with the other.

'Hurrah! That's a good start!' Seffy said.

There was an inventory stuck to the inside of the box. Jean ripped it off and scanned the list, as Seffy pulled out more clothes.

'Ma God, she's sent the lot! Even the two dozen pairs of socks!'

'You can never have too many socks!'

That was true enough, Jean thought. You needed at least two pairs to fill your wellingtons, if you didnae want to get blisters on your blisters.

A few minutes later, the box was empty and the girls were sitting on the floor, surrounded by cord breeches, shirts, ties, boots, sweaters, oilskins, berets and lots of socks.

The smell of rubber and mothballs filled the room.

Seffy examined one of the green jumpers. 'It's all brand new! Golly, it's like being in Dickins & Jones! Whatever did you put in that letter, Jean?'

She pushed her glasses up her nose. 'I mentioned the freezing temperatures and the high probability of bronchitis, pneumonia and rheumatic fever. And I said the ministry would surely have summat to say about their workers not being properly attired.' She shrugged. 'That kind o' thing.'

'Well done! You're such an excellent scribe, Jean. You obviously put the fear of God into our dear divisional officer. She must've packed this lot up the moment she read your letter!' She frowned. 'She hasn't asked for a financial contribution, has she?'

'No. I said the girls all get the minimum wage, due to their age, which isn't strictly true, of course: Peggy gets more. But I said not to think about asking them to pay a penny.'

The next morning, they propped the box on the saddle of Jean's bicycle and wheeled it down the lane. There was no getting the bike from there into the clearing, so they hid it behind a bush and carried the box between them through the thicket.

The girls were sitting around the fire, making the first brew of the day.

'What's in there?' Tich asked, as they lowered the box to the ground.

Jean took a second to catch her breath, then she said, 'Ask and ye shall receive!'

She'd never seen the girls move so fast. As one, they leaped up and in seconds, the box was open and the girls were pulling out the uniforms, with more enthusiasm than they'd ever shown for anything before.

'Look! A tam o' shanter!' Myrtle said, pulling off her headscarf and slapping the beret onto her head.

'Aw, I've always wanted a tammie!' Tich said, rooting around in the box to find one for herself.

Jean twirled her finger. 'Other way round, Myrtle. The badge goes at the front.'

After much trying on and swapping of clothes, until they found their size, every member of the gang was wearing boots, berets and oilskins.

They lined up, without being asked and Seffy walked up and down, hands behind her back, inspecting them.

The difference in the lassies was amazin'. If only they could have a photograph taken for posterity.

'Much better!' Seffy said. 'And I'm sure you're much warmer, too. You can save the other things – the breeches, jumpers and shirts – for best. They're too good to wear every day. Now, you're perfectly equipped for our proper work—'

'When do we start that, then?' Peggy demanded, sticking out her bottom lip.

Ma God, the girl was insolent. Jean could see Seffy take a deep, calming breath before she spoke.

'If you carry on at this rate, we should be in a position to move to the forest next week.'

The gang was unusually quiet.

Eileen looked down at her new overcoat. 'Did yous get these for us?' she asked Seffy.

Jean held her breath. She wouldnae put it past Seffy to take all the credit. It'd been her idea, after all, to get the lassies some better clothing.

But Seffy shook her head. 'It's all down to Jean and her persuasive pen power! It's her you have to thank, not me.'

'Thank you, Jean!' they chorused. Even Peggy was – och, not exactly smiling – but not sulking, at least.

Jean blushed and muttered that it had been her pleasure and was no more than they deserved.

Then she ushered them back to the fire to make their tea.

Chapter Twenty-Three

The next day, Jean cycled to the saw mill.

It was housed in a low, brick building with a corrugated iron roof. As she approached, she could hear the unmistakeable whine and whirr of the saws inside.

She dismounted, pushed her bicycle towards the closed double doors and suddenly spotted him: the conchie, Alec Reid.

He was sitting on an upended log and despite the cold, he was only wearing a shirt and dungarees. His hands were cupped around a steaming mug of tea, but even so, he must have been freezing.

She contemplated turning round and coming back another time, but Seffy had given her time off for this errand and she shouldn't waste it. Besides, it was too late: he'd seen her.

'Miss Ferguson! To what do we owe the pleasure?'

He stood up and the book that had been in his lap dropped to the ground.

How did he know her name? Aw, of course, Mrs Harris had said, 'I'm sure Miss Ferguson is obliged to you' on the night he'd walked her home, a week ago. He was like her, then: he had a good memory for names.

Should she answer him?

It'd been easy to stay silent in the dark, as they'd walked through the woods together. Now, face to face in broad daylight, it was harder to stick to her principles and to Mr Burke's instruction that they shouldnae talk to the conchies.

She couldn't simply blank him; it'd be too rude. And who would know she'd spoken to him, after all? There was no one else around. No, she'd reply but she'd keep any conversation brief and businesslike.

'I've come to see a man about a bike,' she said.

He laughed. 'Not a man about a dog?'

Jean frowned. 'No. Is someone selling a dog? What's a dog got to do wi' it?'

So much for being brief; she'd fallen into the trap of asking too many questions.

'Never mind,' he said, smiling.

'My landlady said there's a fella here – Ron – who has a bicycle he'd let me hire,' Jean said.

'Did she? Aw, well, Mrs Harris knows more than most about this place, eh?' He tapped the side of his nose and gave her a conspiratorial look. 'Why do you need a bike, anyhow? Is yours still not fixed?'

'It's not for me, it's for Rona, my trainee. Once we start measuring the standing timber, it'll be better if we can cycle over there together.'

'All right, wait here a minute.'

Mr Reid went to the saw mill doors, pulled one side open and shouted to someone inside.

'He'll be along by and by,' he said, when he returned. 'They're all on their tea break.'

Presumably, the other workers were drinking their tea together, blithering and havin' a laugh, while he was here on his tod. Literally, out in the cold.

She felt awkward, standing there, holding the bicycle by its handlebars. She stamped her feet; they were freezing in her gumboots, even with two pairs of socks on. She wished this Ron fella would get a move on.

Mr Reid sipped his tea. 'Whatever he wants for the bike, offer him half,' he said.

Jean squirmed. She didnae fancy bartering with some old fella she'd never even met before.

'Aw, don't look at me!' he said. 'I cannae do it for you. He's more likely to put the price up if I get involved!'

Jean had to smile at that.

'Ta very much by the way. For the other night,' she said, not meeting his eye.

'My pleasure. But you'd probably have been fine without me.'

Jean bit her lip. She wouldn't have been fine, not at all. He had no idea how much his non-stop blathering had helped.

She'd listened to every word he'd said. She knew now, amongst a host of other things, that the 'twit twoo' call of the tawny owl was actually a duet between the male and female. And that if there was ever a haze around the moon, it meant snow was on the way. And – most surprising of all – that Mrs Harris, a married woman, and the head sawyer, Mr Galbraith, were, by all accounts, carrying on.

Of course, he might've made that up to shock her into speaking, but if that'd been his plan, it had failed. Jean didn't care for gossip and although she'd been shocked by the news, she hadn't wanted to ask any more about it.

'How're you lassies getting on?' he asked. 'I hear you drew the short straw, having to clear that mess on McIntyre's land?'

Jean wondered how much he knew about the trouble they'd had with the Lost Girls.

She'd just sent off her first report. While she'd alluded to the problems, she hadn't mentioned the girls' outright refusal to work, keeping her fingers crossed that word hadn't got back to Miss McEwen. It was an omission, not a lie. She could just imagine the supervisor pouncing on news of a strike with utter glee: it would be all the proof she needed that Seffy didn't have control of the gang.

'We're nearly done,' she replied. 'We're about to start work on the forest.'

Mr Reid let out a low whistle. 'I bet old man McIntyre's no' happy about that. It's a wonder he's letting you anywhere near it.'

'Aw, well, he has to. The land's been requisitioned by the ministry. I'm a measurer, but the fellers will be moving in soon enough.'

'The *fellas*? I thought you were all lassies?'

Jean shook her head. 'No, not men, I mean—'

He laughed, and she understood, then: he was teasing her.

'Mr McIntyre's not the easiest to deal with, that's for sure,' he said.

Jean agreed with him but she didn't reply. She shouldn't run down the landowner, especially not to someone she hardly knew. It might get back to him.

She kept her eyes fixed on the saw-mill door, waiting for any sign of Ron.

Mr Reid seemed to sense her awkwardness. He sat back down on his log, picked up the battered paperback and started to flick through the pages.

She'd have liked to ask him what he was reading – her eyesight was too poor to see from here – but that wouldn't count as brief and businesslike, so she said nothing.

He stopped after a minute and held it up. 'Siegfried Sassoon. D'you know him?'

Jean shook her head.

'Poet. From the last war. The other men think I'm a cissy. I won't fight and I read poetry.' He gave a resigned smile. 'But I understand why. Most of them have sons and grandsons who are serving, so …' His voice trailed off.

Jean wasn't sure how to reply. She despised the conchies and everything they stood for. Before she'd met Alec Reid, she'd have said they deserved to be ostracised. But he seemed like a decent enough fella. Deluded, of course. But a nice fella, nonetheless.

She was trying to frame her response. Summat that wasnae too friendly but not mean either. Summat neutral. But then Ron appeared and the conversation, such as it had been, was over.

Chapter Twenty-Four

'Peggy Gorman, you're a troublemaker and a bully!' Seffy said. 'I knew the moment I met you, I had to separate you from the others. Away with you to the saw mill!'

She swivelled round and looked at Jean, sitting behind her on the bed. 'You can't say that,' Jean said. 'She'll murder you!'

Seffy threw herself face down on the bed and groaned. 'Why is everything in this godforsaken place so *difficult*? Miss McEwen was right: we did have it easy in Blantyre. I wish I was back there. I wish I was anywhere but here!'

She wished she was back in that snow-covered bothy in Blantyre Forest, where she'd once spent a chaste but wonderful night with Callum. No, stop! She really must stop tormenting herself with thoughts like that.

'You're absolutely doin' the right thing, putting Peggy-with-the-pipe in the saw mill,' Jean said. 'She's stubborn, ill-tempered and a bad influence on the others.'

Seffy turned onto her side. 'I expect she'll kick up a right stink.'

'Aye, but she'll come round. Eventually.'

'I'll tell her she can have her morning cuppa with us on her way to work each day. You and Rona could do that too. It'd be nice to start the day together.'

Jean smiled. 'Like a school assembly? Are ye goin' to make us sing hymns?'

Seffy prodded Jean's thigh. 'Don't mock! I'm thinking of morale. And on that note, we really should try to praise the girls.'

Jean harrumphed. 'For what? Being useless?'

'Oh, come on, they're not too bad now. They've probably never been told they're good at anything.'

'GIRLS!' Mrs Harris was calling up the stairs. 'I'm off out now! Your supper's on the hob!'

'TA VERY MUCH!' Jean called back.

'I wonder where she goes, all dolled up like that,' Seffy said.

Jean made a peculiar face.

Seffy sat up. 'You know something! Come on, tell me everything!'

Jean put up a finger for silence and waited until they'd heard the back door shut before she spoke.

'Now, as you know, I'm not one to spread gossip—' she said.

Seffy gave a squeal of anticipation. 'But—?'

'But apparently, our landlady and the head sawyer at the mill, Mr Galbraith—' She paused, as though she didn't want to say it.

'Never!' Seffy said. 'You mean they're having a dalliance?'

'Aye.'

'Who told you?'

Jean winced. 'That Alec Reid fella, the conchie.'

'You've spoken to him! You swore blind you never would!'

Jean blushed. 'What he told me about Mrs Harris, mightn't be true!'

'Bet it is! She's what my mother would call "blousy". Fancy carrying on with another man, while Mr Harris is doing his bit for king and country. It's a rather poor show. Do you think you can bear to stay in the house of a woman with such low morals, Jean?'

Jean pursed her lips, giving it serious thought.

'I'm joking!' Seffy said. 'Really, what business is it of ours? As long as she's not running a bawdy house, who cares? You know, we're living through quite extraordinary times. Society's turned on its head!'

'You can say that again,' Jean said. 'I think it's terrible. Someone ought to let her husband know.'

'It's probably better he's in the dark. What can he do, if he gets a letter telling him his wife's behaving badly, except brood and get upset? No, let sleeping dogs lie. Of course, if he gets wind of it, comes home and starts chasing Mrs Harris round the garden with an axe, we'll have to take action. You could do one of your famous chin jabs on him, Jean!'

Jean shook her head. 'Anyhow, we've got distracted. We're supposed to be agreeing on what you're gonna say to Peggy. Did you know, by the way, that the saw mill's powered by a steam engine? I'd give anything to see that.'

Seffy rolled her eyes. Honestly, there was no accounting for taste. Peering at a dirty old engine was definitely not her idea of fun.

She took Peggy to one side the next day and said firmly, 'Mr Burke has instructed me to assign someone to the saw mill. And I've decided you're the best one for the job.'

'NO! I won't do it!' Peggy clenched her fists and Seffy took a step back. 'Why me, anyhow?' she asked, sticking out her bottom lip.

'Because you're the oldest, strongest and most responsible. Can you imagine if I put Tich in there?'

Peggy huffed. 'Tich? She's so wee! That'd be a waste o' time!'

'Well, quite. It'll be heavy work, lifting all that timber. And as for Isobel, with those soft hands …?'

Peggy snorted. 'Gawd, no. Besides, Isobel couldnae cope wi' all the men and their wisecracks. She'd be greetin' half the time.'

Greeting, Seffy knew by now, meant crying.

'Precisely! You, on the other hand, are perfectly capable of standing up for yourself.'

That part was, at least, true. Seffy had reasons for rejecting

Eileen and Myrtle too, but she didn't need to produce them.

'Shall we take a walk over to the saw mill later?' she said. 'I'll introduce you to Mr Galbraith, the boss?'

Peggy gave a barely imperceptible nod. 'But if I dunnae like the look of the place, I won't stay!'

And now they were standing outside the saw mill. The air was filled with the sounds of whirring and groaning machinery and it had started to snow. Not the intermittent, tiny flakes of the past week: this was coming down in thick clumps and starting to settle.

'Golly, this'll be a new experience. I've never been inside a saw mill. Have you?' Seffy said. Peggy shook her head. 'It'll be fascinating to see what happens to the logs, won't it?'

'Suppose.'

Goodness, it was wearing, having to be permanently jolly and excited. Working with the Lost Girls was like being in a nursery school.

They turned at the sound of a tractor coming out of the woods, dragging a tree trunk on chains. Alec Reid was in the driver's seat and he pulled up next to them.

'Hello!' Seffy said, smiling broadly, to show she wasn't about to give him the cold shoulder. 'We're with the Women's Timber Corps. Do you think we might take a look around? My colleague will be coming to work here shortly.'

'*Might* be coming to work here shortly,' Peggy said, through gritted teeth.

'Sure,' he said, cheerfully. 'I know who you are. Come on, I'll take you to the main man.'

It was deafening inside the saw mill. The girls immediately put their hands over their ears. A couple of old chaps working on the saws – huge metal wheels with ferocious spikes – laughed and yelled something at them, but it was too loud to hear what they'd said.

Alec disappeared and returned after a few minutes with

a red-headed chap in oil-stained overalls. This must be Mr Galbraith. He weaved between the work benches to reach them.

So, this was Mrs Harris's lover. Gosh, he was younger than her by about ten years and was certainly nothing to write home about.

He scowled at the girls disapprovingly. 'You cannae stand there doin' that all day if you work here!' he said, shouting above the din.

Seffy exchanged a look with Peggy, and tentatively, they removed their hands from their ears. It was so loud! Seffy wished she had a pillow to wrap around her head.

'HOW DO YOU BEAR IT?' she yelled at Mr Galbraith.

'YE GET USED TO IT!' he yelled back.

The awful noise wasn't the only downside of this place: above the not unpleasant smell of pine resin and sawdust, there was an unmistakeable top note of men's sweat. She didn't envy Peggy working here. She'd take the peace and fragrant scents of a forest over this any day.

Mr Galbraith indicated they should move nearer to the doors, where it was quieter. Seffy made the introductions.

'Miss Gorman is to start work here shortly, as per Mr Burke's instructions,' she said.

Peggy looked glum. She hadn't said a word since Alec Reid had brought them inside.

Galbraith scratched his chin and sniffed. 'I never wanted lassies working here,' he said. 'But it seems I've nae choice. Have ye started fellin' McIntyre's woods yet?'

'We start next week,' Seffy said, sounding more optimistic than she felt. She had no idea how much 'training on the job' the Lost Girls had had. She hadn't dared ask. As they'd sent two leader girls running for the hills, they probably hadn't had much.

She turned to |Peggy. 'At least it's nice and warm. You'll be out of the snow! And remember, the pay's higher for working here.'

Peggy shrugged as though she couldn't care less.

Mr Galbraith was looking her up and down as though she were a prize beast in a cattle market.

'Ye look strong enough,' he said, finally. 'Will ye do as you're told?'

'Mebbe,' Peggy said.

Seffy's heart sank but Mr Galbraith gave a short laugh. Perhaps he thought she was joking; Seffy knew she wasn't.

'I was thinking Miss Gorman could start on Monday, if that's agreeable?' Seffy said. 'Can you give us an idea of what she'll be doing?'

Mr Galbraith nodded at one of the young boys. 'That kind o' thing. This laddie's a tailsman, guiding the logs towards the saw blade.'

It was all Seffy could do not to gasp. 'Golly, isn't that rather dangerous?'

'Not if you're mindful and keep your hands well away. And never—' he shook his finger at Peggy '—never wear gloves!'

'Anything else?' Seffy asked, stepping away from the spinning saw wheel. 'She won't be working on those huge saws, will she?'

He shook his head. 'Nah, only the fellas who've been here a while. Now, here's summat else she can do: stacking the sawn timber. And she can saw slab wood for the steam engine on this bench here.'

He hesitated and turned to look at them. 'Ye know, I'm not convinced the lass can do it.'

Peggy's eyes widened. 'What d'you mean, I cannae do it? I'm strong, me! And I was a shop girl afore I came here, so I'm used to standing all day.'

Seffy held her breath. Peggy hadn't cared about being out of the cold or earning more in the saw mill. But being told by a man that she wasn't capable of working here, might just have clinched it.

'I've more brawn than any o' these wee laddies and auld fellas!' Peggy said. 'Here, gi' me a go. I'll show you now! Gi' me a log to carry or summat to stack!'

'You carry on, I'll wait outside!' Seffy said, taking her chance

151

to escape. She felt as though a weight had been lifted from her shoulders. It looked as though Peggy was going to stay. She was finally getting rid of the girl!

The others weren't listening. Mr Galbraith was walking Peggy over to a stack of timber, presumably so she could demonstrate her lifting prowess.

Seffy slipped out through the double doors. She rubbed her ears. They were ringing and she'd only been in there a few minutes.

Ah, that was better. Peace and fresh air. Oh, and snow. Lots and lots of snow.

Chapter Twenty-Five

Basingstoke, Hampshire, England

Missy shivered as she pushed her cart down the long, damp corridor, heading for the wards. It seemed especially heavy today and dash it, one of her new lace-ups had started squeaking. She could hear it each time she took a step, even over the wheels rattling on the concrete floor. Boy, that was gonna drive her crazy.

She was a little over a week into the job, and now she didn't feel so awkward being alone with so many fellas, all vying for her attention. She supposed it was a problem most girls would kill for.

Tomorrow, she and Juliet had the day off and they were taking the train to meet up with the fellas on the coast. She could hardly wait and nothing – not the cold, or the heavy cart, or the darned squeak in her shoe – was going to dampen her spirits.

A nurse passed her in the corridor and wished her a good day. Missy was in awe of the nurses, who floated around with veils in their caps, so capable and elegant, expertly administering to the men.

They were real busy tending to the sick and injured, but they always had time for a smile and a greeting. All except Matron who, on the odd occasion that Missy had seen her, seemed real stern.

She probably looked down on the General Duties Officers because they weren't medical staff; they were more like social workers.

She'd reached the Burns Ward and stopped outside, as always, to prepare herself. She thought of it as pausing to put on her poker face.

It was best to reverse in, so she backed through the swing doors, pulling the cart in behind her. Immediately, she recognised the familiar voice of Cheeky Chas.

'Here's the Sister, sent from heaven! Say, whatcha got for us today?'

The ward mail had come round, and those fellas who'd received post were busy reading their letters from home and shouting out their news. Missy had noticed that the patient the others called Rabbit never got mail. And he still didn't want anything from the cart.

'Anything for you?' she asked. He shook his head. 'No, nothing? OK, well, one of us will be around tomorrow and we'll ask you again then.'

'OK, Squeaky,' he murmured.

Missy frowned. Had she heard that right? Had he called her 'Squeaky'? He must've heard her shoe making that dumb noise when she came onto the ward.

She could hardly ask him to repeat it. She watched him carefully for a few seconds but it was impossible to tell what was going on underneath all those bandages. She sighed. Rabbit sure was frustrating. She wondered if she was ever gonna get through to that fella.

She moved on to the other patients.

'Now, Dexter, I got a copy of that magazine you like. Shorty, here's another of those detective books you keep devouring. Can you slow down a little, please?'

While they were exclaiming over what she'd brought and thanking her, Missy quietly slipped something onto Brain's bed. It was a romance; his favourite. The other fellas would tease him mercilessly if they saw them, so she passed the books over covertly.

She spent another half hour on the Burns Ward, before heading off.

Next on her list was the ward nicknamed 'Charlie'. It was all crutches, casts, canes and concussions. Most of the patients were army dispatch riders, which made Missy think she'd never get on a motorcycle, and she'd tell Callum to be sure he didn't either.

Regardless of their rank, injuries or the province they came from, the fellas all had one thing in common: their desire to talk about home, Canada; and getting back there as soon as possible was their constant preoccupation. Missy was more than happy to indulge them: she was missing home too, although that feeling of being constantly on the verge of tears was wearing off now.

As well as chatting to the fellas, she gladly looked at family photographs and wrote letters for patients who couldn't write themselves. And she had to reassure the others who still hadn't heard from their folks.

'Keep writing, guys,' she said, cheerfully. 'Your letters from home are surely winging their way over the ocean and just taking a little while to arrive.'

She hoped that was right and she wasn't raising false hopes because she felt responsible for these men now: for their well-being and for their happiness.

Please God, if ever Callum was injured and recovering in a hospital some place, she hoped he'd get the kind of treatment these fellas were getting: the best medical care and friendly girls to keep up morale and make them smile.

Chapter Twenty-Six

The South Coast, England

Two weeks after he'd been refused a transfer to Scotland, Callum was summoned back to Captain Coomber's office.

Jeez, he hoped it wasn't bad news. No, the padre would be here in that case and it was just him and Coomber. Maybe one of his men had been caught misbehaving. Drunk and disorderly, the usual.

It was silent in the office, as the captain finished reading – and then signing – a wad of papers.

Callum waited.

In the distance, came the sound of marching feet and someone barking orders, as one of the units carried out a drill.

The captain looked up finally and put the cap back on his pen. 'Ah, Fraser,' he said, as though surprised to find him there. 'You know, you remind me of someone.'

'Sir?'

'Yep. Myself! Mrs Coomber and I have been blessed with four beautiful girls—' he tapped one of the photographs on his desk '—but if I'd had a son, I like to think he'd have been somethin' like you.'

Callum scratched his nose. That was unexpected. And kinda embarrassing. Had he been hauled in here so the captain could tell him he was a decent kinda guy? No, there must be more to it than that.

'You're better than you think,' Coomber said. 'You've got a steady head on those shoulders. Don't think I haven't noticed how you're first to volunteer for a task or to break cover on manoeuvres. The Canadian army needs good men like you. And if you carry on like this, you'll make lieutenant. You'd be pleased about that, huh, Staff Sergeant?'

Callum felt a thud of disappointment deep inside his chest. He'd been summoned to talk about a future promotion. He'd been hoping for something else.

A promotion was the last thing he deserved and he sure didn't feel like he had a steady head right now. His head was a mess. Not only his head: all of him. He had no appetite, he couldn't sleep. Missy was over here – hell, he was seeing her again tomorrow – and Seffy had no idea. He was deceiving them both and he still didn't know what he was gonna do about it.

But he nodded, as the captain expected. 'I would, sir.'

'OK, well, a word to the wise.' Coomber jabbed his finger in the air, emphasizing each word. 'Don't. Let. Women. Mess. Things. Up!'

Now he was about to be dismissed. He glanced at his boots. There was a scuff mark on the toe of the left one. He'd polish that out when he got back to the hut.

The captain inhaled. 'But I've been thinking. About your request.'

Callum's head jerked up. 'My request, sir?'

'Sounds like you need some time to get your thoughts in order, Staff, so, I'm open to what you asked.'

This felt unreal. He hardly dared breathe, let alone speak.

'I'm prepared to have you sent on a temporary basis to Number Thirty-Six Company. They're up in the Highlands, so you can

157

have yourself some of that weather you've been missing so much.'

Oh, boy. Was he serious? Gee, that was the best news ever. He wanted to jump for joy, or shake the fella by the hand but he had to stay calm, eyes fixed ahead, hands behind his back.

At least Coomber didn't seem to expect him to talk yet.

'They need more good foresters up there right now. And after the disaster in Dieppe, we don't want too many men down here on the coast. You know what we're mustering for, right?'

'I – yeah, I reckon I do, sir,' he said. You'd have to be a fool not to. 'But I don't want you thinking I'm running away from that, or from my men.'

Coomber shook his head. 'It'll be a while yet. You'll be back by then, Staff. This is only to give you time to get your head around the right course of action. I can't let you go just yet – you'll need to wait a couple o' weeks, but I'll start making the necessary arrangements.'

'Could I take Private Johnson with me, sir? Please?'

He was pushing his luck now but he'd promised Gordy he'd ask, if he got the chance.

Coomber raised his eyebrows. 'What, you wanna take your best buddy with you now?'

'Johnson's a good forester, sir. He's like my right-hand man in the woods. And his wife is up in Scotland. They've got a baby on the way. They haven't seen each other in months.'

Coomber was a family man; mentioning the baby might just swing it.

The captain rubbed his chin and thought for a few seconds. 'OK, here's what we're gonna do. Draw me up a list of the ten fellas you wanna take with you – all good lumbermen, mind – and I'll get you transferred to that company. They're working someplace in Aberdeenshire—'

'*Aberdeenshire*?'

'Yeah, I know it's not Morayshire but it's the best I can do.'

'No, sir, that's absolutely—' It was perfect. It was where Seffy was. Callum sent a swift prayer of thanks up to heaven. Someone was looking down on him, for sure. '—that's real good of you, sir,' he continued. 'I sure do appreciate it.'

'I'll wire them now to say you're coming at the end of the month, to boost their manpower and do some good felling. OK?'

Callum couldn't help grinning as he saluted his saviour. 'Yes, SIR!'

He was going to Scotland! To the same place as Seffy. He was gonna get the chance to talk to her; maybe, finally, get things straight.

He could hardly contain himself. The moment he was dismissed, he'd bolt across camp to find Gordy and tell him the good news. It was nothing short of a miracle: they were both going back to Scotland.

As he turned to leave, he thought of something. 'Can we keep this to ourselves, sir? About my request?'

Coomber pursed his lips. 'You want it to seem like you had no choice in the matter?'

Callum nodded. If Verne found out, it'd get back to Missy. And she'd have every right to wonder what in hell's name he was doing. She shouldn't hear about his redeployment that way. He wanted to break the news to her himself.

'All righty, we can do that. I think that's just about the last favour, right, Staff Sergeant?'

'Yes, sir. I won't ask any more. I … I owe you, sir.'

'You betcha!' Coomber said, turning his forefinger into a gun and pretending to shoot him. Quite the comedian, these days.

Callum laughed at the gesture, as though he'd found it real funny. He was obliged to the guy, big time; it was the least he could do.

Chapter Twenty-Seven

Aberdeenshire, Scotland

Seffy and Jean staggered gratefully through the back door of Laburnum Cottage and started pulling off their boots and damp overcoats.

'I'm dead on ma feet,' Jean said.

'Me too.'

They'd been working like Trojans for a fortnight and – hallelujah – they'd finally finished clearing the site.

Jean and Rona had already spent some time measuring the first section of forest to be felled and marking up the trees. It was ready for the gang to start work from next week.

'You're away to Mr McIntyre's for tea this afternoon, aren't you?' Jean said. 'Will you be all right, on your own?'

Seffy balanced on one leg and shook off her wellington. 'Oh, Jean, you are funny. Do you think I need a chaperone?'

Jean looked offended. 'Have you no' wondered why the fella's invited you? He's got a soft spot for you.'

Seffy pulled a face. It seemed unlikely: he'd never given any indication she was a favourite. But Jean was awfully suspicious of men and their motives, ever since that horrid experience with the Canadian officer.

'We don't know him from Adam, after all,' Jean said. 'Mebbe I could wait outside the house and you could yell, if you need help?'

'That's a jolly kind offer, Jean but—'

'Dunnae fret! She won't be alone!' Mrs Harris said, marching into the kitchen with a mop in her hand. 'I'm goin' with her to Drumlochrie,' she said. 'She can take your bicycle, Miss Ferguson.' She peered at their boots. 'And yous had better not be leavin' dirt all over my clean floor!'

'I beg your pardon but did you say you're coming too, Mrs H?' Seffy asked, moving to block her view of a muddy patch on the stone flags.

'Aye! Who else is going to mek and serve the tea?'

Seffy turned to Jean. She hoped she wasn't smarting because she hadn't had an invite. 'What'll you do this afternoon, while I'm fraternising with the enemy?'

'Aw, don't you worry about me,' Jean said, crisply. 'I've got letters to write! To Irene, Morag, Enid and all ma other pals.'

'Jolly good! Give them my best, won't you? I'll bring you back some cake, if there's any to be had!'

Now, Seffy and Mrs Harris were cycling up the long narrow drive to McIntyre's house. There was a fast-flowing river a few yards off the left.

'That's the Dee,' Mrs Harris said, nodding at it. 'The royal estate's just over that wee hill.'

Seffy imagined this would be a pretty spot in nicer weather but it was all rather bleak at present. It wasn't snowing but there was still a layer of snow on the ground, which would no doubt freeze later and the light was already fading. She was glad she wouldn't be pedalling back down here alone later.

'Mr McIntyre would've given you a lift, if I couldn't have brought you,' Mrs Harris said, as if reading her thoughts. 'He'd never let a lady cycle home alone in the dark.'

Seffy frowned. That didn't sound like the man she'd met.

'I'm not sure I'd have accepted,' she said. 'I've seen the way he drives!'

Mrs Harris chuckled. 'Aye, he's like a different fella when he gets behind the wheel. But he's safe, as long as you hold on tight! He loves his wee cars! He told me once he drove tanks in the last war. I wasnae sure whether that was a joke or not, mind.'

McIntyre didn't strike Seffy as the kind of man who made jokes, so presumably it was true about the tanks. Perhaps he'd been injured during the war too, which would account for the limp.

'There's the house now,' Mrs Harris said.

It stood alone, large and gloomy with an air of neglect, rather like its owner. The name – Drumlochrie – was engraved on one of the stone pillars at the entrance.

'It's an awfully big place for just one person,' Seffy said, angling for information. Perhaps there were others living here, after all. It certainly looked as though it could house at least a dozen.

'Aye, but he doesnae use all the rooms. There was a wife, once, but—'

'She left him?'

'In a way,' Mrs Harris said, dismounting as they reached the front door. 'She died, awful young. In childbirth.'

Oh, God. Seffy felt terrible now. She must learn not to be so flippant.

'The bairn, too.'

Nooo. Could this get any worse?

Mrs Harris shook her head. 'But don't, whatever you do, ask him about any o' that. It was a long time ago, but if he's reminded, he'll be plunged into an awful gloom.'

Seffy swallowed. What a terribly sad tale; no wonder McIntyre was miserable. She was starting to wish she'd never agreed to come.

They propped their bicycles against the wall and Mrs Harris let them into the house.

The hall was covered in dark wood panelling and the only

sound was the loud ticking of a grandfather clock.

Mrs Harris hung up their coats, took an apron down from one of the hooks and put it on. She ushered Seffy into the drawing room and disappeared to start preparing their tea.

McIntyre was standing at the far end, facing a roaring log fire. He was wearing his customary kilt and there was a black labrador at his feet. The dog got up and padded towards her, tail wagging.

The room was vast, with tapestries and dozens of dusty antlers on the walls, and all manner of ornaments and lamps crammed onto shelves and tables. How could he bear to live in such a museum of a place? It clearly lacked a woman's touch.

'Ah, good to see you, Miss Mills,' McIntyre said, turning. 'Or, should I say, 'Lady …'? What exactly is your title?'

Seffy frowned. He must've been talking to Mrs Harris.

'Um … it's Lady Baxter-Mills,' she said, as she weaved her way through the furniture to reach him. It took so long that she had an urge to giggle. It was practically a maze. At one point she found herself blocked in by two armchairs and an occasional table and had to retrace her steps.

'Thank you for inviting me,' she said, when they were finally able to shake hands. 'And please, it's simply 'Miss Mills' these days. As my supervisor pointed out when I joined the Corps, 'Lady Baxter-Mills' is rather a mouthful.'

McIntyre nodded and shook her hand with a firm grip. Up close, he looked younger: about Father's age. His hair – if a trifle long – was at least neatly combed and his face was clean-shaven. It was rather a noble face. He must, once, have been rather dashing.

'This is Tam,' he said, gesturing to the dog which had flopped back down at his feet. 'Tam o' shanter. Do you like dogs, Miss Mills?'

He seemed more relaxed than usual. Seffy exhaled. Perhaps this would be all right. 'Yes, I adore them!' she said, bending to pat Tam. 'I miss mine so much.'

The chap couldn't be all bad if he liked dogs. And judging from the way Tam was contently curled up, dogs liked him.

They sat in front of the fire, with an occasional table between them. Usually, at this point in a social gathering, Seffy would make a polite comment about her lovely surroundings: 'Charming place you have here,' or 'What a delightful room!' But she really couldn't. It would sound as though she were being sarky. She wondered if she dared asked for a tour of the house. She might be able to make a few subtle suggestions for improvement.

'Whilst we're waiting for the tea,' he said, 'let's talk about your gang in my woodland.'

Goodness, he'd cut straight to the chase. She should've brought a notepad and pen. Jean would interrogate her later and she didn't want to forget anything important.

'Very well,' she said, leaning forward in her seat and telling herself to concentrate.

'How are those lassies gettin' on? Any more walk-outs?'

'No,' Seffy said. She tapped the edge of the table. Touch wood. 'Actually, I wanted to let you know that we've finished clearing the site. We're ready to start felling.'

He flinched, as though her words had caused him actual pain.

'You really don't want us there, do you?' she said.

'I most certainly do not. There's been a forest on that land for centuries!' He gave a resigned shrug. 'But it's wartime. Sacrifices have to be made.'

'And apparently, it takes five trees to keep each British soldier fighting in this war,' Seffy said. She frowned. 'Or perhaps it's four? Do you know, it might actually be six.'

He laughed – a most unexpected sound – then immediately became serious again.

'I must admit, I didnae think you'd get to this stage. Not wi' those wild wee lassies. But listen up, Miss Mills. There is one oak in the heart of the forest which I absolutely insist you leave be. Not a branch of that tree is to be touched, do you hear? Let alone—' he swallowed '—felled. Can you guarantee that?'

164

Seffy was taken aback. Golly, what a responsibility. She didn't dare guarantee anything, especially once the Lost Girls were let loose with axes and saws.

Oh, blast. Why wasn't Jean here? This was Jean's area of expertise, not hers.

'I'm sure – at least, I expect that can be done,' she said, carefully. 'But we'll need some means of identifying the tree. Perhaps you could tie a red ribbon around it?'

He didn't smile.

'No, wait. There's a more scientific way,' she said. 'The measurers mark all trees due to be felled with a scribing pen. As long as Miss Ferguson is made aware, she'll ensure it's not marked.'

Seffy wondered whether it would actually be as simple as that, but for now, at least, he looked satisfied.

'And might I make a request of you, Mr McIntyre? If, for any reason, you need to speak to my lumberjills, will you do it through me? And let me sort out any problems?'

He raised an eyebrow. 'You're expecting more problems, then?'

'No, this is just a precautionary measure.'

'Aye, well, they're certainly a feisty bunch. And there's one that seems worse than the rest. Stout lass. The ringleader.'

'Peggy Gorman, yes. But she won't be felling. I've assigned her to the saw mill.'

'Good idea,' he said. 'Divide and conquer.'

Mrs Harris coughed. She was standing in the drawing room doorway, staggering under the weight of the tea tray.

Seffy shot out of her seat, managed to find a shorter route through the furniture and lifted the giant teapot off the tray. As well as crockery, teaspoons, a jug of milk and a bowl of sugar cubes, Mrs Harris had brought a plate of biscuits.

'Crunchies!' she said, proudly. 'Yesterday's batch.'

'Lovely,' Seffy said, already wondering how she could smuggle some into her handbag for Jean.

Seffy placed the teapot on the table and they sat back while

Mrs Harris poured the tea.

Once she'd left them, there was an awkward silence as they sipped from their cups. Seffy wracked her brain for a topic of conversation. Ah yes, the war. Men always liked to talk about the war.

'The newspapers are awfully optimistic about the end of hostilities, aren't they, Mr McIntyre? What's your opinion? Is it the beginning of the end?'

He put his cup down, looking grave. 'Aye, I should say so. They'll be sending in the troops next. Poor blighters.'

Seffy swallowed. 'Sending in …?'

'Across the Channel. On to the continent. They're massing on the south coast now, of course. Getting ready.'

Seffy felt faint. Action, at last. Of course! What had she thought Callum's company was doing down there? They weren't playing at being soldiers: they were getting ready for the final push.

He tilted his head and looked at her with a concerned expression.

'Do you have friends or family serving, Miss Mills?'

She could hardly think how to answer. She took one of the biscuits from the plate he was holding out.

'Thank you. I … er, have brothers in the air force and – yes, friends, of course. Friends in the forces.'

She tried to smile.

McIntyre bit into his biscuit and grimaced. 'Ma God!' he said, when he'd finally managed to chew and swallow, and could speak again. 'She's done it again! I nearly broke a tooth last time she made some o' these.'

It was so unexpected – and such a relief after that grim sending-in-the-troops talk – that Seffy burst out laughing. To think, she'd once wondered whether he and Mrs Harris might be having an affair. The very idea seemed quite preposterous now.

She peered at her own biscuit. It didn't look too bad: golden and oaty. Perhaps a little overbaked, but it was so long since she'd had a treat like this, her mouth was actually watering.

He was watching her. 'I dare you.' He raised a warning hand. 'But easy does it!'

She tentatively nibbled the edge of it, then took a large bite.

'I'm right, aren't I?' he said.

Seffy could only nod. It was like having a biscuity gobstopper in one's mouth. She'd like nothing more than to spit the bloomin' thing out. At least McIntyre had the decency to look away and stroke his dog while she battled with it.

Finally, it was soft enough to wash down with a mouthful of tea.

'Phew!' she said, looking at the rest of the biscuit in her hand. 'They should make these in munitions factories!'

He laughed.

'Gi' the rest o' that to the dog. That's what I'm gonna do!'

'Do you think I might have a look around, when we've finished our tea?' Seffy asked.

'Look around?'

'The house?' she said. 'It must be very old. I'd be … interested.'

He shrugged. 'Aye, sure you can. There's not much to see and half the rooms are closed up but you're welcome.'

When Seffy and Mrs Harris got back to the cottage later, Jean was sitting at the kitchen table.

'How was it?' she asked.

'Good,' Seffy said. 'He had sugar! I had three cups of tea and two lumps in every one.'

Jean tutted. 'I didnae mean the tea! Did you discuss the forest and the work to be done?'

'Oh, yes! He's going to check the site we've cleared over the weekend and as long as he's satisfied, we can start felling on Monday.'

'We should be all right then?' Jean said.

'Absolutely. I'd say we've done a bally good job! Oh, there was one thing. He said there's a particular tree, an oak, that we mustn't touch, on pain of death!'

Jean's eyes widened. 'It'll depend where it is. I'll have to see it before I can say whether it's possible. You didnae make any promises, did you?'

Seffy couldn't quite remember but she shook her head anyway.

'You know, he's rattling around in that huge house quite alone, Jean.'

'Am I supposed to feel sorry for him?'

'He gave me a guided tour, and there's the most marvellous long gallery on the first floor. It would make a perfect dorm for the Lost Girls!'

Jean blew out her cheeks. 'There's nae chance of him agreeing to that! He can barely stand the sight o' the lassies!'

'Oh, I know, but it's a pity, all the same. It would've been ideal.'

Mrs Harris had been busy putting the kettle on and hanging up her coat in the hall.

Seffy waited until she was out of earshot and lowered her voice.

'I'd have brought you back a biscuit, Jean, but quite honestly, it was like eating bullets!' She rubbed her jaw. 'You wouldn't have thanked me.'

'Now, then!' Mrs Harris said, reappearing. She took cups and saucers out of the cupboard. 'I shall mek us a brew and as Miss Ferguson missed out, I've brought back some of ma special crunchie biscuits! Och, dunnae look so downhearted, Miss Mills. I've enough for you as well!'

Chapter Twenty-Eight

The South Coast, England

'OK, so me and Verne wanna head into town and take a look around. Are you two coming?' Juliet asked.

The two couples had just had a joyful reunion at the station and now they were standing outside the first café they'd come across.

Callum had his arm around Missy. 'I wanna be on our own,' he whispered into her ear. She wanted that too, so they agreed to split up: Juliet and Verne would catch up with them later.

The café had looked OK from the outside but it wasn't quite the quaint little tea shop Missy had been hoping for. They were short-staffed, the woman at the till said, and instead of waitress service, you had to place your order at the counter.

Callum pulled a face. 'Do you wanna go someplace else?'

Missy shook her head. She didn't want to make a fuss and besides, if they switched to another café, the others wouldn't know where to find them. It wasn't so bad: it was warm and not too busy. It would do.

They chose a table next to the window, so they could look out at the distant grey sea. Missy smiled up at Callum as she sat down and he winked back. They were together and that was all that mattered.

He hung his drill jacket on the back of the chair. He looked real smart in his shirt and tie. She was proud to be with him.

She'd noticed, as they'd walked arm in arm from the station, that folk had looked at them admiringly. Sure, they weren't the only ones on the street in uniform but she guessed they must look the part: young and in love and doing their bit for the war effort.

The menu was a chalked-up blackboard stuck to the wall. Missy could kill for a cup of coffee but of course, that wasn't on offer.

'Shall we have a pot of tea and a sticky bun each?' she said.

She wondered how 'sticky' the buns would be – the British had no sugar, after all – but she'd risk it.

Callum went up to the counter. It took a few minutes to order because they were out of sticky buns and the woman had to check if they had an alternative.

He called across the café, telling her all this and she called back, 'It's OK, honey, get me anything!'

His jacket had slipped from the chair and fallen onto the floor.

As Missy bent to pick it up, she felt the weight of something in one of the inside pockets. Probably his wallet. She'd go take it over to him before the woman totted up the bill and he had to pay.

She slipped her hand inside the pocket. Wait, that didn't feel much like a wallet. She pulled out a paperback. Was it some kind of diary? She turned it over. It had a bright orange cover; it was a book of short stories. But Callum didn't read, so that was kinda odd. Oh, but maybe it was a gift for her? How sweet and thoughtful! She should put it back right away and act all surprised when he produced it.

Callum was still at the counter, counting out coins in his hand. He wouldn't be back right away.

She couldn't resist it. She flipped open the book. And nearly died. There was a dedication written on the inside cover, in what was, without a doubt, a woman's hand:

To Callum
Happy Christmas!
Try this one for size, you might even like it!
With very best wishes
Your S xxx

The whole room tilted and swooped away for a second What did that mean? Three kisses! And who, in heaven's name, was 'S'?

She'd written the date underneath her initial: *Christmas 1943*. Christmas just gone. Three weeks ago.

Up at the counter, Callum was thanking the woman and tucking his wallet into the pocket of his slacks.

Before he turned around, Missy slipped the book back where she'd found it and draped the jacket over the chair. It was lopsided but there wasn't time to straighten it. She must've looked flushed and guilty because that was sure how she felt but Callum didn't seem to notice.

'I got us carrot cake,' he said, sitting down.

'Your jacket fell. I was just putting it back.'

Her voice sounded strange, not like her. She reached out and brushed the sleeve, where it had picked up a little dirt from the floor.

Her head was spinning. What had she just seen? Worst case, she'd found clear-as-day evidence that Callum had another girl. A girl whose name began with 'S' and who'd given him a gift so dear that he carried it next to his heart.

And best case? She couldn't think of one.

She felt light-headed. Good job she was sitting down.

The woman arrived with the tray of tea and cake, and set it out on their table. Before she left, Missy asked her discreetly where the ladies' cloakroom might be found.

She stood up. 'Excuse me, a minute, Callum. Don't pour the tea yet. It needs a while to brew.'

In the lavatory, she pressed her hands against the cold basin

171

and stared at herself in the mirror. Her heart was racing, she could hardly think straight but apart from slightly flushed cheeks, she looked the same as always.

What the deuce was she gonna do?

Should she say something? But then he'd think she'd been snooping in his pockets. And in any case, what could she say?

Tell me the truth: do you have someone else? Have you met a girl over here?

No, that wouldn't do. It was too hostile and direct and, if she were being honest, part of her didn't want to hear the answer.

If it'd merely been a fling, she could forgive him. No, not forgive but *understand*. They could talk it through like adults and put it behind them. Because everyone knew British girls were throwing themselves at Canadian men, and what normal fella, lonesome and far from home, could resist?

As long as it – whatever 'it' was – hadn't meant anything. After all, she flirted with guys on the wards every day. She hadn't considered it flirting but now she thought about it, it was: teasing, giggling and pretending to slap the fellas' hands or get cross when they overstepped the mark.

Callum had wanted to be alone with her and perhaps this was the reason: he wanted to explain.

Maybe this 'S' – a Susan or a Sandra – had taken a liking to him and he couldn't shake her off? She could be a barmaid in one of the pubs the fellas frequented or the daughter of a British family that invited troops for Sunday lunch.

She imagined Callum showing her the book and explaining everything. And he'd swear on his life that there was nothing going on.

'Here,' he'd say, 'she insisted on giving me this book for Christmas. I'm showing you because I don't want any secrets between us, Missy.'

And he'd rip up the book, right there and then, to prove it meant nothing.

Missy exhaled, splashed a little water on her face and reapplied some powder. There, she felt calmer now.

By the time she got back to the table, the tea was ready to pour. 'I have something to tell you,' she said, as she stirred her tea in the cup. 'The Fieldings have had a few barn dances while you've been away—'

Callum frowned. 'Uh huh?'

'I shoulda told you before. I've danced with some of the fellas. The Fieldings and others.' She shrugged. 'I thought you should know.'

Callum laughed, a little uncertainly. 'Okaaay,' he said. 'That's all right, honey. You're allowed! I didn't expect you to live like a nun while I was away.'

Missy nodded and looked down at her cup and waited. But he didn't offer any confessions of his own.

How could she possibly bring up the subject of his ma's necklace now? She wasn't even sure she still wanted to be engaged! No, that wasn't true. But the doubts that had been simmering under the surface since their reunion were crowding in now.

They'd been apart for two years. What had Callum been doing all that time? And more importantly, who'd he been doing it with?

They drank the tea and ate the dry-as-a-bone carrot cake, and Callum didn't seem to notice she was quiet.

When he finally got round to what he wanted to say, it was nothing to do with that dumb book. It came as such a surprise, it took her breath away.

'I'm gonna start lumbering again,' he said. 'Temporarily. Back up in Scotland. There's a group of us going—'

'NO! Why you?' She'd cried out so loud that folk on nearby tables turned to stare. 'Tell them your fiancée has come all the way from Canada! They can't!'

He reached for her hand and squeezed it. 'Honey, they can. It's real bad timing and it's not fair on you but—'

'Why didn't you tell me before?'

173

He spread his hands. 'I swear, I only found out yesterday. It's not forever, it's only temporary. A few weeks, couple of months at most and I'll be back and—'

'—and?'

The word seemed to hang in the air but he just shook his head. He had nothing more to say.

Later, when the others arrived in the café, Juliet instantly guessed something was up.

'Are you OK, Missy?' she asked.

When she told her sister the news, Juliet gave Verne a hefty nudge. 'Hey, you'd better not be going too!'

He put up his hands. 'Not guilty! This is the first I've heard of it!' He frowned at Callum. 'I don't get it. Sending fellas back up to Scotland to start felling again? Ain't that a backward step? Sounds kinda fishy to me.'

Callum shifted in his seat and looked uncomfortable. Missy wondered whether he'd had a say in which fellas to take and Verne hadn't even come close to being picked.

'I guess they've sent too many fellas to join the combat troops and the British are falling short of timber,' Callum said. 'That's what we came for, after all, to fell trees. I don't mind the infantry but at heart, I'm a lumberjack. I prefer working in the forests.'

'Yeah, sure, me too,' Verne said. 'But in Scotland? I've never known rain like it! Sure, it's pretty an' all – reminds me of Canada a lot – but the weather's diabolical! Rather you than me, fella!'

On the train back to Basingstoke, Missy sat in silence.

Juliet probably thought she was upset about Callum's redeployment and sure, that was part of it. But worse – much worse – was that darned book she'd found, and the words and kisses inside it.

Telling Juliet would only make things worse. Although her sister had never said anything, Missy sometimes had the feeling she didn't entirely approve of Callum.

Oh boy, but it had hurt, when he'd talked about going back to Scotland. He hadn't been able to hide his excitement. Neither had he said he was sorry he had to go.

Well, that was fine and dandy. If he was determined to throw himself into his work, she would do likewise. And that way, the time would pass real quick until they could be together again.

'It's only short term,' Juliet said, leaning across and patting Missy's knee. 'And you're still a lot nearer to him than when we were back in B.C. Say, we can go visit! Next time we get a good chunk of leave – a week or so – we'll head up to Scotland. What do you say?'

Missy nodded. She'd like to see Scotland. Callum's folks came from there, on his ma's side, and the place was so dear to him. He was pleased to be returning; she supposed she should be glad for him.

Oh, but what if he'd met this girl up there? And he wasn't merely happy because he was starting lumbering again but because he'd be with her real soon? No, she couldn't think like that, she'd go crazy. He wouldn't do that to her, not Callum. He was the faithful type.

'And hey, we've got a weekend off soon,' Juliet said. 'Let's arrange a girls' trip to London. We'll ask Laura along. That'd be fun, huh?'

Missy agreed it would. It would be a distraction and that was exactly what she needed right now.

She sat back in her seat, grateful that Juliet seemed happy to chatter away and didn't expect her to join in.

'You know,' Juliet said, 'someone told me the other day about a Red Cross girl who came to England to surprise her fella, only to discover he'd been repatriated a week before she arrived. And he'd wanted to surprise her!'

Missy frowned. 'You mean …?'

Juliet was laughing. 'Yeah, they crossed in the middle of the Atlantic! He was on his way home and she was heading over here!'

Why was that funny? It was even more of a disaster than arriving in England just before your fiancé was redeployed to Scotland.

'So, you see,' Juliet said, 'these kinda things happen all the time. But it's never the end of the world. They work themselves out in the end.'

That was easy for her to say: Verne wasn't being sent hundreds of miles away.

Missy's mind snapped back – as it did every thirty seconds or so – to that darned book. Verne most likely didn't have one of those in his jacket pocket, either.

She thought about the message on the inside cover.

At least it had only said, 'With very best wishes'. Whoever she was, this 'S', she hadn't written 'love'.

Chapter Twenty-Nine

Aberdeenshire, Scotland

'Here he comes again,' Isobel said, as the girls glimpsed McIntyre hobbling through the oak trees. 'What on earth's he doing?'

Seffy put her finger to her lips. 'Shush!'

When the girls had arrived in the forest that morning, they'd found McIntyre already there.

For one heart-stopping moment, Seffy had thought he'd come to forbid them from starting to fell, but apart from a brief word with Jean about the precious tree-that-must-not-be-touched, he'd barely acknowledged them.

He'd limped between the oaks, leaning on his stick, patting each tree in turn and murmuring something indecipherable.

As the girls had set up the fire for tea, he'd disappeared from view, heading deeper into the forest. Now, as Isobel stamped out the fire, and Jean and Rona cycled off to start measuring, he was making his way back towards them.

'He's saying goodbye to his trees,' Seffy said. She glared at the gang, daring them to scoff, but for once, they were silent.

McIntyre's shoulders were hunched, his cap pulled down low. He looked pale and miserable. The genial host of last Saturday had disappeared.

'He's had a good deal of loss in his life, I think,' Seffy murmured to herself.

Tich had heard her. 'Ma granddad was cross like him all the time after ma wee granny died,' she said. And then, in the next breath, she said, 'Aw, look! That's so bonny! It's snowin' again!'

'These trees are not to be hacked!' McIntyre bellowed, as he approached them.

Here we go again, Seffy thought, men assuming only other men could make a proper job of things.

'What d'you mean, "hacked"?' Peggy demanded, hands on hips.

Goodness, that was all they needed: Peggy – who wasn't even part of the felling team – getting all high-handed.

Seffy stepped between her and McIntyre. 'Don't worry, sir, we're perfectly capable. There'll be no hacking.' In a lower voice, she said, 'Peggy, isn't it time you set off for the saw mill?'

'Aye, off you trot!' Eileen said, with a grin. 'You dunnae want to be late on your first morning!'

Peggy pulled out her bottom lip.

Seffy braced herself. *Please don't let her refuse to go. Not in front of McIntyre.*

An icy-cold gust of wind blew into the clearing. It sent the bare treetops rocking and snowflakes swirling all around them so that, for a few moments, Seffy felt as though she were standing in a snow globe.

A couple of the Lost Girls screamed and grabbed their berets.

'Right, I'm away, then,' Peggy said, clearly enjoying their discomfort. 'It's awful warm inside that saw mill. I might even have to tek off ma jumper!'

She raised a hand to them and traipsed off towards the lane.

Seffy felt like punching the air and yelling 'Good riddance!' But her problems weren't over: she still had McIntyre to deal with.

'You know,' she told him, 'in the last place I worked, our output for the year was only a fraction shy of that produced by men before the war. And they'd been experienced lumberjacks.' It was true. Jock, their foreman, had told them and he'd been impressed.

McIntyre sighed. 'That's all very well, Miss Mills, but you're working with a different gang now.'

He raised his eyebrows and looked doubtfully at Tich, Eileen, Myrtle and Isobel. The implication was clear: he had no faith in them. The girls glared back. They were undoubtedly affronted but, unlike Peggy, they lacked the confidence to answer back.

Seffy looked at her gang of four, togged up in their oilskins, boots and berets. At least they were properly kitted out now. But the question in her own mind, as well as McIntyre's, was could they actually fell trees?

'Be assured,' he said, 'I'll be keeping a close eye on you. If your work's not up to scratch, I'll be lodging a formal complaint.'

He turned to go.

'And don't fell every one!' he called back, waving his stick in the air. 'Leave a scattering of trees, to ensure natural regeneration.'

Seffy pulled a face behind his back and gave him a sarky salute. It was hardly professional, but honestly, did he have to be such a grouch? He'd been perfectly polite on Saturday, over tea, but now she was here as a lumberjill, not a lady, his tune had completely changed.

'Wha' did he mean?' Tich asked. 'Regener ... whatsit?'

'We've got to leave some trees standing,' Seffy said. 'Then the forest will re-grow naturally. Although it'll take a long time.'

'And how will he judge if our work's not up to scratch?' Isobel asked.

'I suppose, if we're slapdash, or if we cut the trees too high. In my last place, we worked alongside Canadian foresters. When they first arrived, they used to fell trees at knee-height and leave huge stumps behind. Such a waste.'

'Och, we'd never do that!' Myrtle said, shaking her head.

'Listen, girls,' Seffy said, 'Mr McIntyre's going to look for any excuse to throw us out of the forest. So, we mustn't give him any reason to find fault. Let's make a start. Eileen, do you want to show me how you cut in?'

'Cut in?' Eileen queried.

'You know, using an axe to make the first cut in the base of a tree?'

'We call that laying in,' Eileen said.

'Very well, laying in, then. Off you go.'

Within seconds, Seffy had to yell 'STOP!' before Eileen did some serious damage.

'Eileen's the best at layin' in, an' all!' Tich said.

Oh, this was hopeless. So much for the girls having learned on the job. They didn't seem to have a clue. It wasn't entirely unexpected but she was going to have to start from scratch and teach them to fell properly. Which would all take time. Blast!

She wasn't a trainer; it was a while since she'd actually felled a tree herself. But if she didn't teach them, they'd never get the forest cleared and she'd be stuck here forever. Miss McEwen's words rang in her ears: 'You have to stay until the job is done!!'

'Right, gather around!' Seffy said.

She thought back to her early days in the Corps, when she'd been taught to fell by Jock and Miss McEwen. She vaguely remembered they'd given the lumberjills a rousing introduction to the work. She should do likewise.

'Felling is a terrifically interesting and highly skilled job!' she said. 'My old foreman told me even men who've been lumberjacks for ten years or more, will admit they're still learning!'

'What hope is there for us, then?' Isobel said, and the others muttered their agreement.

Seffy ignored her. This would be like training a dog: one had to ignore bad behaviour and praise the good.

'Let's look at cutting – I mean, laying in,' she said, trying not to think about Eileen's shocking attempt of a few minutes ago.

She picked up her axe. 'Now, the stance is crucial. You have to make a triangle in the trunk, in the place you want the tree to fall.'

She slapped her hand against the trunk. 'This is hardwood, so if you don't give it a good old whack, the axe can bounce off the bark and get you in the leg.'

The girls squealed. Goodness, they'd have to stop that if they wanted to be taken seriously as foresters.

'Plant your legs square on to the tree, bend your knees a little and—' Seffy swung the axe with ease. After a few blows to demonstrate, she asked Myrtle to take her place.

'Well done!' Seffy said, with enthusiasm, as she watched Myrtle strike the base of the tree. 'You're not making a bad job of that at all!'

Myrtle lowered her axe and looked at Seffy warily. 'Are you havin' a laugh?'

Goodness, she'd over done it.

'Of course not!' Seffy said. 'I'm always deadly serious when it comes to felling. Now, we have to throw the tree: saw it off at the root, using the crosscut. I kneel to do this but you can stand if you prefer. Who wants to do this with me? Tich, how about you?'

Finally, and to Seffy's immense relief, the first tree was down.

The girls had clearly enjoyed yelling 'TIMBERRR!' – Tich had even done a celebratory dance – but not much else about the process.

'Now comes the snedding,' Seffy said. 'Axes and saws at the ready! All the branches and the top need to come off. Pile it all up, then we'll burn it. Unlike those chaps who left the copse in such a mess, we'll tidy up as we go along.'

'Snedding?' Eileen said. 'We call that brashing.'

Seffy took a deep breath. 'Very well, brashing it is.' They could call it Aunt Dolly's drawers if they liked, as long as the job got done.

'Sometimes I think I wouldnae care if a tree fell on me,' Myrtle mused, looking up into the canopy. 'At least then, I could get away from here. I'd be nice and warm and cared for in a hospital bed.'

'You wouldn't,' Seffy said. 'Because if a tree fell on you, Myrtle, you'd be dead.'

There was a moment's silence, then the girls burst into laughter.

Seffy looked around, surprised. 'I wasn't joking.'

'I know you weren't,' Eileen said. 'It was just the way you said it. "You'd be dead!"'

Her impression of Seffy's English accent made everyone laugh again. Even Seffy had to smile.

They were a curious bunch. Awfully rough around the edges and blunt to the point of rudeness at times – heaven only knew how badly they must've behaved to make those other leader girls leave.

But despite everything, she was starting to like them.

Chapter Thirty

Basingstoke, Hampshire, England

It had been a few days since Missy had discovered the book in Callum's pocket and he'd announced his move to Scotland.

What a day that had been. And she'd missed her chance to talk about turning his ma's necklace into a ring. She'd have to wait until they were together again. She wouldn't attempt that kind of conversation on the telephone after what had happened last time.

A girl could easily feel glum with all those thoughts zipping around her mind, but she was doing her best to stay cheerful.

At least she had this weekend to look forward to. Juliet, true to her word, had arranged for the two of them, plus Laura, to have a girls' trip away and meet up with some of their Red Cross pals. That would surely take her mind off her woes.

As she pushed her cart around the wards and saw all these brave young fellas laid up, it helped put her problems into perspective. Things weren't perfect between her and Callum but at least they had their health and they had each other. She must hold on to that thought.

There were new fellas on the wards most days. They came in looking ghostly pale and withdrawn, wincing in pain or maybe at the memories of what they'd been through, but once they started teasing her or even flirting a little, Missy knew they were on the mend.

But not him. Not Rabbit.

He'd been here a couple of weeks now, about the same time as her. He was always sitting up when she arrived on the ward, propped up with pillows. His head was still covered in bandages with just a gap for his mouth and, apart from huffing and murmuring, 'Here comes Squeaky' when she pushed the cart in, he didn't speak.

She tried not to mind him calling her Squeaky. It could've been a little joke between them. But he always sounded irritated, like she was a fly he thought he'd put out the window but which had found its way back in. He made her feel like a pest.

That afternoon, she asked him again, real polite and gentle, if he wanted anything and, as usual, he shook his head.

'Heck, I wouldn't bother with him, Sister,' the guy in the next bed said. 'He just sits there, dumb like that the whole time.'

That was mean and, although Rabbit hadn't reacted, he must've heard. He wasn't deaf, after all. It couldn't be much fun, not able to see or move, and who knew how much pain the poor guy was in?

Missy scowled at the fella who'd just spoken and shook her head to show her disapproval. She wouldn't be doing her job if she simply ignored a patient. There must be something she could do to help Rabbit.

She ran her eyes over the cart and picked up one of the newspapers. She leaned closer to his bed to speak quietly to him.

'Hey there, Rabbit,' she said. 'It's Officer Gilbert again. I've got a newspaper here. There are cartoons and jokes at the back. Would you care to have me read some of them out to you? I—'

She gave a little 'Oh!' of surprise as he grabbed the newspaper.

'Would you care—' he yelled, as he raised his arm, almost whacking her in the face with his elbow '—to stick this where the sun don't shine?'

184

He hurled the newspaper to the other side of the ward, making fellas yelp and duck. Some covered their heads with their arms.

All hell broke loose. Men were shouting and cussing Rabbit, outraged by the way he'd spoken to her, but also, she guessed, mighty shaken up by that unexpected missile flying through the air.

At the sight of Rabbit sitting there, calmly, apparently oblivious to everything going on around him, hot tears pricked the back of her eyes. No, she would not cry.

But gee, she'd never felt so humiliated.

My God, they were making such a hullaballoo. And it was getting louder as guys further down the ward, called out, wanting to know what was happening.

She needed to calm them down before some of them tried to get outta bed – regardless of wounds and drips – to box Rabbit's ears.

'Hey, guys, keep the noise down, please!' she said. 'It's OK! I'm all right.'

Behind her, the door opened and the men started to quieten down until there was, finally, silence.

It was Matron. She walked slowly down the ward and picked up the newspaper from the linoleum floor. She folded it up and tucked it under her arm.

'What is going on in here?' she asked, gazing around. Her voice was calm.

The fellas stared back. No one answered.

Matron jerked her head at Missy who followed her meekly out into the corridor, letting the door swing closed behind her. Thirty pairs of eyes watched her go.

'What happened in there, Officer?' Matron asked.

Missy took a deep breath and tried to compose herself. 'I offered to read something to Rabbit. That's the guy with all the bandages. I was just doing my best to distract him, but he took offence, I guess, and he yelled and threw the newspaper across the ward.' She shrugged. 'It set everybody off. He's … he's darned rude!'

Matron nodded but didn't speak straight away. She was always so steady and unruffled. It was kinda catching. Missy could feel herself starting to calm down.

'Lance Corporal Grant is very angry,' Matron said.

So that was the guy's name. She heard the reprimand in Matron's voice that she knew his name and Missy hadn't.

'And—' she raised a finger to stop Missy speaking '—he's also very scared.'

Scared? Hell, she'd been scared when Lance Corporal whatever his name was, had almost hit her. The way he'd spoken to her! No one had ever spoken to her like that. She imagined telling Callum and him getting real mad.

'Do you want me to take you off that ward, Officer Gilbert?' Matron asked.

Missy frowned. That was unexpected. Did Matron think she couldn't cope with the fellas in there?

'Because that would be a pity. Some of the patients in Burns—' Matron inclined her head towards the door '—are in pretty bad shape, as I'm sure you realise, and, well … they like you. I've heard good reports about your work in there.'

Missy blinked hard. She'd expected to get a dressing-down and instead, someone was telling her she was good at her job.

'No, I wanna keep it,' she said, firmly. 'Please, Matron.'

She liked the fellas on that ward and she shouldn't let that Rabbit get to her. There were hundreds of fellas in the hospital. Most of them greeted her on a daily basis like a long-lost sister or a pal, but she couldn't expect everyone to like her.

That evening, she didn't think about Callum and that darned book quite as much as she had over the past few days. Her mind was full of what had happened today on the ward. Could she have done anything differently, handled it better?

'Wanna talk it through?' Juliet asked, as the girls sat together in the sitting room. 'Whatever it is that's bothering you?'

Missy said no, thank you. She might tell Laura, later but she had no desire to tell Juliet. She'd only say she should've done this or that. Juliet always knew best.

This situation with Rabbit was vexing but there must be something Missy could do to make it better. And she wanted to work it out for herself.

Chapter Thirty-One

Aberdeenshire, Scotland

It had snowed almost non-stop for a week. The snow was two feet deep on the roads and deeper in the drifts. It was a struggle just to reach the forest each morning, and Seffy was frustrated by their lack of progress.

Just as the Lost Girls were picking up the rudiments of felling, too.

She didn't want them to start slacking – the longer they took, the longer it would be until she could move nearer to Callum – but the girls were glum and wanted nothing more than to huddle around the fire, keeping warm.

This morning, she'd given in and allowed them to linger there long after tea break should have finished.

'Here comes Jean!' Isobel said, looking up.

Jean was stomping purposefully towards them through the snow, with Rona close behind. The measurers had given up trying to ride their bicycles and were now walking everywhere.

Jean's spectacles had steamed up and her cheeks were flushed. As the pair got closer, Seffy could see the grin on Rona's face.

Something had happened.

'Good news!' Jean announced.

'The war's over?' Tich said, hopefully.

Seffy's heart leaped. Oh, wouldn't that be wonderful! But one look at Jean's face told her it wasn't that.

Jean tutted. 'Not that good. But we're officially snowed off!'

'Is that the same as browned off?' Eileen asked. 'Because we're definitely that.'

'Aren't you pleased?' Jean said. 'We have permission to down tools! We've got the next week off!'

As they finally understood, the girls started to cheer.

Myrtle looked up at the mottled grey sky and the ever-descending snowflakes and cried, 'God bless you, beautiful snow!'

They were hugging one another now and jumping up and down, more animated than Seffy had ever seen them. It must feel like all their prayers had been answered.

Seffy couldn't share their joy. This was simply another delay.

'Who says we're snowed off?' she asked Jean.

'Mr Burke. He telephoned the saw mill and Alec drove out to gi' me and Rona the news. It was good of him. The tractor kept getting stuck in the snow and he had to dig himself out.'

Snowballs were whizzing past their heads. The girls had wasted no time in starting their unexpected holiday.

'I can see you're not best pleased, Seffy,' Jean said, 'but it makes sense. There's no point even trying to work in this weather.'

'Yes, I suppose so,' Seffy said. 'OUCH!' Someone – she suspected Tich – had just struck her on the head with a well-aimed snowball.

'Peggy still has to work,' Jean said. 'The saw mill's staying open while they've got timber to process. I expect that went down like a lead balloon!'

Seffy smiled at the thought. It jolly well served petulant Peggy right, to miss out on a few days off.

A few days off …? The christening of Emerald's baby was later this week. The timing of all this couldn't have been better. Her mind was racing with possibilities. Could she …? No, it was a ridiculous idea. But why not? Today was Tuesday and they'd been given the whole week off. Goodness, she might be able to get to London after all!

She'd have to allow the best part of two days to get there and the same to get back but she could still spend a couple of days in London. What a genius idea! It would be utter bliss to get away from this hellhole and to be in civilisation again.

'Seffy, could we have an advance on our wages?' Isobel asked, interrupting her thoughts. 'Me and Eileen are thinking of headin' home.'

'Ask Jean,' Seffy said. 'She's in charge of wages.'

'No!' Jean said. 'I should've made it clear but we're to stay put, in case the weather suddenly changes. And in any case, how would you get to the railway station? It's five miles away and the roads are blocked. There's nae chance of anyone getting there!'

Seffy exhaled, deflating like a balloon. Of course. What had she been thinking? Sometimes she was awfully dense. They were marooned here, cut off by the snow. She wouldn't be able to reach the railway station either.

The disappointment was like a heavy weight pressing down on her chest.

'What's up wi' you?' Jean asked. 'You look like you've lost a shilling and found a penny.'

'Oh, nothing,' Seffy said. 'I had a silly idea of going to London, to my godson's christening. But ironically, the thing that's freeing me to go – the snow – is also preventing me from leaving.'

Jean gave a small cough. 'Not forgetting Mr Burke's firm instruction that we're to stay here and not go gaddin' about.'

Seffy tutted and waved her hand. 'Oh, heavens, who's to know, if we all keep schtum? I wouldn't even have minded Isobel and Eileen nipping off home. I am leader girl, after all. Surely that must count for something? Anyway, it's a moot point. As you've just pointed out, there's no possibility of anyone getting anywhere near a train, so that's the end of that.'

Jean was silent, which Seffy took as a sign of disapproval.

It was a pity there weren't any Canadian Forestry Corps companies around here. They had the very latest equipment. They'd probably have bulldozers fitted with snow ploughs which would've cleared the roads in no time.

But she was simply tormenting herself now. She should simply put the whole harebrained scheme out of her mind once and for all.

The snow didn't seem quite so wonderful now. It looked enchanting but it was jolly inconvenient if you wanted to get anywhere.

She suddenly felt awfully low. How were they going to fill their time, stuck here with nothing to do, waiting for a break in the weather?

Isobel and Eileen had quickly got over their disappointment at not being allowed to leave and had joined the snowball fight. They were dodging behind trees and screeching like banshees each time they were hit.

'What is this, playtime?' Jean asked, but Seffy rather envied the girls; she wished she could be as carefree.

A blackbird flew in front of her, low to the ground, making an alarm call.

'Oh, I wish I had wings and could just fly down to London!' she said.

Jean frowned. 'Human beings will never fly. Our bodies are too heavy and our muscles too weak.'

'For goodness' sake, Jean, just indulge me for once!'

Why did she have to take everything so literally?

'Ouch!' Seffy yelled. Another snowball had reached its target: smacking her hard on the cheek this time.

'Right, Myrtle the Turtle, you've asked for it!' she said, bending to scoop up a handful of snow. She patted and shaped it quickly into a snowball.

She glanced around. There! She'd spied something that could

only be Myrtle's shock of frizzy hair behind an oak tree. Seffy took a few paces forward, raised her arm and waited.

Myrtle's head peeked out. Seffy hurled the snowball with all her might and it hit the girl right in the face.

'Bullseye!' Seffy cried.

Everyone was in fits. Even Myrtle, which only went to show she could be a good sport, when she wasn't busy moaning.

Jean was standing a little apart from the others showing no inclination to join in.

'Do you know what date it is today?' she said. 'Twenty-fifth of January. It's Burns Night tonight. And although Hitler's killed the haggis—'

'The rotter!' Seffy said.

'Has he?' Tich asked, wide-eyed.

'Aye,' Jean said, 'there are no onions to be had and you cannae have haggis without onions. But there's still whisky. Shall we drink a toast to the Bard tonight?'

'And celebrate being snowed off?' Rona said.

Jean looked at Seffy for approval.

'Yes, why not!' she said. It wasn't like Jean to suggest anything so frivolous. It should be encouraged. 'Good idea, Jean. Let's all meet up in The Drover's later for a drink.'

'I'll tell Peggy,' Eileen said.

If you must, Seffy thought.

Chapter Thirty-Two

When Seffy woke late the next morning, it was strangely silent and there was a purplish light at the edge of the blackout curtain. She peered out. It was still snowing and the thick carpet of snow was muffling all sounds.

It was a queer feeling to have the whole day ahead, with nothing to do. She felt too restless to stay in bed, so she quietly washed, dressed and headed downstairs, leaving Jean still gently snoring.

The kettle on the range had just started to boil when there was a knock on the back door. It took her a moment to realise it was the conchie, Mr Reid. He was covered in snow from head to foot. Even his eyelashes had a coating.

'Oh, hullo,' Seffy said. She couldn't think what he might be doing there. 'Has Mr Burke telephoned again? Is there a change of plan?' she asked.

'No, it's nothin' like that.'

'Right. But shouldn't you be at work?'

'I sent a sick note wi' one of the laddies. They all think I'm a malingerer, anyhow. I shan't be missed.'

He was carrying two planks of wood over one shoulder. Perhaps Mrs Harris had asked him to prove his manliness by putting up some shelves?

'I'll call Mrs Harris down,' Seffy said. 'Leave that wood outside and come in.'

'Actually, it's you I've come to see, Miss.'

He lowered the planks and stood them up on their ends. He also had two wooden sticks tucked under one arm.

It was like a puzzle. Seffy's gaze flitted from one component to the next, trying to work it out.

'I was talking to Jean last night in the pub,' he said, 'and she mentioned you wantin' to get to the railway station. These might be the answer to your prayers. They're skis!'

'Skis? Gosh, wherever did you get them?'

'I made them at the saw mill last winter, in the evenings when everyone else had gone home.'

'Do they work?' Seffy asked.

He laughed. 'Aye! I've just skied here from ma digs. Took a fraction of the time it would've taken to walk.'

Seffy could see now that they were much more than mere lengths of wood: they'd been varnished and carved, so that they curved up at one end.

But what did he mean, the answer to her prayers?

Jean must've heard their voices: she appeared at Seffy's side, rubbing her eyes.

'What's goin' on? The whole house is freezing with that door open. Is the poor fella not allowed in?'

Jean had certainly changed her tune. Seffy remembered when she wouldn't even pass the time of day with 'the poor fella'.

She wasn't sure whether Mr Reid *was* allowed in. Mrs Harris wasn't exactly a fan. But she was in bed and, hopefully, would stay there for a while.

Seffy opened the door wider. 'Entrée!'

Jean beckoned him over to the range. 'Here, come and warm yourself up. You look perished.'

Golly, she was fussing over him like a mother hen. He was certainly a decent sort of chap. Jean could do worse than set her cap at him. Oh, but she'd have to sort out her hair. No one could fall in love with a girl whose hair was as straight as a horse's mane.

He was explaining to Jean how he'd found a potential solution to Seffy's predicament.

Jean listened carefully, then turned to Seffy with a frown. 'Have you ever skied before?'

'Of course not! Has anyone? Apart from you, obviously, Mr Reid. How did you learn, by the way?'

'Alec, please,' he said. He shrugged and looked faintly embarrassed. 'I've skied with my family since I was young.'

'In Switzerland, no less,' Jean said.

'Erm, yes. Before the war, of course,' he said.

Mr Reid – Alec, as she was now to call him – was clearly from a well-to-do family. He'd been abroad, he was educated. He could've been an officer but instead, he was labouring in a saw mill in the back of beyond.

Seffy wanted to ask more about his time in Switzerland but Jean cut in.

'When is this christening, anyhow?' she said. She sounded cross.

'Friday afternoon,' Seffy said.

'And today's Wednesday. You'd have to leave first thing tomorrow to have any hope of getting there in time. It's impossible! You cannae learn to ski in twenty-four hours!'

Seffy's chest tightened. Whenever someone said she couldn't do something, she immediately wanted to prove them wrong.

'Don't be such a killjoy, Jean!' she said. 'Let's hear what Alec has to say. For once, there's someone here who knows more than you!'

Jean looked offended but, honestly, anyone would think she didn't want her to even try to get to London.

'You'll need to go to Waverley Station in Edinburgh,' Alec said. 'And from there you could catch *The Flying Scotsman* down to London.'

Seffy gasped. 'Does it really fly?'

'Almost! It's the most incredible locomotive. It can get up to

195

a hundred miles an hour. It does the journey to King's Cross in seven or eight hours. But I don't know how much it costs. It's probably a king's ransom.'

'Seffy's got money, haven't you?' Jean said.

Seffy blew out her cheeks and ignored that slight dig.

'I *did* have money. I won ten pounds not so long ago in a bet with my brother. But there's hardly any left. That's a super idea about *The Flying Scotsman* though. I'll see if I can afford it when I get to the station.'

Alec nodded. 'It'd certainly be the fastest way to get there. And quite an experience. I shall want to hear all about it!'

'Right, so that's the trains sorted out,' Seffy said. 'But be honest, is there the remotest chance of me learning to ski by tomorrow morning?'

She wanted to laugh. The whole thing sounded so ridiculous.

He pulled off his hat and pressed his back further into the warm range.

'I wouldnae be here if I didn't think it were possible. If we were talking about alpine skiing – shooting down mountains at top speed – then Jean's right, you couldn't master it that quickly.'

'However …?'

'However, this is a little more straightforward. You'll be on the flat, mostly and I can teach you how to tackle an incline. It's all about technique.'

'Same as felling a tree. That's all about technique, too!' Seffy rubbed her hands together. 'Shall I give it a go? At least the snow will make a soft landing if I fall!'

'When you fall!' Jean said, shaking her head.

They wrapped up against the cold and went outside, where it had almost stopped snowing. There was just an occasional flake swirling around.

Some of the village children were speeding down the snow-covered lane in front of the cottage at high speed, using wooden trays as sledges.

'Hey!' Alec yelled, good-naturedly, leaping out of the way as a small boy nearly collided with him.

'You're the conchie!' the boy said. 'We're no' to talk to you, mister!' he added, as he gathered up his tray and started the hike back up the slope.

Poor Alec. Even the children were against him.

They headed for the track that led through the woods which was now a swathe of white virgin snow, sparkling in the winter sunshine.

Alec strapped the skis to his boots, picked up the sticks and gave a demonstration of cross-country skiing. It was rather a strange action – straight limbs moving back and forth – but it certainly had the desired effect: He glided across the snow, seemingly without too much effort.

'What's your balance like?' he asked, as he stopped just shy of Seffy's feet. 'A good sense of balance definitely helps.'

Seffy frowned. She'd never thought about it. But she could ride a horse, so maybe that would help?

When it was her turn, Alec fastened the skis' leather straps over her boots.

'I feel like one of those clowns with the huge shoes,' she said. 'It's jolly strange.'

'Here, take your poles.' He placed a stick in each of her hands. 'Off you go!'

She did as instructed and to her surprise, didn't immediately keel over. She was moving! She was skiing!

'Kick, push and glide!' Alec yelled. 'Push down on the snow to propel yourself forward.'

'Whee!' she yelled after a few yards. 'I can do it!' And promptly toppled over.

Jean and Alec were laughing, as they ran over to help.

Alec pulled her up.

'You made it look so easy!' Seffy said, bending to wipe the snow from her legs.

'You're doing very well,' he said. 'You're a natural!'

They practised for what seemed like hours, and before he left, to struggle back to his digs on foot, Alec handed something to Seffy.

'It's a compass, so you'll know if you're going in the right direction tomorrow. You need to head due east for the station. I take it you can read a compass?'

'Of course! And so can Jean. We were in the Women's Home Defence Corps!' Seffy said.

He shook his head, not understanding.

'It's like the Home Guard. But for women,' Jean said. 'Unofficial, of course. Before we arrived here, I thought I'd mebbe set up something similar with this gang, but—'

'—we soon realised they were a lost cause!' Seffy said. 'Can you imagine Peggy's reaction if we'd dared suggest drills and training outside working hours? Anyway, it would've been a distraction. Our aim has always been to get the work done in double-quick time, then move on and forget we were ever here!'

Seffy set off at first light the next day, to give herself as much time as possible to get to the station.

It suddenly seemed a rather daunting undertaking.

She had no idea whether she'd even be able to ski for five miles and, despite the compass, there was every chance of getting hopelessly lost. Everywhere looked the same when it was covered in snow.

Jean was up early too, ostensibly to see her off, although Seffy suspected it was more in the hope of dissuading her from going than to wish her bon voyage.

They stood outside the cottage and Seffy hoisted her bulging haversack onto her back.

'Now, are ye absolutely sure about this?' Jean said. 'I hate to be a harbinger of doom—'

'No, you don't, Jean. But go on.'

'Well, imagine if you get stuck in a snowdrift and you're still floundering there as the light fades. I mean, you could—'

'—freeze to death?'

Jean nodded. 'It's a pity you don't have a flare that you could send up in an emergency.'

Seffy sighed. 'I don't have a flare but I do have two arms and two legs to dig myself out of a snowdrift and a very loud voice to call for help, so I'll just have to hope for the best!'

'I don't suppose Mr Burke'll be too happy if he finds out you've abandoned us.'

'Abandoned you?' Seffy gave a hollow laugh. 'We've been snowed off! Other girls would've left if they could. I just happen to have found a way of doing it. All thanks to you, by the way, for *talking* to the conchie!'

Jean blushed.

But it was true, and rather ironic, that if Jean hadn't changed her mind about speaking to Alec – and goodness, they had looked pally in the pub last night – he'd never have provided Seffy with her means of escape.

'Anyway, Mr Burke won't find out,' Seffy said. 'Who's going to tell him?'

'What'll you do wi' the skis? You can hardly take them on the train,' Jean said.

'I'll charm the stationmaster into letting me leave them in his store, and if I still need them on the way back, they'll be waiting for me.'

There! She'd batted away yet another of the obstacles Jean seemed determined to put in her way.

'Look, it's only a few days,' Seffy said. 'I'll be back before you know it.'

'When? When'll you be back?' Jean asked.

'Tuesday. That's the plan, anyhow. Let the gang run wild until then and try to relax, Jean. Read a book or something!' She almost added, 'Build a snowman!' But that would've sounded facetious.

Jean would never do such a thing.

She bent down to tighten the straps around her boots, picked up the sticks – or poles, as Alec called them – and stood for a moment, gazing at the straight white runway ahead.

She took a breath of icy air. 'Righto, then!'

Jean was hugging herself and shivering. A few words of encouragement wouldn't have gone amiss.

'I won't wave,' Seffy said. 'Might tip over.'

Jean smiled at that, at least.

'Go on, get yourself inside. It's cold,' Seffy said. She bounced on the skis a couple of times. 'I'm off then. Goodbye!'

'Farewell!' Jean said. 'Haste ye back!'

Chapter Thirty-Three

That evening, Jean and Mrs Harris ate their shepherd's pie in silence at the kitchen table.

It had been a long, empty day since Seffy had left that morning.

Jean had tramped through the snow and knocked on a few neighbours' doors to ask if they'd be prepared to offer billets to the lumberjills to no avail, but otherwise, she'd done little except get under Mrs Harris's feet.

And write her second report for Miss McEwen.

The report was due to be sent at the end of this week and in the draft she'd written today, Jean had spilled the beans about Seffy's unauthorised trip to London.

Oh ma God, was she a terrible snitch? This was exactly the kind of information Miss McEwen was hoping for. She'd have Seffy's guts for garters. She might be hauled back to Blantyre, with no chance of a transfer down to England now.

Och, no, she couldn't do it; she couldn't be so mean.

But she was furious with Seffy for disobeying orders and leaving her in charge of the Lost Girls. She'd tried saying all sorts to make her stay but Seffy had dismissed every objection out of hand, as though it were all just a jolly caper.

She still mightn't send it. It was only a draft. She might write it up quite differently and not mention Seffy's misdemeanour at all. She'd sleep on it, but if she still felt this cross in the morning, then that report would be in the post as soon as the snow cleared and Jean could get to the post office.

Seffy had to learn that you reap what you sow.

'No luck finding your lassies new lodgings, then?' Mrs Harris asked.

Jean was about to say they weren't *her* lassies, but of course, in Seffy's absence, they were. She shook her head.

'The problem is word's got round that they're more trouble than they're worth!' Mrs Harris said. 'And what's all this I hear about them playing darts in The Drover's?'

Jean put down her knife and fork. 'The lassies are playing darts?'

None of them had mentioned darts when they'd all been in the pub last night.

'Aye, tramping through the snow to get there every evening. Where there's a will, there's a way. Turns out they've taken to the arrows like ducks to water and Davey McAllister – he's the landlord – is no' happy!'

Jean's heart sank. She'd have laid bets on something like this happening the minute Seffy disappeared.

'It's not that he minds lassies in his pub—' Mrs Harris went on.

'What, then? Are they muscling in on the auld fellas' game?'

She had to wait while Mrs Harris chewed long and hard on a piece of gristle.

'It's not the darts,' she said, finally. 'They're no' buying any drinks! They're in The Drover's from opening time to last orders and they have no more than a couple o' shandies between the lot of them! Davey's got a living to earn!'

'Has he spoken to them about it?' Jean asked, cringing at the thought. She could just imagine Peggy giving him a mouthful.

'I dunno. You'd best go up and speak to him. You're the boss now, after all, since Lady Muck did a bunk!'

Jean cleared her throat. 'Remember what I said, Mrs Harris? If you wouldnae mind keeping it under your hat, you know, about Seffy being away?'

'Aw!' Mrs Harris slapped her hand over her mouth. 'Of course!'

Jean pushed her plate away, no longer hungry.

She didn't want to speak to Mr McAllister: she hated confrontation. But the Lost Girls couldn't be allowed to upset the villagers. It was all very well for Seffy to say 'let them run wild' but how could she? They were her responsibility.

At least the pub wasn't far away. She'd do it now: she should strike while the iron was hot. She grabbed her overcoat, pulled on her boots and ran to The Drover's, slipping and sliding in the snow and grateful for the dim light afforded by her torch.

As she pushed open the door and blackout curtain, she wondered what her mother would say if she could see her waltzing into a pub alone, like a lady of the night.

It was a relief to find Alec sitting alone at a table by the door.

'Jean! You're becoming a regular! Come and take a seat.' He sounded pleased to see her.

'Are the lassies here?' she asked, looking around. She could only see fellas at the bar and around the fire.

'Aye, they're here all right. Queens of the oche! Davey McAllister's on the warpath. He's down in the cellar, fetching up a barrel, but he'll be back any minute. You should probably have a word.'

Jean nodded. That's what she'd come for, but she was glad to have a few minutes to compose herself.

She tugged off her coat and sat down.

'Any word from Seffy?' Alec asked.

Aye, he would ask that, before anything else. It'd been so obvious, as he'd fussed over Seffy yesterday, that he liked her. Jean didnae want him for herself – it wasn't that – but if he and Seffy fell in love, she'd have to trail around wi' them like a gooseberry or else be on her own.

Perhaps she should warn Alec that he had stiff competition

for Seffy's heart from a very handsome Canadian fella? Och, no, it was nothin' to do wi' her.

She shook her head. 'I've heard nothing. I'm assuming no news is good news.'

She'd been wondering how Seffy was getting on all day. If she'd managed to catch *The Flying Scotsman*, she'd be in London by now. As much as Jean was cross with her for disobeying orders and abandoning her post, she hoped she'd arrived safely.

The girl was certainly brave. Jean could no more have put on those skis and launched herself into the unknown than flown to the moon.

Alec must've heard something in her voice because he was looking at her curiously.

'I'm sorry,' he said. 'Did I do the wrong thing, giving her the skis?'

Jean flushed. 'Not at all. I dunnae know why you'd think that.'

'Because—' he said, smiling. 'Seffy was too excited to notice but I could tell you were put out about her leaving. Were you wishing you were going to London, was that it?'

How could she explain how vexed she was, without sounding spiteful? She'd never been to London and sure, she'd like to see the place. But what really irked her was the way everything fell into silver-spoon Seffy's lap.

Take the christening. She'd been so keen to go, it was almost as though she'd willed it to snow.

And men fell over themselves to help her. Alec had even bunked off work to bring her the skis. Would he have done the same for her, if she'd been the one trying to get to England?

She took a deep breath. 'I was peeved with her, in truth, for leaving me in the lurch. Those lassies can be a handful, especially Peggy.'

'Aw, don't fret about Peggy. She's already winnin' the fellas over at the saw mill. She's further up the pecking order than me, that's for sure. I think that wee pipe helps. She'll soon be one o' the lads!'

Jean nodded. It sounded as though Alec was keeping an eye on her, which was reassuring.

'And is that the only reason you're irked with her? Because she left you in charge?'

'No. Our instructions were quite clear: we were to stay put. Seffy disobeyed. She broke the rules.'

'Ah, I see. You wouldnae do that? You never break rules?'

Jean shook her head. 'The thing about rules is, you don't have to think, you just have to follow them.'

Alec laughed. 'But I don't want someone else telling me how to think: I want to think for myself. I don't want to be a sheep!'

Jean frowned. Was that what she was? A sheep?

'In any case, you're mistaken, Jean Ferguson! You do break rules. You started that day at the saw mill, when you spoke to me properly, for the first time. Now, why did you do that?'

Jean was flabbergasted. She'd never expected to have to justify her actions to a conchie.

'I … well, it would've been rude not to reply when you'd addressed me so directly.'

'Aye, and you're not a rude person. I accept that. Anything else?'

She shrugged, not sure where this conversation was going. 'I suppose, it seemed like the right thing to do.'

Alec finished his pint and put down the glass. 'So, your moral compass was telling you not to be rude. And speaking to me – even though it was against the rules – felt like the right thing to do?' He nodded. 'Hmm, interesting. Did you sort out the bicycle wi' Ron, by the way?'

Goodness, that was a sudden change of tack. She could hardly keep up with him. Aw, but this was fun. She couldnae remember the last time she'd had to think hard about something.

'The bicycle? Oh, aye. He wanted a shilling a week but I offered him sixpence and he accepted.' She looked down for a second and added, shyly, 'I took your advice.'

'Good for you! See, you should have more confidence in yersel',

Jean. You're more capable than you think.'

He was being kind but she was still full of doubts. She was mithering about that report. If she omitted to mention Seffy going AWOL and Miss McEwen found out, she'd be for the high jump. She might even be accused of aiding and abetting Seffy's crime.

'A penny for them?' Alec asked, tilting his head.

How could she tell him she was considering reporting Seffy? He'd think she was a terrible telltale and she couldn't bear that.

There was one concern she could share with him, though.

'I'm wondering whether Seffy will ever come back,' she said.

He looked surprised. 'She wouldn't do that, would she? Desert her post and all of you?'

'She hates this place and she's gone back to her old world. Mebbe she'll decide to stay there.'

'You think she has an easy life, is that it? Because she's posh and … everything?'

Jean knew what 'everything' meant. Because Seffy was rich and titled, charming and beautiful. All the things she wasn't.

'But you never really know another person,' Alec said. 'What you see on the outside isn't the whole picture. Seffy didn't want to come here, she's made that very clear. So that's one thing that didn't go her way, isn't it?'

'What she said yesterday, about wanting to get the work done and forgetting we were ever here,' Jean said, 'that didnae apply to me, by the way. She was talking about herself.'

Jean had wanted to shake Seffy when she'd said that. Alec had looked so hurt, and after all he'd done to help her.

He waved his hand dismissively. 'Aw, I didnae take offence. Folk don't always mean everything they say.'

Jean studied him across the table. She shouldn't like the fella: she despised conchies. But once you got to know him, Alec Reid was hard to dislike. How was he so wise and sure of himself? She'd never met anyone so young who had such an old head on his shoulders.

He nodded at the bar. 'Davey's back now. Let's go up. What'll you have to drink?'

The barman, who'd always seemed so pleasant up to now, scowled at Alec but nonetheless served him and took his money for Jean's shandy.

'Oi, Miss!' he yelled, as Isobel sauntered past, presumably heading for the lavatory. 'This here's the bar, and it's open for business should you feel the urge to splash out on a drink?'

Isobel must've heard him but she walked on without a backward glance, which enraged him even more.

He jabbed a finger at Jean. 'You're one o' them, aren't you?' He slammed her drink down on the bar so hard she thought the glass would break. 'I'm on the verge of banning every one of yous from ma pub!'

Jean took a deep breath. It had been a shock, being bawled at like that. The fella's face had been so close to hers she'd felt spittle on her cheek. She could feel Alec bristling beside her, but she didn't want, or expect, him to leap to her defence.

Stay calm and think. How would Seffy reply? She wouldn't get on her high horse. Seffy favoured a softer approach.

'Mr McAllister,' Jean said, politely but firmly. 'These lassies are working hard for the war effort—'

He made a scoffing sound.

'—and they're young and they dunnae earn very much at all.'

He shrugged, as if to say, 'What's that to me?'

Jean raised her voice. 'If they were soldiers, off duty in here, would you not cut them some slack? These girls are soldiers of the forest!'

Aw, it was useless. He obviously couldnae care less. There wasn't another pub for miles and if the Lost Girls were banned from The Drover's, morale would hit rock bottom. They might never get the girls back to work. She felt her resolve drain away like water down a plughole. She couldnae sort this out. Seffy should be here, taking charge.

'There you go.' An auld fella, leaning on the bar next to Alec, was holding out a sixpence between gnarled fingers. 'I'll put summat towards a drink for the wee lassies.'

Another man placed his cap upside down on the bar and dropped a couple of pennies into it. 'Aye, me too. I hear they're doin' good work.'

Alec raised his eyebrows at Jean.

'Ta very much, gentlemen,' she said. 'That's good of you.'

The landlord crossed his arms and watched, with pursed lips, as others made their way around the bar and dropped pennies, sixpences and threepenny bits into the cap. He looked thoroughly ashamed, as well he might.

After only a couple of minutes, there was at least enough for three shandies. And the coins were still coming.

'There!' the first fella said, with a nod. 'That's your Timber Girls' fund!'

Timber Girls? Jean winced but didn't correct him. If fellas wanted to keep the girls in drinks and good spirits, well – within reason – they could call them whatever they liked.

Chapter Thirty-Four

Hammersmith, London, England

When Seffy was shown into the drawing room, Emerald leaped out of her armchair with a joyful squeal.

'Darling girl! You made it!'

'Don't come any closer!' Seffy said, putting out a warning hand. 'I've been travelling since first thing and I'm filthy!'

'Come here, silly moo! As if I mind that!'

The girls embraced, although Seffy felt so scruffy that she didn't dare hug Emerald as tightly as she'd have liked.

'You managed to wrangle some leave, then?' Emerald asked.

'Hmm, in a way. Oh, it's so good to see you and to be here! I can hardly believe it!'

Emerald laughed as she ran her eyes over Seffy's clothes. 'Goodness, have you come straight from the woods?' She tugged at Seffy's overcoat. 'Are you wearing actual slacks under there?'

'Yes! Get your hands off! Don't worry, I won't show you up: I've brought a frock for the christening.' She held up the haversack. 'All in here. Much more practical than a suitcase.' She blew out her cheeks. 'Do you think I might have a quick wash and get changed?'

'We can do better than that. Shall I ask Aggie to draw you a bath and you can have a wallow?'

'Oh, that would be utter heaven!' Dear Emerald, she knew her so well.

'Don't be too long though because we've got tons to catch up on!' Emerald said. 'I want to know everything! Oh and do be ready to leap out of the tub if the sirens go off, won't you?'

The bath was so deliciously hot, Seffy could only just bear it. It was filled with mountains of iridescent bubbles and she had a whole bar of soap to herself and actual shampoo. She folded one of the fluffy towels to make a pillow, leaned back and closed her eyes. It was total bliss.

If the alert sounded, she'd throw caution to the wind and stay put.

Oh, but what a day she'd had!

Her journey to the station had started well enough. It had stopped snowing and the only slight niggle had been the glare from the sun on the snow, which had made her squint and yearn for sunglasses. She'd actually managed the skiing quite well, until she'd reached a steep slope and had completely forgotten how to slow down.

Everything had flashed past in a dazzling white blur. She'd tried leaning forwards but that'd only made her go faster. She'd been considering throwing herself into a snowdrift – it was one way of stopping – when her left ski had struck something hard. She'd been catapulted forwards and received an almighty cold slap, as she'd landed face down in the snow.

It was a wonder her only injury had been a bump to the head. Nothing had been broken, including the skis, and although she wasn't entirely sure whether she'd been knocked out – everything had certainly gone fuzzy for a while – she'd seemed to be in one piece.

Now, she lifted her hand out of the bathwater and touched

the quail's-egg-sized lump on her forehead. Ouch, it was sore.

After a few more minutes, she reluctantly got out of the bath. Perhaps she could have another one tomorrow?

She wrapped herself in the dressing gown that had been laid out for her use, made a turban of a towel and padded back to her room on the deep pile carpet. The house had central heating. She actually felt warm for the first time in months.

Her haversack had been unpacked, clothes put away and her pyjamas were folded neatly on the bed.

Seffy exhaled. She remembered this. Oh, and how she'd missed it. She would never take it for granted again, as long as she lived.

She pressed the eiderdown on the bed. It was thick and soft and would undoubtedly be as warm as toast and she'd be able to stretch out like a starfish and not worry about kicking Jean.

'Is everything to your liking, ma'am?' Aggie the maid asked, coming into the room.

She could've kissed the woman. To her liking? It was paradise.

'Ah, that's more like it,' Emerald said, when Seffy joined her in the drawing room. The room was softly lit with small lamps and a fire was blazing in the hearth.

Seffy pulled a curl of her hair over her forehead. She'd examined the bump in the bathroom mirror and it was rather a corker. She knew it would tickle Emerald to hear about her skiing escapade but she didn't want to act the fool, at least not this evening.

'Turn around,' Emerald said. 'Let me look at that dress. You do have the most marvellous figure, Seffy. And here's me, with no waist to speak of!' She squeezed her sides and pulled a face.

Seffy smoothed down her dress. She was in fine fettle these days, it was true. She was fitter than she'd ever been in her life; she could never go back to the sedentary lifestyle she'd once led.

Oh, but she was forgetting poor Emerald, who was feeling like a frump.

'Nonsense!' Seffy said. 'You'll soon get your figure back. You've just had a baby!'

'I know, it's silly. Bertie's quite happy. Says there's more of me to love! Now, do come and sit down. Shall we have a sherry?'

Seffy giggled. This all felt terribly grown-up. She'd never been here before – Emerald and Bertie had married just as Seffy had joined the Timber Corps – and she was rather in awe of this magnificent house, of which her chum was mistress. They'd always be the best of friends – goodness, they were like sisters – but thanks to the war, their lives had certainly taken different paths.

For the next hour they sat in front of the fire, catching up on news from family and friends. It wasn't all good: Emerald knew of several chaps – brothers and sweethearts of girls they were acquainted with – who'd been killed in action or who were MIA.

Seffy sighed. This was no good. All this talk of war was bringing them down.

She lightened the mood by telling Emerald about her new posting in Aberdeenshire: the bitter cold, the outrageous Mrs Harris and the rebellious gang of girls.

In no time at all, Emerald was exclaiming and giggling.

'A pipe?' she said, shaking her head. 'She actually smokes a pipe?' She wiped a tear from the corner of her eye. 'Now, would you like to see the baby?'

Goodness, the baby! Seffy had completely forgotten about her godson, the whole reason for her being here! Was that frightfully bad form? She might be sacked as godmother before she'd even started.

'Absolutely!' she said. 'I'd love to see the little man!'

The nursemaid brought him downstairs, bathed and ready for bed.

He looked like all babies – that's to say, he looked like Mr Churchill – but he was rather sweet and Seffy happily agreed to hold him.

She rocked and jiggled him in her arms, as she'd seen other women do but perhaps with too much enthusiasm because he promptly started to cry and was whisked away by the nursemaid.

'Now he's here I wouldn't change him for the world,' Emerald said, a little wistfully, 'but I was rather hoping for a girl. And I'd have called her after you, Seffy.'

Seffy pulled a face. 'Gracious, don't inflict my awful name on anyone! My aunt once took great pleasure in telling me that Persephone means "bringer of destruction"!'

As she waved her arms around, her sleeve caught the edge of a lamp and sent it crashing to the ground.

They laughed.

'See what I mean?' Seffy said, bending to retrieve it.

'Dear Seffy, you haven't changed a bit!' Emerald said. 'Still making me laugh.'

'Oh, I'm not like this in Scotland,' Seffy said, checking the lamp for damage and placing it back on the table.

'Aren't you? I thought it was a lark, being a lumberjill? Otherwise, really, what's the point?'

Seffy shook her head. 'It was a lark in the old place but not now. Jean, my deputy, is a very prim and proper miss, and we're like chalk and cheese. And as for the gang I'm supervising, I have to mind my ps and qs with them for fear they'll go on strike again. The one who smokes the pipe is quite scary!'

'And what about the landowner? Is he anything to write home about?'

'McIntyre? He's ancient. Served last time and has the wounds to show for it. He's miserable.'

'Like Mr Rochester?' Emerald asked, hopefully. She'd read *Jane Eyre* at school and had never forgotten it.

'More like Scrooge.' Seffy sighed. 'Actually, I'd rather forget about the lot of them! They've made my life a total misery for the past month. Let's talk about something else. Oh, the baby's name! You still haven't told me. What did you plump for, in the end?'

'Henry Bertrand Jamieson!'

'Did someone say Bertrand?' It was Bertie, peering around the

213

door and grinning at them.

'There you are, darling!' Emerald cried. 'Look, Seffy's managed to get here, after all! And now I'm with my two favourite grown-ups in the whole world!'

Bertie came in, looking awfully dapper in his army uniform and kissed them both on the cheek.

'Wait until you hear what Seffy's been up to in the grim north,' Emerald said. 'She's got chilblains and all sorts!'

Seffy squirmed. She was sure her trials and tribulations were nothing compared to Bertie's role, gallantly fighting the enemy.

'Good journey?' he asked her.

'Yes, thank you. I lucked out and managed to get a ride on *The Flying Scotsman*!'

'You never did!' Bertie said. 'I'm green with envy!'

Seffy giggled. It had been quite an experience although she'd felt seriously underdressed, in her breeches and boots, surrounded by women wearing tailored suits, gloves and hats. And, as Alec had guessed, even travelling third class had cost a fortune. She certainly wouldn't be going back that way – she'd have to stick to the common or garden trains for her return trip – but speed had been of the essence on the way down and it'd been worth every penny.

At King's Cross Station, there'd been posters plastered all over the walls. Seffy had happily ignored the one that asked house-wives to 'PLEASE FINISH TRAVELLING BY 4 O'CLOCK AND LEAVE THE BUSES, TRAMS AND TRAINS FREE FOR WAR WORKERS!' because she was hardly a housewife, and she was definitely a war worker.

But the poster that asked, 'IS YOUR JOURNEY REALLY NECESSARY?' had made her think twice.

Spoilsport Jean would say it was definitely not necessary but Seffy had decided it was. Because without this trip, she'd have been in danger of going stark, staring mad.

'Charming place you have here, Bertie,' she said.

He smiled and patted Emerald's hand. 'We like it, don't we darling? But Emmy and the baby won't be staying here much longer. It's not safe.'

Emerald pulled a face. 'Yes, we're being evacuated next week. Going to Salisbury to stay with my aunt.'

'Aunts can be great fun!' Seffy said.

'Yours might be, mine definitely isn't. But at least we've managed to fit in the christening. Bertie got leave and you got here from the ends of the earth, so it's all worked out jolly well!'

The nursemaid was back. 'I think he's hungry, ma'am,' she said.

'Of course!' Emerald said, taking the baby from her. 'I'll have to feed him before dinner or no one will get a moment's peace. Why don't you two go on through to the dining room and I'll join you shortly?'

Chapter Thirty-Five

The next morning, after a blissful night's sleep – and thankfully, no alerts – Seffy was woken by the sound of Aggie coming into her room.

Emerald was standing in the doorway, in her dressing gown.

'Are you awake?' she asked, jiggling on the spot. 'I couldn't wait a moment longer!'

'Yes, of course! Come in!'

Aggie was drawing back the curtains and light was flooding in.

Emerald climbed onto the bed, while Seffy propped up four feather pillows behind her and sank back into them.

'I feel like a French queen, receiving visitors in her boudoir,' she said.

Emerald grabbed her hands and scowled at them. 'Except no queen ever had hands as rough as these! Remind me to give you some cream.'

Seffy thanked her but she knew it would take more than a dash of Pond's to restore her hands to their former glory.

She licked her lips. 'Is there any tea going? I've been dreaming of tea in bed for yonks!'

Emerald stopped Aggie as she was leaving the room and asked for a tray of tea for two.

'You angel!' Seffy said. 'Do you know, in my paltry billet I have to make do with one pillow and it's as flat as a pancake.'

'Gracious, it all sounds rather primitive!' Emerald lay across the end of the bed, toying with the edge of the eiderdown. 'I do think you've absolutely proven your point, Seffy. I know this whole caper started out as a bet with Percy but haven't you taken it a bit far? Can't you tell them you've had enough?'

Seffy laughed. Dear Emerald, she had no idea.

'It doesn't work like that. I've signed up for the duration. I have to stay!'

'Can't you go AWOL? Come and stay with me in Salisbury! It'd be a hoot!'

'I did try to leave the Timber Corps once,' Seffy said. 'But it turned out lumberjills are tied to the service by an Essential Work Order. We can only withdraw from the service – barring illness or marriage – with the permission of the Ministry of Labour.'

'I'm sure you could get a doctor to sign you off with nervous debility or something, if you really wanted to,' Emerald said. 'Can't your father pull a few strings?'

Seffy shook her head. 'I couldn't do that, Em. I'm committed now. But that doesn't mean a few days of pampering and relaxation aren't most welcome!'

Emerald shifted position and propped her head on her elbow.

'And at least they gave you leave to come down here. We must be grateful for that. Now, why are you looking so sheepish all of a sudden?'

'Actually, I didn't have permission at all,' Seffy said. 'We were snowed off and I absconded, much to the horror of my second-in-command.'

She felt suddenly rather ashamed of herself. Had it been terribly selfish, to simply up and leave?

Emerald was waggling a finger. 'Tut, tut, Seffy! Aren't you supposed to be setting a good example to those wayward girls? I'm only teasing. I'm perfectly delighted that you're playing truant! And once this silly war is over, you can come home for good, darling. You'll have done your bit, we're all so terrifically proud of you. But won't you be the teensiest bit pleased when it's all over and better days have come?'

Seffy nodded. She couldn't argue with that. But it was hard to imagine the end of the war and what she might be doing then.

'Any news on the chap front?'

Seffy smiled. She'd wondered how long it would take Emerald to get around to that.

'There are no men to speak of in the new place,' she said, 'but remember my Canadian chap? I've been writing to him and I've applied for a transfer to the New Forest, so I'll be nearer to him. And to you, in Salisbury, of course!'

She'd expected Emerald to brighten at the news but she looked grave.

'Whenever you talk about him you always get that dreamy look on your face,' she said.

Seffy laughed. 'Do I?'

Oh, how she wished she'd had more notice of this unexpected trip to London. Callum was on the south coast, not a million miles away and there might have been a chance to meet up, even just for a few hours.

'But … Don't take this the wrong way,' Emerald said. 'But don't you think you might be wasting your time?'

Goodness, that was a low blow. And unexpected. Seffy was lost for words.

'Has he ever made a commitment, told you how he feels, given you anything definite?'

'He gave me his cap badge!' Seffy said, laughing.

'Other gals get diamond rings and promises, and you're happy with a cap badge? What's happened to you? All that fresh air has sent you doolally! Didn't you once tell me he was engaged to a girl back home?'

Seffy nodded, dolefully. She really didn't want to be reminded of that.

'And presumably that situation hasn't changed?' Emerald said. 'The chap's toying with you! Or is it simply a matter of wanting what you can't have? No, hear me out. I have to say it or I'll never forgive myself. You're twenty-two years old, dear Seffy. You need to find someone who's all yours. Why should you *share*? Don't you want a home and a proper grown-up life?'

Like me. That's what she meant.

Yes, once this would've been Seffy's dream; but not anymore.

She looked fondly at Emerald. She knew her friend only wanted the best for her. But was she right? Was she nothing but a distraction for Callum until he could get home to his fiancée?

'What did he give you for Christmas?' Emerald asked.

Goodness, this was turning into the Spanish Inquisition.

'As yet …' Seffy said, 'nothing.'

She was irked with Emerald now. She couldn't be fagged to tell her that Callum wanted to deliver her present in person. It would sound too lame.

Try as she might, she wouldn't be able to make Emerald understand. No one could understand apart from Callum and her. Because when they were together, there was something special between them, something that defied explanation.

'What happened with you and Teddy?' Emerald asked. 'You've never told me. Did you throw him over because of the Canadian?'

'"The Canadian"? He does have a name you know!' Honestly! She hadn't traipsed the length of the country for a ticking off. 'It's Callum,' she said, when Emerald didn't respond. 'Staff Sergeant Callum Fraser.'

There it was again: that stomach flip she got just from saying his name. Didn't that prove something?

They should talk about something else. She didn't want to fall out with her best chum over a man.

Seffy knew what would cheer Emerald up.

'What time's the christening today?' she asked. 'And is there any chance of a spot of shopping beforehand?'

Chapter Thirty-Six

That afternoon all the christening guests had gathered for a pre-event drink at Emerald's place. They were milling around in the drawing room as Seffy dashed in and tried to catch the eye of the footman with the drinks tray.

'Late as usual, I see, Seffy,' a deep woman's voice growled behind her.

She turned and came face to face with Fiona-Three-Fiancés. They hadn't seen one another since they'd been debutantes.

There was a wedding band on the girl's left hand, clearly visible as she swigged her glass of champagne. Clearly, one of the three fiancés had come good.

'Oh, hullo, Fiona, how lovely to see you after all this time,' Seffy said.

Should they kiss? No, the moment had passed.

'Yes, I am a trifle late. I went shopping. Couldn't get a cab for love nor money!'

She'd been to all her favourite haunts: Liberty's, Harrods and Fortnum and Mason. It had been such a wonderful treat but everything had seemed so expensive. Had it always been so costly? And as she didn't have many coupons, or much cash, for that matter, thanks to the extravagant *Flying Scotsman*, she'd only bought a small gift for Jean and a pair of stockings for herself.

But it had been a delight to simply browse and feel human again. Shame Emerald hadn't been able to come too, but she'd had to prepare to receive her guests.

Another face from her past loomed into view.

'What've you been doing with yourself, Seffy?' Marguerite Rollason asked, looking all superior in her WAAF uniform. 'Last I heard you were working on the land and you'd gone completely feral!'

'I'm in the woods, rather than on the land, actually,' Seffy said.

She looked around for Emerald, wishing she'd come and rescue her but Emerald and Bertie were circulating. She could hardly expect them to spend all afternoon with her.

'Don't mind if I do!' Seffy said, deftly swiping a glass of champagne from a passing footman's tray. She took a big gulp. She was going to need this if she were going to get through today.

Some other girls had joined their circle. None of them had been particular pals of hers at school but Emerald must've kept in touch with them.

Seffy drank some more of her champagne. She'd enjoy letting it slip, in a moment, that she was the baby's godmother and, therefore, quite clearly Emerald's most particular friend.

'Did I hear you're a lumberjack?' one of the girls asked. 'I say, is that a smudge of dirt on your nose?'

They laughed, as Seffy touched her nose self-consciously, before realising she'd said it in jest.

Blast them all. If she got huffy, she'd be accused of not being able to take a joke; she'd simply have to take the teasing on the chin.

As well as Marguerite, there were one or two others in WAAF and WREN uniforms, looking terrifically smart. Seffy felt at a distinct disadvantage, but she could hardly have worn her uniform of breeches and boots to a christening.

'I say, who are they?' Marguerite asked, suddenly perking up.

Two RAF chaps had just arrived and were standing in the doorway. Seffy's heart leaped as she recognised them. That was Teddy! And Percy! Thank goodness, a couple of allies.

She jumped in the air and waved. 'Cooee! Over here, boys!'

'Friends of yours?' Marguerite asked.

'I should say so,' Fiona said. 'Seffy and Teddy Fortesque were an item for yonks, before she gave him the heave-ho. And the other's her brother. He's a twin, so I can't tell which one it is.'

'It's Percy,' Seffy said, not taking her eyes of the men, who were threading between groups of people, making their way over.

Teddy looked the same as ever: perfectly dashing in his blue RAF uniform, the buttons shining like gold. What was it about a man in uniform? It made them all seem so smart and authoritative. They had a frightfully attractive air of purpose about them.

'They're like modern-day knights in shining armour,' Jean had said, when they'd discussed it in bed one night.

On closer inspection, dear Teddy looked a little weary but his face lit up as he reached her and hugged her tight. Seffy felt the rough worsted uniform against her cheek and caught a whiff of cigarettes.

'Careful of my drink!' she said, laughing.

'Hello, you,' Teddy said, releasing his hold on her. 'How are you? How's the forest?'

'Tickety-boo. How's the sky?'

Before he could reply, Percy squeezed through the circle of girls, demanding his turn and gave her a superstrong, brotherly hug. This time, there was no hope for the champers and half of it tipped out onto the carpet but she couldn't mind. Teddy and Percy were here!

She had no real desire to introduce everyone but as the girls were looking interested – and hopeful – good manners prevailed and Seffy quickly did the honours.

'We're terribly late!' Percy said. 'There's rubble everywhere and the taxi had the devil's own job to find a way through We were worried you might've already left for the chapel.'

He looked so grown-up. Her little brother! He was at least three inches taller than the last time she'd seen him.

'Seffy was late too,' Fiona said.

'Seffy's always late,' Teddy said.

Seffy felt affronted for a second until he added, 'Because she's an optimist!'

'Am I? Is that anything like a Methodist?'

He roared with laughter and the other girls joined in politely.

'No, but am I? An optimist?' she asked.

'Yes you are, Sis,' Percy said. 'You never give up and you always find a way through.'

Was that true? She'd never thought of herself like that. But she supposed she did like to solve problems. She'd arranged for Grace and Gordy to marry before the company moved out of Scotland and she'd steered Joey and Ralph in the right direction, romantically. The only thing she didn't seem able to fix, was her own dire situation with Callum.

'Anyway, what are you chaps doing here?' she asked. 'I had no idea you were coming. Why didn't anyone tell me?'

'We're VIPs, we had to be here,' Teddy said. 'We're the godfathers!'

'Never!' Seffy thumped his arm. 'I'm the godmother!'

Percy was chatting to the other girls now, so she and Teddy moved away. Teddy accepted a glass of champagne from a footman, downed it quickly and took another.

'You didn't answer my question,' Seffy said. 'How's the sky?' His smile faltered for a second before he pasted it back on. 'Is … is everything all right?' Seffy asked. He'd gone awfully pale and his bottom lip was trembling. For one terrible moment, she thought he might be about to cry.

She put her hand on his forearm. 'Shall we get some air?'

As they crossed the drawing room, skirting around the other guests. Seffy noticed Emerald watching them from a seat in the corner. She gave a satisfied nod.

Oh, honestly! They were simply two friends nipping out for a chat. There was nothing more to it than that.

They slipped out through the front door and stood under the portico. Teddy offered Seffy a cigarette, which she refused and then lit one for himself. When he'd taken a few drags and relaxed a little, he started to speak.

'Quite a few of the chaps haven't made it,' he said, hesitantly. He bowed his head. 'And it rather knocks the stuffing out of one, after a while. You go down to breakfast after being out all night and if a plane's gone down, that means seven men – pals – aren't there, sitting with you.'

He looked up and valiantly tried to smile but his lips were quivering. Seffy's heart went out to him. What could she do to help? She felt totally useless.

She stroked his arm. 'None of us knows or can understand what you've been through, Teddy. I'm sure it's been – it is, horrendous.'

She wondered if he were worrying that he might be next. She could hardly say, 'It's going to be all right' because that would be utter nonsense. She didn't know, any more than he did.

He continued smoking his cigarette in silence and staring out at the traffic passing the house.

'You know, I keep you in my prayers every night, Teddy,' she said. Which was true. She had so many people on her prayer list that it took forever to recite the names. Her brothers, Tol and Percy, were on the list too, of course. And Callum.

Teddy turned his head and gave her a quick, grateful smile.

'And thank you for taking Percy under your wing, so to speak,' Seffy said. 'I know you've been looking after him.'

'It's not a hardship,' he said. 'Any member of your family is practically one of my own.'

He grew more serious and he looked straight into her eyes. She'd forgotten how direct he could be and how, when he spoke to you, it was as though you were the only person in the world.

225

'It's so good to see you, Teddy,' she said.

'Ditto, old bean.' He flushed slightly and looked down at his shiny black shoes. He looked jittery, and she felt rotten. They'd been close once and she'd ended it all, resorting to that terrible 'let's remain good friends' cliché. Had she done this to him?

'Hey, it's me, Seffy,' she wanted to say but instead, she said, 'Now, are you all set for this christening and for taking on your godfatherly responsibilities? It's a serious business! When we recite our vows, we have to renounce the devil, you know!'

She giggled and nudged him playfully but he didn't return her smile.

'Seffy, don't answer me now—' he placed a finger briefly across her lips '—but if you ever thought that there might be a chance for us … for my part, I'd marry you tomorrow, if you'd have me!'

He gave a short laugh, as though it were a joke. But it clearly wasn't.

Goodness, where had that come from? Was it the two glasses of champagne talking or did this have something to do with his recent, awful experiences? Did he want to grab life while he still could?

Eighteen months ago, before Seffy had joined the Corps, those words, 'I'd marry you tomorrow', would've been music to her ears but now she simply couldn't imagine marrying Teddy. She liked him very much – she loved him – but as a brother, nothing more.

But given what he'd just told her, and the terrible times he was going through, how could she dash his hopes?

'You're not saying no!' he teased. 'Allow a chap to dream a little, won't you?'

So, although it was on the tip of her tongue to tell him how she really felt, she couldn't do it.

He'd asked her to stay quiet and she would.

Chapter Thirty-Seven

'What are your plans for this evening, Sis?' Percy asked, once the christening was over and they were all back at Emerald and Bertie's house.

His eyes were bright. 'Do you fancy coming out with Teddy and me? We're meeting up with some pals. Canadians, mostly. They're a super crowd. Come along, it'll be fun!'

Canadians? Goodness, what were the chances? Of course, it wouldn't be *those* Canadians, – Number Thirty-Four Company of the Canadian Forestry Corps, to which Callum belonged – but nonetheless, it would be nice to hear that glorious accent again. And it would be a wheeze to be out on the town after so long.

She started to say she'd love to come but then stopped herself.

What was she thinking? Had she completely forgotten her manners? She was Emerald's guest. It would be the height of rudeness to simply disappear for the evening.

'Don't mind me,' Emerald said. She must've overheard. 'You bright young things head out and enjoy yourselves! You can tell me all about it in the morning!'

Seffy was thrilled. She didn't even think about the likelihood of any bombing. After all, one couldn't spend one's whole life anticipating danger.

Later, as Seffy and Teddy stood in the hallway, while Percy attempted to flag down a cab outside, Emerald appeared, carrying the baby on her shoulder.

'Be nice to Teddy,' she whispered to Seffy.

'I'm always nice!' Seffy whispered back.

Before they stepped outside, Teddy placed Seffy's overcoat across her shoulders. 'Here, put that on, before you catch a chill.'

She slipped her arms into the sleeves. Tonight, she would enjoy being looked after. It would make a welcome change from having to be strong and forthright and look after everybody else.

'That was a big sigh,' Teddy said.

She hadn't even realised she'd done it.

'Relief,' she said. 'Relief at being back.'

Once the taxi had delivered them into town, they linked arms – with Seffy in the middle – and made their way down the street towards the dance hall. Teddy and Percy lit the way with pocket torches, which they were careful to direct down at the pavement.

'I thought we were supposed to be meeting some Canadians?' Seffy said.

'We are!' Teddy replied. 'Here they come now.'

Seffy peered into the darkness. She could see nothing but the ghostly shapes of a group of young women coming towards them. They weren't easy to make out but their overcoats were flapping and they appeared to be in khaki uniforms. They were strolling along, arm in arm, clearly used to the blackout and talking loudly in accents that definitely weren't Home Counties.

'What are they doing here?' Seffy murmured.

'I should close your mouth, dearie, in case you swallow a fly,' one of the women said.

She'd brushed close to Seffy as she passed by in a waft of scent and made a bee-line for Percy.

These were the Canadians? Women? And not just any women:

they were in the services.

Percy and Teddy had let go of Seffy's arms as they were swallowed up by the group. Now, they were busy greeting their friends and discussing where they were 'heading out to'.

There were about a dozen girls and there was a lot of shrieking and laughing. The chaps had completely forgotten about her. No one had even bothered to introduce her. Perhaps she should simply slip away, shoot back to Emerald's in a taxi and say she had a beastly headache?

But suddenly Teddy was blocking her way.

'Hey, Seffy! Not so fast! Where are you going? Come along, they don't bite!'

He took her arm and steered her towards the Canadians.

'Girls, I'd like you to meet a very good friend of mine, Lady Persephone Baxter-Mills.'

'Gee, that's a mouthful,' one of the girls quipped. 'I'm just plain old Dorothy Miller from Winnipeg!'

In the ensuing laughter, another girl said to Seffy, 'Take no notice of sourpuss, there. We're delighted to meet you. Any friend of Teddy's is a friend of ours!'

A few introductions were made. The girl who'd spoken to her was called Juliet, then there was Laura and after that, too many others to remember. More young people out on the town – chaps, as well as girls – were joining the group now, hugging and exclaiming as they recognised pals and fellow Canadians.

Finally, the group moved off, meandering slowly down the street.

Seffy gathered that the girls were over here with the Canadian Red Cross. They must be nurses.

'We've come to be near our husbands, as well as to do our bit for the war effort,' one of them told her.

They were all married, then, and they seemed awfully grown-up. They spoke in loud, clear voices and their accents were, like the rest of them, rather glamorous. Seffy wasn't easily intimidated but for a while, amongst these women, she was a little lost for words.

They were talking about British girls who were marrying *their* men 'left, right and centre'.

'They think Canada is going to be like the States,' one of the girls said. 'They've seen the States in movies – the big cars, the houses with refrigerators and servants – and they think Canada is the same.'

'And isn't it?' Seffy asked.

'No, not at all. Sure, we have big cities too but a lot of Canada is rural – it's prairie land – and those girls might find themselves living in a shack, with no electricity or running water.'

'It sounds like one of our billets,' Seffy muttered but the girl had turned away.

Seffy found herself at the back of the crowd standing next to a quieter girl. She was dark-haired, pretty and small, with elfin features and she looked a little anxious.

'Not worried about the raids, are you?' Seffy asked. 'There's truly no need. It's surprising how quickly one gets used to them.'

'Yeah, I lived here for a little while,' the girl replied. 'I'm not real keen on London, I must admit. My sister – that's her there, the loud one – she adores it here. It's a mighty fine city, but I guess I'm more of a country girl at heart.'

'Oh, me too!' Seffy said.

There wasn't time to continue their conversation. Someone slapped the girl on the shoulder and said, 'Come on, change of plan. We're heading out to the Beaver Club!'

Percy and Teddy had reappeared. Teddy slipped his arm through Seffy's, just as the girl turned to her and asked, 'Are you coming too? You'll like it!'

The Beaver Club was just off Trafalgar Square and it turned out to be a 'home from home' for Canadian servicemen and women.

Teddy had clearly been here before.

'They have lounges for everything,' he explained when they arrived. 'Billiards, darts, table tennis, chess, cards and a writing room, where the chaps can write letters home, and a reading room full of newspapers from all over Canada.'

'They can even get a haircut,' Percy added. 'Or have their clothes repaired.'

It was impressive. Especially the canteen. There were rows of metal containers, each filled with delicious-looking food: meat and gravy, piles of potatoes and vegetables. Seffy inhaled. It smelled divine.

There was more food here than the whole Blantyre camp had eaten for their Christmas dinner. She couldn't remember the last time she'd seen such a marvellous spread. Probably at someone's wedding before the war.

If only she could stuff piles of it into her handbag and take it back for Jean and the Lost Girls.

Teddy was laughing. 'Your tongue's almost hanging out, Seffy. Shall we see you in a little while then? Why don't you go and tuck in and we'll see you later in the lounge? There's dancing in there. You can hear the music from here.'

He pointed down a corridor and Seffy nodded, not taking her eyes off the food.

She picked up a plate from the stack and moved to where a girl in a white apron was poised in front of the food, wielding a huge metal serving spoon.

'What can I getcha, honey?' she said.

Golly, even the serving staff were Canadian. It was as though they'd imported part of Canada to London, lock, stock and barrel.

'Might I have a bit of everything?' Seffy asked. 'But I'm not actually in the Canadian forces, as you can probably tell. But—' she turned to see Teddy and Percy looking back at her, amused looks on their faces '—I am here with some Canadian friends. If that's all right?'

'Sure, that's fine!'

'Jeez, Miss, you look like you haven't eaten in a month of

Sundays!' a passing uniformed soldier said, as Seffy sat at a table with her plate piled high.

She had a mouthful of chicken and had to quickly swallow it before she could reply. 'Some of us are on rations, you know!'

She felt rather like a poor relation, which was ridiculous. This was her country and yet, in this Beaver Club she felt as though she'd entered another world. There was enough food here to, quite literally, feed an army.

It was the end of the night and Seffy had enjoyed herself although she'd eaten so much that she'd struggled to dance.

She was ready for bed. She'd had a busy couple of days and it was all catching up with her.

Everyone staggered out onto the street and there were fond farewells and cabs were hailed.

Seffy hadn't had another chance to talk to the dark-haired Canadian girl – their paths hadn't crossed again all night – but now they found themselves standing next to one another on the pavement. They shook hands and wished each other farewell.

'I do beg your pardon. Remind me of your name again,' Seffy said, embarrassed that they'd probably been introduced but there'd been so many new faces and names, she'd forgotten.

'My name? Oh, it's Miranda!'

The girl's chum was laughing and trying to drag her towards a waiting taxi.

'Very nice to meet you,' Seffy said. 'I'm—'

'Oh, I know who you are!' Miranda said. 'Teddy told us! Now wait – let me get this right. Lady Percival. No?'

Seffy laughed and Miranda joined in. The girl was, Seffy realised, more than a little tipsy.

'Persephone,' Seffy said. 'It's a bit of a mouthful, as your friend said earlier but—'

'Oh, Dorothy's no friend of mine!' Miranda said, slurring her words a little.

She squealed, as her pal grabbed her around the waist and told her, mock-sternly, 'You're coming with us right now!'

'Guess I'd better go!' Miranda said.

She climbed a little unsteadily into the taxi after her friend, and once inside, she wound down the window. As the taxi pulled away from the kerb, she waved at Seffy.

'My real name's Miranda,' she called out. 'But all my friends call me Missy!'

Seffy gave a jolt of surprise. Had she said 'Missy'? How strange! That was the same name as Callum's fiancée.

She was being silly. It didn't mean anything, of course. Missy was probably a commonplace name in Canada, like Margaret or Joan over here. But still, it was an odd coincidence. Seffy felt suddenly rather unsettled.

She wished she'd had the chance to ask Miranda whereabouts in Canada she came from. She had a sudden urge to know.

'What's up, Seff? You look like you've seen a ghost!'

It was Teddy. He'd placed his hand gently on her forearm and she'd jumped. Goodness, she was nervy. What was the matter with her?

He followed her gaze down the street. 'Game gals, aren't they?'

She had to agree. They'd voluntarily come halfway around the world and into a war zone. It was awfully brave. They could've stayed in Canada and done their bit for the war packing parcels for POWs.

As for 'Missy', she really shouldn't let it bother her. It couldn't possibly be the same girl.

She'd always imagined Callum's fiancée to be homely. The kind of girl who'd started a bottom drawer when she was ten years old and was simply waiting for her man to come home from the war, so they could marry.

He'd never described her like that – he'd never described her at all – but that's how Seffy imagined her. She'd be too feeble to get on a boat and sail across the Atlantic.

The girl Seffy had met tonight – Miranda or Missy or whatever she'd called herself – hadn't been quite as brash or bold as the others but Seffy imagined she had an inner strength.

Shame they hadn't been able to talk for longer. She'd rather liked her.

Chapter Thirty-Eight

Aberdeenshire, Scotland

'Where's Seffy?' Isobel asked, when Jean arrived at The Drover's Inn on Saturday night. There'd been no sign of Alec at his usual table when she'd arrived, so she'd bought herself a drink and gone straight to the back of the pub.

The Lost Girls had been so grateful the other night when they'd realised how Jean had stuck up for them and, as Eileen put it, 'Got McAllister off our backs', that they'd insisted she join them for a game of darts tonight.

'We'll treat you to one of our free drinks!' Isobel had said. 'And as you're good at adding up, you can be scorer.'

Jean wasn't sure darts was that complicated. Did you need to be a measurer to calculate the score? But she couldn't see any harm in joining them.

'All right,' she'd said. 'Count me in.'

Rona had nudged her. 'Very funny! Jean's made a joke!'

Now, Isobel was looking for Seffy over Jean's shoulder. She daren't reveal that Seffy was in London. It would only stir up discontent. Heaven only knew how long Seffy's absence would remain a secret, though. Mrs Harris knew, for one, and she was hardly the soul of discretion.

Jean crossed her fingers behind her back. 'Seffy couldn't come. She's poorly. Touch of influenza.'

She hated lying but fortunately, the girls – self-obsessed at the best of times – were having too much fun to worry about Seffy. Apart from Isobel's enquiry and a half-hearted 'Aw, shame' when Jean mentioned the flu, no one else even noticed she was missing.

Jean leaned against the back wall and watched, as darts thudded into the board every few seconds.

The auld fellas, rather than begrudging the Lost Girls' presence, seemed to be relishing it. They didn't even mind Peggy barking at everyone like a sergeant major on a parade ground.

'You goin' to have a go?' Tich asked Jean.

'I've never played before,' she admitted.

'Doesnae matter. None of us – apart from Peggy – are much cop. You cannae be worse than Eileen. She's a chucker.'

'I am,' Eileen agreed. 'I just throw it and hope for the best!'

'JEAN! Come and have a go!' Myrtle said.

One of the men held out a dart. 'Come on, lass. Stand on the oche, straight onto the board. Aye, that's the way. Aim just to the left of the bullseye, where the eight and the sixteen meet.'

To Jean's surprise, all three darts landed where they were supposed to. It was rather a thrill; she seemed to have the knack.

'Beginner's luck,' she said modestly, as everyone congratulated her.

She was conscious that, where darts were concerned, Peggy considered herself Queen Bee and sure enough, she soon had something to say.

'It's because you took ages, Jean. Do that in a match an' you'd be disqualified. It's one thing lining the dart up but you measured the distance and worked it all out afore you threw!'

Jean shrugged and exchanged a smile with Tich. She was a measurer, that was what she did.

Later, during a break from the game, the girls asked Peggy

how she was getting on at the saw mill.

'How do you find Mr Reid?' Jean asked.

'All right,' Peggy said. 'He's one of them conchie doodahs. The other fellas won't speak to him but I do and he sticks up for me. Not that I need him to, mind.'

'How does he stick up for you?' Rona asked.

'He tells the fellas to have more respect and not to curse so much because there's a lady present.'

'A lady? Who's that then?' Tich asked, making everyone – including Peggy – laugh.

'Why won't the fellas talk to him?' Myrtle asked. Clearly, Mr Burke's instruction about not talking to conchies hadn't registered with the Lost Girls.

'They think he's a coward because he's no' joined up,' Peggy replied.

'And what about Mr Galbraith?' Jean asked. 'What's his excuse for not enlisting?' She knew his position as head sawyer was probably reserved but she wanted to hear what the girls thought.

'He says he's medically unfit for service,' Peggy said.

'Medically unfit?' Rona laughed. 'Bet that means flat feet!'

'Or ingrowing toenails!' Isobel said.

'Or dandruff!' Tich said. 'Or—' she laughed so much she couldn't speak for a minute. 'No, I cannae say it!'

'You have to tell us now, Tich!' Jean said.

'PILES!' she screeched.

Alec arrived in the middle of the girls' hysterics, holding a pint of beer.

'What's so funny?' he asked.

'They're being awful rude about your boss!' Jean said.

Alec smiled. 'Very pleased to hear it. But take care. He and his lady friend have just come in. They'll be coming through any minute. Galbraith likes to throw a few arrows on a Saturday night.'

The game had started up again and there was an ever-increasing chorus of cheers and groans, as fellas and lassies took it in turns to play.

Alec took a seat in the corner, where he had a good view of the board.

'Do you play?' Jean asked him.

'I'll gi' you two guesses.'

She could've kicked herself. Of course, being a conchie, he wouldn't be allowed.

'Would you like to?' she said.

'Now you're rubbing salt into the wound, Jean! Sure I would but—' he shrugged. 'They'd never let me. I'm only allowed to watch!' There wasn't a trace of self-pity in his voice.

Jean sat down next to him.

'I've been thinking about what you said the other night. About my moral compass and everything,' she said.

'Aye?'

'The thing is, I don't think ma thoughts are fully formed. No, dunnae laugh. I'm not sure what I think about so many things. But you seem so clear on what you believe in and what you will and won't do.'

'But I'm not!' He twisted his pint glass on the table. 'When France fell and it seemed likely we were next, I felt terrible. I have to join up now, I told myself …' he tailed off.

'But you didnae,' Jean prompted. She didn't want him to stop talking.

He looked at her with soulful eyes. 'I couldn't. I dunnae want to fight, Jean. No one has the right to kill another person, I strongly believe that. War's not the answer.' He raised a finger. 'And I know you're gonna say, what is the answer, and I don't know! I lie awake at night, trying to work it all out. I honestly have no idea.'

Jean nodded. At least he was being honest. Aw, but it was so interesting; she could talk like this forever.

'Could you have gone to jail? For refusing to enlist?' she asked.

He shook his head. 'That battle was won by the men in the last

238

war. Hardly any conchies go to jail now. But when I went before the tribunal, to plead my case, they said if I wasnae gonna fight, I had to do my bit in other ways. Not unreasonably.' He smiled and raised his glass at her. 'Working in a saw mill, for example.'

'JEAN!' Peggy yelled. 'It's your turn. Put your fella down for a minute and come up here!'

Jean turned scarlet. The whole pub must've heard. What if Alec thought she'd told the lassies they were courting? Oh ma God, she wanted to die.

She made her go on the darts last as long as possible – ignoring Peggy's impatient tutting – so she didn't have to return to Alec's table straight away.

She threw the darts well, again. It wasnae just beginner's luck. She really could do this. Everyone said so.

'Would you like to join the team?' one of the auld fellas asked.

'What team?' Jean asked.

'The mixed league darts team for The Drover's Inn,' Peggy said. 'But you'll have to speed up, mind!'

'What d' you say?' the auld fella asked. 'No one can touch Peggy, of course, but we need another good player.' He gave Jean a gummy smile. The game had stopped. Everyone was waiting for her reply.

Afterwards, she wondered how she'd had the nerve to say it but she was emboldened by a few port and lemons and by her sudden loyalty to someone who, despite the odds, was now a good pal.

'I will join your team – ta very much for asking – but only on one condition,' she said. She glanced at Alec, sitting in the corner. 'That Mr Reid is allowed to play darts here.'

There was a shocked silence, then all the men put in their two pennyworth.

'Over ma dead body!'

'I'll no' play with the likes of him!'

'It's no' right!'

Jean felt her face burning. She wished Seffy were here; Seffy

239

would've backed her up.

Alec was shaking his head and waving his hand, telling her not to do this but she'd started now.

'Listen to you all!' she said. 'You're like bullies in the playground!'

If the Lost Girls started sniggering now, she'd lose her nerve but they were quiet. Peggy had even stepped a few feet nearer, so that she was standing at her shoulder.

'We're none of us perfect,' Jean went on. 'And when this war is over we'll all have to look into our hearts and ask ourselves the same questions: Did I do enough? Did I do what was right?'

She looked at Mrs Harris, standing next to Mr Galbraith. Mrs Harris bowed her head and shuffled a few inches away from him.

'And that's for Him to judge, not us,' Jean said.

'That's all well and good, lass,' one of the men said, 'but the conchie still cannae play.' He held up a dart. 'Now, who's turn is it?'

Jean slunk back to the table where Alec was sitting. She felt foolish.

'Thanks for trying,' he said, 'but they'll never change their minds about me. In my home village, people turn their backs on me when I walk down the street. Hey, I didn't realise you were so religious, Jean. All that "He will judge us" business was very impressive.'

She shrugged. 'To tell the truth, I'm not religious but … it sounded all right, didn't it?'

He gave a firm nod. 'Aw, but you've sacrificed your place on the team for me.'

'It doesnae matter,' Jean said. 'I'm still glad I did it.'

Alec smiled and raised his glass at her. 'We'll make a rebel of you yet, Jean.'

Chapter Thirty-Nine

London, England

On Saturday night, Seffy, Percy and Teddy were planning another night out on the town.

Bertie had been obliged to return to his unit but Emerald said she'd come too, as a last hurrah before she was dispatched to Salisbury with the baby.

'Are we meeting up with the Canadian gals?' Seffy asked Teddy. She'd like to speak to Miranda – alias 'Missy' again and set her mind at rest.

'No, I didn't arrange anything,' he said. 'Sorry, if I'd known you were keen, I would've. But never mind, we may well bump into them. They tend to hang around the same venues as us. We'll keep an eye out!'

Emerald and Seffy linked arms as they walked along the pavement, giggling and exchanging confidences. It was like the good old days, when, as debutantes, London had been their playground.

Seffy wondered whether she should tell Emerald about her encounter with Missy last night and how it had sent her into a spin. It couldn't possibly be Callum's fiancée, could it? She was being silly and Emerald would surely tell her so.

241

But, on second thoughts, Emerald might roll her eyes and accuse Seffy of being obsessed with 'the Canadian'. It would ruin the whole evening. After yesterday's lecture on the subject, she felt inclined never to mention Callum to her friend ever again.

No, she should put the whole matter out of her mind and focus on enjoying herself. She was out on the town, for goodness sake, with her best chum, her darling brother and dear Teddy. Heaven only knew when she might get the chance to do this again.

She squeezed Emerald's arm.

'What's that for?' Emerald asked, laughing.

'Just to say, it's so lovely to be with you. I'm having a ball!'

They moved from one dance hall to another and Seffy didn't sit out all night. It was so much fun, twirling around the dance floor with Percy and Teddy and with other dashing chaps who cut in and asked if they might have the pleasure. This was what it was to be young and alive! She'd almost forgotten what it felt like.

It had gone midnight before she finally had to stop dancing.

'Golly, you lot have worn me out!' she said. 'And I don't tire easily! Shall we catch our breath for a few minutes, Emerald?'

They sat at one of the tables at the back of the dance hall, while Teddy and Percy went off to get more drinks.

When Teddy returned, alone, he looked at Seffy with concern.

'I say, are you quite all right, old girl?' he asked, as he placed two G&Ts on the table.

'I'm a little tired, that's all,' she said.

'You don't seem yourself, somehow. You've got a whacking lump on your head and every time you move, I can see you wince, as though you're in pain.'

It was true, her legs and midriff were aching – presumably from skiing all that way– and she still had the bump on her head.

Teddy was the only one who'd noticed.

'Unless it's me you're pulling faces at,' he said. 'Is that it? Am I being terribly crass or dull?'

Dear Teddy, he cared about her so much and he could be so

funny at times.

'Crass or dull?' she said. 'You? Never!' He pulled a funny face and she laughed. 'Oh, Teddy, I do love you!'

He looked instantly hopeful and then ecstatic.

'Do you? Do you really, Seffy? Oh, God, I'm so glad because I feel exactly the same way! I love you too! Always have, always will!'

His words were tumbling out. She couldn't stop him. All she could do was listen in horror.

What had she said? She wished she could take it all back. It had been a throwaway comment; the kind of thing she might've said to her brothers or to Emerald. She didn't love Teddy in *that* way.

'Oopsie, just noticed, there's no ice in that G&T,' he said, looking into one of the glasses. 'I'll nip back to the bar!'

Perhaps he was embarrassed or wanted to collect his thoughts. In any case, he'd gone.

Emerald rested her hand on Seffy's arm and leaned into her. 'You're not interested in Teddy, are you? Not in that way. Sorry, I couldn't help overhearing. You know, you really should tell him he misunderstood you. Nip it in the bud now, Seffy. That's my advice.'

She flinched. She couldn't. How would she even start to say something like that?

'You can say it kindly,' Emerald said.

Emerald was right, she should tell him but how could she? The moment had passed. Tomorrow, or the next day, he might be up in the air again, fighting the Luftwaffe.

She couldn't be that cruel.

Teddy was coming back from the bar now and Seffy held her breath. She could feel Emerald's gaze on her, urging her to do the right thing.

But – oh, the relief – he was with Percy and a couple of RAF chaps they must've met at the bar. She couldn't say anything now.

With a bit of luck, it had been the drink talking and by the morning, Teddy would have forgotten he'd ever said it.

All thoughts of the faux pas with Teddy went out of the window when, as they were leaving the dance hall, they bumped into the Red Cross girls again, out on the street.

They were in a similar, large group to the night before, which included Canadian servicemen. Seffy heard their booming Canadian accents way before they appeared.

It was awfully dark and there were so many people milling about that it took a minute to spot Missy in the crowd. Seffy recognised the loud, tall girl first – the one Missy had pointed out as her sister. Missy was standing behind her, with the friend who'd hustled her into the cab the night before.

'Hello again!' Seffy said, falling into step beside them. She could hear Emerald calling her name from further down the street but this was too important an opportunity to miss. She'd catch up with Emerald just as soon as this had been resolved.

'We met last night, do you remember?' Seffy said. 'I didn't get chance to ask about the war work you're doing over here?'

'Hi!' Missy said. 'Sure, I remember you. Good to see you again! We're over here with the Red Cross—'

'But we're not nurses!' the other girl said.

They laughed.

'Everyone thinks we're nurses,' Missy said, 'but we're working with injured servicemen in a military hospital in Hampshire. We're only in London for the weekend.'

She seemed in a better mood than last night. She was certainly chattier. Perhaps she'd had a few more drinks.

'What about you?' the other girl asked Seffy. 'Are you doing war work?'

'If you're allowed to tell us, that is!' Missy said and giggled. 'We were talking about you in the cab home last night. We wondered what you did. My sister said you were a society girl but I said no, you were probably a spy!'

'Or a movie star,' the other girl said.

Seffy was flattered: they'd been talking about her. As she wasn't in uniform, it was only natural that they might wonder what she did.

'I could hardly admit it, if I were a spy!' she said. 'But I am involved in war work actually. I'm based up in Scotland as—'

'SCOTLAND?' Missy screeched. Yes, she was definitely more than a little tipsy.

She spun around to face Seffy. 'Say, you must know my fiancé! He worked up in Scotland too. In Morayshire!'

Seffy's heart skipped a beat.

'He was lumbering up there,' Missy said.

Seffy's throat had gone dry. She swallowed, feeling herself start to sway.

But this was ridiculous. There were thousands of Canadian foresters in Morayshire. Missy must think everyone knew everyone in little old Blighty.

She laughed. 'I hardly think—'

'Staff Sergeant Callum Fraser! That's his name. Did you ever come across him?'

Suddenly everything seemed far away, as though Seffy were viewing it all through a misty pane of glass. She could hear noises – someone calling her name and another sound that she couldn't place but that seemed vaguely familiar.

It *was* her! This was *the* Missy – Callum's fiancée – standing in front of her, in the middle of London.

And she was beautiful and brave, and she'd come all this way to be with him.

Percy grabbed Seffy's arm, making her jump. 'There you are, Sis. You nearly gave me heart failure. Thought we'd lost you! Didn't you hear the sirens? Come on, quick! We've got to get to the shelter!'

He tugged her arm but she resisted and turned, straining her neck to look back. There was no sign of the Canadian girls. It was as though she'd imagined them.

'Where've they gone?' she said.

Teddy was there now, taking her other arm. 'The Canucks have gone that way but there's a shelter down here that's nearer.'

'Do hurry, Seffy!' Emerald was saying. And then, to Teddy, 'She's being awfully strange. Do you think she's quite all right?'

No, she wasn't all right. She'd had the most awful shock. She didn't think she'd be all right ever again.

Chapter Forty

Aberdeenshire, Scotland

By Monday morning, as Jean had anticipated, much of the snow had melted. There was still a thick covering on the hills but the roads were clear enough to cycle to the saw mill.

She was expecting to find a message from Mr Burke but if not, she'd telephone his office and ask whether they should start thinking about returning to work.

The Lost Girls wouldnae be happy but they couldn't really complain. They'd played a lot of darts over the past few days and – with the exception of Peggy – they'd had some unexpected leave on full pay. It was time to pick up their tools again.

While she was at the saw mill, Jean intended to kill two birds with one stone and find out how Peggy was getting on. Alec thought she was settling in all right, but she wanted to check for herself that Peggy wasn't causing trouble or driving Mr Galbraith to distraction.

It would make a good topic for her next report: 'Lumberjill Miss Gorman at the saw mill'. Aye, that'd do nicely. Because, after a great deal of soul searching, she'd decided not to report Seffy for going AWOL. She was due back from London tomorrow and despite Jean's initial concerns, she had to admit she'd coped all right in Seffy's absence.

Seffy had behaved badly but that didn't mean Jean had to do likewise. When she'd really thought about how much trouble Seffy would be in, if she'd blown the whistle on her, she couldnae do it.

It'd mean fudging her report but so be it. She'd already lied to anyone who'd asked, telling them Seffy was laid up with influenza. This was simply one more transgression to add to her growing list.

As she reached the saw mill, she spotted Alec heading out into the woods on the tractor and they waved at each other.

Peggy arrived as Jean was pushing open the double doors and followed her inside, trailing in clumps of snow on her boots.

It was quiet. The machinery hadn't started up yet.

Peggy was wrapped from head to toe in her overcoat, gloves, hat and scarf. Only her eyes were visible.

'Morning, Peggy,' Jean said. 'Can we have a wee chat before you start work?'

Peggy pulled down the scarf over her mouth. 'What, are ye checking up on me?'

'Not at all! But you've been here a fortnight now and I want to see how you're getting on. I have to write an official report, see.'

Peggy perked up.

'We could use Galbraith's office,' she said. 'He's allus the last to arrive, so he won't be needin' it for a wee while.'

They sat on either side of the desk. Jean pulled a notebook and pen out of her pocket and removed her coat. Peggy took off her woolly hat but kept the rest of her outdoor clothes on, as though she wasn't planning to stay.

'Now,' Jean said. 'How're you getting on? Are you learning a lot?'

'I'm learning a lot o' new curses!'

Jean frowned. 'Anything else?'

'I'm on the machinery now!' Peggy said.

'You're on the saws?'

'Aye! I get paid more. And it's more exciting than lugging timber around all day.'

Wasn't that rather too soon? Surely Peggy needed to gain more experience first? But Jean knew little about Peggy's job here. It was Seffy who'd discussed it with Mr Galbraith when Peggy started and, of course – Jean felt a flash of irritation – Seffy wasnae here.

'And once the snow clears,' Peggy went on, 'I'm to learn to drive the wee tractor. I'll get more money for that, too. Mr Reid is gonna teach me.'

Goodness, that was brave of him.

'Don't you have to be over twenty-one and have a licence?' Jean said. She was pouring cold water over Peggy's plans but you had to be realistic about these things.

'Nae problem! I'm twenty-two! And so long as I stay off main roads, I dunnae need a licence, Mr Reid says.'

'That's excellent!' Jean said, remembering she was meant to praise the girls. 'Good for you.'

'It's awful dangerous, mind. You have to watch out for stumps and uneven ground 'cos if you catch the underneath o' the tractor, it can stop sudden, like, and you'll be catapulted off!'

'Gracious me!'

Peggy was getting into her stride now. 'Aye, and, if a tree's too heavy, the tractor'll rear up on its back wheels and topple backwards onto the driver. I could be crushed to death!' She looked at Jean. 'Are you no' writing all this down?'

Jean hastily made a few squiggles on her pad.

'You will be careful, won't you, Peggy?' she said.

It sounded as though Peggy was trying to run before she could walk. Jean should probably have a word with Alec and Mr Galbraith and see if they could rein her in.

'Now, tell me what else you do here …' Jean said.

Half an hour later, when Mr Galbraith turned up, Peggy hastened from the office to start work. That was a good sign, Jean thought.

At least she wasn't dragging her heels.

There'd been no message from Mr Burke, so Jean asked if she might use the telephone.

'And then, if you can spare me a couple o' minutes, I'd like to ask you about Peggy,' she said and received a grunt in reply.

She'd only just been connected to Mr Burke's office, when an ear-piercing shriek rang out from deep within the saw mill.

Mr Galbraith froze for a second, grabbing the edge of the desk and staring in horror at Jean. Then he leaped to his feet and ran out. Jean dropped the receiver and followed him.

The saws were running now and the sound was deafening.

Peggy, looking very young and pale, was staggering towards them. She was cradling her right hand.

She had to shout over the noise of machinery. 'I THINK I'VE CHOPPED MA THUMB OFF!'

Jean's stomach plunged. She couldn't be serious. If this was Peggy's idea of a joke …

'If you really had, you couldnae stand there and say that,' Mr Galbraith said, with a sneer.

Some instinct for self-preservation made Jean look away, as Peggy removed her top hand.

It was just as well, because she must've been telling the truth.

Jean leaped clear – with a scream – as Mr Galbraith's head rolled back and he fainted, collapsing heavily at her feet.

Pandemonium broke out, as fellas came running from all directions, in a panic. But none of them seemed to know what to do. They needed Alec, Jean thought. Where was he?

A couple of wee laddies flung themselves to the floor and fussed around Mr Galbraith, who was out cold.

'NOT HIM!' Jean yelled, pointing at Peggy. 'HER!'

Peggy was still standing motionless, gripping her hand and staring at it in disbelief as bright red blood splashed onto the floor.

'SOMEONE TURN OFF THE MACHINES, SO WE CAN HEAR OURSELVES THINK!' Jean shouted.

'She needs to put her arm in the air,' an auld fella said.

'She needs one of those tourniquets!' another said. 'But I cannae do it.'

Jean stepped over Mr Galbraith and put a comforting arm around Peggy's shoulder. 'That's it, squeeze your hand tight. You'll be all right.'

'It doesnae hurt, that's the odd thing,' Peggy said.

Jean felt sick but she was doing her best not to show it. 'You're probably in shock,' she said.

The saw mill suddenly fell quiet: the machines had been turned off.

Alec stormed inside, his face full of concern. He leaped over Mr Galbraith's prone body without giving it a second glance.

'What's happened?' he said. 'Why are the machines off?'

Peggy showed him her hand and an auld fella looking over her shoulder let out a groan.

Alec didn't flinch. He closed his hand gently around Peggy's.

'Someone bring out a chair!' he yelled. 'And I need clean rags. Quick!'

The chair appeared in seconds and Alec held Peggy's shoulders to steady her as she lowered herself onto it. He must be afeared she was about to pass out, Jean thought.

Someone else brought rags and thrust them at Alec, who started to wrap them tightly around the injured hand.

Jean looked away, as the blood soaked through the first rags in seconds.

'Where is it?' Alec asked, looking around at the floor. 'Where's the thumb?'

Jean slapped her hand to her forehead. Ma God, of course. They'd all been so busy running around like headless chickens, no one had thought about that.

'I cannae stomach looking for it,' one fella said.

'Me neither!' said another.

'Aw, for goodness sake!' Jean said. 'I'll find it. Which machine were you on, Peggy?'

She found it without too much effort: a strangely white little nubbin resting on the side of the machine. She tried not to look too closely and pulled out her handkerchief – clean that morning – and used it to pick up the thumb.

'I have it!' she called out. 'Someone find me something to put it in!'

Alec, in the meantime, had run outside and returned with a huge handful of snow. They put the thumb, still wrapped in the handkerchief, into a box and packed the snow around it.

'What now?' Jean asked.

'I'll take her to the cottage hospital, on the tractor,' Alec said, helping Peggy to her feet.

'But there's still so much snow everywhere!'

'I'll just have to dig us out if we get stuck. Go and telephone them, Jean. Tell them what's happened and that we're on our way.'

Back in Mr Galbraith's office, Jean's knees started to shake. She had to sit down and put her head in her hands. Aw, this was useless, but she needed to pull herself together before she could even think about telephoning the hospital. She couldnae believe what'd just happened.

This was her fault. She'd jinxed everything, by being smug and telling herself nothing bad had happened in Seffy's absence.

A strange buzzing noise made her look up. The telephone receiver was dangling on its wire where she'd dropped it and someone was evidently still on the line.

She picked it up. It was Mr Burke, demanding to know what had happened.

'There's been an accident,' Jean said, with a trembling voice and then the whole story came out.

'What in hell's name was the lass doing on a saw?' he said. 'Was she unsupervised?'

Jean opened and closed her mouth. She didn't know.

'Meet me at the saw mill at midday,' Mr Burke said. 'I shall bring the welfare officer and I expect you, Galbraith and Miss Mills to be there and to explain yerselves!'

Chapter Forty-One

By a stroke of luck, when Seffy's train finally arrived at Ballamar, there was a Bedford lorry parked outside the station.

A group of lumberjills were helping the railway chaps to unload the timber, and when Seffy explained she was also in the WTC, they happily agreed to give her a lift home.

She retrieved the skis from the stationmaster's store, relieved that she wouldn't need to use them. Although there was still plenty of snow on the higher ground, she'd seen from the train that the snow had melted from much of the roads.

'Where've you been?' one of the girls asked, as they sat together in the back of the truck.

'I've been in London for a few days,' Seffy said, hoping this wasn't going to turn into a long conversation. She really wasn't in the mood.

'LONDON? That's a way! Did you set off last week?'

Seffy yawned. 'Something like that. I'm hoping for a little peace and quiet now I'm back.'

She'd set off yesterday, glad to escape Emerald's anxious enquiries about her health. She'd tried to act as normal as possible, but after the shock of Saturday night, she knew she hadn't been her usual self.

She hadn't told Emerald about her discovery and not only because it would confirm Emerald's bad opinion of Callum: she simply couldn't bear to say it out loud.

She'd been quiet and withdrawn for the rest of her stay and had tried to pass it off as fatigue, but Emerald hadn't been fooled.

'You're not worried about that Teddy business, are you?' Emerald had said. 'Why don't you write to him and explain how you feel? So that he's not under any illusion that you're going to do something silly like marry him.'

Seffy had assured Emerald that she would write to Teddy once she was home but she couldn't think about that now. Her head was spinning.

At least she'd managed to sleep for much of the long journey north. It had been heaven to lapse into oblivion for a while and forget how Callum Fraser had played her for a fool.

'If you've been away, you won't have heard about yesterday's accident at the saw mill,' the lumberjill sitting beside her said.

Seffy's stomach swooped away.

'Wha … what accident?' She could barely get the words out.

No one knew for sure what had happened; they'd only heard rumours.

'I heard someone lost an arm,' one of the girls said.

'No, it was worse than that!' another said. 'I heard someone was killed!'

They dropped her off at the top of the lane and despite being weighed down with her haversack and the skis and poles, Seffy almost flew down the hill.

She dumped the skis at the back door and burst into the kitchen.

Mrs Harris was sitting at the table, smoking a cigarette.

'What happened at the saw mill?' Seffy demanded, breathlessly.

Mrs Harris sighed. 'It was that wee lassie you put in there.'

Peggy! She might have known.

Mrs Harris blew out a plume of bluish smoke. 'She lost her thumb.'

'NOOO!' Seffy's haversack fell from her shoulder as her hands flew to her face. *Please say that wasn't true.*

'And that's not all.' Blast the woman, she was enjoying this. 'The weasel fella came and gave Jean and my – Mr Galbraith – an almighty dressing-down. "What did they think they were doin', allowing a lass on a saw like that?"'

'But Peggy wasn't supposed to be on the saws!' Seffy said.

'That's as mebbe. But she was and now—' Mrs Harris shrugged '—she's a digit down. And poor Jean had to bear the brunt of it from the weasel fella. She didnae tell on you, mind! She said you were in bed wi' the flu.'

Seffy swallowed. Peggy had been maimed, Burke had been there and Jean had had to take the blame for the accident. This was a complete nightmare.

She found Jean sitting on the settee in the front room, writing a letter. The coal fire was burning brightly. She looked up when Seffy came in but didn't speak. She looked hollow-eyed and sombre.

Seffy didn't quite know where to start.

'I'm so dreadfully sorry,' she said. 'I hear you got it in the neck from Burke. And poor Peggy! That's so terrible. How did it happen?'

Jean recounted the story in a monotone voice, as though she'd already told it a dozen times.

'She'd walked two miles from her lodgings in the freezing cold. I had a chat with her when she arrived and she still had her gloves and all her outdoor clothes on, then. When she started work on the saw, she says she forgot to take off the gloves.'

'Which – to be fair – Galbraith had warned her about,' Seffy murmured. She shook her head. 'I bet she was feeding in a log, it got caught in her glove and carried her hand into the saw?'

'Aye, that's it. It would've been worse without Alec's quick thinking. Feckless Mr Galbraith did nothing except pass out. But

Alec … he took charge. Thank God he was there.'

She looked at Seffy reproachfully. *Unlike you* was the clear implication.

'I hardly dare ask, but how is she?' Seffy said.

Jean shrugged. 'Put it this way, she won't be thumbing any lifts from now on. Not wi' that hand, anyway.'

Seffy grimaced. 'They couldn't fix it? Sew the thumb back on?'

'Nope, it was splintered. Alec told us when he got back from the hospital. The welfare officer said she could go home for a few days' compassionate leave. But she didnae want to. She's holed up at her billet and I expect the old dear's waitin' on her hand and foot.'

Seffy nodded. 'I'll go and see her later, if she's up to visitors.'

She threw herself down in an armchair and put her chin in her hands. She was close to tears.

'I feel dreadful. You were absolutely right, Jean, I should never have gone to London. I'm completely to blame.'

Jean's silent rebuke was almost unbearable.

But finally, she sighed and said, 'You weren't to know she'd go on the saw.'

'But I put her in the saw mill,' Seffy said. 'I didn't like her – she was too much trouble. I just wanted her out of the way. Out of sight, out of mind. I should've kept a closer eye on her.'

'Aye, but Peggy's wilful and determined. When she sets her mind to summat, it's hard to stop her. Rather like someone else, sitting not a million miles away.'

Jean had raised her eyebrows and there was the trace of a smile on her lips. Thank goodness.

'Guilty as charged,' Seffy said, quietly. 'Do you hate me? I wouldn't blame you.'

'I did hate you, aye, for a wee while. Especially when Mr Burke was tearing into me about the accident.'

Seffy winced. She could imagine. Jean was a good girl; she'd probably never had a ticking off like that before.

'What did Burke say?'

Jean rolled her eyes. 'Aw, he let us have it wi' both barrels – me and Mr Galbraith. Told us we were irresponsible, slack and negligent. Mr Galbraith got more stick than me. He's been given a written warning.'

'Quite right, too,' Seffy said. 'He's supposed to be in charge, after all. Thanks for covering for me and for taking the flack, Jean. I owe you.'

Jean shrugged. 'Aye, well, what's done is done. You got there all right then, on the skis?'

Goodness, that felt like a hundred years ago now. It was hard to believe it'd only been five days since she'd set off across the snow.

'Yes. I came a cropper at one point.' She pulled up her fringe to show Jean the bump. 'Think I might've knocked myself out. But otherwise, it was fine.'

'And how was London?'

How could she say it had been anything other than marvellous?

'Oh, yes … the christening was lovely and my chum was pleased I'd made the effort, so …'

This was awkward; they were making small talk. Seffy sensed that Jean was still annoyed with her but, being the good egg she was, she was doing her best not to show it.

She nodded at the letter on Jean's lap. 'Who're you writing to?'

'The Land Army Benevolent Fund. Look, here—' Jean picked up a magazine lying next to her and passed it to Seffy. 'I read about it in *The Land Girl*. The fund provides money for girls finding it difficult to manage. I'm applying for the Lost Girls. They struggle on their paltry wages. Even Peggy, who earns more than the rest. That's why she was so desperate to work on the machinery: she wanted more money. And now she's paid the price.' Jean blew out her cheeks. 'Anyhow, I thought it was worth a try.'

Seffy nodded and flicked through the magazine.

'Good idea. You're a whizz at letter writing, Jean. If anyone can get that funding, you can. Oh, what's this?'

A piece of paper, covered in Jean's neat handwriting, had slipped out from between the pages and fluttered to the floor. Seffy bent down and picked it up. A letter – no, a report of some kind – addressed to Miss McEwen, of all people!

She spotted her own name and frowned as she read,

> *... and Miss Mills left the area and travelled to London, explicitly disobeying orders received from HQ regarding avail-ability to start work.*

She blinked, hardly able to believe her eyes.

'Have you been telling tales ... on me?' Her voice faltered as she looked at Jean's panic-stricken face. 'Wait, you have!'

'Noo!'

'Jean, I don't have rocks for brains! I recognise a report about *me* when I see one!'

Jean was red-faced and flustered. 'No, I mean, that was a draft. I must've forgotten to burn it. I burned the final version—'

'There was a final version?'

'I was never gonna send it!'

Jean stood up and tried to grab the paper but Seffy put it behind her back.

'Why would you do such a thing?' she asked.

Jean's face had crumpled; she was almost in tears.

'Miss McEwen made me promise to write a fortnightly report, detailing what we – what you, specifically – had been up to,' she said.

Seffy gasped. This was treachery!

'She wouldnae let me come, otherwise. I felt truly rotten but I needed to get away from Blantyre and it was more money—'

'Oh, you Judas! You sold me for thirty silver coins!'

'I did no such thing! I thought better me than someone else.'

'Someone else who might've actually been a friend? Miss McEwen told you to report on me and you didn't think to tell me?'

Jean shook her head and threw herself back down on the settee. 'But I've not told her anything she could hold agin you! It's been hellish difficult! I've not told her about the strike, or the grief we've had from the landowner, or the problems wi' the lassies—'

'And what about this?' Seffy pulled the now-crumpled report out from behind her back and waved it in the air.

'I wasnae going to send it! You have to believe me! I was cross wi' you and it helped, writing it all down Here, gi' it to me and I'll put it on the fire.'

Betrayed again. First by Callum, now by Jean. What had she done to deserve this?

'I thought we were a team!' Seffy said, ignoring Jean's offer to burn the report. Goodness, she felt quite choked up. 'We could've managed this together, if you'd only told me. We might – heaven forbid – have had a bit of fun with it! Oh, but I forgot, Jean, you don't understand fun!'

Jean's eyes flared. 'I do! I like fun as much as the next girl! But I'm not frivolous and daft! I don't run away from ma duty! I've got a black mark against my name for the first time in my life because of YOU!'

She burst into tears and, moments later, Seffy did the same.

Mrs Harris – who must've been listening at the door – bustled in.

'Cripes!' she said. 'There's enough fighting in the world wi' out you two joining in! Here – and here!' She pulled a not entirely clean handkerchief from each of her cardigan sleeves, like a magic trick, and handed them one each. Seffy didn't dare refuse hers.

Mrs Harris waited until they'd stopped crying and dried their tears.

'Are you done with your bawling now,' she said, 'or do I have to bang yer heads together?'

Seffy touched the bump on her forehead. 'Please don't.'

'Are ye pals again now?' Mrs Harris said.

Goodness, this was like being back at school.

Jean gave Seffy a watery smile. She managed a watery smile back.

'Because ye cannae share a bed and no' speak to one another,' Mrs Harris said. 'I did it myself for years and I dunnae recommend it!'

Their screaming match had been like a thunderstorm: sudden and loud but now it was over, the air definitely felt clearer.

'Friends?' Seffy asked.

'Friends,' Jean confirmed. 'But – there's one thing that's unavoidable. I'm sorry, Seffy. I won't mention London, of course, but I'll have to put Peggy's accident in ma report. Miss McEwen is bound to hear about it from Mr Burke.'

Seffy nodded. 'I understand, Jean. Do your worst! I'm joking! No, honestly, it's fine. It's no more than I deserve.'

Chapter Forty-Two

There was a letter on the kitchen table for Seffy the next morning. Jean hoped it'd cheer her up because she'd been awful quiet since her return from London. They'd made up after their row, but last night Seffy had hardly eaten any supper and she'd gone to bed early.

Jean wondered whether her low mood was solely down to that business with the report and Peggy's accident, or whether something had happened while she'd been in London.

Mrs Harris was stirring brose at the stove. 'I forgot to tell you yesterday, Miss Mills, but that letter came for you whilst you were away.'

Seffy brightened momentarily but her face fell again as she looked at the handwriting on the envelope. She opened it slowly and unfolded the letter.

'It's from him,' she said, dully.

'From your fella? The Canadian?' Jean asked.

Why didn't she seem pleased?

'Oh, yippee doo,' Seffy said in a flat voice. 'He's being redeployed to Scotland.'

'Redeployed? But that's good news, isn't it?'

'The bally nerve of him!' Seffy said, ignoring her and reading on. 'He wants to come and see me and deliver my Christmas present!'

She slammed the letter down on the table and yelled, 'Don't bother!' at it.

Jean and Mrs Harris exchanged alarmed looks across the kitchen. Perhaps that knock to the head had left Seffy a wee bit unhinged.

Jean didn't understand. This was the fella Seffy had been mad for. The one she'd wanted to move heaven and earth to be near.

'So … you dunnae want to see him?' she asked, tentatively. 'I didn't have much luck with those Canadian fellas myself, as you know. But I always thought yours seemed all right.'

Seffy stuffed the letter back into the envelope. 'Actually, I do want to see him but not in the way he expects. I want to tear him off a strip, Jean, tell him to stuff his stupid present and then never see him again as long as I live!'

'But why?'

'I discovered something when I was in London,' Seffy said. Her shoulders slumped. 'Oh, but I can't tell you, Jean. You'll think badly of me.'

Jean shrugged. 'I mightn't. If he's crossed you, then I'll be on your side. We're pals, after all, aren't we?'

Mrs Harris was placing steaming bowls of brose on the table in front of them now. 'And a trouble shared is a trouble halved!' she said.

'Has he met someone else?' Jean asked. It was the only thing she could think of.

Seffy huffed. 'He's always had someone else. Not just someone, but a fiancée. I've always known.'

Jean tried to make her face a mask. She took a dim view of that kind of behaviour, if she were honest, but her loyalty to Seffy was outweighing that now. She was surprised, though, that Seffy would settle for someone who wasn't free, when she could have her pick o' men.

'While she – his fiancée – was tucked safely away in Canada, there was always hope, you see,' Seffy said, sounding more sad than angry now. 'And I could put her to the back of my mind. But she's not in Canada any more: she's here. And by complete chance, I met her, in London!'

Jean gasped. 'You met her? The fiancée? And he hadn't told you she was here?'

'Not a word of it. Not even in that letter—' Seffy flicked a finger at it contemptuously.

'Mebbe it's a good thing you went to London, then,' Jean said. 'Because otherwise you might never have known.'

Poor Seffy, she was hurting. Of course, she was angry with the fella for stringing her along. But she must still have feelings for him, else she wouldn't be so upset.

Seffy pursed her lips. 'I hadn't thought of it like that. Perhaps that trip to London was meant to be.'

'Does he know how you feel about him?' Jean asked. Because it was obvious that Seffy still loved him.

Seffy shook her head. She looked defeated. 'Not in so many words but what does it matter, now …?'

'I know nothing about love,' Jean said. 'But I do know about facts. And if the fella doesnae have all the facts, then how can he make the right choice? Her or you?'

Seffy lifted up her spoon and immediately put it down again. 'Oh, Jean, that's sweet of you but he'd pick her over me, I know he would. You see, he made her a promise. He's committed to her.'

'I think you should be brave and tell him how you feel,' Jean said.

'A good Scottish laddie, that's what you both need!' Mrs Harris called out from the sink.

The girls raised their eyebrows at each other. They were hardly going to take advice on men from the likes of her.

'Turns out,' Seffy said, 'Callum's not the man I thought he was.

I played with fire, Jean, and I've been well and truly burned!' She exhaled. 'But better to find out now, I suppose, than …'

She trailed off and inclined her head towards Mrs Harris, obviously not wanting to discuss this further in front of her.

'Oh!' She'd clearly remembered something. 'On a jollier note, I've got something for you, Jean. I brought it back from London.' Seffy reached down and lifted a brown paper bag onto the table. 'Go on, open it!'

They were going to be late for work if they didn't get on wi' breakfast but Seffy was trying to cheer them both up and Jean didnae want to disappoint her. She reached into the paper bag and pulled out a box.

'What's that, then?' Mrs Harris asked, coming closer.

Jean read the label. 'It's an "Ann Barton Permanent Wave Set".'

'Isn't it a super idea?' Seffy said. 'We can perm your hair here and save the expense of going to a hairdressers! Rita Hayworth, eat your heart out!'

'Whatever will they think of next?' Mrs Harris said, nodding approvingly.

Seffy was so pleased with herself that Jean could only thank her and try to match Mrs Harris's enthusiasm.

'Ta very much! That's … aye, like you said, a super idea.'

In truth, she thought the kit looked complex and dangerous. No, she was quite happy to leave her hair as it was. It wasn't as though there was anyone around here she wanted to impress.

She would put the kit under the bed and pray that Seffy forgot all about it.

'Come on, then, Seffy,' Jean said. 'Let's eat up and get to work in that forest again! And remember, when you see the gang, you've had influenza!'

Chapter Forty-Three

The South Coast, England

Before Callum left for Scotland, he and Missy arranged to meet in their favourite little coastal town. She was starting to think of it as their place.

'Shucks, I can't go, I have to work that day,' Juliet had said when Missy told her the plan.

Missy had laughed. 'I don't need you to hold my hand. I'm a big girl now, Juliet, I can manage that journey alone!'

She'd gotten used to the British trains now. And as for the fellas – sure they still whistled and asked if she had a light, any excuse to talk to her – but she could handle them. The secret was to look purposeful, like she had somewhere to be. And she did; she had to be with Callum.

Sure, she couldn't pretend she didn't still have niggling worries about him. When was he gonna say something about the book or this 'S' person? If he was never going to mention them, she'd have a tough decision to make: whether to let it drive her crazy or let it go.

Callum had been over here a while now and of course he'd met all kinds of people. Missy didn't know what her man did every minute of every day but what girl did? As long as the trust was there. And mostly it was. Mostly, she trusted him with her life and her happiness.

If his head had been turned by a pretty face, there was nothing she could do about that. And one day, they'd be leaving here and they'd never come back. Whatever had happened, would be in the past. Right now, she had to think about her – their – future.

They'd found a real nice tea shop in town this time and a chatty waitress who made them smile and sat them at a good table in the window.

'Juliet says, if we get enough leave, me and her could travel up to Scotland,' Missy told Callum. 'You could show me around. I'd really like to see the place. It might be the only chance I ever get.'

They talked about Scotland and made plans for when she might visit. It was the best chat they'd had in a while.

Callum took off his jacket and wiped his forehead with the back of his hand. It sure was fuggy in here. Missy liked it but the windows were steamed up and it was too warm. He couldn't breathe.

He watched her across the table as she lifted the teapot and carefully poured them each another cup of tea.

She was a sweet girl and he sure did care about her. He wanted to protect her and make her happy.

But Seffy had tapped into some other part of him.

When he was with her, he could be himself, that was the only way he could describe it. He couldn't get her out of his head.

He worried that he'd inherited his pa's flaw; the flaw that had made Pa drink and yell and, most likely, have other women, too. Callum didn't wanna be that man.

'Mom and Dad send their love,' Missy said, glancing across at him. 'I got a letter yesterday.'

Callum nodded and smiled. 'Give 'em my best, won't you?'

Mike and Barbara were good people. Callum had always held Mike up as an example of the kind of man he'd like to be:

267

hardworking and respectable, a family man, one of the good guys.

'Looking forward to Scotland?' Missy asked, with a smile, as she passed him his cup.

There it was again: that guilty stabbing sensation in his chest. He hadn't thought about what he was gonna do or say when he got to Aberdeenshire and saw Seffy. He only knew that he needed to see her, face to face. Writing letters wasn't the same.

He wouldn't have even made this transfer request if Missy hadn't come over. She had no idea that she was the catalyst for his move back to Scotland.

'How long will you be there?' Missy asked, and he said he really didn't know. A few weeks. Not long.

It had been a whole month since the telephone conversation when Missy had asked about his ma's necklace. She hadn't broached the subject since. Maybe she'd changed her mind. Callum felt rotten though because although the line had been bad, he'd still been able to hear her. He'd been buying himself time. He'd had his own plans for that necklace. Missy's idea for turning it into a ring had come right outta the blue.

Missy placed both hands flat on the table and looked straight at him. 'Now,' she said, 'I wanted to talk to you about your ma's necklace, Callum.'

Ah, so she hadn't changed her mind, after all.

She explained how she'd like to have the necklace made into a ring, if he agreed, maybe with some extra gold added, but hopefully, it wouldn't be too dear.

It was everything he already knew but had to pretend to be hearing for the first time.

Callum took the necklace out of his pocket and placed it down on the table in front of her. 'There it is.'

Missy smiled and examined it. 'Oh, boy, I'd forgotten how pretty it is.'

She looked at him expectantly.

'Sure,' he said, 'we can do that, Missy. We can look see if there's a jewellers in town someplace. Maybe the nice waitress can tell us. Whatever you want, honey, that's what we'll do.'

He exhaled. It wasn't what he wanted but he felt better about everything now. He'd given Missy the choice.

'Whatever I want?' she asked, her eyes lighting up.

'Whatever you want.'

He had a bad feeling, like something was coming that he wasn't ready for.

She put her fingers on the necklace and slid it slowly back across the table towards him.

'You keep this,' she said. 'It shouldn't be changed; I see that now. I don't need a ring.'

'You don't?' Boy, she'd changed her mind awful sudden.

'No. Leastways, not that kind. We don't have to do everything all traditional, the old way. We're a modern couple, aren't we?'

Were they? Callum had no idea where this was going.

Missy leaned across the table and took his hands in hers. 'I know we can't do anything until you're back from Scotland, honey, but let's forget about the engagement ring. Let's just get married!'

Chapter Forty-Four

Basingstoke, Hampshire, England

The next time Missy came on to Burns Ward, Petey Morrison was in the middle of one of his shaggy dog stories.

Petey was a laid-back kinda fella and he sure had the gift of the gab. Back home, he lived with his wife and kids in a real backwoods place. He was always spinning tales about his adventures with mountain cats and snakes, ravines and quicksand. Missy guessed half of it wasn't true but it didn't matter: it kept the fellas amused. There was always a lot of laughter on the ward when Petey was telling a tale, and laughter sure was the best medicine.

Missy was in a good mood herself that day. Callum was about to head up to Scotland, and though she wouldn't be seeing him for a while, once he was back, they were getting married. Every time she thought of it, a thrill coursed right through her.

Petey was telling a story about a bear and it made Missy remember something.

'One time, we had a bear out back with a bucket on its head,' she said. Immediately, she had all the fellas' attention.

'A bear wearing a bucket?' Petey laughed. 'Hey, I can't beat that! Go on, then. Tell us!'

Missy hesitated. She felt kinda mean interrupting Petey's story but he didn't seem to mind, and the fellas were urging her on, so why not?

'It was a few years back now,' she said.

'Speak up!' Private Mitchell yelled from a few beds down.

Missy raised her voice. 'OK! Can you hear me now? I spotted a bear tearing around our backyard, with this metal pail stuck on its head.'

'How big?' Chas asked.

'The bear or the pail?' Missy asked.

She hadn't meant to be funny but it was a lovely sound when everyone laughed.

'Hey, shut up, Chas, and let the Sister tell the story!'

'So, anyhow,' Missy said, 'it was shaking its head like crazy but it couldn't get the bucket off.'

'What kinda bear was it?' someone asked.

Missy shrugged. 'I dunno. A brown one? A black one?'

'A grizzly? You don't wanna get anywhere near a grizzly!'

There was a row then between a couple of fellas about which type of bear was the most dangerous. While they were debating, Missy had time to push the cart around a few more cots, handing out Winchesters and a couple of books, before the guys finally stopped bickering and declared themselves ready for her to continue.

'Of course, the poor critter was going out of its mind,' she said.

'Sure,' Petey said. 'It couldn't eat, it couldn't drink—'

'It couldn't see!' Rabbit said.

So he was listening, was he? It was always pretty hard to tell what was going on with him, all quiet and wrapped up in those bandages.

'So, anyhow, my dad wanted to have the bear shot,' Missy said.

'Best thing for it,' Brains said, with a firm nod. 'Put it out of its misery.'

A few of the fellas jeered then and objected to the idea of the bear being shot.

'I wouldn't allow it,' Missy said. 'I felt so sorry for it and I wanted to save it. It was just a case of could we catch it safely? And get the bucket off its head?'

The door swung open, a nurse reversed in, pulling the medication cart, followed by another nurse, and the fellas groaned.

Missy stood up fast and mouthed 'Sorry!' at the nurses, because that was an even worse welcome than 'Here comes Squeaky'. But they shook their heads, no matter. They were used to it.

She started to push her cart towards the door. When the fellas were having medical interventions, she had to leave the ward.

'Hey, you're not going, are you, Sister?' Chas called out.

'No, you can't stop there!' Brains said.

Missy laughed. 'You know I have to leave now. I'll come back in a little while. I'll finish the story then!'

'Pinky promise?' Brains asked.

She lifted her little finger and wiggled it in the air. 'Pinky promise!'

The next day, when Missy wheeled the cart onto Burns Ward, Rabbit said, 'Hey.'

No mention of Squeaky.

She frowned. 'Are you talking to me, soldier?'

'What happened to the bear?' he asked, in a disinterested kinda way.

It had been a couple of weeks since he'd hurled the newspaper across the ward and she was still wary of him. She was tempted to say, 'What's it to you?' but that would be petty and unprofessional, and she wanted to live up to Matron's view of her, that she was good at her job.

She stopped the cart at the end of his cot and let her hand rest on the metal frame.

'I told you all yesterday, when I came back in. I finished the story then.'

Rabbit shook his head. 'Must've been asleep.'

The fella in the next bed caught her eye and mimed someone giving him a jab. He nodded at Rabbit and she caught on that the nurses must've given him something that had knocked him out.

'Oh, I saved the bear, all right,' Missy said. 'Now, do you want anything from the cart?'

'But how?' Rabbit asked. 'How d'you do it?'

She narrowed her eyes. Not that he could see her. She glanced at the books stacked in a neat row on her cart, spines uppermost. She looked at the titles for a moment and then selected one.

'If you like tales of derring-do, Lance Corporal,' she said, 'I have just the thing for you. *The Last of the Mohicans* by James—'

'—Fenimore Cooper,' he said.

'That's right. And if you'll let me read you the first few pages, I'll tell you about the bear. Do we have a deal? Shake on it?'

He sighed and she imagined that, under all those dressings, he was trying to roll his eyes.

He held out his bandaged right hand and, oh, so gently, she took it in hers and moved it up and down, just a couple of inches.

'Deal,' he said.

'So,' Missy said, a short while later. 'My dad and my boy – my husband – managed to corral the bear against a fence and then they wrestled it to the ground. One of them held the bear around the neck and the other pulled the pail off. And then they got the heck out of there and let the bear run away.'

'Good job,' Rabbit said, nodding.

'Yeah,' Missy said, looking down at the book she'd just been reading to him. 'Very good job indeed.'

Chapter Forty-Five

Aberdeenshire, Scotland

It was Tuesday evening, a week after Seffy's return from London. She and Jean were writing letters in the front room, with the fire burning and the gramophone softly playing.

'Thank goodness for Mr Galbraith,' Seffy said. 'I love having the place to ourselves. I wonder if he could be persuaded to take Mrs H out more often?'

Jean shook her head, without looking up. 'Go ahead and ask him, if you like. If you want to encourage infidelity.'

Seffy sighed. It was no good, she couldn't put this off any longer. She must compose a reply to Teddy.

She'd received a letter from him yesterday. He must've dashed it off almost as soon as they'd parted.

With everything else going on – the shock of meeting Missy, the tortuous journey back to Scotland and then Peggy's accident – Seffy had barely given Teddy a second thought, but now, those innocent words, 'I do love you, Teddy!', had come back to haunt her.

His letter was amorous, to say the least, and she was horrified. He clearly still held a torch for her and she'd unwittingly set it alight.

She was kicking herself now for not taking Emerald's advice. She should've taken the bull by the horns and cleared the whole matter up with him while they were still in London. Now, she'd have to do it by letter and there could be no room for misunderstandings.

She chewed the end of her pen, then wrote,

Dearest Teddy.

No, that wouldn't do. He wasn't her dearest, that was just the point. Fancy giving him false hope with the very first word! She screwed up the paper with a sigh and tossed it into the fire.

Jean looked up. 'Not wasting paper, are you, Seffy?'

'Wasting paper, wasting time. Oh, I don't know what I'm doing!'

She ripped off a fresh sheet of paper and started again.

Dear Teddy,
I hope you are well. It was lovely to see you in London recently. We did have a blast, didn't we? And of course, it was super to be with the old crowd again.

She stopped herself from writing *It was just like old times* and instead, bit the bullet and wrote *I must apologise if, due to overexcitement and possibly a little too much white wine, I gave you the wrong impression.*

Oh, this was excruciating! She was cringing as she wrote it, but she absolutely must not fudge it. It wasn't fair on the chap. If she was too vague, she'd only leave him hanging, wondering what on earth she meant. She must be crystal clear.

She glanced at Jean, who'd finished writing her letter and was folding it in half and placing it in an envelope.

'Jean?' she said. 'I need your advice.'

* * *

'So, to be clear,' Seffy read, 'as much as I value our friendship and hope it can continue, anything more is out of the question. Any romantic attachment that we once enjoyed should be considered over, with no possibility of it ever being revived.'

Jean gave a firm nod. 'Aye, that'll do it.'

Seffy winced. 'You don't think it's a trifle harsh? It sounds like something a solicitor would write. And that "ever" is awfully final.'

Jean clicked her tongue. 'You said you wanted to be clear. That's clear!'

She was right, of course. Oh, but poor Teddy. Seffy had thrown him over once before and also by letter. It seemed the coward's way out but what alternative did she have? She couldn't possibly wait until the next time she saw him or – heaven forbid – until another billet-doux arrived. She'd been too namby-pamby the first time she'd called a halt to their romance. She mustn't fall into the same trap.

This letter would do the trick. Jean was an expert letter writer, after all, and sometimes you simply had to be cruel to be kind. She thanked Jean for her help.

She would cycle into Ballamar at the first opportunity and post it before she chickened out.

The back door slammed. The girls jumped and looked at one another, aghast.

They heard Mrs Harris's unmistakeable laugh and a man said something indecipherable in reply.

'It's them!' Jean said.

'Oh, blast, she's brought him back!' Seffy said.

Jean started gathering up her things. 'Come on, I'm no' staying here, in this den of iniquity.'

Seffy giggled. 'Oh, Jean, you are funny.'

'I mean it. Let's go to The Drover's. There's a league match in there tonight. We can go and cheer the lassies on.'

* * *

'Hello, there!' Davey McAllister said to Seffy, when the girls reached the bar. 'Are ye all better now?'

Jean had to smile, as Seffy did a sterling job of touching her throat and saying, 'Just about, thank you,' in a croaky voice.

It was the first time she'd managed to persuade Seffy to go to the pub since she'd got back from London. She'd clearly not been in the mood before, but she'd brightened tonight, especially once she'd got that letter to the RAF fella done and dusted.

'The league match'll be starting soon,' Davey said. 'It should be a good night!' He glanced at the cap laid out on the bar. 'Now, there's enough in there for a couple o' drinks, ladies, if ye want to avail yerselves?'

Jean shook her head. 'No, that's for the lassies. We'll buy our own, ta very much. Two halves o' shandy, please.'

When they made their way to the back of the pub, there was Alec, standing at the oche with a dart in his hand.

Seffy frowned. 'I thought you told me the other chaps wouldn't let him play?'

Jean was mystified. 'That's right. I did ma best but they weren't havin' any of it.'

Peggy was holding court at a nearby table, surrounded by the other five girls. It was only just over a week since the accident and her right hand was still bandaged.

When Jean and Seffy had visited her, she had, understandably, looked awful peely-wally. And – most unlike her – she'd been quiet, although she'd perked up when they'd produced the slab of tablet they'd brought her. By the time they'd left, Peggy had eaten most of it.

Now, she was laughing and shouting instructions to all and sundry. Considering what she'd been through, it was amazing. She seemed back to her old self.

'That's all doon to me,' she said, nodding at Alec. 'I told the fellas how Mr Reid stopped me bleedin' to death and got me and ma thumb through the snow to the hospital.'

'I wonder what they did wi' it?' Tich said. 'Your thumb? Seeing as they couldnae sew it back on?'

'Aye, I've wondered that myself,' Peggy said. 'I could've kept it mebbe, in a jar?' She cackled. 'Summat to scare the kiddies with, one of these days, eh?'

As the girls watched, Alec finished his turn and an auld fella, who'd just hobbled in, walked up to him and shook his hand.

'See?' Peggy said. 'He's a hero at the saw mill and now everyone's buying him pints and shaking his hand. And he's allowed on the arrows.' She pulled a face. 'He's useless, mind!'

'At least we dunnae have to take cover when he plays!' Eileen said. She turned to Jean and Seffy. 'Peggy's started playing wi' her left hand and the darts go everywhere. Look, there's one up there, in the ceiling!'

Peggy chuckled. She was clearly enjoying being the centre of attention.

Jean didn't mind Peggy taking all the credit for the change in the fellas' attitude to Alec. What did it matter, after all, as long as they were being kinder? But she hoped her wee speech of the other night might've helped a little, too.

Peggy was waving her good hand at Jean.

'Will you join our team now, Jean? You said you would, if Mr Reid was allowed on the arrows.'

'Aye, you did,' Myrtle said.

'Startin' from tonight?' Peggy said. 'I cannae play 'til I've practised some more wi' ma left hand. Come on, say you will!'

'We need you!' Eileen said. 'And we won't tek no for an answer!'

Jean looked at the girls' hopeful faces. It was nice to be wanted.

Seffy was smiling at her and nodding slowly. She looked impressed.

When Jean had told her how she'd stood up for the girls when Davey McAllister wanted to ban them and how they'd then invited her to play darts, she could tell that Seffy had only been half-listening.

But now, Seffy must be able to see how much progress Jean had made wi' the Lost Girls.

'Will you play?' Rona asked.

'Aye, all right then,' Jean said. 'I will.'

Later, in the match interval, Jean sat with Alec at a corner table. The pints that the fellas had bought for him were lined up on the window ledge behind them.

'You'll be fair blootered if you drink all those!' Jean said, laughing.

'Aye and I'm lookin' forward to it!' he said.

It was the first chance they'd had for a proper chat since the accident.

'How did you know what to do?' Jean asked. 'Wi' the tourniquet and packing the thumb in ice like that?'

Alec shrugged. 'I know a wee bit o' first aid. I wanted to be a doctor, at one time. Before war broke out.' He gave a wry smile. 'I prefer putting people back together than ripping them apart with a bullet. I might still do it one day.'

'Train to be a doctor? Go to university?'

'Aye, if they'll have me.'

Jean thought about telling him how she'd put off her mathematics degree to do her bit for the war effort and that she might go back and do that later, too. But that was a story for another time.

'You've forgiven Seffy for her wee trip to England, then?' he asked.

If only he knew how close she'd come to dropping her pal right in the mire.

'Aye,' Jean said. 'Though she brought me back a strange gift: a home perming kit.'

He pulled a face. 'I have no idea what that is.'

'Put it this way, I'll no' be using it. Else I'll end up with hair as frizzy as Myrtle's!'

Alec laughed. 'You should hear yourself, Jean. You sound so indignant! If you want my opinion, I think you've very nice hair. You should leave well alone.'

She felt herself start to blush. He was a nice fella, Alec Reid. How could she ever have thought otherwise?

Chapter Forty-Six

Callum parked the truck at the top of the incline and told Gordy to stay right there.

'I won't be long,' he said.

Gordy was curled up on the seat, his overcoat wrapped around him like a blanket.

'Take as long as you like, buddy. I'm gonna have me a snooze.'

As Callum jumped down from the cab, Gordy said, 'Hey, you're not gonna say it on the doorstep, are you?'

Callum rolled his eyes. 'Course not. What d'you take me for?'

He slammed the door, switched on the torch and made his way down the icy lane.

He was filled with a nervous kinda dread but he was also as skittery as a puppy. After six whole months, he was gonna see Seffy again. Boy, he'd missed her.

It'd been tough, finding this place in the dark, with barely any lights on the truck and no signposts. He'd had to concentrate real hard, so they didn't end up in a ditch. But he'd been glad to have something to focus on; it had stopped him thinking about what lay ahead.

'Whatcha gonna do, bud?' Gordy had asked on the way.

'I've gotta tell her the truth,' he'd said. 'I'm getting married.

I've gotta end it with Seffy, once and for all. I can't see her no more, or write.'

Or think about her, which was gonna be nigh on impossible.

'Gee, that'll be tough,' Gordy had said.

'Yeah, but otherwise it's not fair. On either of them.'

'I get it, buddy. You've made your choice.'

But that wasn't it. He hadn't made his choice: Missy had come to England and decided she wanted to get married over here. That had made the choice for him.

He found Seffy's place – Laburnum Cottage – at the end of the row of tiny houses. The gate was hanging off its hinges so he leaped over it and knocked on the door.

It was opened by a middle-aged woman.

'Sorry to disturb, ma'am – sir.' He'd spotted a ginger guy standing behind her. 'But might I speak with Miss Mills?'

The woman looked at him suspiciously. 'Who're you?'

'A friend. She's expecting me.' She wasn't necessarily expecting him tonight but he'd written and told her about his move to Scotland, so she knew he'd appear at some point.

The woman looked doubtful. 'I dunno. She's never mentioned no American to me.'

She mightn't have mentioned an American, ma'am, he wanted to say, because I am actually from Canada. But there was no point. He knew, to the British, they were one and the same.

The fella in the hallway must've taken pity on him because he said, 'They're all in the pub.' And gave him directions. It was only down the road.

Callum raced back up the hill and climbed into the cab.

'Wake up, Gordy, we're going to the pub!'

It was unexpected, the thought of Seffy in a bar. That sure didn't sound like her but perhaps, in this new place, she had new habits. It was pretty remote, there probably wasn't much else to do.

As they walked in, he gazed around, looking for a flash of blonde hair, but there was no sign of Seffy, only a bunch of old timers sitting up at the bar.

This was frustrating; he was bursting to see her.

They couldn't stay long – he and Gordy were passing through and they'd taken an unofficial detour – but he wanted to arrange to meet up with her, so they could talk sometime soon.

Maybe they could go out someplace and have a little time together before he had to say it? Or would that just prolong the agony?

He tried to ignore the voice inside his head that was saying, 'Hold your horses, fella. Haven't you come to say goodbye?'

He pulled off his cap, ordered a couple of beers and scanned the room.

'Looking for someone, pal?' the bartender asked.

'Yes, sir. The lumberjills? I was told they were here.'

He didn't say which one in particular; he didn't want the whole bar knowing his business. He and Gordy were clearly a novelty and he sensed everyone around them watching and tuning in to their conversation.

The bartender nodded. 'They're away in the back. Ah, but I cannae let you go through. It's the final o' the league darts competition. You'll have to wait, son. They cannae be disturbed for anyone.'

Darts? Were they watching or playing?

Gordy made a sympathetic face. 'That's too bad, bud. Guess we got our timing wrong, huh?'

OK, he could wait. A little while, at least. He'd waited six months already.

'Here's one o' them now,' the bartender said, indicating a beefy kind of girl with curly hair. She was standing a few feet away. She took a couple of coins out of a cap on the bar and tapped one impatiently on the counter.

She had a bandage around her other hand. A recent injury; it looked like she'd lost a thumb.

He and Gordy exchanged a look.

'What d'you reckon? Saw mill?' Gordy said and Callum nodded.

Wow, this sure was a rough kind of place, where women worked in saw mills, played darts and bought their own drinks.

He couldn't imagine Seffy in here. She'd told him in her last letter that this new posting was 'interesting' and he was sure getting a flavour of that now.

'Excuse me, Miss,' Callum said. 'I'm looking for a friend and you might be able to help. Seffy Mills? Is she here?'

The beefy girl looked him up and down. 'Who wants to know?'

'My name's Callum Fraser. Could you do me a real big favour and tell her I'm here, please?'

'It'll cost you,' she said. 'A wee dram.'

Jeez, she wasn't joking. Callum nodded at the bartender, who took down a bottle of whisky.

'And I may as well take one for Seffy too, while you're at it,' she said.

'Seffy drinks that stuff?' Callum asked.

'Sure she does!'

Boy, she'd changed, if that were true.

Callum added a second whisky to the order and the girl disappeared into the back, a glass in each hand. She managed it OK, even with that nasty-looking injury. He wondered if she'd deliver his message or simply forget it once she was back with her pals.

He thumped the bar. Darn it! He was real tempted to push his way through the old guys standing around and to hell with their precious game. It would be enough just to glimpse her, for now, even if they weren't close enough to speak.

He strained his ears, listening for that cut-glass accent and tinkling laugh. But he could only hear the rhythmic thump of darts hitting the board and gruff Scots voices. Nothing that sounded like Seffy.

'It's a serious business, the darts league,' the bartender said.

'Sure, I can imagine,' Gordy said, rolling his eyes at Callum.

'If oor team wins, they'll be drinking all night,' the guy went on. 'We'll have a lock-in.'

The girl was back, without Seffy.

'She says she doesnae want to speak to you and you know why!'

'No, hold on – wait – what exactly did you say to her?'

Callum had grabbed the girl's arm, to stop her leaving. She looked pointedly at his hand until he let go and apologised.

She sighed. 'I said, "There's a yank at the bar asking for you," but I couldnae remember your name and she said, "What does he look like?" and I said, "Ugly as sin!"' She laughed. 'No, not really. I said, "He's no' bad looking and he's wearing a green uniform."'

'And, wait – she said she wouldn't speak to me?' Callum asked.

'Aye, that's right.'

The girl shrugged and walked off.

This didn't make any sense. Why wouldn't Seffy speak to him? She'd been her usual cheery self in that last letter. There'd been no sign of anything wrong. Other than she wasn't too happy about the place she'd been sent.

There must be some mistake.

He rubbed his temple and breathed out, hard. OK, he'd had enough. He'd tried being patient and polite but he was going through now, to sort this out.

He made to move towards the back of the pub but Gordy caught hold of his sleeve and held him tight.

'Not so fast, buddy!'

'Now, I want no trouble here!' the bartender said. 'The lass doesnae want to speak to you and that's an end to it!'

Gordy released his grip and patted his arm.

'That's too bad,' Gordy said. 'But we're gonna have to start headin' back soon anyway, bud. I don't want them thinking we've gone AWOL and start cancelling my leave.'

Sure, Gordy had Grace to think of. When that baby was born, he'd wanna go see them straight away.

What had happened to make Seffy react like that? Had she met someone else? Someone she drank whisky and played darts with?

Or was she mad because he hadn't sent a gift at Christmas? No, Seffy wasn't like that. And besides, he'd written and explained he'd be bringing her present in person.

No, it was something else.

'Women, eh?' the bartender said, all pally again, now Gordy appeared to have Callum under control.

He didn't reply. He didn't wanna be the fella at the bar, pouring his heart out to the fella behind it.

'I'll wait,' he said.

The bartender's smile vanished. 'No, you won't, pal. You'll be on your way now.'

'Let's go, buddy,' Gordy said. 'Come on, she's made it easy for you. If she won't see you, you can't tell her. You're off the hook!'

Callum finished his pint and put the glass down. 'No, I won't leave it like that.'

'Come back some other time then and clear this up. It's probably nothin', right?' Gordy said.

Callum bit his lip and nodded, slowly. He would come back. He owed it to Seffy to tell her properly, face to face. Like a man.

Chapter Forty-Seven

The girls had just finished their morning cuppa in the forest and were about to start work.

Jean, looking deadly serious, ushered Seffy to one side. 'There's summat I need to tell you,' she said.

'Go on,' Seffy said, bracing herself.

She hoped it didn't have anything to do with Callum. It'd been a shock when he'd turned up at the pub last week and a part of her regretted refusing to see him. But he'd taken her by surprise and she wanted to be prepared for this confrontation. And the darts match – which The Drover's team had gone on to win – had been at a critical point. It would've been disloyal to have abandoned the girls simply because Callum Fraser had clicked his fingers.

There'd been no sign of him since. Perhaps he'd never come back. She'd missed her chance to tell him what she knew and what she thought of him.

But what Jean wanted to say had nothing to do with Callum. It was yet another issue with the Lost Girls.

'Myrtle's got some unwanted guests,' Jean said.

'Never!' Seffy said. 'Is she entertaining men at her billet?'

'No, she's got head lice. I was standing over her as she set up the fire and I saw her hair move.'

Seffy gasped. 'Nits?'

'Aye, those too. Nits are the eggs.'

Seffy scratched her scalp. It was making her itchy just thinking about it.

'Can't we simply suggest to Myrtle that she might want to wash her hair and drown the blighters that way?'

'The water wouldnae be hot enough to kill them,' Jean said. 'I saw it on a public information film. She's probably already passed them on to the others. We'll all have to be treated, to be on the safe side. Shall we ask the girls to come to the cottage tomorrow night and do it then? Mrs Harris'll be out wi' her fancy man; we'll have the place to ourselves.'

'I don't suppose we have much choice,' Seffy said. 'But I can't say I'm looking forward to it. It'll be a *lousy* evening!'

'Ha, ha,' Jean said. 'Very funny.'

Seffy made the announcement the next day, at morning tea.

'The welfare officer has notified us of a nasty epidemic in the area,' she said, twisting the truth somewhat. 'There's no nice way of putting it: it's head lice.'

Tich and Isobel shrieked; Peggy looked unperturbed. Seffy could've sworn someone murmured, 'Not again!'

'No need to panic,' Jean said, 'We simply need to take precautionary measures. Can you all come to our digs tonight and we'll treat everyone's hair.'

Peggy folded her arms and glowered. 'I'm no' sure I like the sound o' this.'

That was all they needed: Peggy in a rebellious mood again. Despite the accident, she was still a feisty madam.

She'd insisted on returning to work at the saw mill, much to Seffy's surprise. In Peggy's shoes, she wasn't sure she'd have wanted to go back.

She definitely wasn't allowed anywhere near the saws again,

but Peggy was adamant she could still lift timber and learn to drive the tractor and Mr Burke had agreed.

'Look, Peggy, it won't hurt, it doesn't take long and we'll be doing it too,' Jean said.

'It might be fun!' Seffy said. 'A party! Erm, of sorts.'

'Will there be food and drink?' Myrtle asked.

'It won't be much of a party otherwise,' Eileen said.

Seffy could tell by the exasperated look on Jean's face that she'd said the wrong thing but it was too late now.

'I'm sure we can rustle up something,' Seffy said. If all else failed, she could give them each a dram of her whisky. There was still half a bottle left.

Peggy was pretending to consider the invitation but was clearly weakening at the thought of being fed and watered.

'All right,' she said. 'I suppose we could come. What time do ye want us?'

That evening, Seffy wondered what Mrs Harris would say if she could see the lumberjill invasion of Laburnum Cottage.

It seemed even smaller with six additional girls draping themselves over the kitchen chairs and pressed up against the range, towelling their hair dry.

Jean had bought a bottle of Lethane from the chemist in Ballamar and a fine-toothed comb, which, she'd told Seffy earlier, was to remove the nits – the louse eggs.

'Best not mention eggs,' Seffy had said, curling her lip.

Everyone's hair had been shampooed at the kitchen sink and thoroughly combed. Now they had to wait for it to dry before Jean could apply the Lethane.

'We've got a few buns in, there's tea and we even have milk,' Seffy said. 'Shall we have them now?'

It wasn't much but it was the best they'd been able to manage.

Once everyone's hair was dry enough – Myrtle's frizzy bonce

had never really looked wet – they took it in turns to sit in the 'delousing throne', as Seffy christened it, while Jean dabbed the oil all over their scalps and the girls rubbed it in.

'Poo, it stinks!' Rona said, pulling a face as she stood up from the chair and let Eileen take her place.

Once the Lost Girls had been treated, Jean did Seffy's scalp and Seffy did hers.

'Right, that's done,' Jean said. 'But now, we mustn't wash our hair for ten days!'

'Ten days?' Isobel said. 'But I wash mine every Thursday night!'

'Not this week, you don't,' Jean said. 'You need to leave the Lethane on so it can kill all the lice when the eggs hatch.'

The room was filled with screams.

'I told you not to mention eggs,' Seffy said.

'But it's all right to wash it as soon as the ten days are up?' Isobel asked.

'Aye,' Jean said. 'By then, everything will be dead.'

There was yet more screaming. Seffy stuck her fingers in her ears.

It was only when the noise died down that they heard knocking at the front door.

'It's probably the constable!' Jean said. 'I expect the neighbours thought someone was being murdered. I'll go.'

But it wasn't the police. When Jean returned, alone, she told Seffy that her Canadian fella was at the door, asking for her.

Callum. He wasn't giving up, then. And he'd caught her off guard again.

Oh, blast her stupid heart. It had leaped for joy when Jean had said he was here. She must remember what he'd done and how much she loathed him for it.

'Is it that yank again?' Peggy asked. 'He's keen! Do ye owe him money or summat, Seffy?'

'Are you going to speak to him?' Jean asked. 'Will you be all right?'

Seffy touched her hair. It was lank and – she sniffed her hand – stinky.

'How can I go to the door like this?' she said. 'I'm covered in nit oil!'

'He won't care,' Myrtle said. 'Not if he really likes you.'

Jean had disappeared for a minute but she was back now, holding out her balaclava.

Seffy snatched it up. 'Yes, that'll do. Thank you, Jean.'

She waited until she was in the hall before pulling it on, to avoid having to listen to the girls' opinions. She probably looked ridiculous but never mind: this wasn't a date.

She was about to give Callum Fraser a piece of her mind. If she was wearing something resembling a hangman's hood, then so much the better.

Chapter Forty-Eight

The front door was wide open and the full moon was shining down.

Callum was silhouetted in the doorframe. His arms were crossed over his chest, as though he were hugging himself. He was stamping his feet against the cold.

He must've heard her come into the hallway because he stopped stock still and stared into the gloom.

'Seffy, is that you?'

She remembered that voice: deep and mellow. It had sent a tingle down her spine. She didn't reply but stepped nearer, so he could make her out.

'Oh, there you are,' he said.

She still hadn't spoken.

He rubbed his jaw. 'Look, I wanted to come see you last week. I came to the pub. But they said you didn't wanna see me. Was that right? Oh, and I sent you a whisky by the way. Did you ever get it?'

She had no idea what he was talking about.

'No,' she said. 'I don't even like whisky.'

'Darn it! I knew I couldn't trust that girl!' he said.

'Ah, well, trust is a funny thing. You can't trust anyone these days.'

He must've heard the bitterness in her voice. He breathed out hard, sending plumes of icy breath into the air.

'Say, I don't know what's up or what I—' He cocked his head and peered at her more closely. He let out an involuntary laugh, which he tried to cover up with a cough. 'What's with the hat? Is this a bad time? Were you washing your hair?'

A moment ago, he'd sounded so bewildered that she'd almost felt sorry for him but now! Was he actually laughing at her?

Seffy tugged the balaclava down. 'My hair's wet, if you must know. And I'd rather not catch double pneumonia.' She knew she sounded uppity and he'd understand why soon enough. 'I can't invite you in,' she said. 'I've got a houseful.'

Right on cue, the girls in the kitchen erupted into gales of laughter.

'Sure, that's OK.' Callum spread his hands. 'Look, my Jeep's back there, in the lane. Shall we go sit in there and talk? It'll be warmer.'

Seffy hesitated. She shouldn't go. She should say her piece and send him packing. She imagined the satisfaction of slamming the door in his face. But she'd rather not make a scene on the doorstep, like a common fishwife. Not while she still had a modicum of pride. It would be more private in the Jeep.

'Very well,' she said. She grabbed her overcoat from the hook and he flicked on his torch and led the way.

They sat in the Jeep and Callum turned on the engine but as Seffy had left the passenger door open, it was still cold.

He sighed. 'You can shut the door, Seffy. You're perfectly safe.'

'It's not that,' she said. 'I'm not keen on small spaces.'

She hated feeling hemmed in. And there was also the small matter of the Lethane, which stank of turps mixed with petrol. With adequate ventilation, hopefully, he wouldn't smell it.

This felt so odd. Last time they'd been together, they'd hardly been able to keep their hands off each other. Now, they were distant, like polite strangers.

Callum twisted in his seat towards her. 'Hey, it's been a while, huh?' His voice had softened. He lifted a hand, as though to touch her cheek, but pulled it back. 'I've—'

He'd been about to say he'd missed her, she knew it. He'd stopped himself. She'd missed him too. Until she'd realised the man she was missing wasn't the man she thought he was. Her chest tightened, as her anger flared up again.

'How are you, Seffy?' he asked.

'I'm well, thank you,' she said, curtly. 'How are you? Or, perhaps more to the point, how is your fiancée? Did Missy enjoy her trip to London?'

There was silence for a moment.

'What?' he said. 'How do you—?'

'Oh, I've met her!' She'd imagined saying those words so many times. Triumphantly. Caught you out, Callum Fraser! Her heart was beating ten to the dozen. 'She seems nice,' she said. 'There's just one problem: she's not in Canada, as you'd led me to believe!'

He took a sharp intake of breath.

'When, in God's name, were you planning to tell me?' she demanded.

It was too dark to see his face but Seffy could picture how he must look: utterly horrified.

'You've met Missy?'

'I have! Turns out it's a very small world. We were both in London a couple of weeks ago. Are you going to tell me it wasn't her?'

Callum groaned and threw back his head. 'No, she's here all right. But what are the chances …? Did you tell her who you were?'

Ah, of course. He was concerned she might've ruined everything by revealing herself to be Callum's – what? Other woman? Close friend? What exactly had she been to him?

'No!' she said. 'I rather regret not having had that interesting conversation. The sirens went off and the small matter of running for our lives rather took over.'

He sighed. 'Sarcasm really doesn't suit you, Seffy.'

'Well, lying doesn't suit you!'

He banged his hand on the steering wheel. 'I've never lied!' he said, through gritted teeth. 'I told you I was engaged pretty much from the start. But I thought I had months – years even – to sort out this whole mess.'

'A mess! Is that what I am? Charming!'

He shook his head. 'Not you. Me. I'm the mess. Look, I wanted to tell you she was over here but I didn't wanna do it by letter. I wanted to explain in person.'

Seffy sighed. What was there to explain? His fiancée was here, in Britain – goodness, they were probably seeing each other every weekend – and he hadn't told her! Those were the facts.

'Has she been here all this time?' Seffy asked. 'All the time that you and I …' She had a sudden vision of their kiss in Greta Green.

'No!' he said. 'No!'

Oh, this was stupid. She wasn't going to sit here listening to this for another moment. She started to swing her legs out of the open door but he grabbed her arm.

'Let go of me!'

'Just listen!' he said. 'I swear on my life, I didn't know she was coming!'

'Don't insult—' She was going to say 'Don't insult my intelligence' but he was talking over her, clearly desperate for her to believe him.

'She got here before Christmas but I didn't find out straight away. She just turned up, with the Red Cross! It's the truth!'

He'd let go of her arm.

'Oh, you must think I was born yesterday!' she said. That was it: she was leaving.

'No, I don't. You were born 19th September 1921.'

She stopped, her legs dangling from the Jeep. 'How do you know that?'

Callum gave a deep sigh. 'Because when we were out on the loch and we saw the Northern Lights – do you remember?'

'Yes.' How could she forget? It had been one of the best nights of her life.

'Well,' he said, 'that was your twenty-first birthday.'

No, this was all a trick. So what? He had a good memory for dates and events. It didn't mean a thing. He was still a rotter.

She climbed out of the Jeep, but before she could take more than a couple of steps, he'd leaped out of his side and raced around to block her way.

He was a bulky shadow looming over her now. But he didn't touch her again.

'Let me get past,' she said.

'Look, Seffy, please. We need to talk but not like this. Not in the dark and cold, while you're so angry!' He held up his hands. 'Sure, I understand why you're angry, but I am not that man. I can't believe you'd think that of me!'

When she didn't reply, he merely stepped to one side and shone the torch so she could find the path and make her way back to the cottage.

'I'll come back Saturday, after work!' he called after her. 'Midday. And we'll talk then!'

When you've calmed down. That's what he meant.

'We'll see about that!' Seffy yelled back. The nerve of him! She was shaking and not just from the cold.

296

Chapter Forty-Nine

Basingstoke, Hampshire, England

'You're what?' Laura said. 'You're writing to Rabbit? Why would you do that?'

The girls were on their break, sitting in the Red Cross Room and Missy was penning another note to him.

'Because – haven't you noticed – he doesn't get any mail. I'm trying to cheer him up. That's our job, isn't it?' Missy said.

'Yeah, sure, but … what kinda things do you write?'

'Oh, silly stuff. I tell him about the Up patients' ping pong tournaments, I write about the book I'm reading to him, *Last of the Mohicans*. And funny things that happen. Remember how that guy pretended to blow his nose on the nurse's veil? I wrote about that. I try to make him smile.'

Laura rolled her eyes. 'Not an easy task! What, and then you just drop the letter in the ward mailbox?'

Missy nodded.

The first time she'd written to him, she'd been on the ward when the post had been brought round. She'd watched as the post guy had called out, 'Lance Corporal Grant?' and placed the envelope carefully in Rabbit's bandaged hand. 'There you go, chum. Letter for you.'

His head had jerked back in surprise and he'd turned the envelope over and over, as though he couldn't quite believe it, until Chas, in the next bed, had said, 'Here, buddy, toss it over. I'll read it for ya.'

Missy's heart had been in her mouth. What if she'd raised false hope? Maybe Rabbit had a best girl back home he'd been longing to hear from? He was gonna be mighty disappointed when it turned out the letter wasn't from her.

She hadn't been able to watch. She'd busied herself with the other patients.

'Hey, Sister, I learned a new card trick!' Mikey had called out. 'Come on, pick a card, any card!'

She'd gone over to Mikey's bed. But she'd still been able to hear Chas and Rabbit.

'Dear Rabbit,' Chas had read, and immediately Rabbit had asked. 'Who the hell's it from? Skip to the end!'

'Gee, I can't make it out. The writing's small. It looks like "Squeaky" or summat. Does that make sense?'

Missy had held her breath.

'Hey, Sister, was that your card?' Mikey had asked. 'Five of diamonds?'

Darn it, she hadn't been paying attention.

'Sure! That was it! Well done! That's a great trick, Mikey.'

She'd tuned back into the fellas' conversation.

'Yeah, that makes sense,' Rabbit had said. 'OK, read it.'

Now, Laura was shaking her head and looking kinda disapproving.

'OK, but remember, Miranda, what I said about not getting too attached? That guy – Rabbit – he's pretty beaten up. He's got skin grafts and surgery ahead of him and—'

'—I know! Look, I'm just being friendly. I'm happy! I guess I want everyone else to be happy, too.'

Laura looked at her properly then. 'Yeah, you are real chirpy these days. Is it the trip you're planning, up to Scotland? No, it's more than that, I can see by your face! What's goin' on, huh?'

Missy checked that no one else was close enough to hear, then she confided in Laura about her wedding plans.

'Callum has to get permission from his commanding officer and that'll take a little time. They have to do checks. Make sure he's not already married, for one! Then we have to get a licence and book the church and banns have to be read. It's only gonna be a small wedding but there's still a ton of stuff to do. Oh, and don't tell my sister, OK?'

'Juliet doesn't know?' Laura asked.

'No, it's a secret. Keep it under your hat!'

And then she turned back to the letter she was writing to Rabbit.

Chapter Fifty

Aberdeenshire, Scotland

It was late on Saturday morning. Eileen and Myrtle were at either end of the crosscut saw, making light work of a huge Douglas fir.

'Gi' it a shove, then!' Tich called, from twenty yards away.

Seffy smiled. After all their complaining, the Lost Girls finally seemed happy in their work. Goodness, she'd even heard Isobel humming 'You Are My Sunshine' earlier.

There wasn't any sunshine – in fact, today was decidedly grey – but the temperature was warmer now and the days were drawing out. There were still a few weeks to go, but the end of winter was in sight.

The girls got up from their kneeling positions and removed the saw from the trunk. Myrtle stood back, while Eileen gave the trunk a firm push. It slowly started to tilt and then gathered speed.

'Don't forget—' Seffy started to say but her words were drowned out by a chorus of 'TIMBERRRR!'

With a whoosh and a gratifying thud, the tree crashed to the ground.

'Super! Well done!' Seffy said. The girls were already fetching their saws and knives, to start stripping the tree.

She glanced at her watch. Almost midday. She'd have to leave soon, if she was going to keep that appointment with Callum.

It would jolly well serve him right if she didn't turn up. She wasn't fuming any more, but she was still peeved at him for putting her through the mill. After due consideration, she'd decided he probably had been telling the truth – he hadn't known about Missy coming to England – but she'd rather have found out almost any other way than by coming face to face with his fiancée like that.

'Does he seem happy she's over here?' Jean had asked, as they discussed the matter in bed one night.

And the short answer had been no.

'I wouldn't be surprised if he feels pushed into a corner,' Seffy had said. 'But maybe he was simply downplaying his happiness, so as not to rub my nose in it.'

Because there was no doubt in her mind that Callum had come to Scotland for two reasons: to tell her about Missy and to end everything between her and him. He'd said he wanted to talk and that could only mean one thing.

She had butterflies in her stomach at the thought. Oh, blow it. She would go and see him. It was time to face the music.

'Girls, I'm sorry but I'm going to have to clock off early today,' she said.

'Oh, aye?' Tich said.

'I'm meeting someone.'

Isobel raised her eyebrows. 'Is it a date?'

'It IS! You look awful sheepish,' Myrtle said.

It was actually the opposite of a date but she wasn't going to share that with the Lost Girls.

She gazed around at the trees that were still standing around them and tutted.

'I feel rotten though because we wanted to get these last few down before the weekend. Then on Monday, we could've moved on to the south side.'

'Nae matter,' Eileen said, as she carried an armful of branches across the clearing. 'We can work over a wee bit. We'll get it done today, won't we girls?'

The others readily agreed.

Goodness, what a change. The thought of getting them to work over their allotted hours would've been unimaginable even a couple of weeks ago. But the girls had got into their stride, they were turning into good lumberjills and even miserable McIntyre hadn't been able to find fault with their work.

At least something was finally going well.

When Seffy arrived at the cottage, the army Jeep was parked in the lane outside. Callum was leaning against the driver's door, arms crossed.

She was seeing him properly now, for the first time in six months. He looked well, and quite as handsome as ever.

He uncrossed his arms and stood up straight as she approached. He was eyeing her warily. They hadn't exactly parted on good terms the other night. He was probably wondering if she was going to start shouting at him again.

'You're late,' he said, casually.

It was on the tip of her tongue to say, 'That's because I'm an optimist!' But today that wasn't true. She was full of dread; her stomach had been churning all morning.

She gave him a quick smile.

He threw his keys in the air and snatched them up again. 'Shall we go for a walk?'

She shook her head. 'I've got a better idea. Give me five minutes!'

She raced upstairs. There wasn't even time for a wash. She swapped her grubby work dungarees for some clean breeches and then ran to the shed.

Callum's eyes lit up as she reappeared, holding a fishing rod in each hand.

'Do you fish?' she asked.

He stepped forward and took the rods without taking his eyes off her. His gaze was intense. 'I grew up on a lake, ma'am. Of course, I fish.'

'This river is called the Dee,' Seffy said, as they stood in the ankle-deep water and cast their lines. 'And somewhere over there – or perhaps it's that way—' she wrinkled her nose, trying to remember what Mrs Harris had told her '—is the royal estate at Balmoral.'

Callum raised his eyebrows. 'Royalty? Friends of yours, huh?'

She laughed. 'Hardly! You do have a strange view of me and my life.'

He was looking out across the grey water. It had started to rain and the far shore was swathed in mist.

'You know, when you wouldn't see me that night in the pub,' he said. 'I thought maybe you'd started dating a prince or a duke or someone like that. Someone more … your style.'

He glanced at her and then back at the river.

What did he want her to say? 'No, actually, Callum, you're much more my cup of tea!' Which was true but she was hardly going to say it now.

'Have you done this before?' he asked, nodding at the line.

She was relieved he'd changed the subject. 'Yes, my grandfather used to take me fishing when I was little. I loved it.'

He looked up and down the riverbanks. 'You do realise we're poaching?' he said. 'In broad daylight? That's why I suggested standing here, near the trees and away from the road.'

They were almost certainly on McIntyre's land – his house was nearby – but Seffy had already decided what she'd say if he caught them.

'It's not poaching if we don't catch anything!' she said.

Callum frowned. 'You mean, if we catch a salmon, we have to throw it back? Hey, I'm not standing here all afternoon in the rain for nothin'!'

But it wouldn't be for nothing, Seffy thought. They'd have been together.

'I think this land belongs to the chap whose forest we're felling,' she said.

'So he wouldn't mind?'

She laughed. 'Mind? He'd probably shoot us! But he's usually roaming around the woods on Saturdays, checking up on my gang and our work, so I think we're probably safe.'

It was so peaceful, standing here in the shallows, amongst the glistening rocks. There was no sound except the pitter patter of rain.

'Isn't it beautiful?' Seffy said, looking around at the green, mist-covered hills.

Callum nodded. 'Sure is. You know, if you like this, you'd love Canada.'

Seffy forgot about the scenery and stared at him. Oh, she did like this. She liked it very much.

She wished she'd never come, though. This was torture.

'Hey! I've got your Christmas present,' he said, suddenly. 'Come on, the fish aren't biting anyway. Let's sit down a minute.'

Callum took something out of his overcoat pocket, then laid the overcoat on the ground and they knelt on it.

He handed her a little wooden box. 'Here. Sorry it's so late, but you'll see what I mean about not trusting the post.'

Seffy's hands were trembling as she opened it. Because this wasn't merely a Christmas present: it was a goodbye present.

The box was filled with wood shavings, nestled inside which was the most beautiful gold pendant, with an opal in the centre.

She gasped and shook her head. 'Oh, no, this is too much, Callum. I can't possibly accept it.'

He lifted the chain out of the box and placed it in the palm of his hand. They bowed their heads closer, to examine it.

'It was my mother's,' he said, 'and her mother's before that. And my ma's folks emigrated from Scotland, which is why, I guess, I've always felt so at home here. It seems right for it to stay in the British Isles and besides, I wanted you to have it.' He gazed into her eyes. 'Something precious.'

Seffy bit her lip. 'No, really, I can't.'

It felt wrong. He shouldn't be giving this to her. Gracious, it was a family heirloom. By rights, he should be giving it to Missy.

'It's awfully kind,' she said, 'but I won't take it, Callum. I can't.'

It was a goodbye present and if she didn't take it, she didn't have to say goodbye.

She got to her feet and stepped away from him.

'Come on, we can't keep skirting around the issue,' she said. 'Your fiancée – a lovely girl, I have to say. I wish I could hate her but I can't – she's come to claim you, hasn't she?'

He blew out his cheeks. 'Yeah. And I have to do the right thing.'

Of course he did. What had she expected? Oh, but it hurt. It was like a knife piercing her heart.

'Give the necklace to your girl, Callum.'

'NO!' He jumped to his feet. 'I've been waiting to give this to you. Seffy. It's not for anyone else!'

Callum held the necklace out to her but she shook her head and put her hands behind her back.

He sighed and looked out towards the river.

'If you won't take it,' he said, taking back his arm. 'Then it's staying here!'

She watched, horrified, as he hurled the necklace into the water.

'Oh, no! What've you done!'

She ran into the water and waded out, at the point where the necklace had disappeared. It was only a foot or so deep and – thank God it was so crystal clear – within a few seconds she'd spotted it, glinting on a stone. She reached down into the icy water and pulled it out.

'I've got it!' she called back, relieved to see it wasn't damaged.

'You have to keep it now!' Callum said.

She ignored him and carried on walking out into deeper water.

'Hey, what're you doing?' Callum called.

Seffy looked out across the river, at the raindrops hitting the surface of the water, making so many circles. It was so peaceful here. A tiny part of her wanted to keep on walking but instead, she stopped and turned back towards the bank.

He was at the water's edge.

The freezing cold water was lapping over the tops of her wellingtons. Her legs and feet were soaked. She swallowed. Maybe this was the moment to be brave.

'What if I said I loved you?' she said, her voice breaking. She breathed in the cold, pure Scottish air for courage. 'That I'd always loved you and that I'd never stop? What then?'

His eyes widened in surprise and then softened, as he stared at her, for what seemed like an age. He put his head in his hands, covering his eyes.

Seffy waited, hardly daring to breath. When he looked across the water at her again, he was grimacing, as though in pain. He gave a little shake of his head.

'If you did say that, Seffy,' he said, slowly, 'I'd have to say, I … I'm real sorry, but I still have to marry Missy.'

Chapter Fifty-One

Callum parked the Jeep outside the cottage and rubbed his face with his hands. Gee, that'd been tough.

Seffy had insisted on walking back alone. He'd had to respect her wishes, even though it'd grieved him to leave her like that, especially as the rain had gotten heavier.

Part of him wanted to sit here and wait for her to arrive, to see her one more time and make sure she was OK.

He was in turmoil. He couldn't stop thinking about what she'd said. Seffy loved him; she'd always loved him. Jeez, if only she knew how much he'd longed to hear her say somethin' like that. But it was too late; that ship had definitely sailed.

He had to move; she wouldn't be happy to see him here. She'd told him, in no uncertain terms, that he had to leave her be now, and he'd promised that he would.

He unloaded the rods and flies from the back of the Jeep and carried them round to the shed in the backyard. The cottage had seemed deserted but as he was propping up the rods in the shed, he heard a noise and turned to find Jean standing in the doorway.

'Hey, Jean,' he said.

She pushed her glasses up her nose and eyed him warily. 'Where's Seffy?'

Oh, boy. He really didn't wanna have to explain everything. Not now.

'We were at the river. She wanted to walk back,' he said.

'She wanted to walk back in the rain?'

'Yeah. I guess she wanted some time alone. She's OK, though. We're good, you know,' he said. That wasn't true. Seffy had been real sore and he'd understood why. 'I brought the rods back in the Jeep,' he said, nodding at them. 'How you doin', anyway, Jean? Long time, no see.'

Jean was one of those measurer girls. He'd heard the best of them could calculate a tree's cubic output just by looking at it. The way Jean was looking at him now was kinda unnerving. She was assessing him: it was like she could see right through him.

'I'm all right, ta,' she said. 'I like it here, better than Blantyre Forest.'

'Good for you. I'm pleased to hear it,' he said. He slapped his palms against his thighs. He wanted to leave but she was blocking his exit. 'Well, I'd better get off.'

'She was all set to go to England, did you know that?' Jean said.

Callum shook his head, not understanding.

'Before Christmas, Seffy applied for a transfer to a Timber Corps camp in the New Forest. Isn't that near where you're based?'

Seffy had wanted to move? This was news to him. Why hadn't she told him?

'Yeah, that's right,' he said. 'I'm stationed down that way. I'll be heading back there in a few weeks' time.'

That was crazy. He'd been doing his darndest to get up here, she'd been angling for a post on the south coast, nearer to him. They were like a couple of magnets, irresistibly drawn to each other.

'But anyhow,' Jean said, 'we were sent here and her plan went to pot.'

'Yeah. Plans have a nasty habit of doing that.' He shrugged.

'You take care, Jean and—' he stopped before he turned away for good '—look after Seffy for me, will ya?'

As she stepped aside, two girls – lumberjills –came tearing into the yard, calling, 'Jean! Jean!'

They almost collided with him but Callum swerved just in time.

'Someone wants you, Jean!' he called back, raising his hand. And with a heavy heart, he walked slowly back to the Jeep.

Chapter Fifty-Two

As Seffy trudged back to the cottage, the rain started hammering down.

She tightened her headscarf under her chin and pushed her hands deep into her overcoat pockets. She was going to get soaked but she didn't care. She was glad she hadn't gone with Callum in the Jeep. She hadn't wanted to drag things out, or say a final goodbye while Mrs Harris and Jean peered out of the window.

She'd told him that was it, the end. He had to leave her alone now.

Please, she'd wanted to add, this poor bruised heart of mine can't take any more.

'Seffy, SEFFY!'

Eileen and Myrtle were running towards her down the lane, arms waving, frantically. What were they doing here, so far from the felling site?

'Thank God we've seen you,' Eileen said, when they reached her. 'Summat awful's happened.'

Something awful had happened, that was true, Seffy thought, but this must be something else. Knowing the Lost Girls, it could be something as 'awful' as Myrtle losing a glove or Eileen forgetting her jammy piece.

'What?' Seffy demanded. This had better not be anything silly; she wasn't in the mood.

'Mr McIntyre's tree's come down!' Myrtle said, wincing. 'You know, the one we weren't supposed to fell?'

Seffy closed her eyes for a second. She felt sick. 'We'll have to tell him,' she said.

'Aw, he already knows,' Myrtle said. 'We've just been to his house. We thought we'd better.'

That explained why the girls were so far from their usual stamping ground. 'Golly, that was brave,' Seffy said. 'And you lived to tell the tale. Did he explode?'

Myrtle shrugged. 'Not really. He went a wee bit pale.'

'And then he drove off to the forest to tek a look for himself. I don't think he believes us,' Eileen said.

He was probably thinking the same as Seffy: that the girls could easily be mistaken. There were hundreds of trees in this forest. The Douglas firs all looked identical, as did the oaks. They might've got it wrong. Please, let them be wrong.

'Come on,' Seffy said. 'Let's go and meet him at the tree. Oh, and we'll need Jean. The voice of reason.'

'Isobel and Tich have gone to get her,' Eileen said. 'Come on. Let's make haste!'

There was no mistake.

McIntyre's special oak was lying on the forest floor, ripped out by its roots. The landowner was standing motionless beside the huge trunk, staring at it in disbelief and soaked to the skin.

He didn't look around when they arrived but asked, quietly, 'What in God's name happened?'

'We were felling another tree and it went the wrong way,' Eileen said. 'I dunnae know why, although there was a sudden strong gust of wind, so …' She shrugged, helplessly.

'We did everything the same as always,' Myrtle said, 'but when

I pushed the trunk, instead of going into the clearing, it landed on your oak and took it down wi' it.'

So, the girls hadn't actually felled the tree; it had been an accident. But that would be no consolation to McIntyre. He was furious. Seffy could see it in his tense, white face and by the way he was holding himself rigid.

For once, his anger wasn't a ranting, raving kind: it was cold and silent, which was worse.

Oh, yell at us, why don't you, Seffy thought. Let's get this over with.

The others arrived then – Jean, Tich and Isobel – dashing through the driving rain, holding onto their berets.

Tich didn't help matters by exclaiming, 'Oh, ma God!' when she saw the fallen tree and slapping her hands over her mouth.

'I'm sorry to see this, Mr McIntyre,' Jean said. 'But I did say it'd be—'

Seffy nudged her, hard.

Jean had warned McIntyre it would be difficult to spare a tree that was surrounded by others that were due to be felled. He hadn't wanted to hear it and now certainly wasn't the time to remind him.

'We could take a cutting,' Jean said, changing tack.

McIntyre spun around and glared at her. 'A what?'

Jean swallowed. 'We could take a cutting from this tree and plant it and with a bit of luck, it'll grow.'

Was that right? Did Jean know this or was she making an educated guess? Seffy knew one could take cuttings from roses but was it possible to do it from trees, too?

'And what good is that to ME?' McIntyre said.

'It won't be this actual tree, of course,' Seffy said. 'As much as we'd like to, we can't bring it back to life. But it would be—' she took a deep breath '—a child of this tree.'

It had sounded ridiculous. And judging from the look on Jean's face, she thought the same.

McIntyre seemed to have calmed down a little. He was staring at the ground, lost in the thought.

When he looked up, he'd clearly made a decision.

'I want you off my land. All of you. NOW!'

Tich cried out in dismay but he put his hand up to silence her.

'No arguing! Take your tools, leave now. I want no trace that you were ever here. I'll be reporting you to Burke first thing tomorrow. I was right all along. I knew you weren't to be trusted in my woods. You're a disgrace to the Women's Timber Corps!'

Chapter Fifty-Three

Jean pushed open the back door of Laburnum Cottage and started pulling off her gumboots.

'According to Alec,' she shouted through the open door, 'there's nae chance of anyone gettin' hold o' Mr Burke until next week!'

Seffy appeared, holding a cup of tea and looking hopeful.

It'd been three long days since Mr McIntyre had thrown them off his land and they hadn't heard a word from anyone in authority since. They were tired of twiddling their thumbs, so Jean had gone to the saw mill on a recce. The change in the place – and in Alec – had been astonishing. The fellas were not only talking to him, they were listening to him, too.

'We've got a temporary reprieve, then,' Seffy said. 'But how does Alec know about Mr Burke?'

Jean stepped into the kitchen in her stockinged feet and smiled.

'Alec's practically running the place. He knows everything! And apparently, Mr Burke is on annual leave.'

The girls sat disconsolately at the kitchen table.

'We really will have to do something soon,' Seffy said. 'This is too dull and we're hardly showing initiative. I suppose we could always send a telegram to Miss McEwen? We might get moved on?'

Jean frowned. 'No, let's keep her out of it.'

Seffy must be desperate, if she wanted to get Miss McEwen involved. But poor Seffy had been let down summat rotten by that Canadian fella at the weekend. She probably wanted to throw herself into her work as a way of forgetting all about him.

They jumped in their seats as someone hammered at the front door.

'That sounds official,' Seffy said. 'Come on, let's go and see.'

It was Mr McIntyre, looking unusually agitated. His red sports car was parked in the lane.

'Are the lassies working in my woods?' he demanded.

'Of course not,' Seffy said. 'You made it quite clear that we were to leave and—'

'No!' he said. He ran a hand through his hair. 'I mean, you dunnae understand. I want—' he exhaled '—I *need* them to start working again.'

Jean gave a jolt of surprise. 'What d'you mean, sir? When?'

'Now!' He pulled out his pocket watch and frowned 'I – it's urgent! No time to explain. Can you round them up? All of them? Except that rough girl. Not her. And wear your dress uniforms!'

Hang on a minute, Jean wanted to say. He'd been rude and ungracious from the moment they'd met him; he'd as good as sacked them the other day and now he was giving orders and expecting them to obey?

'What's all this about?' Jean asked. 'We dunnae wear our dress uniforms for work, by the by. They're only for special occasions.'

'This IS a special occasion!' he said. 'It's an inspection.'

Jean rolled her eyes at Seffy. No doubt he wanted to impress some local dignitary. Or perhaps it was an official from the ministry.

She was expecting Seffy to refuse point blank. Let him explain that to his important visitors! But no, she was nodding at the fella and looking brighter.

'We could whizz around the billets on the bicycles and round the girls up, couldn't we, Jean?' she said.

'Good!' McIntyre said, rubbing his hands together. 'Can you get them into the woods on the south side and start felling again, at the double?'

'No, wait!' Jean said. 'If this is an inspection, we should all be there, not just the fellers. Me and Rona too, and Peggy. It's all of us or none of us! And no dress uniforms.'

She looked expectantly at Seffy and after a moment's hesitation, Seffy said, 'Yes, Jean's right. But Peggy's at the saw mill. You'll have to fetch her.'

'All right, I can do that,' he said, without enthusiasm. 'And then, you'll start felling again?'

He seemed to have forgotten all about his precious fallen tree. Ma God, he really must have his back to the wall.

'Of course!' Seffy said.

'Aye, we'll go back to work on one condition,' Jean said. She took a deep breath. 'That you open up your house to the lassies.'

McIntyre's eyes widened. 'Open ... whatever do you mean?'

Seffy had gasped at her audacity. But she quickly caught on.

'Yes! That's it!' she said. 'The girls have rotten billets and you've got so much room, Mr McIntyre. You're rattling around in the place. If you get a cook and open up your long gallery as a dorm for the girls—'

'They'll pay the going rate, of course,' Jean said.

'Women? In my house?'

'They don't have fleas!' Jean said, crossing her fingers behind her back. She couldn't actually swear to that.

He bit his lip. He was wavering.

'Those are our terms,' Jean said, firmly.

'I cannae do it immediately,' he said.

'We need your absolute word—' Jean said.

'The word of a gentleman!' Seffy added.

'—that the place will be ready to take the girls within a fortnight.' Jean finished.

'A fortnight? But that's no time at all!'

Jean held out her hand. 'Do we have a deal?'

Mr McIntyre huffed and muttered something about being blackmailed.

'Very well,' he said, finally, giving Jean's hand a cursory shake. 'What choice do I have?'

Seffy looked proudly at her fellers, brashing the fir they'd just brought down, while Jean and Rona made a neat pile of the lopped branches.

It had been a mad dash from the moment McIntyre had left them, but they'd done it: the gang was on site and working as he'd requested. And, thanks to genius Jean, they'd secured a new billet for the Lost Girls into the bargain.

Peggy arrived a little while after the others, courtesy of a ride in McIntyre's topless sports car.

'It was a wee bit windy!' she announced, as everyone laughed at her wild tangle of hair.

'It's like a bird's nest!' Tich said.

'Here, borrow my headscarf,' Seffy said. 'That'll soon flatten it down.'

Peggy took it and thanked her.

'I was taken aback, when the McIntyre fella turned up at the saw mill and said you wanted me here,' she said.

'We insisted you came,' Seffy said. 'Isn't that right, Jean? We wanted the whole gang here, reporting for duty!'

Later that afternoon, they heard a car engine on the road.

'That'll be them,' Seffy said.

She felt suddenly nervous. She hoped they weren't going to let themselves, or McIntyre, down.

'Keep going girls,' she said. 'We'll only stop when they get here. They might simply want to observe, or they might want a chat. Make sure there are no saws or axes lying around for anyone to trip over!'

317

A few minutes later, there was a rustle through the trees and a foxy little dog with stubby legs and pointed ears appeared. He was a sweet little thing with a thick caramel-coloured coat and a white chest.

He ran straight up to Seffy and she scooped him up.

Gosh, he was heavier than he looked. He stretched up and licked her face.

She laughed. 'Where have you come from, mister?'

The murmur of voices and the sound of footsteps grew louder. McIntyre – scrubbed up and in a red and grey kilt that Seffy hadn't seen before – was leading the way.

The dog started to wriggle in her arms, so Seffy put him down. 'Dookie, come here!'

A pretty, dark-haired girl of about thirteen had appeared, dressed in a kilt and tartan jacket. The dog ignored her and continued to scamper around the felling site, sniffing and cocking his leg incessantly.

'He's very naughty,' the girl said, in a clipped English accent. She giggled as the dog charged around the Lost Girls' feet. 'Do watch he doesn't nip your ankles. He's a terror for that.'

'He's a darling,' Seffy said. 'I have a dog at home – Trixie – who's quite as disobedient as yours. I miss her terribly.'

The other visitors had reached them now. They weren't in uniform: this wasn't, after all, an official Timber Corps inspection.

A stately-looking woman came first, in a forest-green overcoat with a fur collar and a matching hat. She was with another dark-haired girl, wearing the same kilt and tweed jacket as the first.

This girl was a similar age to the younger Lost Girls – seventeen, or thereabouts – and looked rather familiar. Seffy stared as much as she could without being rude. Who was she? Seffy felt as though she'd seen her before but couldn't place her.

McIntyre was fawning and smiling – a strange sight to see – and the gang had stopped work, despite Seffy's instruction that they should carry on.

The Lost Girls were gazing at the strangers in obvious confusion.

'Is that—?' Rona murmured.

'It cannae be,' Isobel said, letting her axe fall to the ground.

Seffy looked more closely at their visitors. Goodness, it was! She put her hand over her mouth to hide her shock. The woman in the green overcoat was the Queen! It was the actual Queen and the two princesses, Elizabeth and Margaret Rose. They must be staying at Balmoral.

The Queen was smiling at the Lost Girls and admiring the felled tree around which they were all standing.

McIntyre cleared his throat. 'Your Majesties, may I present members of the Women's Timber Corps, who're doing a sterling job for the war effort, here in my forest.'

He turned to Seffy. 'And this is their leader girl—' he swallowed and Seffy thought for one horrible moment he'd forgotten her name, but no, it seemed he was merely pausing for effect. 'Lady—' he started and she winced.

Don't spoil everything, she begged him silently. She didn't want to be announced as a titled lady.

It wasn't the done thing to interrupt when one was being presented to royalty but there was nothing else for it.

'It's Miss Mills, your Majesties,' she said quickly, throwing an apologetic glance at McIntyre. 'That's … er, my name.'

She tucked one leg behind the other, bowed her head and curtsied.

'Ma God, you dropped so low, I though you wouldnae be able to get up again!' Peggy said when the royal party had left.

'How did you know what to do?' Rona asked.

'Good breeding, that's wha' it is,' Tich said, admiringly.

Seffy smiled. All modesty aside, it had been the perfect curtsey. Wait until she told Mummy. Those months as a debutante and the interminable deportment classes had not been in vain.

One didn't like to brag, so she wouldn't mention it now, but of course, she'd met Queen Elizabeth before, when she'd been presented at court. She could've sworn she'd detected a glimmer of recognition in Her Majesty's eyes. But it wouldn't have been proper for the Queen to have singled her out.

The girls had lined up to be properly introduced – what an honour!

The rest of the visit had passed in a blur and Seffy could barely remember what had been asked or how she'd replied but she remembered the Queen had asked about the process of felling a tree and commended them on a job very well done. Her Majesty's kind and encouraging words would keep them going for a long time.

And to be fair to Peggy, she'd kept the story of her terrible injury to herself and not said anything out of turn.

'I didnae breathe the whole time!' Tich said. 'It's a good job they didnae stay long, I was about to pass out!'

'Princess Elizabeth seemed quite taken with our work,' Jean said. 'Perhaps when she's old enough to join the war effort, she'll become a lumberjill.'

The Lost Girls laughed at the thought of it.

'I doubt that one'll be getting her hands dirty!' Myrtle said. 'She'll be queen hersel' one day, remember.'

'No, I think she'll muck in,' Jean said. 'There's a steeliness about her. She's an earnest young woman and she'll take her duty seriously, I'm sure. I have high hopes for her, when the time comes.'

McIntyre returned a few minutes later, looking surprisingly bashful and rather grateful. He twirled his cap around in his hands.

'Well done, ladies. You were a credit to the Corps.'

'Not a disgrace, then?' Tich said.

'How did that come about?' Seffy asked. 'A visit from royalty?'

McIntyre gave a modest shrug. 'I know the family – a little – and

I had a telephone call from the Queen's equerry. The Queen and the Princesses had heard the Women's Timber Corps were on my land and they wanted to see for themselves. But it had to be unofficial and low-key. No photographers or press.'

'To think, we've met our royal patron!' Jean said. 'There's not many lumberjills – or land girls, for that matter – that can say that.'

Thank goodness, Seffy thought, the request hadn't been made a few weeks ago, when they'd have had nothing but a rag-tag group of ruffians to show their Majesties.

McIntyre coughed. 'I think your lassies gave a very good account of themselves, Miss Mills. Didn't speak too much—'

'No! They were struck dumb, for possibly the first time ever!' Seffy said, making everyone laugh.

He cleared his throat. 'As a wee thank you, would you all like to come and take tea with me on Saturday, at three o'clock?'

'Everyone?' Peggy asked.

'Not just Seffy?' Eileen said.

'All of you.' He nodded at Jean. 'All of you, or none of you.'

Chapter Fifty-Four

'I'm sorry about your trees,' Seffy said to McIntyre on Saturday afternoon, as they took a turn around his garden. 'I know you feel the loss of them very deeply. Especially … that particular one.'

His shoulders sagged and he looked away.

She'd wanted to acknowledge what had happened but perhaps she should've stayed quiet. She'd upset him.

'Thank you, Miss Mills,' he said, after a moment. 'It was a blow, I'll admit. But the tree was old, it wasnae gonna last forever. And when you've waited for the axe to fall—' he gave a rueful smile '—quite literally, in this case, sometimes it's not as bad as you'd expected, if you take my meaning.'

Seffy understood completely. She'd always known that there'd come a time when Callum would have to choose between her and Missy. It'd seemed so far off she'd never given it much consideration. And now the axe had fallen, painful though it had been, life went on; she'd survived.

A jubilant shout went up from the first floor of the house, followed by a cheer. She'd left Jean to break the good news to the Lost Girls about their new billet.

McIntyre was stroking his chin. He seemed pensive.

'I've asked around,' he said, 'and that idea of Miss Ferguson's, of taking cuttings from the oak, might actually be possible. We can try, at least. And I'm planning a new wood, in that site you cleared.'

'That's a super idea,' Seffy said. As they strolled below the first-floor windows, she heard a shriek, followed by the thunder of boots rampaging over floorboards. She glanced at McIntyre but he was making no sign of having heard them.

'Isn't there a saying about planting a tree?' he said. '"To plant a tree is to believe in the future"? Summat like that. Of course, I won't be around to see the wood in its full glory.' He looked at her. 'You might be, though, Miss Mills. Come and see the trees, will you, gi' them a pat for me? If you're ever passing?'

Seffy smiled. It was rather unlikely. This place was so remote and not particularly on the way to anywhere. Once she'd left, she doubted whether she'd ever come back.

She stopped. She'd had a sudden vision of herself, all grown-up. A mother – or even, perhaps, a grandmother – strolling hand in hand with a man through McIntyre's wood. She could smell the damp air, feel the cool breeze on her face. They were surrounded by a clutch of children, who were scampering through the trees, kicking up leaves and laughing.

It had only lasted a second, and then it was gone, but it left her swaying slightly. Had she just seen a picture of her future?

McIntyre was looking at her quizzically.

'I will,' she said. 'If I'm ever passing, I promise I'll come and see the trees.'

They walked on a little further and she asked about his plans for the Drumlochrie estate.

Seffy wouldn't say it, but he had no one to leave it to, after all.

'I've been thinking about that,' he said. 'I'd like to leave everything – the house and the land – to the nation. I believe that's possible. Then others can enjoy it.'

Seffy nodded. 'Your legacy.'

McIntyre laughed. 'Och, I'm not sure I'd call it anything so grand! Come on—' he looked skywards '—that looks like rain and the tea should be ready by now. Let's head back into the house.' He gave a wry smile. 'If it's still standin'!'

As they walked in silence across the lawn, Seffy's mind drifted back to the vision she'd had of her future self, walking through a wood that was still to be planted.

She shook her head. It was no good: try as she might, she still couldn't put him out of her mind.

The warm, rough hand that had been holding hers, after all those years, had been Callum Fraser's.

'I think it's a good thing, havin' those lassies living there!' Mrs Harris said, when the three women were back at Laburnum Cottage later. 'It'll breathe new life into the place.'

Seffy raised her eyebrows. 'I only hope Mr McIntyre realises what he's let himself in for!'

'Aye,' Jean said. 'I feel a wee bit guilty. Those girls are only half-tame!'

They laughed but it was true, the Lost Girls were wild. And very excited about the thought of moving into Drumlochrie and living together.

'Did you see them, running amok?' Jean said. 'They were in an especially good mood today, mind, because they've all had money from the Land Army Benevolent Fund. I think they only sat still for five minutes the whole afternoon and that was when you brought out the tea, Mrs Harris.'

Mrs Harris sighed. 'Aye, it was a pity I couldn't have made some o' ma special crunchies but Mr McIntyre said he'd rather I used the sugar for a cake, so there you are. Aw, who's this then?'

Someone had knocked on the back door.

Mrs Harris bobbed up and looked out of the kitchen window. She sat straight back down again, muttering something and crossing herself.

'It's the telegraph laddie,' she said, faintly. 'It's bad news. I can tell by his face. I cannae go. One of yous'll have to read it.'

It mightn't be so bad, Seffy thought. It could be from Mr Harris, announcing he was coming home on leave. Or it could be – no, she wouldn't let herself think it might be from Callum.

Jean had pushed back her chair and gone to open the door.

When Seffy glimpsed the boy standing there in his uniform and black tie, she started to shiver. No, on second thoughts, Mrs Harris was right. This was bad news.

'Seffy, I'm sorry,' Jean said. 'It's for you.' To the telegram boy, she said, 'Wait there a minute.'

She'd left the door open and a chill wind was blowing through the kitchen.

'You read it for me, Jean,' Seffy said. Her teeth were chattering. She bowed her head and clutched her hands tightly in her lap.

Something awful had happened. Nothing would ever be the same again.

She heard the rustle of paper and then Jean took a sharp breath.

'I'm sorry,' she said. 'It's Teddy.'

'Tell me,' Seffy said, not looking up.

Jean's voice was flat and hesitant. 'I'm afraid he's … he's been killed in action.'

Mrs Harris gasped and clutched her chest. Jean went back to the telegram boy. 'No reply,' she said, and shut the door.

'Did you hear me, Seffy? Did you understand?' Jean said, bending down and squeezing her shoulder.

Seffy shook her head, shrugging Jean off. No, that wasn't true. There must be some mistake. Not Teddy. They'd got the wrong chap; they'd got him mixed up with someone else.

'Who'd sent the telegram?' she asked, surprised to find she could speak.

'It was from Percy,' Jean said, gently. 'That's your brother, isn't it?'

Seffy nodded.

Mrs Harris got up and put the kettle on. 'I shall make us all a cup of tea,' she said, quietly.

'Oh, God!' Seffy's hand shot to her mouth.

She'd suddenly remembered the letter she'd sent him. What had she been thinking, sending a letter like that? Poor, dear Teddy must've died with those horrible, pompous words ringing in his ears: 'No possibility of it ever being revived'. She put her head down on the table and howled.

Chapter Fifty-Five

'Is my tie straight?' Seffy asked, turning from the mirror on the dresser to face Jean.

Jean frowned and stepped forward to adjust it. 'Now it is,' she said. 'All set?'

'All set.'

They'd arranged to meet the others half a mile from the church. The Lost Girls would be coming directly from their billet: McIntyre's house.

He'd kept his promise. He'd engaged a cook, increased Mrs Harris's hours and had the long gallery at Drumlochrie turned into a dorm for the girls.

They'd been living there for the past couple of months and although McIntyre was prone to shaking his head in apparent despair whenever he talked about his lodgers, Seffy had it on good authority – Mrs Harris – that he was a different person since they'd moved in.

'He's no' so crabbit!' she'd said.

His attitude to their work had certainly changed. They'd

finished felling the original requisitioned section of forest – meaning Seffy could, in theory, now leave Ballamar – and McIntyre had agreed that the gang could move on to another part of his woodland. He told anyone who'd listen that they were doing a good job.

'Are we quits now, then?' he'd asked Seffy. 'I've taken the gang into the bosom of my home and I'm letting you fell more o' ma trees! What more can you ask for?'

Seffy had raised a finger and said, 'Just one more thing.'

And today was it.

'I'll see you downstairs,' Jean said. 'I've still got to polish my boots!'

Seffy nodded and sat on the bed, grateful for a few minutes alone.

She took out the letter she'd received from Grace yesterday and read it again.

3rd May 1944

Dear Seffy

I hope you're keeping well and those wee scamps aren't giving you too much trouble!

This might be the last letter I write for a wee while as the bairn's due any day. I'll be sure to write as soon as I can and let you know if it's a lad or a lassie.

You asked what I'm hoping for and I have to say a daughter, but I know Gordy wants a son! Either way, it doesnae matter, of course, so long as it's bonny and healthy, please God.

Now, I have some news. There's no easy way to say it but I thought you should know.

Callum Fraser is getting married on Saturday 13th May, near where they're stationed, on the south coast. The reason I know is that he's asked Gordy to be his groomsman (that's what they call 'best man').

I suppose you heard his fiancée came over from Canada? I expect they saw no reason to wait.

328

I know you're over him now, like you said in your last letter, and you probably dunnae care but this might still come as a wee shock. I hope I've not upset you or done the wrong thing in telling you. Don't shoot the messenger! I just thought you should know.

Sending you hugs and best wishes.

Ever your good friend,

Grace

There it was, in black and white. Callum was getting married next Saturday.

She'd known that was his plan, she shouldn't have been surprised and yet, reading Grace's words had been like a punch to the stomach.

It was queer to think she'd never see or speak to him again. Even if she knew how to get in touch, she wouldn't. What would she say? 'All the best and have a happy life?'

She shuddered at the thought of being mere friends, after all they'd meant to one another. She could never do that.

Enough, now.

She put the letter back in the envelope and placed it in her sock drawer, next to Callum's opal pendant.

'Are you ready?' Jean called up the stairs.

'Ready!' she replied.

As they walked towards the kirk, Jean said, 'You dunnae have to transfer to England, you know. I could put a word in wi' Miss McEwen. I bet she'd let you stay here. Or go back to Blantyre, if you'd rather. Whatever you want to do.'

Seffy frowned. 'If Miss McEwen's moved heaven and earth to get me a posting in the New Forest, she'll have my guts for garters if I don't go!'

Jean shook her head. 'Not necessarily. Circumstances have changed, after all.'

Circumstances certainly had changed. And it was dec

Jean to make the offer, particularly as she was due to take over as leader girl here if Seffy went to England.

But although she'd found it hard to think straight after what had happened with Callum and then, that awful business with Teddy, Seffy was clear on one thing: she needed to get away from here.

'No, Jean, I'm still going to go. I need a new challenge. I need to keep this—' Seffy tapped her head '—fully occupied! You can have the bed all to yourself!'

It wasn't so bad here now: the Lost Girls had turned into the kind of gang she'd originally hoped for, but this place held so many memories and most of them weren't good.

She'd never forget standing in the freezing river as Callum told her he'd chosen Missy over her or sitting at the kitchen table, finding out that Teddy had been killed.

Dear Teddy. The feelings of guilt over that blasted letter would never leave her. She should've trusted her own instincts: she'd known the wording was too harsh. She'd regretted sending it the moment she'd dropped it into the letter box.

They rounded the bend in the lane. They could see the Lost Girls in the distance, waiting for them.

'You know,' Jean said, 'You were specially chosen for this place.'

Seffy looked at her. 'What d'you mean?'

Jean sighed. 'I wasnae supposed to tell you. The bigwigs in the WTC heard what you did last summer and thought you could handle the Lost Girls. They thought you'd be up for a challenge.'

Seffy gave a hollow laugh. 'It's certainly been that!'

Jean smiled. 'I thought you should know. You've been awful low for the past few weeks, and I understand why, but you've got … well, a lot of folk admire you, Seffy. I …' She cleared her throat. 'And I'm one of them.'

'Here they are!' Peggy yelled, as Jean and Seffy reached them.

The girls were clearly excited to be wearing their dress uniforms for the very first time.

Before they set off, berets were adjusted, ties were re-tied, Isobel had an actual lipstick and let everyone borrow it. And then, they marched – Seffy at the front, Jean bringing up the rear – to the church.

They hadn't practised their marching as much as they should but if they were a little out of step, Seffy was sure no one would mind.

As they entered the church and marched down the aisle, Seffy spotted several familiar faces in the pews: Alec, Davey McAllister from the pub, the saw mill chaps, the darts team gents and Mrs Harris, sitting next to Mr Galbraith.

The applause started as a ripple and moved through the congregation like a wave until everyone was clapping.

It was probably not the done thing to clap in the house of God, and the rector was frowning, but heaven help him, Seffy thought, if he tried to stop them, because they were clapping loud enough to raise the roof.

They'd reached the front now and there was McIntyre, using one of his pews, at last. Gracious me, he'd had a haircut.

The looks on the girls' faces as they took their places in the pews! They were bursting with pride and so was she.

They weren't the Lost Girls anymore; they seemed to have found their place in the world. For now, at least.

'Seffy!' Someone was calling from the pew behind, as the applause was dying down.

Seffy turned in her seat. It was Joey. And next to her – golly, she could hardly believe it– were Enid, Morag, Belinda and Flora. All the Macdonald girls. Oh, and there was Aunt Dilys at the end, waving.

Seffy laughed. 'What are you doing here?'

Joey lowered her voice to a whisper. 'It was Jean's idea. She wrote and told us you were moving to England. We wanted to see you before you left.'

'But how did you get here?'

'We're on a "Women's Home Defence special exercise"!' Joey said, giggling. 'Your auntie borrowed the truck and drove us here.'

After the service, everyone gathered outside the church. As Jean busied herself introducing the Lost Girls to the Macdonald crowd, Seffy sought out her aunt and gave her a peck on the cheek.

'Thank you so much for bringing everyone today,' she said. 'It's so lovely to see you all.'

Dilys sniffed. 'Well, we couldn't miss your passing out parade! You're moving on then, to a camp in England? I heard there was some doubt about whether you'd actually go.'

Seffy bit her lip. She didn't want to burden her aunt with the whole sorry tale of her and Callum.

'Not changed your mind, have you?' Dilys said, looking stern.

'No, Aunt,' Seffy said, firmly. 'I'm sticking to my plan. I'm going.'

'Good girl. Always move forward, that's the ticket!'

'Oi, Seffy!' It was Enid, holding out a large white envelope. 'This came for you. Sorry, it was a wee while ago. I kept meaning to forward it on but I kept forgetting. And then I heard we were coming here, so I thought I'd bring it.'

The letter was either from Tol or Percy. Their handwriting was almost identical. Silly sausage, whichever one it was. They'd sent it to her old address at Blantyre.

'Go on then,' Dilys said. 'I can see you're dying to read it.'

Seffy sat down on the church steps and opened the envelope. There was a letter inside – ah, it was from Percy. And – how odd – another, sealed and stamped envelope with her handwriting on the front.

She quickly scanned Percy's letter.

Sis, this came for Teddy, a couple of days after we lost him. I recognised your handwriting and rather than let it go into the box of personal effects, I swiped it. Sorry for the delay in posting it. I thought you'd like to have it back.

Seffy's mouth had gone dry. Could it be …? She checked the postmark and turned the envelope over. It was still sealed.

Relief washed over her. Teddy had never read her letter! That wonderful possibility had never occurred to her. It must've got delayed in the post. Please God, he'd gone to his grave with hope and some measure of happiness in his heart.

She read the next few lines of Percy's letter.

Teddy was so happy, those last few days, he'd written. *The flights were good and he had you and—*

She couldn't read any more.

She wiped a tear from her eye.

Dear Teddy, such a sweet boy, didn't deserve to die like that. But what a relief: he'd died thinking she loved him. Whatever else happened in this godforsaken war, she would always be grateful for that.

Chapter Fifty-Six

The South Coast, England

Missy's shoes made a satisfying clickety-click as she walked up the path to the church. It was a sunny spring morning in England. The perfect setting for saying 'I do.'

A pretty tortoiseshell cat slunk out from behind a gravestone and stopped in front of her, demanding to be petted. Missy put her small bouquet into her left hand and bent to stroke it.

'Hey, I bet that's lucky,' Gordy called out from the church entrance. 'A cat crossing your path on your wedding day.'

She straightened and smiled at him. 'Hi, Gordy. Are they all set in there?'

He nodded. 'All set.'

There wouldn't be many inside the church: a few fellas from Callum's company and a couple of girls from the café where they were holding their reception. Missy suspected the girls were more interested in meeting Canadian soldiers than witnessing her marriage but they'd boost the numbers a little.

Verne hadn't been invited, of course. He and Juliet had been kept in the dark about the whole shebang.

Had she been getting married back home, her sister would've

been matron of honour and Dad would've given her away. Missy felt a tiny pang at the thought. It sure wasn't the wedding she'd dreamed of since she was a little girl, but at least they were doing it properly, in a church. And when they got back to Canada, someday, they'd have a proper knees-up.

She was in her uniform and the lack of a white dress had given her a moment of regret but she'd pushed the thought aside. At least she was wearing her strappy shoes with a heel. No way was she going to wear those mannish black lace-ups on her wedding day.

Anyway, who cared what she was wearing or who was or wasn't here? Soon, she'd be Mrs Callum Fraser and nothing else mattered.

Callum had suggested walking into the church together but Missy had said no. If she couldn't walk down the aisle on her father's arm, then at least the groom should be in his rightful place, at the altar. They'd be walking down the aisle together at the end of the service, in any case, as man and wife.

Gordy – who was also the groomsman – had agreed to walk her down the aisle. 'Ready?' he asked now, holding out the crook of his arm.

'Do you have the ring?' Missy whispered, as they stepped into the church. He tapped his pocket. 'Sure, I do.'

After the welcome by the minister, they sang the first hymn and then the service started. It was galloping along so fast, it was making Missy panic. She wanted to slow it all down and remember every second. She glanced at Callum, standing beside her, so tall and handsome – and serious – in his uniform and wondered what he was thinking.

The minister cleared his throat. 'Should anyone present know of any reason that this couple should not be joined in holy matrimony, speak now or forever hold your peace.'

There was silence. Dust motes floated in the sunshine streaming through the stained-glass windows. Someone coughed. The cat that Missy had petted outside, padded up the aisle, meowing loudly.

'Does anyone *human* have any objections?' he said, and everyone laughed.

That minister was quite the joker. Missy exchanged a smile with Callum and felt the tension she'd been holding slip away.

'I DO! I have a reason! In fact, I have three!'

Missy's stomach dropped like a stone. A woman had yelled out from the back of the church.

She knew that voice. Juliet.

This was like some kind of nightmare and at the same time, inevitable. Missy had known this was all too good to be true: deep down, she'd been expecting something to go wrong.

Everyone turned to watch, as Juliet marched down the aisle. She was in uniform; she was furious. Her hair had escaped its bun and was flying around her face.

'And you are?' the minister asked.

'I'm the bride's loving sister.'

Loving? Was this some kind of sick joke? Missy heard nervous laughter from the fellas in the front pews.

At least there were only a handful of people here to witness her deep, searing shame. Couldn't anyone do something? Tell Juliet to shut up or drag her outside? But no one moved.

She'd reached them now. Her face was coated in a sheen of perspiration;

'And what are those reasons, Madam?' the minister asked.

Callum stepped in front of Juliet and gave her an icy stare, daring her to speak again. He put up his finger for silence.

'I just wanna say—' she started.

'I think you've said enough!' Callum said. 'What are you doing, Juliet?' He turned to the minister. 'Can we go someplace a little more private?'

Callum put his hand in the small of Missy's back, gently

336

steering her as they were led into a cool room at the back of the church.

There was a large hardback book laid out on a table, complete with a pen and pot of ink and two wooden chairs. Here, Missy supposed, they would've signed the register, had they managed to get that far.

The minister looked at Juliet. 'Now, madam, what reasons do you have against this marriage?'

Juliet glanced at Missy and then back at the minister.

'First off, it'll break our parents' hearts if she gets married over here.'

Oh, that old chestnut. Sure, they'd be a little sore but they'd get over it. Juliet was making a complete fool of herself.

'And Callum,' Juliet said, turning to him, 'everyone knows you only proposed to Missy because our father told you to!'

Missy gasped as though she'd been punched. The barefaced lie! Why would she say that? And why wasn't Callum immediately refuting it?

'Those objections are not legal impediments to this marriage taking place,' the minister said.

Missy let out a little 'Oh!'

There, thank God. Juliet had simply wasted everyone's time and ruined her – *their* – wedding day.

She mustn't forget this was Callum's special day too. She wanted to smile at him but her lips were quivering and, in any case, he wasn't looking at her. His head was bowed, his gaze fixed firmly on the floor. She wished he'd hold her hand or say something reassuring.

'However,' the minister said, gravely, 'I appreciate that, for the bride and groom, there may be … um, repercussions. Take a few minutes – or as long as you need – to discuss this. Then, if you still wish the ceremony to go ahead, we will proceed.'

When they were alone, Missy said, 'That's not true, is it, what Juliet said about Dad making you propose?'

Callum groaned up at the ceiling. He looked back at her and reached out for her hand, but she snatched it away. Why didn't he answer?

'No, he did not *make* me! I respect your dad and I owe him a lot but even he can't tell me what to do with my life!'

That was no doubt true. Callum knew his own mind; he was his own man.

He spread his hands. 'But, honestly? I suppose, at the party that night, he gave me a nudge in the right direction. I-I should've thought of it myself.'

Wait, so there was something in what Juliet had said?

Missy narrowed her eyes. 'So, all that under the stars, romantic, down on one knee stuff wasn't actually your idea?'

Callum gave a hollow laugh. 'Sure, it was my idea. Your dad suggested I might like to propose, he didn't tell me how to do it!'

Missy put her hand on the back of a chair to steady herself. It was true, then: Dad had 'suggested' he should propose, like some kind of arranged marriage! And apparently 'everyone knew'! How mortifying. She should be angry – with both men – but she just felt beaten down and numb.

'Missy, I—' Callum started to say.

But she'd just thought of something. She dashed to the door and ran out into the church which was, thankfully, deserted. The minister must've told everyone to get some air. But Juliet was there, at the back, sitting alone in one of the pews.

'What was the third?' Missy said.

Juliet turned. 'Pardon me?'

'You said there were three reasons but you've only told us two.'

Juliet walked slowly back down the aisle towards her, twisting her hands, uncertainly. 'It's probably nothing. I shouldn't—'

'Tell me!'

They were standing face to face now. Juliet placed her hands on Missy's shoulders and took a deep breath. 'I was gonna say

338

to Callum, "I don't think you love my sister in the way that you should".'

'What does that mean?' Missy shrugged Juliet's hands away and took a step back.

Juliet winced. 'It's something Verne said to me in a letter once, about Callum and—'

'And?'

'—he thought he might've had something going on, with a British girl.' She paused. 'Missy, did you know there were female foresters working with the fellas up in Scotland? Lumberjills, they called them.'

Missy's heart was thudding, her mind was racing. She knew nothing, about anything. She shook her head. 'Uh, huh.'

'I had no idea either, but apparently, they were working alongside our fellas for months. There were dances at the camp and all sorts. How d'you think Gordy met his wife? She was one of them.'

The pieces slotted into place: Callum had someone else! Stupid, stupid! She'd pushed all the doubts to the back of her mind and made excuses. They were shy, they needed time, blah blah. Heck, she'd never even had the nerve to tackle him about that dumb book!

'Are you OK?' Juliet said. 'You're not gonna do something crazy?'

Missy swallowed. In a funny kinda way, she was OK. And as for the crazy part, she'd already done that. She'd known Callum wasn't a hundred per cent committed to this marriage but she'd pushed for it. And now, it had all blown up in her face.

'How did you find out about the wedding?' Missy asked.

'One of the guys let something slip to Verne and he wired me. I dropped everything. I've been all over looking for you. Turns out, there are three churches in this town and of course, you had to be in the last!'

Juliet smiled briefly, then her shoulders slumped. 'But, I guess, I was working on a hunch. I don't know for definite about Callum. You should talk to him. I'm sorry, I shouldn't have come.'

'You should! I'm glad you did.'

They hugged one another. Missy couldn't remember the last time they'd done that. Must've been way back when they were kids.

'You think I did the right thing?' Juliet asked.

Missy patted her shoulder. 'I do.'

Callum was leaning against the wall, deep in thought. He stood up straight when Missy entered the anteroom and gave her a questioning look.

'Would you mind turning out your inside pocket?' she said. She was calm and resolute. 'No, the left-hand side.'

His mouth twisted for a second, then he did as she asked, wordlessly pulling out the paperback and holding it out to her. He couldn't meet her eye. The orange cover was worn and soft. He had it there, even on his wedding day.

Missy gave a slight shake of her head. She wouldn't take it or ask what 'S' stood for because if she didn't know the girl's name, then she didn't exist.

But she would ask him something. There was still a tiny chance for them, if he gave her the right answer.

'Callum—' he looked so big and strong and yet, there was a vulnerability, suddenly, in his face that made the words stick in her throat. Come on, she told herself, don't be a coward.

'Do you love—?' She stopped. She'd been going to say, 'Do you love me?' but she changed it at the last moment. 'Do you love another woman?'

He didn't flinch. He stood stock still and looked at her – really looked at her – and his eyes flickered for a second before he said, 'I do.'

Chapter Fifty-Seven

Basingstoke, Hampshire, England

'You're late!' Teresa the Limey said when Missy rushed into the Red Cross Room later that day.

'I apologise. I had to change. I'll work over.'

She'd been to the boarding house first, almost colliding with Laura on the front porch.

'Hey, what're you doing here?' Laura had asked. She'd looked around. 'Is he –?'

'No!' Missy had said. There hadn't been time to explain. 'Ask Juliet when she gets here. She'll tell you. I've gotta get changed and go to work!'

'But I'm just heading out to the hospital to cover your shift, Miranda, like we agreed!'

Juliet had been a little way down the street behind Missy and she'd reached the boarding house then. 'Best let her go, Laura,' she'd said. 'She's determined to go to work.'

Laura had shrugged, still looking unsure. 'OK,' she'd said. 'But you'd better hurry, Miranda!'

Missy had quickly washed, changed her tunic and run all the way to the hospital, only realising when it was too late to go back, that she hadn't changed her shoes. Now, she ignored Teresa's huffing and started tossing packs of cigarettes, newspapers and craft materials onto the half-empty cart. It wouldn't have killed the woman to have topped up the provisions while she was waiting.

'Having a nap, were ya?' Teresa asked, stifling a yawn.

'No, actually,' Missy said. 'I've been in church. Today was supposed to be my wedding day.'

Teresa froze in the middle of putting on her headscarf. '*Supposed* to? What, didn't he want to get married?'

It was the most she'd ever said to Missy, in all these weeks.

'Oh, I reckon he wanted to get married, all right.' Missy got behind the cart and gave it a firm shove. 'Only not to me!'

She smiled to herself as she steered the laden cart down the corridor. The shock on Teresa's face had given her a kind of grim satisfaction.

She hadn't intended on telling anyone, other than Laura, but it had kinda burst out of her. Knowing the Limeys, the gossip would be all over the hospital by tonight. Everyone from patients to porters would know that Officer Gilbert had been stood up at the altar.

At least, that's what the Chinese whispers would make of it. That wasn't exactly what had happened. Truth was, in the end, she'd been the one to call it off.

She didn't doubt that Callum loved her, in his own way. He would've married her, if she'd wanted to go ahead with the ceremony, but how could she marry a man who, by his own admission, loved someone else?

'Good luck with your girl, Callum,' had been her parting words to him.

She'd nodded at the paperback in his hand. He'd simply bitten his lip and shaken his head. She didn't know what that meant. It wasn't any of her business any more.

She took a deep breath. The worst thing that could've happened, had happened. And the sun was still shining and she still had work to do.

Amid the hollowness inside her, lurked a strange kind of relief. Deep down, she'd known it hadn't been right.

Even when she'd been standing at the altar, about to make her vows, she'd felt unsure. She'd put it down to nerves but it must've been more than that.

As the cart rattled down the corridor and she started to pick up speed, Missy glanced through the small square windows. There were daffodils flowering in the grounds. Bright, bouncy splashes of yellow. Spring, at last.

The Burns Ward – her favourite – was her first port of call and she was glad. It felt like a return to normality. She liked to feel needed; to be essential to someone's life.

She paused outside the door and exhaled, feeling a little drained but all right.

She hadn't been on the ward for a couple of days; they'd have missed her. There'd be new family photos for her to admire and the projects would have advanced. She sure hoped Nugget hadn't lost any more stitches off that scarf he'd been working on.

And of course, there was Rabbit. Mr Sarky. She'd be glad to see him again.

She reversed in, pulling the cart behind her and glanced at his bed.

It was empty.

Woah, that was a shock. The noises in the ward – the fellas' joyful shouts, the whoops and cheering – were muffled momentarily. She leaned on the cart.

Then suddenly, the voices were back, loud and demanding.

'Oh, hiya, Sister! Where've you been? Nice shoes, by the way!'

'Do you have a *Herald* on there, please, ma'am?'

'Hallelujah, she's here! I'm all outta smokes!'

'Come see Nugget's scarf, Sister! Hold it up, buddy! It's now a tie!'

The bed wasn't simply empty, as though he'd gone out in the

wheelchair for a smoke. It had been completely stripped of all bedding. There was nothing left but the mattress.

She looked at Chas in the next bed. 'Where'd he go?'

'Oh, yeah, Rabbit's gone.' He lifted himself up to peer at the cart. 'Say, do you have any basic kinda books? You know, without too many words in 'em?'

Gone? Was there something they weren't telling her? Rabbit couldn't have been discharged. He was still wired up to a drip and covered in bandages. He was too darned sick!

She pasted on a smile, nodded at the fellas, handed out books, gum and cigarettes with barely a word, all the time scouring the ward for any sign of him. But there was no one wrapped up in bandages like an Egyptian mummy.

He wasn't there.

'We have no idea where Rabbit is,' Shorty said. 'Woke up this morning and he was gone! Gone down his rabbit hole!' He laughed at his joke. 'Hey, Sister, where—?'

She'd left the men and the cart and burst back through the door and out into the corridor. She had to find a nurse, or a doctor and *beg* them to tell her what had happened to him. Even if it was bad news, she needed to know.

She yelped as someone grabbed her arm from behind and held her in a firm grip.

Matron.

She peered at Missy from under her cap with her beady bird eyes. Her mouth was set. Oh, boy, she looked real mad.

'A little behind on your rounds today, aren't you, Officer?' Matron said. With her free hand, she made a show of lifting up her watch. 'I'd have expected you to be on Charlie Ward by now.'

'Yes, ma'am.'

'And you seem to have mislaid your cart.'

Missy started to say she'd left it on the ward but she stopped. Matron was peering down at her feet.

'My, that is interesting footwear. "Mary Janes", isn't that what they call them?'

Shoot, could this get any worse? She should be wearing her flat lace-ups but instead, she was prancing around the hospital in strappy heels, as though she were at a party. She braced herself for a severe dressing-down.

Matron released her arm. It was sore but Missy resisted the urge to rub it.

'About the shoes,' she said. 'I – the thing is – I just …'

'He's down there on the left. Side room A,' Matron said. 'He's had an operation, so don't stay long. He's – don't RUN!'

Missy had gone racing, helter-skelter, down the corridor, not even held back by those darned shoes. Relief and gratitude coursed through her like fire.

'Thank you, Matron,' she muttered to herself.

He was still here, she hadn't missed him!

Run, rabbit, run.

Missy pushed open the door. Was this him? He was lying flat on the bed and half his bandages were gone, so she couldn't be sure.

He looked asleep but as she stepped inside and gently closed the door, he moved and pushed himself up with difficulty, until he was sitting with his back against the metal bedframe.

'Hi there, Rabbit,' she said.

She didn't know what she'd expected, but not this: it was the same strapping young man – his limbs too long for the bed – but now with most of his bandages removed. No more rabbit ears. He had thick, dark hair.

She stepped closer. His eyes – nice eyes – were brown and they were fixed on her. The skin on his face was red and puckered but it wasn't so bad. He was a good-looking fella.

'Hey, there, Squeaky,' he managed. His voice was a little croaky, as though he hadn't used it in a while.

She was shy, all of a sudden. It was the first time they'd seen each other and it was weird. She shook her head at the strangeness of it all. 'How did you know it was me? I changed my shoes.'

He managed a smile. A little crooked but a smile nonetheless. 'Yeah, but you didn't change your scent. Or your voice.'

A wave of embarrassment washed over her. She hoped he wasn't disappointed. She was warm from all that running. Her face was probably shiny. She wished she was wearing a little powder.

He looked around and frowned. 'Where's your cart?'

'Oh … I left it some place,' she said, waving her hand dismissively.

'Careless.'

'Yeah.'

She studied him more closely. 'Can you see?' she asked, remembering – too late – that she shouldn't ask the fellas about their injuries.

He nodded slowly. 'This one's a little fuzzy.' He pointed to his left eye. 'But the other's fine and dandy.'

'You can see me, then.' She gave a silly little 'ta dah' movement with her hands and immediately wished she could take it back.

'Sure can. And you're not at all how I imagined.'

Thank you, sir, she thought. Kick a girl while she's down, why don't you? In his mind's eye, she'd probably been a cross between Marilyn Monroe and Lana Turner.

She gave a little shrug.

'No, Squeaky,' he said, firmly. 'You're a million times better.'

The door opened and a nurse stepped into the room, carrying some dressings and what looked like a blood pressure monitor. She took one look at them and turned on her heels.

'I'll come back!' she said.

Missy was still reeling from being told she was better than he'd imagined, when Rabbit said, 'Where've you been, Squeaky?'

She couldn't go through all that. He'd hear it on the hospital grapevine soon enough. She'd lost Callum, but in a weird kinda way she'd found herself.

She hoped, in time, all that upheaval would start to feel like something that had happened to someone else, a long time ago.

'You know, my name is really Missy.'

'Well, mine's really Robert but I guess we'll always be Squeaky and Rabbit. What d'you say?'

'Yeah, I guess …'

What was this 'always'? There was something comforting about the word, though. It was a balm after the turmoil of the last few hours.

'You'd better get some rest,' she said, repeating a line she'd often heard the nurses use.

'Don't be a stranger!' he said, in his usual sardonic way, as she turned to leave. 'I'm thinking of our Mohican friends. We're only up to chapter twelve, right? The story ain't finished yet!'

Chapter Fifty-Eight

'Are you sure you're all right, Miranda?' Laura asked.

It was lunchtime, a few days after the wedding-that-wasn't. The girls were sitting on a bench in the hospital grounds. Their eyes were closed and they'd turned their faces up to the sunshine.

'I'm A-OK. Really. And please, Laura, would you mind calling me Missy?'

'Sure, but—'

'Miranda's my real name and I had some highfalutin' idea about using it over here and becoming a different person but I guess I'll always be little Missy from Invermore, B.C.!'

Laura laughed. 'I don't want you to be a different person. I like the person you are. But sure, I can call you Missy. I think it suits you better than Miranda.' She paused. 'Have you heard anything from … Callum?'

Missy opened her eyes and the two girls looked at one another. 'No and I don't expect to.'

She could say it without bitterness. She couldn't hate him; she couldn't even be mad at him. She felt a little sad, that was all.

Laura looked as though she was bursting to say something. 'I didn't tell you this before because you were busy with your … plans and our lives were heading in different directions but now that you're not, you know—'

Missy laughed. 'Spit it out, girl!'

'OK, well, here's the thing. You know there's gonna be an invasion, right? That's why all the troops are on the coast?'

Missy nodded. It was a sobering thought but it was all anyone could talk about. Everyone knew it was coming; it was just a matter of when.

'I've been asked if I'd be willing to go overseas too,' Laura said. 'Once it's happened, I mean. The troops will still need support; there'll still be a lot of work to do. I've said I will. Why don't you come too!'

Missy frowned. 'Where would we be going?'

'Probably France to start with, then maybe Belgium or the Netherlands. Married Red Cross girls aren't permitted to go but now – well, now you could. What do you say?' Laura's eyes were shining. 'It'll be an adventure!'

'What'll we be doing?' Missy asked.

'Same as here. We'll be assigned to a Canadian hospital, still part of the Red Cross. But we have to get parental permission, so once we get the call, you'll need to send a cable to your folks right away. Might be worth sounding them out real soon.'

That was it, then. For a moment, she'd been excited: Laura's enthusiasm was infectious. But Mom and Dad would never agree to it. It had been difficult enough persuading them that she should come to England.

Over supper, that evening, Missy mentioned the opportunity to Juliet.

'But, like I told Laura, Mom and Dad would never give permission, would they?' Missy said. 'Especially as you wouldn't be coming this time!'

Juliet pursed her lips. 'You know, you came to England as a girl and you're gonna leave as a woman. Try them. You might be surprised.'

And to her amazement, they agreed.

When Missy told Rabbit she'd be leaving Basingstoke sometime soon and heading for Europe to be a welfare officer, he said, 'Sure you are. This place was always too small for a gal like you.'

If only he knew how scared she'd been: a frightened little mouse, wishing she'd never come. And now? She'd toughened up, that was for sure.

She was a little disappointed by how well Rabbit was taking the news of her leaving. She'd thought she meant more to him, that he might even say he'd miss her. But she was just another Sister to him, after all.

'What does your husband have to say about it?' he asked. 'Or are you hoping you'll meet up with him out there?'

'Oh, no,' she said quickly. 'I don't – that's to say, I don't have a husband.'

He frowned. 'Aren't you officers all married? I thought that's why you'd come over, to be with your fellas.'

Missy blushed, ashamed of the deception. 'Some of the girls are married. My sister, for one. But we made out we were all married to keep you fellas at arm's length.'

He nodded, looking thoughtful.

Missy toyed with the edge of the coverlet. Matron would scream blue murder if she caught her like this, sitting on the edge of the bed, idling.

'I was supposed to get married,' she said. 'A couple of weeks back but it didn't work out.'

It had served her right. She hadn't come here for the right reasons; she hadn't come to serve her country, she'd come for herself.

'That's too bad,' Rabbit said. He was watching her closely. 'But if you don't mind me saying so, you don't seem too cut up about it.'

'No,' she said. She brushed some non-existent fluff from her tunic. 'I'm OK.'

A look of uncertainty flashed across his face, before he asked, 'Will you write to me, when you're out there, Squeaky? Proper letters? Not because you feel sorry for me?'

'I will write, yes. But you have to write back!'

She glanced at his hands. They were still bandaged. 'You'll have to dictate your letters to one of the girls,' she said. 'But don't ask the Limeys! They hate me, so heaven knows what they'd put!'

'Sure. I'll ask Laura,' he said.

'No, you can't. Laura's coming with me.'

And then they talked a little about Laura and what a great girl she was, and Rabbit said he was glad Missy had a good buddy like that, going along for the ride. They could look after one another.

'OK, then,' he said, finally, 'I'll ask one of the others. Should I ask Juliet?'

Missy nodded. 'Yeah, you can ask her.'

'But if someone else is writing my letters, I won't be able to put anything … you know …'

'Fresh?' Missy suggested.

At the same time he said, 'Saucy.'

They laughed again – Missy blushing at her own nerve – and Rabbit wincing because it hurt whenever he moved. It didn't matter, he said, it was a good kinda pain.

'Well,' Missy said, slowly, not meeting his eye. 'I guess the fresh, saucy stuff will just have to wait!'

'Until you're back,' he said, with a firm nod.

'Until I'm back,' she agreed.

Chapter Fifty-Nine

The New Forest, Hampshire, England

Seffy sat on a log in a forest glade and stretched out her bare legs. What bliss, to wear shorts at long last and to feel the sun's rays on her limbs.

She could easily sit here all day, admiring the view of the sparkling blue English Channel but this was strictly a five-minute break. She was forewoman, after all: she couldn't be seen to be slacking.

'It's not a bad old life, is it Vida?' she said to the bay mare grazing nearby.

Because war might be raging but the sun came up every day and there were still reasons to smile.

Grace's baby had been born safe and sound – the daughter that she'd been hoping for – and only this morning, a letter had arrived from Jean, announcing she'd moved into the dorm at McIntyre's place. Apparently, living with the Lost Girls was proving to be 'good fun.' It'd made Seffy happy to think of Jean having fun.

She threw her head back, marvelling for a moment at the conifers stretching up into the sky, straight as soldiers on parade.

She closed her eyes and exhaled.

Coming here had been the right thing to do. She'd only been here two weeks but she felt revived, like her old self again. And if her thoughts sometimes flipped to Callum Fraser, well, she was getting awfully good at flipping them straight back.

She had new pals. The girls on the dragging team were a good bunch.

'Where've you been working up to now?' one of them had asked. 'Because you're twice as strong and capable as the rest of us!'

Seffy had laughed and said, 'Sometimes I feel as though I've been at the North Pole. But I've actually been in the Highlands of Scotland.'

The girl had shaken her head. 'Cor, that must've been tough.'

'It was! But it did me the power of good. When you've almost frozen to death in a Scottish winter, you can cope with anything!'

Seffy missed it. Not the cold, but the woodsmoke and the morning mists, the swathes of purple heather, the glitter of frost. And most of all, she missed her friends.

She'd go back one day. She was a Highland girl, after all.

Vida gave a gentle snicker and as Seffy opened her eyes, someone slapped her playfully on the shoulder from behind. She jumped and then laughed, as she saw her colleague, Claire.

'You've caught me slacking!' Seffy said. 'I was just having a breather. You know, that view is really rather stunning. It's like an oil painting.'

Claire smiled. 'Don't apologise. You've earned a rest. But do you mind if I take her?' She walked over to Vida and picked up the horse's lead rein.

'Go ahead,' Seffy said. 'I'll catch you up.'

She put her face up to the sun and closed her eyes again. Just two more minutes.

She heard the jangle of chains and the thud of hooves as Claire led the horse away. There was nothing then but birdsong and the rustle of leaves overhead.

And footsteps, getting closer.

Seffy sighed. What now?

She opened her eyes, turned her head and saw a tanned, muscular man standing in a patch of sunlight a few yards away.

Callum.

She stood up. Was that really him or was she dreaming?

He pulled off his cap and held it in his hands. He was wearing a white shirt, loose at the collar and dungarees. He looked exactly the same as the very first time she'd seen him.

She should be cross; he was supposed to be leaving her alone. But part of her was simply overjoyed to see him. Her bruised old heart always betrayed her.

'What are you doing here?' she asked.

'Ah, Seffy, cool as ever,' he said, walking slowly towards her.

'What do you mean?'

'I mean, you're always so serene.'

Serene? Her stomach had just done a hundred loop-the-loops and her heart was racing.

'The girls back there told me where to find you. Although –' he smiled – 'they made me help them on the crosscut first.'

'Who told you I'd moved down here?' she asked.

'Grace told Gordy and …' he shrugged. 'Look, I'm guessing – this might sound kinda arrogant but –'

'Go on,' Seffy said.

'I thought … maybe … you wouldn't have come to this part of the country if you never wanted to see me again.'

'I might!' Seffy said. 'I mightn't have been thinking about you at all! What if I simply fancied some sea air, a change of scene, a new challenge …?'

Those were the reasons she'd given herself for moving down here. But they'd sounded weak and unconvincing, as she'd reeled them off.

Who'd she been trying to kid, as Callum might say?

But really, what was he doing here? Had he come to torment her, to ruin the peace she'd found?

354

'How's married life?' she said, the words bursting out before she could stop herself.

Callum raised an eyebrow. 'I'm sure it's great. For those who are married.'

What was that supposed to mean? More games. Seffy's chest tightened.

'I didn't get married, Seffy,' he said. 'I'm not – I didn't do it.'

Was that true? How did she not know this?

'Why not?' she asked.

He cleared his throat. 'Because I love someone else. Someone I've loved from the moment I saw her. What you said, at the river, about loving me? I wanted to say it back, so bad …' he bit his lip. 'but I couldn't. Do you understand?'

This was all too much to take in. Callum wasn't married. He was still free. And he loved her.

He was gripping the cap tightly between his hands now. 'I just wanna say one thing and then, if you want me to go, I'll leave and wish you nothing but a good and happy life.'

She put up her hand. 'Wait! Just so you know, I won't be a nobody again!'

He frowned. 'You? You'll never be a nobody. You'll always be a somebody.'

'No, you don't understand! I want to be sure what I mean to you, Callum.'

He let his cap fall and took her hand. 'I want you to be my wife. Will you marry me please, ma'am?'

'Ma'am?'

He swallowed. He was nervous; it was the first time she'd ever seen him not completely in control.

She made him wait for the count of ten.

'No,' she said. 'And yes.'

His face broke into a grin and he shook his head. 'I've been working myself up to that for days! And I reckoned on that question only having one of two answers.'

'Well, you didn't reckon on me!' Then, more seriously, she said, 'Staff Sergeant Callum Fraser, I will marry you. But not quite yet.'

He narrowed his eyes. 'Just to be clear, that's the 'yes' and the 'no'?'

'Precisely.'

'So, when?'

'When this blasted war is over. I have important work to do and if I marry you and have to give it up, I'd go bonkers. I'd be worrying, you see. Because we all know what's ahead.' She glanced out at the English Channel. 'Far better to be occupied, in mind, body and soul! I'm needed.'

'You certainly are,' he murmured.

He put his hands around her waist and pulled her closer. Seffy reached up, put her arms around his neck and they kissed. And kissed. And kissed some more.

'Was that the only way to make me shut up?' she murmured, when they finally pulled apart.

He laughed. 'Something like that.'

'I still have your mother's necklace,' she said. 'And when you come back, safe and sound, I'll swap it for a wedding ring. Do we have a deal?'

'We do,' Callum said.

They hugged one another close and kissed again and through the trees, the lumberjills' cry rang out, 'TIMBERRRRRR!'

A Letter from Helen Yendall

Thank you so much for choosing to read *The Highland Girls Report For Duty*. I hope you enjoyed it! If you did and would like to be the first to know about my new releases, you can follow me on social media or via my website (details below).

I was recently told by a writer of historical non-fiction that historical fiction authors have it easy because we can 'bend the truth.' And it's made me think, very hard, about whether I do that.

Of course, I make up most of my characters (sorry!) although I spend so long with them, they feel real to me.

And I hope I can be forgiven for making up some place names. My group of Canadian characters, for instance, come from the imagined lakeside town of 'Invermore' which is based on the real lakeside town of 'Invermere' in British Columbia.

'Ballamar' – the nearest village to Seffy and Jean's billet – is an amalgamation of 'Braemar' and 'Ballater' – real Scottish villages, near to Balmoral but which I couldn't use because there was no train station near them in 1944 and I needed Seffy to be able to ski to a railway station in order to get to London.

But I haven't changed 'Basingstoke', which was the real location for a Canadian military hospital during WW2 war ('Canadian Neurological and Plastic Surgery Hospital No.1').

As much as possible, I do stick to the facts.

For a while, I didn't think it was going to be possible to bring Missy, Callum's fiancée, over to Britain from Canada. Ordinary folk didn't travel for pleasure during WW2 and certainly not across the Atlantic. If I'd 'bent the truth' and sent Missy to England for a holiday, readers would, quite rightly, have thrown my book across the room.

But then I read about the Canadian Red Cross Corps (CRCC) Overseas Detachment and discovered that 641 Canadian female volunteers had travelled to Europe during the war.

They'd worked in hospitality (at the four London Maple Leaf clubs, for example), as ambulance drivers, in administration, as nurses and, of course, some had been General Duty Officers, like Missy, helping to rehabilitate injured Canadian servicemen.

I couldn't have written about Missy's role in the CRCC without Lois Macdonald Cooper's fascinating book, 'Wartime Letters Home' (Borealis Press Ltd 2005), a collection of over 300 letters that she wrote from Basingstoke and continental Europe, to her parents in Canada, when she was doing the same role as Missy.

In writing *The Highland Girls Report For Duty*, I couldn't resist including a little nod to our lovely late Queen, Elizabeth II and I took the liberty of including Dookie, the royal family's first corgi, in the scene.

Bending the truth? In fact, Queen Elizabeth and the two princesses did visit a group of lumberjills working in Invercauld, near Balmoral during the war (although almost certainly without a corgi in tow!). It was a photograph of that visit that inspired the scene in my book.

Although the future Queen Elizabeth didn't become a lumberjill, she played her part in the war effort. In 1945, when she was eighteen, she enlisted in the ATS (Auxiliary Territorial Service), the first female of the Royal family to be an active duty member of the British Armed Forces.

Whenever I look at photographs of the girls and women who

served in the Women's Timber Corps, I get a little lump in my throat. They look so happy and fulfilled. Most are now, sadly, no longer with us but what a fine example they set, of grabbing life's opportunities and working hard for what you believe in.

I hope you loved *The Highland Girls Report For Duty* and if you did, I would be so grateful if you would leave a review. I always love to hear what readers thought, and it helps new readers discover my books too.

Thank you
Best wishes
Helen Yendall

Twitter/X: @helenyendall
Facebook: https://www.facebook.com/helen.yendall
Instagram: https://www.instagram.com/helenyendall23/
Website: https://blogaboutwriting.wordpress.com/

A Wartime Secret

England, 1940. Can Maggie keep her family – and her secret – safe? An emotional and heartbreaking wartime novel for fans of Diney Costeloe, Dilly Court and Mandy Robotham.

When Maggie's new job takes her from bombed-out London to grand Snowden Hall in the Cotswolds she's apprehensive but determined to do her bit for the war effort. She's also keeping a secret, one she knows would turn opinion against her. Her mother is German: Maggie is related to the enemy.

Then her evacuee sister sends her a worrying letter, missing the code they agreed Violet would use to confirm everything was well, and Maggie's heart sinks. Violet is miles away; how can she get to her in the middle of a war? Worse, her mother, arrested for her nationality, is now missing, and Maggie has no idea where she is.

As a secret project at Snowden Hall risks revealing Maggie's German side, she becomes even more determined to protect her family. Can she find a way to get to her sister? And will she ever find out where her mother has been taken?

Scotland, 1942.

The lumberjills, the newest recruits in the Women's Timber Corps, arrive in the Scottish Highlands to a hostile reception from doubtful locals. The young women are determined to prove them wrong and serve their country – but they're also all looking for something more …

Lady Persephone signed up to show everyone she's more than just a pretty face – but it'll take more than some charm and her noble credentials to win handsome Sergeant Fraser over.

Tall, strong Grace has led a lonely life working on a croft, with just her mother for company. All she wants is to find her place in the world – even if that's a thousand miles from home.

And Irene misses her husband terribly, so until he returns home from the front line, she's distracting herself with war work. But one distraction too far leads to devastating consequences …

Can the lumberjills get through their struggles together – even when tragedy strikes?

The Highland Girls on Guard

Scotland, 1943. It's a long, hot summer in Scotland but the Women's Timber Corps have more than forest fires to worry about.

Upper class **Seffy** has spent months proving herself to the other young women, but when new recruits arrive, she quickly feels lost again. She distracts herself by helping set up a Women's Home Defence Corps, but the idea soon meets resistance from the locals.

Dependable **Joey** had turned her back on love since she ran away from heartbreak to join the Corps, but when she crosses paths with a soldier deployed nearby, she feels a connection with him she's never felt before – but will she be burned by love again?

And young **Tattie** is desperate to impress the other women and make a new life for herself, far away from her troubled home. But her willingness to impress leaves her at risk of being used …

As the summer beats on, can the Lumberjills pull together and protect the forest – and each other?

Acknowledgements

Many thanks to my agent, Robbie Guillory and the team at HQ, particularly Seema Mitra and Teresa Palmiero, for helping to make *The Highland Girls Report For Duty* the best it could be.

By its very nature, writing is a solitary pursuit and it can be lonely. Many thanks to the friends and organisations that have supported me and still keep me going, in particular: Sophie Mansfield and the members of Sunny Side Up; Sue Ablett and Evesham Festival of Words; the Romantic Novelists' Association; The Saga Sisters, Jane Bettany, Chris Cherry, Ruth Goldstraw and Sally Jenkins.

Finally, a special thanks to my husband. If he didn't take charge of dinner most nights, while I slave over my laptop, we would never eat. Thank you, Alan, for the support and the sustenance.

Dear Reader,

We hope you enjoyed reading this book. If you did, we'd be so appreciative if you left a review. It really helps us and the author to bring more books like this to you.

Here at HQ Digital we are dedicated to publishing fiction that will keep you turning the pages into the early hours. Don't want to miss a thing? To find out more about our books, promotions, discover exclusive content and enter competitions you can keep in touch in the following ways:

JOIN OUR COMMUNITY:

Sign up to our new email newsletter: http://smarturl.it/SignUpHQ

Read our new blog www.hqstories.co.uk

𝕏 https://twitter.com/HQStories

f www.facebook.com/HQStories

BUDDING WRITER?

We're also looking for authors to join the HQ Digital family!
Find out more here:

https://www.hqstories.co.uk/want-to-write-for-us/

Thanks for reading, from the HQ Digital team